FIONA

FIONA

The Viking Treasure Huntress Series
Book Two

ANN BOELTER

annboelter.com

 Trademark Publishing Company

www.annboelter.com

Published by Trademark Publishing Company, Colorado.

Printed in the United States of America
First Printing: April 2022
ISBN: 978-1-7326565-6-7 (paperback)
ISBN: 978-1-7326565-5-0 (ebook)

Cover Design and Interior Formatting by

www.emtippettsbookdesigns.com

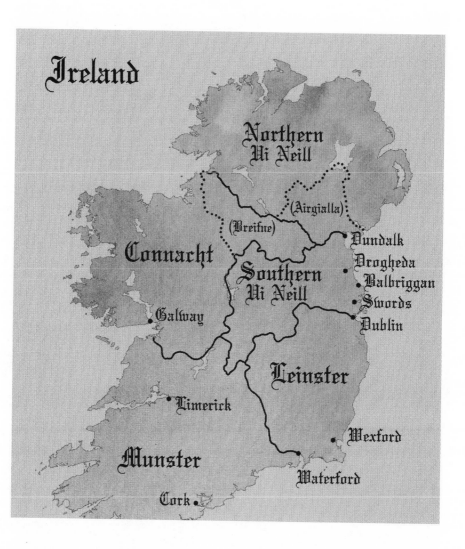

The following section, *The Creation of The Treasure Huntress*, is included to provide essential background information for those who have not yet read the first book in the series, **NENA**, and those who might like a refresher. This excerpt was originally printed as the **NENA** Prologue and contains no new material, so if you've recently finished **NENA**, please feel free to proceed to the Prologue for **FIONA**.

~Ann

The Creation of the Treasure Huntress

Southern Coastal Norway - Circa 900 AD

Sigurd eased open the door and swore under his breath as the telltale squeak still announced his arrival.

"You don't have to creep; I'm awake." Leila's quiet voice came from the shadows.

"Sorry to wake you. I'll fix that tomorrow. I swear."

"It's alright, Sigurd. And you didn't wake me. I heard you talking to someone. Did we have a visitor?"

"No." Sigurd closed the door behind him and made his way through the interior of the small cabin to stoke the fire.

"Who was it?" she asked.

"No one." He evaded her question. "Are you cold? Would you like something to eat?" He moved to the bed and bent over to adjust the furs around her. She seemed paler than usual this morning. His heart twisted.

"No one? I recognized his voice, so I know he's been here before."

"It was just a peddler."

"You never could lie to me, Sigurd, so why would you try now?" Leila chided him.

"The healer says you shouldn't waste so much energy being stubborn," he grumbled.

"The healer says it's my stubbornness that's kept me alive this long," she countered, ignoring his gruffness.

He looked at her fondly and shook his head. "A deal then. You drink a cup of broth and I'll tell you who he was."

"Agreed," she conceded.

Sigurd moved quickly to the pot suspended over the fire before she could change her mind. He gave it a cursory stir with the long wooden ladle, then tested the broth with his finger. It was only lukewarm, but she couldn't drink anything too hot anymore. He picked up a large mug, then set it back and chose a smaller one, not wanting to give her any excuse to back out. Getting her to eat was usually a battle.

He returned to the bed and helped her sit up, then propped furs and blankets behind her for support. He tried not to dwell on how light she had become, or how he could feel her delicate, almost birdlike bones just beneath her skin. He held out the cup and waited before removing his fingers to make sure she had a steady grip on it with both of her hands.

Smiling to himself, he shook his head as he watched her resolutely swallow small sips of broth one after another. She wasn't hungry, but she would finish the cup to get the information she sought. In that moment, Sigurd was actually happy that the stranger had returned, though he'd been infuriated at the time by the man's audacity.

Leila finished the last small swallow and handed him the empty cup.

"Satisfied?" she asked.

He took it and pretended to make a full inspection of the inside.

"You are such an oaf," she said affectionately.

He grinned at her.

"So, who was he?" she asked.

"Truly, he is no one you know. No one I knew until he first came here a couple of weeks ago. His name is Jarl."

"A jarl? Aren't we so important then, to have warranted two visits from a jarl."

"Not *a* jarl," he corrected her. "Jarl is his given name, not his title."

"Strange," she murmured. "Why would someone name their boy that?"

"I don't know. Maybe his brothers were already named King and Prince." He smiled at her, and they shared a quiet laugh.

"And he was here before? What does he want?"

"He wanted me to build him a ship."

"And what did you say?"

"I told him no, of course."

"Because of me."

"No. Because I'm too old, and because I prefer to spend my time with you."

"You are not too old, and if I were not here, you would have agreed," she murmured.

"You are here—and I thank the gods for that every day." He took her hand. It felt cold and thin. He rubbed it between his palms, trying to share some of his warmth.

"He had a nice voice," she commented. "Was he nice?"

"He seemed alright."

"You always said you wanted to build one more ship—that you had some grand ideas."

"That was before..."

"Before I got sick," she finished for him.

He nodded and shrugged.

"I would like for you to build one more ship."

"I cannot leave you."

"You won't have to. We shall build it together."

Sigurd frowned at her and shook his head.

"I'm not delusional. I realize I can no longer be of help with saw or hammer or plane, as I was before, but I can still give you direction and supervision—and I know how much you always liked that." She paused and smiled, waiting for him to react to her last words, but Sigurd did not take the bait at her teasing. He only shook his head no.

"Since I cannot help with tools, and you do not seem to appreciate my offer to oversee the project, I could use every day to summon the goodwill and power of the gods to bless each piece of the craft as you build it. Njord to ensure good weather. Frey for prosperity." Leila could see her words were not swaying him. "And it's spring," she continued. "The weather will soon be fair. You could carry me every day to the building site with my furs and blankets so I could watch as you work. That way we would still be together. You can do what you enjoy, and I will be able to see you create something magnificent. You know I always loved that—and to be in the forest in summer." Her voice trailed away as she imagined it. "The fresh air will be better for me than being cooped up here in the dark," she added.

Sigurd stroked her smooth, slightly graying blond hair back away from her face, not seeing the drawn skin or the dark circles under her eyes—seeing only the beautiful strong young woman he had fallen in love with so many years ago. Even in her suffering, she would put his needs and desires above her own. He knew she felt she was a burden to him. How could she not know she was his life?

"I love you so much," he murmured. "But I cannot do what you ask."

"I want you to do it for me. For us." She smiled a weak smile at him. "So there will be some part of us that will live on after I am gone."

He didn't wish to deny her anything, but he could hardly agree. It would be too much for her. He could easily carry her every day as she had asked, and would do it gladly, but the weather would be fair for a healthy person. She was so thin and weak now, that even in the warm cabin she often took a chill. Being exposed to the cool wind that rolled in off the fjord could kill her. Sigurd could not bear to be the reason that they lost even one minute of the time they had left together. He looked at the stubborn set of her jaw and knew he wasn't going to get off so easily. She had clearly prepared further arguments.

"Even if I were to agree, and that is an *if*, I've already told him I would not. Twice now, in fact."

"You could go find him and tell him you changed your mind—tell him you will make him the greatest ship ever built."

Sigurd shook his head. "First, I would have no idea where to look for him, and second, I will not leave you." His tone brooked no argument.

"Another deal then?" she asked.

His eyes narrowed as he cocked his head. "What did you have in mind?"

"If he returns and asks again, you will agree?"

"I've already refused him twice," he reminded her

"Then you should be safe in making the deal. Though I like my odds; the fact that he returned after you refused him once, tells me he is persistent."

Sigurd thought of the two times he had run the man off. The first time his refusal had been rude and clipped, but this second time, the threats if he were ever to return again had been explicit. The man would not be back. He was safe to make this pact with her. "And if I agree, and he does not come back, that will be the end of it?"

She nodded.

"Very well then. To have peace and quiet on the subject—if he returns, I will agree to build his ship, and you can help me. But only if he returns. I will not seek him out."

Leila smiled a genuine smile and leaned her head back in the furs. "Now it is in the gods' hands."

It was the happiest he had seen her in some time. Sigurd felt only a little guilty knowing it would never come about. It was for the best and would still give her something to look forward to—something other than her sickness to dwell upon. Seeing her in such a good mood lifted his own spirits. He returned to the cooking area to pour himself a cup of mead.

"Would you like some?" he asked her. She was still smiling, lost in thought about their deal, but looked up and shocked him by accepting.

"Yes, I think I would. Just a little."

He reached up to the shelf for the oxhorn cup that was her favorite and blew the dust out of the inside. The intricate silver inlay around the rim accented the natural black and gray swirling pattern of the animal horn. He poured only enough to fill the bottom tip, then carried it to her and took a seat next to the bed.

"A toast?" she asked as she took the cup from him.

"A toast," he agreed.

"To our ship," she said, and raised her oxhorn.

He shook his head and raised his own. "To our ship," he said and touched the rim of his cup to hers before lifting it to his lips. In a practiced move, he raised the horn only slightly, and waited for the liquid to make its way over the curve before flooding toward him. He held a mouthful for a few seconds before swallowing. It had been a long time since he'd drunk anything other than water, and he savored the slightly sweet alcohol bite on his tongue. It was good—better than he remembered. He lifted the oxhorn cup once again to his lips.

A bold knock sounded at the door.

Sigurd sat dumbfounded in his chair and stared at the door, then glanced at Leila. She was trying unsuccessfully not to smile.

"Aren't you going to see who it is?" she asked. "It might be another peddler." Her smile widened.

He stood and moved toward the door, his mind racing. It couldn't be. He had threatened the man's very life less than an hour before. It couldn't be him. But who then? Living so far from the village, he could count on one hand the number of visitors they'd had in the past two years. He paused and took a deep breath before lifting the latch and pulling open the door. The hinge squealed in his ear.

"Apologies, for the intrusion," Jarl said before Sigurd could speak. "I could not leave without making another attempt. You say there are plenty of other shipbuilders, and I know that there are, but you are the best. Everyone knows it. Everyone agrees. They say your ships are far advanced beyond anyone else's. That is what I need, and I will do anything to have one. If it is not more gold, then just tell me what it will take to persuade you. I will pay anything you ask. Anything you need or desire, I will secure it."

Sigurd said nothing, only stared at him.

"Don't be rude, Sigurd," Leila prodded and smiled approvingly at the tall young man who stood outside the door. "Invite him inside and offer him a drink."

Sigurd opened the door a little wider and stepped back, still staring at Jarl with a mixture of incredulity, anger, and confusion.

"Please come in," Leila said. "Pay him no mind. He is more than a little shocked to see you, I think, but he'll find his tongue soon enough. We were just talking about you." Her words jolted Sigurd from his stupor.

"Leila, this is Jarl. Jarl, this is my wife, Leila."

"It is my greatest pleasure to meet you, Jarl. Apologies that I do not get up to greet you. I've been ill."

"No apologies required. Gratitude for inviting me into you home," Jarl said, then turned to Sigurd whose stare now held a mixture of consternation and resignation. "Have you reconsidered my offer then? Will you build it?"

Sigurd didn't answer, only glanced to the bed where Leila awaited his response as eagerly as Jarl did. Dammit. He was trapped. Why had he ever agreed? The deal had been safe. What kind of a man came back after being threatened with death? How had she known? And how could the gods play such a cruel trick on him? He could not build a ship and care for her at the same time. Hell, he doubted he could even build a ship alone; she had always helped him in the past. But he had made a deal with her. He looked back at Jarl.

"I will, but there is an additional price to be paid."

"Name it."

"As you can see my wife needs special care."

"I will hire women from the village to tend to her."

"I can tend to my own wife," Sigurd growled. "But I will need fresh meat delivered regularly and firewood cut."

"Done," Jarl agreed and waited for the next.

"And I will require a sturdy horse to drag the cut trees to my work site."

Jarl nodded. "And I am more than willing to help. I'm strong and good with an axe. I know nothing of shipbuilding, but I'm a quick learner."

"Stop right there." Sigurd interrupted him. "I have no need of your assistance, nor do I want it. You will not come to the building site unless invited. That is not negotiable. If you cannot agree, the deal is off. Are we clear?"

Jarl frowned. "Yes, but..."

"Not negotiable," Sigurd repeated.

Jarl nodded. "Understood."

"You can come here to the cabin and hang the meat in the larder, and I'll show you where to stack the firewood. I'll start when you bring the horse."

"I'll be here tomorrow with the horse and the first half of the payment. So the sum I offered before is acceptable?" Jarl asked.

Sigurd scowled and nodded curtly.

With a quick nod to Leila, Jarl hastened to the doorway before Sigurd could change his mind. The hinges squealed their final taunt at Sigurd as Jarl pulled the door closed behind him.

"You should allow him to help, at least with the felling of the trees and the hauling," Leila said after Jarl had gone.

"Woman," Sigurd threatened, his eyebrows raised.

"Only that part. To find the right trees will take you far from the building site, and I will be left alone while you are gone," she reasoned.

He considered her words. "Perhaps you are right. He can help, but only for that."

Leila watch as Jarl unchained the latest log from the horse's harness. He wore only a leather vest, and the muscles of his upper arms bulged, well defined from the labor. He led the animal for a drink before he tied it up, then walked up the hill to check on her, as he had done after each previous load.

"Is there anything I can get you?" he asked.

"No. I'm fine. But maybe sit and rest for a moment."

"I should get back. Sigurd will be..."

"Sigurd will be inspecting and rejecting the next forty trees before he finds one he likes. You have a moment." She smiled.

He smiled back and nodded before stretching out on the ground next to her furs.

"Things are going well. Sigurd seems to be pleased," she said.

"Pleased is not how I would describe him, but you know him better than I."

"He is gruff now, but soon he will not be able to help but be excited."

"Why did he change his mind?" Jarl asked.

"He didn't. When he told me you had come, I wanted him to build it, but he refused, so we made a deal. Only if you returned a third time would he agree."

Jarl smiled and shook his head. "So that is why he stares at me so strangely. You know, I was well on my way back to the village when I felt compelled to turn around. I had to try again. Thank the gods that I did."

"Yes, thank the gods," she murmured. Leila took in the strong cut of his jaw, his thick wavy chestnut hair, and the traces of the dimples still visible from his smile. He was quite handsome. "Are you married, Jarl?" she asked.

"No."

"Someone special then?"

He shook his head.

"Pity."

"It is for the best. When the ship is finished, I intend to sail her to many foreign lands, and amass a great fortune. Having a wife left at home would only be a worry."

"Perhaps."

"I need to get back. If Sigurd were to discover me sitting here with you..." Jarl shook his head as he stood. "Are you sure there is nothing else I can get you? Did you try the apple cobbler? The woman where I'm staying made it especially for you."

"Yes, it was very good," Leila replied, though she had only taken a small bite earlier to appease him. "But it is not necessary for you to bring such things. I do not eat much."

"All the more reason to continue, until I find what you really like." He smiled at her again before he turned to leave, his dimples giving an odd softness to his chiseled face.

"Jarl," she called after him.

"Yes?"

"There is one thing you could bring me."

"What is it?"

"I would have coal and parchment. I have a few ideas for your ship that I would like to share with Sigurd. If I could sketch them during the day when they are fresh in my mind, I could show him at night."

"I'll bring them tomorrow," Jarl agreed.

Leila loved seeing the spark back in Sigurd's eyes. There was a spring in his step as he moved about the cabin—pouring them each a cup of water while he waited for the latest stew Jarl had brought to warm over the fire. True to his word, after the logs were hauled, he had refused any further help from Jarl and had banished him from the work site—though Jarl more than continued to live up to his end of the bargain. Not only was their shed already filled to the eaves with split firewood and their larder full of a variety of fresh and smoked meats, he always brought something extra, some specially prepared food—a loaf of fresh baked bread, a pie, a pouch of soup or stew. She had pointed Jarl's extra efforts out to Sigurd in hopes that he would ease his restriction and accept Jarl's help, but he had not.

After they finished eating and he had cleared away their dishes, Sigurd showed her his crude sketch of a dragon's head and neck. The skeleton frame of the ship was complete, and he was preparing to start on the bow. "What do you think?" he asked.

"It's nice, but..."

"But what?"

"You have made similar before."

"Yes," he said, as he glanced back at his scribble, his brow furrowed as he tried to identify what she didn't like about it.

"This one needs to be different," she challenged. "Special."

"I could use another animal, I suppose, but which would be better than a dragon?"

"Why not all of them?"

He looked at her blankly, and Leila was sure he must be thinking she had lost her mind.

"I have given this a lot of thought, so hear me out before you speak," she continued. "Why not use the dragon's head, but give it scales on its neck, each the size of a man's hand. On each scale you can carve the symbol of another animal. Then the ship can possess and draw from the power of all, rather than just one."

"That would take meticulous carving," he said frowning, but she could tell he was excited by the idea.

"It would, and you can do it."

"Bear, bull, horse." He started to list under his breath.

"Fish, gull, ram," she added. "I can sketch them for you. Not the whole beast, only a symbol of their greatest strength—their essence, if you will. Like this." She picked up the coal and began to sketch an eagle's head and beak, curved to fit into the shape of a dragon's scale, then a porcupine's spiny back, a panther's paw print. She looked up at him. He nodded.

"And the dragon's head? I suppose you have an idea for that as well?" he asked.

She smiled and nodded before pulling a completed sketch from the middle of the stack of blank parchments.

Sigurd whistled between his teeth.

Her eyes searched his face. "What are your honest thoughts?" she asked.

"Honestly? I think you overestimate my skill as a carver."

"I do not."

"It is stunning and beautiful, but...well, the detail is too fine. It would not hold up to what a ship must—storms, battles."

"I thought of that, too. What if it was made from ironwood?"

"Ironwood?"

"Only the head."

"That's impossible. It would be hard enough to carve this detail from a soft wood, but ironwood? Impossible," he repeated.

"Not impossible," she disagreed. "Difficult, yes, but not impossible. And if it could be done, would it hold up?"

"Aye," he said, nodding and frowning at the same time. "If it could be done, it would probably outlast the rest of the ship."

She smiled and nodded. "Good."

"I didn't say I would do it," he protested. "There are other concerns."

"Like?"

"Like...like the color of the wood would not match, for one." He stammered, struggling to come up with something. He noticed her smug expression. "But I see you have thought of that as well."

"I had thought to save that for another day; I knew you would be concerned about the carving and thought it might be best not to overwhelm you."

"Spill it, woman. What else do you have planned for my ship?"

"Our ship," Leila corrected him before continuing. "You and I have accumulated much gold over the years, have we not?"

"Aye. Our raiding was always successful."

"We have no children left to leave it to, and have more than we can spend. Certainly more than I will ever spend, and even if your next wife enjoys silks and jewels, there should be plenty to accommodate her."

"Do not say such things. Even in jest. You know there will never be another woman for me. So yes, we have plenty of gold."

"Could some of it be melted down and somehow...wiped or dipped on the head and scales? I'm envisioning it thicker on the head—to make it appear as if it were made from solid gold, then becoming less and less down the neck in the scales, until it melds into the natural golden color of the wood at the bottom in the body of the ship."

"You would dip the wood in gold?"

"I don't know how it would be done—dip, pour...burnish it somehow." She was shocked when he did not reject the idea immediately.

"I shall have to give that consideration. I don't know if it can be done. Perhaps I could consult the blacksmith. He might know a way."

Leila smiled again, suddenly very tired. "Good."

Sigurd carried her to the work area every morning. Once he was satisfied that she was snug and warm in her mound of furs and had water and food within her easy reach, he went to work in the vale below. Sometimes she napped. Sometimes she sketched. Sometimes she sat just watching him.

Leila loved seeing him like this. Happy. Productive. Creative. He was in his element. She would not let her failing body take that from him—would not have him reduced back to the sad man who was watching her die. She fought back the nausea, refusing to succumb to it—pooling all of her strength whenever he would come to show her something or ask her advice. She would not let him see how weak she was becoming. How fast it was happening now. When he returned to his work, she would collapse into her furs, exhausted by the effort.

Sigurd worked like a man possessed. He loved what he did. Loved that they were taking on this enormous project together. He wanted desperately for her to see it to completion. He carried her to see each of the dragon scale carvings up close as he completed them—her visions brought to life with his chisel, blade, and rasp.

Jarl was often waiting for them at the cabin at night. Sigurd didn't like it, but he didn't complain, not after seeing Leila eating the special things Jarl brought for her. She seemed stronger to him. Whether it was the fresh air, or the excitement of the shared project, or the extra food she managed to eat so as not to offend Jarl, he didn't know, but he was not about to risk changing anything.

Sigurd held her up to show her the latest scale he had completed, a raven's eye.

Leila nodded. "It is good. It will give the ship the protection of raven's sight."

"That leaves only one," he said. "Will you show me your idea now?"

She nodded again. "I have the last sketch back at my furs. Can you guess it?" she asked as he carried her back up the hill. "I'll give you a hint. It is the most cunning, powerful animal of all."

"Surely we have not missed an animal with such power," he said "And you say the most powerful? More powerful than the dragon?" He could see she was enjoying stumping him so he continued to guess long past when he had tired of the game.

"Do you give up?" she finally asked.

"Aye," he smiled.

"It is man."

He frowned as he gently positioned her back in her nest of furs. "But men will be on the boat. What have you drawn? A sword? A shield? A battle-axe?" He reached for the sheaf of paper, but she pulled it tight against her breast.

"What is the most important power the gods have bestowed upon man?"

He shook his head as she handed him her last sketch. He balked. "This?" he asked.

"It is love. More powerful than a man's battle-axe. More powerful than his sword or shield. More powerful than even his mind. It is so powerful, it can make him do things his mind tells him are impossible or foolish. It can give him resolve or courage when he has none. It is his greatest strength, and it's the true essence of man—like the raven's eye, or the crab's claw, or the scallop's shell. We have added all the great animal powers to make the ship stealthy, fleet, and strong, in order to protect her and to make her invincible in battle. We have ensured all of those things. Now we must ensure that this ship is blessed not only to find the physical riches that her captain seeks, but to make sure he finds the greatest treasure of all."

Sigurd stared at her, shocked by the profoundness of her thoughts. "I would so easily give up everything I ever had and live the poorest pauper, if it meant spending more time with you." His face twisted with the pain that he was normally able to hide.

She smiled as she touched his cheek. "I know. And I you. Which is why this one is the most important. It will capture the essence of that love, our love, and be the most powerful blessing of all."

He nodded and brushed his eyes.

"And the position of the last scale?" she asked. "Where is it?"

"Where you requested—just above the waterline on the starboard side."

"Over the dragon's heart," they said simultaneously, sharing a smile.

"I'm not sure what Jarl will have to say about it." Sigurd frowned.

"If you do not think he will want it, or is ready for it, then don't tell him."

Sigurd glanced back at the sketch of the two figures entwined in a loving embrace. No details, easy to carve, but so clear, as were all her drawings, capturing and expressing the pure essence of whatever it was she had drawn.

"I will do it."

"And if Jarl notices it and complains, then tell him you were only honoring the fancy of a dying woman. He seems very serious. Driven. I don't think he would understand or appreciate the truth. It will be our secret. And Sigurd, I have one last request, if you agree. We did not build this ship for coin. Jarl has paid enough already with his deposit to more than cover any costs. Do not accept the remainder of what is owed. Instead, tell him when he no longer feels the drive to seek riches, he must give the ship to someone else. Someone worthy. No coin or favor is to ever change hands for her. He must swear to that and agree to make subsequent captains swear to it as well. That way she will always end up in the hands of someone deserving."

"I like that," Sigurd agreed. "The idea that something we created will go on forever, enriching the lives of good men."

"And women," she added.

"And women," he agreed, then paused. "I have finally thought of a name for her," he said quietly. "What do you think of the Treasure Huntress?"

Leila smiled and nodded. "It is a good name. May she provide her captain with all the physical riches he desires until she is able to seek out the true desire of his heart."

She was weakening. For the past weeks Sigurd had known and had focused on finishing the ship's bow. She had fought so hard against the coming of the end, as she had fought by his side when they were younger. She was the strongest person he had ever known, but she would not live to see the ship complete—would not take a short cruise around the fjord as he had envisioned. He knew that now. Thankfully, she would at least see the dragon finished.

"I'm very tired today," she murmured after he woke her to tell her it was done.

"We'll go home early," he said as he wrapped her in her favorite fox fur blanket before picking her up. "For a while you were getting better. You seemed stronger. You will again. You just need to eat more," he said as he carried her down the hill for her inspection.

"I felt it, too, but it was not to last. I think it was like the last glorious blaze the suns sends forth every evening before it gives in to the night."

"Don't say such things," Sigurd admonished her.

Leila turned to look at the ship as they approached. "It is perfect." She smiled wanly as her finger traced over the gilded carving of the couple. "Absolutely perfect, Sigurd. I'm so proud of you."

Sigurd lifted her higher for her to view all the symbols, from the golden dragon's head down to the last of the gold-dusted scales. It was not difficult. She weighed nothing anymore; her body had been ravaged from its long fight.

"I am so happy. I just want you to know, you have made me happy my entire life—and now with this.... It is perfect." She wiped a tear from his cheek. "Please don't cry. Do not be saddened when I go. It will be soon now."

"Don't say that." Sigurd shook his head.

"Shush. I must and you know it. Promise me you will not be sad when I am gone—that you will think of our time together with happiness."

"I cannot make that promise."

She smiled again. "Then promise me you will try."

He nodded, unable to speak.

She glanced back at the ship. "Finish her when I am gone. Finish her with all the care you have put into her so far. It will help you through the hardest times. And know that you will not be alone. I will still be here watching and helping you."

"We should get back to the cabin. It's already getting cold." He changed the subject, heartsick at the path it had taken.

She nodded, and he began the trek home.

"Would you like some fish roe?" he asked after he'd gotten her settled into the bed. "I see Jarl caught a fat one in the fish trap today, and there is still some of the fresh butter he brought before." It was one of her favorites—one of the few things she had eaten lately. "I could fry it for you."

"Yes, that would be nice."

He brought her the plate. "Here you go. This will make you feel better. You need to keep up your strength."

"Gratitude, Sigurd. Just set it there. I'll rest a bit and then I'll eat it." Her voice trailed away.

Something in her tone disturbed him—something more than her normal physical weariness. Sigurd pulled his chair closer to the bed and took her hand. She did not awaken. Tears flowed silently down his cheeks as he sat watching her breathe—slow peaceful breaths.

As she drew one longer staggered breath and exhaled, he knew it was her last. The skin and muscles of her face relaxed and her hand went limp in his grasp. Her body was finally free from the fight it had kept up for so long. Sigurd wiped the tears from his face as he stared at the form of the woman he had loved his entire life. He would do his best to honor her wishes. He owed her that and so much more. To fight through his grief to do so would be only a fraction of the fight she had put up to stay with him.

Jarl saw the huge cloud of dark smoke and started to run; that was no cooking fire. Gasping for air, he burst into the small clearing surrounding Sigurd and Leila's cabin. Everything appeared normal. He glanced toward the work-site. No smoke was coming from that direction; the source was somewhere near the fjord. Relieved, he paused briefly to catch his breath, then walked to the cabin and knocked on the door—softly at first, then harder. When there was no response, he opened it and peered inside. The cabin was empty, and while that was not unusual during the day, something was off. Jarl scanned the small space again. The copper pot that always hung over the fire was missing, as was the honey crock he'd brought for Leila when he had discovered her sweet tooth.

Jarl stepped back outside and followed the now-diminished smoke spire to the fjord. There he found Sigurd sitting on a rock staring out over the calm open water. Traces of smoke lingered over its smooth-as-silk surface.

Jarl knew only one thing burned on open water. A burial ship. He sat down next to Sigurd without speaking.

"She loved the water on days like this," Sigurd said. "The gods honor her with it today. She had a special connection to the gods—always did. Whatever her desire—other than her health. She thought I hadn't been building any ships since she took ill, but when I realized she would die, I built one for her. I never told her. I didn't want her to think I was ready for her to leave me. I didn't want her to give up." He glanced at the rabbits Jarl had on a tether, then at the pouch that he knew would contain some type of fresh stew. "There will be no need for you to continue to bring food."

"A deal is a deal," Jarl disagreed.

"I will finish your ship, have no fear."

"I do not fear that. I know Leila would haunt you if you did not."

Sigurd looked at him at that and smiled a tired smile. "Aye, that she would."

Jarl nodded. "As she would me if I left you to your own devices to feed yourself."

Sigurd only nodded his acceptance and looked back out over the water.

"I have need of your assistance tomorrow," Sigurd said, his voice surprising Jarl as he arrived at the cabin. Never once during the long winter had he ever found Sigurd at home during the day. "She is ready to launch. I had thought to try to do it myself, but today I could hear Leila's words as clearly as if she'd been standing next to me. 'Don't be such a stubborn oaf,' she said, and I suppose she's right. Be here at dawn."

"I will," Jarl said, barely able to control his excitement.

Sigurd nodded and walked inside the cabin, closing the door behind him.

"I have never seen anything like this," Jarl murmured as he turned to Sigurd in wonder. "The bear, the bull." He turned back to the ship and his fingers traced over the symbols.

Sigurd watched him closely as Jarl continued to examine the scales. He was close to the lovers now. They were right in front of him, over the heart of the dragon as Leila had wanted, but Jarl continued past them, noting the details of all the others—the eagle, the fox, the horse. It was as if the lovers were invisible to him.

Sigurd smiled. Leila had been right. Jarl was not yet ready to see it. But he would in time. Of that Sigurd was certain; Leila would see to it. When she put her mind to something, no man would be able to resist her for long. "She is the Treasure Huntress," he said.

Jarl nodded. "She's perfect, as is her name. I'm only sorry Leila could not see it."

"She saw the most important parts, and I will describe the last to her when I see her again in Valhalla." He noted Jarl's doubtful gaze. "She is in Valhalla," Sigurd said with conviction. "You knew her only as gentle and weak, but when she was younger, she was fierce—a shield-maiden with no equal. Many an opponent fell to her blade." He smiled seeing the memory. "Men were afraid of her, but to me, she was the most perfect woman the gods had ever created. I thought to have no chance with her, of course. I was a decent fighter, but not a great one. My skill lay, well...," he glanced at the ship, "in other forms. But the gods must have taken pity on me, or maybe they knew that by giving me a woman so far beyond my reach that I would cherish her with the proper honor she deserved. That is the only reason I can possibly think of that an average man like me was chosen by a warrior goddess like her. And she was a warrior. Even in the end, she fought as no other could."

Sigurd shook his head. "But I digress. Building this ship made her last days—our last days so much better, and I thank you for that. She thanked you for that. You gave us something far more valuable than your coin, so you owe nothing further. Leila wanted you to..." He paused as he searched for words. "She wanted you to get more than you bargained for," Sigurd finished with a strange enigmatic smile.

"Even at the original sum, I will have already received that. This ship is easily worth ten times what we agreed," Jarl protested. "I do not wish to start off with bad luck from a cheated purchase."

"It is I who have changed the sum so there is no cheating, and it will not be without cost to you. There is an additional stipulation. When you lose the desire to seek further riches, you must gift the ship to someone else. Someone worthy of her. She cannot sit idle and forgotten at a dock, nor can she ever be sold. She must forever serve a captain who is driven to hunt for true enrichment—in whatever form that takes for him." He smiled the strange smile again. "This edict must be passed down to each captain who follows you. You must swear to it, as must they. It is not negotiable."

"I swear. But I would swear it, and still pay you the agreed upon sum."

Sigurd shook his head. "It is what Leila wanted."

Jarl nodded. "Very well, but know that it is only under protest that I accept." Jarl paused, his eyes drawn back to the ship's sleek lines. "What will you do now? Begin another? I must say when people see her, they will flock to your doorstep."

"I will never build another ship."

"You say that now, but when you are over..."

"Jarl, a man hones his craft during his lifetime. Every ship I have ever built was an improvement on the last." He looked at the Treasure Huntress. "I could never build another ship even close to her equal—much less improve upon her. When you realize you have reached your zenith, it is time to quit. There will be no satisfaction and no joy in building something inferior.

And the Huntress...." His voice trailed away momentarily. "With Leila, I built something that exceeded my wildest fantasy. Anything else would be a disappointment. I have hung up my tools for good, and there they will stay."

Jarl wanted to argue—to point out that even what Sigurd considered to be his inferior boats were far superior to any others. It was why he had come—why he had refused to take no for an answer. But he could see in Sigurd's eyes there would be no point. His decision was made. Perhaps when his grief had passed, he might change his mind.

"Others will still come...as I did."

Sigurd shrugged. "They will be turned away. Leila was the only reason I accepted your offer. She is gone now, and the next will not be met with such favor or kindness. You can tell that to any man who asks you. They will not be welcome here."

"As you wish. But I fear they will not believe me. They will think I am only trying to discourage them to not have competition."

Sigurd wasn't listening. He was staring at the ship. "I thought it would be impossible for me to see her go," he murmured.

For a moment Jarl wasn't sure which *her* Sigurd was referring to—the ship or his late wife. He realized it was probably both.

"Leila put every last bit of her strength into this ship, and I know she's a part of it. I must admit that after she died, I wasn't sure I could do it—to give up that last piece of her, but...," He smiled a small smile. "It is not so painful as I imagined it would be. I understand now. Her spirit is in there, and she wants to be free. She was trapped in her weak body for so long, but now she's strong again. She'll protect it, you know—and you and the captains who follow you. Of that I have no doubt. She was a ferocious fighter...and an amazing lover." His voice trailed off. "But a word of advice—don't ever cross her. You do not wish to feel her wrath."

Jarl nodded. "I shall return tomorrow with a crew to sail her."

"There's no need. The two of us can take her to Grimstad. I'll return home from there on foot," Sigurd said as he jumped from the dock onto the deck of the boat.

"But we have to pass through the rocks outside the harbor," Jarl protested. "The channel is narrow there, and the winds unpredictable. Two men cannot maneuver a ship this large. I would hate to have her damaged—or worse."

Sigurd only looked at him as if his concerns were foolish. "She's large, but she'll handle nimble like a fox. You'll see. I know the ship, Jarl, and you must learn to trust her."

Jarl was torn. He did not wish to deny Sigurd, but the ship was far too valuable to risk on what seemed like a whim. He glanced up at the golden dragon's eye and swore that it was measuring him. He shook his head and took a deep breath.

"Very well then," he muttered. "Off to Grimstad." As Jarl stepped on board, he had the odd impression that he and Sigurd were, in fact, not alone. He dashed the thoughts from his mind. All that talk of Leila's spirit had gotten inside his head.

"You take the helm," Sigurd said as he moved quickly around the ship, tightening lines, loosening sails. "She's yours now."

Jarl took hold of the rudder. It felt warm to the touch. From the sun, he chastised himself—nothing more. Yet still he could not shake the feeling the ship had a spirit of its own—not necessarily the spirit of Leila as Sigurd had claimed, but a spirit all the same. Jarl shook his head and gripped the handle tighter. It felt good in his hand.

"To our first of many adventures, Huntress," he murmured. "May the gods bless us with good fortune." At his words, the sail dropped under Sigurd's masterful care, catching a breeze that Jarl swore had not been there before. The great ship glided out into the fjord.

Prologue

Southern Coastal Norway – Circa 909 AD

Sigurd stepped up onto the familiar long flat stone and stomped the slushy spring snow from his boots. After gently lowering his rucksack, he walked to the outermost tip and stood staring out over the ice. The first sign of thaw that had appeared as a thin strip near the shore only a week ago, was now a visible wide band rimming the entire fjord. He smiled as he unclasped his thick bearskin cape. Shrugging it off, he returned to the rucksack. "I have a special treat today, Leila," he said over his shoulder.

".…."

"Aye, I know it's been awhile, but it's not the same—talking to ice; I much prefer when there's at least some open water." He turned and held up two oxhorn cups. One, ornately rimmed with fresh-polished silver, sparkled in the sunlight.

".…."

"What are we celebrating, you ask? Do I need a reason to visit my wife?"

".…."

Sigurd chuckled. "Ah, you know me too well. I just heard news that a fleet has been assembled for another journey to the East. Finally. After four years trapped by war in Daneland, I'd begun to fear you would never leave that place."

".....""

He pulled the bung from a small barrel and filled the two oxhorn cups. "This is my latest mead and I'm eager for your opinion. I unsealed it only just this morning to celebrate. I worried it might not be ready, but I think it's...well, here, I shall let you decide." He leaned over and poured the golden liquid from the decorated horn into the water, then dragged the bearskin closer and sat down on it with his legs dangling over the edge. "What do you think?" he asked. "Very good, eh? My best, perhaps?"

".....""

"I believe the improvement to be from the honey. I purchased it from a late merchant ship—one of the last to arrive in Grimstad before the harbor froze last fall. It was supposedly harvested from bees who live in an endless field of sweet clover—I paid a goodly sum for it."

".....""

He smiled ruefully. "Yes, I know it sounds far-fetched, and I thought it to be a sham at the time. But I sought news of you, and I've found that a large purchase aids in the loosening of men's tongues. I had no expectations for the honey, but now I think there might be something to it. Don't you agree?"

".....""

Sigurd sat in silence sipping his mead. "Even when there's no word, somehow I know you're not lost to me. I can still feel you. Yet that's no excuse, mind you—nor is it a release for the future. I don't think it too much to ask that you send more frequent word of your adventures. I try to envision you in strange lands, but it's difficult for me; you were always the one with the imagination. The Treasure Huntress is a testament to that. And it's not as though I expect you to dispatch travelers to my door. I've come to not mind the trips to town so much. This place isn't the same without you, and being among people doesn't vex me as it used to.

".....

"Bah, how can you ask that? I told you there'd never be another woman for me and I meant it. And whilst we are on the subject, how is it that Gunnar is still with no wife? Four years in Daneland and you could find no worthy Dane woman to capture his heart?"

".....

"You have a plan for him?" Sigurd cocked his head. "Well...I'm listening."

".....

"I must wait to hear it?" he exclaimed with mock indignation, then chuckled. "Very well." Sigurd tipped his head back and closed his eyes, enjoying the warmth of the sun on his face. "At least spring is here. Once the last of the ice melts, there'll be many ships and more news. With mild days like today, it won't be long. I shall continue to traipse back and forth to Grimstad, hanging about the docks like a beggar waiting for the scraps you see fit to toss me."

He smiled as a thought occurred to him. "What I would give to one day crest that last hill and see you there."

Chapter 1

Gunnar wiped the light salt spray from his face and glanced up at the sail, still taut and full from the unusual east wind. It had been so since they rounded the tip of the Jutland Peninsula and left the protection of the Danish coastline. The Treasure Huntress now skimmed across the deep open water towards her goal with the men having yet to touch an oar. Gunnar smiled to himself, his spirits as light as the great ship. They were making record time with virtually no effort.

The winter winds should have reversed a month ago and been coming from the west by now—should have been blowing directly into their faces. The entire crew should have been rowing into a strong headwind, yet most of them sat lounging in the shade of the ship's side bulwarks. Only the helmsman's efforts were required to keep them on course.

That it was a gift from the gods was the only explanation. And, if the gods continued to favor him so, perhaps while he was conducting his brief business in Dublin, the winds would shift and push them home again with equal speed. No, not home. After the past four years, Aalborg would never be home to him. The thought gave him pause. But if not Aalborg, then where? It wasn't Loshavn, the Norwegian village of his birth. He hadn't returned there since avenging the death of his wife, Brigitta. And now that his sister, the last of his close family, had married the Danish jarl and moved away, he doubted he ever would.

He thought again of Aalborg. The name alone was now capable of stirring dark emotions. After returning from the East as the new captain of the Huntress, he'd gladly accepted his sister's invitation to overwinter there with her new family. It had been a fine winter—filled with ease and indulgences. He'd only just begun to plan his return to the East that following spring when the feud between the two Dane kings, Holger and Beghel, had escalated to all-out war.

Sworn to King Holger, his sister's husband had immediately begun raising an army. Gunnar had no choice but to join them. The war had naught to do with him, but he could hardly repay their generous hospitality by abandoning them with an enemy at their doorstep. By all accounts, it was to be a quick, decisive victory for Holger, but days had stretched into weeks, then months, then years of bloodshed and carnage. So many had died, and for what? For a rich king to become richer? He scowled. No, Daneland would never be home.

Perhaps he would settle with Jarl and Tryggr at their fledgling settlement in the East. Besides his sister, they were the closest things he had to family—assuming they yet lived. He pushed aside the guilt that question and his long absence raised. He would know soon enough.

Gunnar exhaled as he stared out unseeing over the wind-whipped chop. Perhaps he was destined never to settle—to sail the Huntress until he was too old to hold a sword, or to fall in battle and be sent to Valhalla—possibly on this very trip. He didn't worry over it. His destiny was already set; he knew that. It had been determined by the three spinners at his birth. Only by living would he discover what they'd planned for him.

The bow of the boat dipped slightly deeper into a wave, spraying his face once again with a light salty mist.

"The winds couldn't be more perfect; we make excellent time to Ireland."

Gunnar turned and nodded acknowledgment to Rask, his newly appointed second-in-command and the youngest of his three new brothers by marriage. The sides of Rask's head were fresh-shaven; the skin, still glistening from the scraping, was red in places where the knife blade had cut too deep. His remaining dark hair was pulled back along his crown into a thin single braid down his back.

"The gods must favor your decision then," Rask continued as he returned his razor-sharp knife to its sheath. "Many of the men questioned the wisdom of going so far out of the way to purchase slaves instead of capturing them along the way, but this will surely quell their concerns."

Gunnar was well aware of what the men thought of his decision to sail west before east, but none of the others dared to voice it, and Rask shouldn't either. Orders were to be obeyed without question or whispered doubts—certainly not to be joined and given credence by his second. Gunnar knew he should discipline him then and there, but the unexpected favorable winds had put him in such a good mood, he let it pass. There would be plenty of opportunities to correct Rask in the future—of that Gunnar was certain.

Making Rask his second had not been an easy decision. Strategically, it was a sound move to have a Dane high in his chain of command when so many Danish ships were joining this next fleet to the East. Being a brother to the jarl of the prosperous Aalborg, made Rask a good choice. And to his credit, he was intelligent and a naturally gifted fighter—equally skilled with sword, axe, and knife. But he was young, and with youth, those same strengths and natural abilities were drawbacks, tending to make him overconfident, quick-tempered, and more than a little arrogant. What had ultimately tipped the scales in Rask's favor was something Gunnar's father had told him long ago when he was still a boy.

"Son, you can temper and hone a flawed piece of steel until it's perfect on the outside, but it will never make a great sword. It will either never hold a proper edge or will break at the first hard test of it. Men are the same. You can give any man authority, but few will make great leaders. Like the sword, when challenged with adversity, a man who is weak on the inside will break, no matter his physical strength. To lead, you must be strong here." He had placed the flat of his huge palm against Gunnar's chest. *"Never forget that."*

Gunnar never had.

Rask was forged from leader's steel, Gunnar was sure of it, though much tempering and honing were still required. He glanced around the boat at the other men but found none better suited to the position. His third-in-command, Olag, was a prime example. An accomplished veteran fighter, Olag lacked that certain something—that inner strength that other men looked to when things got tough—something intangible but very real.

"I thought this day would never come," Rask said over the wind. "You've no idea how I've longed for this."

Gunnar nodded. "The Treasure Huntress agrees." He rested his hand on the golden arched neck of the ship. "I'm sure it is she who has summoned this wind."

The two men stood in silence staring out over the white-capped expanse ahead. There was not a cloud in the sky, and the normally dark blue-gray water of the North Sea sparkled like a brilliant sapphire.

Gunnar didn't share the actual reason for this early trip. As the captain, he didn't need to, and in truth, there was no credible reason. He could have justified it in many ways. He could have said it was to sea trial the ship, or that by purchasing instead of capturing the slaves needed for the arduous journey east, he was avoiding risk of injury to the crew. He could even justify Dublin over Hedeby, the slave-trading center that would later be only a short detour from their route, because the slaves were cheaper in Dublin.

But none of those excuses held merit. Maintenance to the Huntress had never been neglected so a sea trial was unnecessary. After four years of war, this crew was unusually seasoned and battle-ready, making it unlikely they would be injured while capturing slaves. And while it was true that the slaves would be cheaper in Dublin, even Hedeby's inflated prices were paltry in comparison to what he would receive for all those who survived the trip. The people of the East placed high value on pale-skinned slaves.

The reason for this trip was simple. It would be another month before they could begin to venture east. A month spent sitting idle in Aalborg, waiting for the rivers and lakes in the wilds of Rusland to thaw enough for them to pass. A month spent chafing with boredom. The Treasure Huntress had beckoned him with adventure now.

"When we return home from the East, will you take Magnild as wife?" Rask asked.

The question took Gunnar by surprise, but he didn't have to think about it. "No," he replied.

"Why not? Is something wrong with her?"

"Magnild's a fine woman, and I've enjoyed her company, but I have no desire to call her wife."

"Someone else then?"

"No, and why do you ask? Has my sister put you up to prying?"

Rask shrugged. "She would like to see you also marry a Dane—to remain close and settle in Aalborg. But I, too, am curious. All of the other men your age are married. Why not you? There are plenty who would have you."

"I was already married," Gunnar said, choosing to ignore *men your age.*

"I know of your first wife, Brigitta, but they say she's been gone many years now. Do you still mourn her?"

"Mourn?" Gunnar pondered the question, then shook his head. "No, not mourn, but her death left an empty hole inside me that it seems no other woman can fill. And what of you? All this talk of marriage—is it because some maid has captured your heart and will become wife upon our return?"

"Me?" Rask shook his head. "No. Never."

"Never is a long time," Gunnar disagreed.

"This is my life as it was meant to be. To travel to strange lands. To explore. To raid. I will become rich and enjoy many fine women along the way. My eyes cannot wait to behold the oddities and wonders that, as of yet, I've only heard described in the songs of skalds. Having a wife would be an obligation forcing me to curtail my adventures and return."

"You could take a shieldmaiden as wife and raid together," Gunnar countered.

Rask shook his head. "Even a shieldmaiden would eventually expect to settle and raise a brood. Look at your sister."

"Your brothers have many ships, and now that the war between Holger and Beghel is over, they will surely return to raiding. Why not sail with them?"

"Well, first, they are *my brothers'* ships as you and everyone else knows; I would make my own way. Second, none of their ships can hold a candle to the Treasure Huntress. And third, they are content to raid the same tired villages and coastal towns in North Umbria and East Anglia. I've suggested many times that we go south to Frankia and beyond, but they will not. They say there's plenty of coin to be had in England, and it is familiar."

"There's much to be said for that. And clearly, they are successful."

"Yes, but you of all people surely understand—if it were only about coin, you would have retired long ago."

Retired? And long ago? Just how old did he think he was?

"I want more than that," Rask continued.

"And what of children? Or when you are old?" Gunnar refrained from saying *like me*. Rask's impression still rankled him; he was only nine-and-twenty after all. "Then will you seek a wife?"

"The Treasure Huntress will be my wife. Together we will travel the world—maybe even discover new lands. How could a life in any one place, seeing the same things, the same woman day after day, ever compare to that? As for children?" He shrugged. "If the gods will it, there will be bastards along the way. I have no need or desire to change their dirty swaddling and bounce them on my knee."

"Time has a way of changing what a man needs and desires," Gunnar murmured.

"It hasn't changed you."

Rask was wrong about that, but Gunnar didn't correct him. Time had absolutely changed him. Many times. Changed him from a hot-headed youth seeking adventure, to a happily married man with desires only for the simple family life that Rask condemned, to a man bent on revenge, to this—what was he now exactly? Other than fulfilling his oath to Jarl and Tryggr, he had no goals, no burning desires, nothing to prove or accomplish.

"Land!" One of the men behind them shouted. Grateful for the interruption in the conversation and his thoughts, Gunnar squinted ahead at the hazy, thin gray line on the horizon.

Chapter 2

After following the Scottish coast north, they skirted through the Orkney Islands, then dropped down through the North Channel into the Irish Sea. From there, they hugged the Irish shoreline south, never once making landfall. They didn't need to; they had plenty of provisions and the northern Irish were rumored to have grown more aggressive, having recently retaken several cities after routing the occupying Norse forces.

Early in the morning of their tenth day at sea, Gunnar ordered the men to take in the sail while he studied a small port town with his scope. Only a few fishing vessels remained at the docks. No warships or fortifications that he could see. It was exactly what he'd hoped to find. Satisfied, Gunnar put the men to oars.

They rounded the natural breakwater and entered the harbor, the Huntress slicing silently through the calm protected waters. Gunnar directed the crew to the outermost tip of the longest dock. As they drew near, the men on the starboard side pulled in their oars, and the boat drifted the last few feet, ending with a gentle rub of wood and crunch of barnacles.

"Dublin is surely close. Why are we stopping here?" Rask asked.

"Dublin requires sailing deep into a bay and potentially a trap. This tiny harbor affords easy access back to open water where no ship can match the Huntress, much less outrun her. We'll take measure of any dangers here. If the winds of war are quiet and it's safe, we'll continue on to Dublin. Secure the boat and guard it closely until I return." Gunnar jumped from the boat onto the weathered timbers of the dock, his body automatically compensating for the sudden steadiness after the rolling of the ship.

"Where are you going?" Rask asked, clearly frustrated at being left behind.

Gunnar ignored him. Rask was going to have to learn that a second wasn't always entitled to answers. As he strode up the dock, seemingly unconcerned, Gunnar was keenly aware of everything going on around him. The few men on the fishing vessels that remained at the dock were working on various repairs. There were no furtive whispers, no scurrying to sound an alarm. Some had stopped to stare at the ship, but he was used to that; the Huntress never went unnoticed or unappreciated. Satisfied that the looks were only in awe and nothing nefarious was being plotted, he continued up into the small town.

He paused outside a smithy, surprised and disappointed to find it quiet and empty. Blacksmiths were usually valuable sources of information and most were hard at work by first light, but the forge here was cold. Gunnar turned, looking further up into the town.

A man stumbled from a doorway ahead, then stood blinking blindly in the sunlight. Gunnar glanced at the wooden sign suspended from an iron pole above the man's head. He couldn't read the words, but the faded red image of a dragon under the lettering was clear. He smiled. Though crude in comparison to the intricate detail of the Huntress, it was still a dragon; the gods were practically shouting the way. Stepping past the drunkard, Gunnar reached for the brass handle, pulled open the heavy oak door, and ducked inside.

"What'll it be, love?" A raspy female voice hailed him.

"Ale," he replied as his eyes adjusted to the dim light and swept through the dark, musty interior. The few drowsy patrons remained leaning over their cups, oblivious to his entrance. Gunnar made his way to a table in the corner. From there, he evaluated the barkeep, another potentially good source of information, but quickly eliminated him. The barkeep was built more like an elf than a man, and smaller men were often resentful of his size. While there were exceptions, any information would likely be costly and not necessarily reliable.

"Here you go, love." The full-figured serving wench set a large chipped tankard down with a thud onto the aged wooden table. Froth sloshed over the side. Middle-aged and broad in the beam, she was past her prime but still attractive. Gunnar smiled to himself. She would be equally if not more informed than the barkeep and, unlike small men, women typically responded quite favorably to him.

"Are you hungry?" she asked. "There's a lamb stew that actually has some meat in it, and the baker dropped off fresh bread this mornin'. I'd make sure you got some of that and not the last of the old weevily stuff." She paused. "Or are there other appetites you might be needin' satisfied?" She leaned over suggestively.

Gunnar took a moment to admire the display she'd placed temptingly close to his face—creamy mounds of pale bosom that threatened to escape from her bodice at any moment. He braced himself for a wave of sour body odor, but was surprised by only the faint scent of lavender—a whiff of fresh, clean scent, amidst the rank tavern smells of smoke, stale ale, sweat, and vomit. She smiled, revealing a mouth that still contained all of her front teeth—another pleasant rarity in a place like this.

"I do, in fact, have other needs. And I have silver," he added, setting a small pouch on the table with a clink. "But unfortunately I've not the time to satisfy them all," he declined her offer, giving one last admiring glance at her breasts. "I'm here on business and need information, for which I'm happy to pay."

"You wish only to talk?"

"I wish to do a great many things," he murmured as he reached around and gave her ample behind a squeeze, "but only have time for talk now."

She smiled. "We could always talk while..."

"With your generous endowments, I fear I'd not be able to keep my head straight for conversation."

"Aren't you honey-tongued," she said as she smoothed a stray wisp of her hair. "And handsome, too. Not that a handsome man has need of sweet words to get a woman to do his bidding. We could still go to my quarters...to ensure you have my undivided attention," she suggested.

Gunnar nodded. "Lead the way. And bring something to drink for yourself on my coin. Whatever your preference."

"That would be poteen," she replied, her voice raised in question.

"Poteen?" he asked.

"Have you never had it before?"

"Perhaps by another name?"

"Some of the local lads who are trying their hand at making it are calling theirs whiskey, but there's no other name that I'm aware of, love. I'll bring two cups. If you've never had it, you're in for a treat."

"Poteen then." He nodded.

The woman hurried behind the bar to retrieve an unopened jug, then waved for him to follow. They passed through a side door and up a narrow flight of steep stairs—so steep that even though he followed close behind, her ample swaying hips were at his eye level. Upon reaching the upper landing, she opened the first door on the right. Gunnar followed her inside. The room was cramped but clean, with a bed, a small table, and two chairs. The shutters to the single tiny window were open, letting in bright morning light and fresh air. The woman took a seat at the table. Gunnar sat across from her.

"What is this place called?" he asked while she unstoppered the jug and poured a small amount of light amber liquid into two tin cups. The portion was so small, he assumed it to be expensive. Before he could tell her there was no need to be sparing, she held out a cup to him.

"This fine establishment is The Red Dragon," she said.

"No, the town; what is it, and are we close to Dublin?"

"You be in Balbriggan, and aye, Dublin is less than twenty miles from here." She raised her cup to him briefly before tossing it back.

Gunnar did the same, coughing violently as his throat contracted and spasmed. "By the gods, that's like drinking fire," he gasped when he finally caught his breath, his eyes watering.

"Aye," she agreed and poured herself another. "And like fire, it'll warm you all the way down."

"What did you call it?"

"Poteen. But mind yourself, love. A single cup packs the punch of ten ales."

Gunnar grinned and nodded for her to refill his cup but took only a small sip this time.

"So what is it you wish to know?" she asked and leaned back in her chair, her face flushed from the climb and the drink.

"First, so you know you'll be paid." Gunnar set a small chunk of silver on the table.

"And all you want to do is talk? For that much?"

"Yes. The information I seek is important to me, and in my experience, women in your position tend to be well-informed."

She smiled, nodding in agreement as she slipped the silver into her massive bodice. "I do have ways of hearin' things that other folks might not."

"I've come to purchase slaves."

She frowned. "You'd have to go to Swords or Dublin for that. We've no slave traders here. Is there something else you seek?"

"I intend to go to Dublin, but needed first to verify it's still safe there... for my kind?"

"Aye. Safer than many places these days. It was rough those first years after they chased the Viking king, Sihtric, away. Everyone feared him to return to reclaim it, so all Vikings were viewed with suspicion. But since he seems satisfied to remain in Wales, things are quiet and all merchants are welcome again."

"Good, then perhaps you've heard of a slave trader there who might be more reputable?"

She took a deep breath, momentarily lost in hard concentration, anxious to live up to his expectations and earn her coin. "What type of slaves are you after? I've heard of a slaver who specializes in exotic slaves from afar. They say he has some with unique-shaped eyes and others with beautiful skin the color of coal."

Gunnar shook his head. "I'm looking for male slaves, healthy and strong."

"I hear pretty regular of two lads, Tibbot and Quillen, who specialize in laborers, but I recently heard complaints that Quillen has a bad run of flux in his stock, though he would deny it, I'm sure."

"You see. This is why I came to you. For the truth. So Tibbot it is. Where might I find him?"

"He's in Swords. Anyone in the harbor there should be able to point you in the right direction." She paused. "But you do know there's a heavy tax on slaves being collected from every ship that leaves the Swords or Dublin Bay? Swords is only about ten miles from here. If you were to travel by road, you could avoid payin' it."

Gunnar considered her information. The cost of the tax itself didn't concern him near as much as the fact that someone was able to collect it. No one would willingly pay such a tax if it could be avoided, so they must have effective ways of enforcing it. Possibly warships or blockades. Either posed significant risk to a single ship, even one as extraordinary as the Huntress.

"Then it seems I'm in need of a horse," he said. "And not some broken-down nag, mind you. I want a decent horse, sound of wind and limb."

She chuckled. "Then you'll want to avoid the smithy closest to the harbor. With the condition of some of his beasts, you'd be faster afoot, though I hear he's been feelin' poorly and has taken to his bed these past days. Follow the road out front to the top of the hill. Take the left fork. Down a piece on the right-hand side, you'll come across a hostler. His name is Larkin. Tell him Cora sent you, and tell him I said to treat you right."

"Gratitude, Cora. You've been most helpful, and I'm most appreciative."

"I could make you appreciate me even more." She raised her eyebrows.

Gunnar smiled. "I'm sure that you could. And know that I'll make every effort to conclude my business swiftly, hopefully leaving time for leisurely activities before I sail." He stood and made his way to the door.

She followed him and placed her hand over his before he could lift the latch. "There's an alehouse on the outskirts of Swords. The Red Stag. Anyone there'll know the way to Tibbot's, I'm sure. And one last thing, love, before you go. If you be purchasin' slaves today, take care. There've been stories of raiders freein' slaves of late."

"Raiders?"

"A dangerous bunch from the stories told, and brazen they be. Attackin' good men such as yourself in broad daylight after they've made legitimate purchases. They take the slaves and disappear like banshees on the wind. Rumor has it they be rogues, seeking to swell their ranks with men who'll be loyal to them."

"Gratitude, my lady. Your caution is well received and will be well heeded." He winked at her.

She smiled. "I would hate to have anything mar this handsome face is all." She stretched up on her tiptoes and brushed his lips with a kiss, her breasts pressing soft and full against his forearm. The light scent of lavender again teased his nostrils, and for a moment he was tempted to give her a toss. But if he was to get to Swords and back before dark, he didn't have time for the delay.

"Put mind to ease. My men can handle themselves, and, thanks to your valued counsel, I'll take necessary precautions."

Chapter 3

Gunnar left the tavern and hiked the hill following Cora's directions. He found the hostler just as she described, and when he mentioned her name, the man bypassed the first two stalls with lesser animals and opened the third, leading out a sturdy dapple gray mare.

Cora was not only informative but well connected. The gods were making this easy. Gunnar nodded his approval and the man handed him the rope, before returning with a strapping bay gelding. Again Gunnar nodded. After counting out the proper coin, he waited while the two were saddled, then mounted the bay.

———————◆———————

He hailed Rask from the end of the docks and waited for him without dismounting.

"We're off to meet with a slaver," Gunnar said as he handed him the gray's reins.

"By horse?"

Gunnar nodded.

"These are fine animals for hacks," Rask commented as he swung aboard the mare.

"The hostler came well-recommended."

"By who? I thought you said you'd never been here before."

"Doesn't matter, but if the slaver they recommended turns out to be half as good, we shall be very well-served."

Gunnar and Rask drew in rein outside the open gates and let the horses cool while they surveyed the grounds inside. They'd pushed them hard and made good time, but the steeds seemed no worse for wear. Cora had been correct about their quality and about the Red Stag Tavern; several men had known of the slave trader, Tibbot, and were happy to provide directions.

"Unusual place for a slaver," Rask commented, and Gunnar agreed. The gates were open and unguarded, revealing a short, glistening white drive that led to the front of a sprawling residence. Gunnar stared down at the drive. He'd never seen anything quite like it. He pushed the bay forward to examine it closer. What he'd first thought to be fine white gravel was actually a mixture of crushed oyster and cockle shells. When the sun touched a piece just right, the glossy inner pearl coating sparkled.

"I see no sign of slaves—do you think we have the wrong place?" Rask asked.

"No. This is as described, only grander than I was envisioning," Gunnar replied, though he too was puzzled. From all indications, this was a lesser lord's estate, and he'd never known a lord to be involved in the slave trade, at least not openly. Gunnar pointed to another wood structure behind the stables. "I think that's where our business lies. Those must be the slave quarters."

They were met outside the stables by a middle-aged man who looked them up and down with disdain, even though his drab brown clothing indicated he was a servant. "State your business," he demanded.

Gunnar peered around him into the building he'd thought might house the slaves but saw only the dwindling remains of winter stores—assorted grains, fodder, dried peat blocks. Perhaps they had the wrong place after all. "We were told your master bartered slaves. We've come to make a large purchase, but I see none. Is this the correct place?"

"Aye. His lordship has a great many slaves."

Gunnar looked around again. "Then where are they?"

"Wait here. I'll fetch his lordship for you. He'll take you to them."

"Make sure you convey to him that we are in a hurry and that our purchase will be sizable."

The servant frowned at the prodding but turned and set off for the house at a brisk pace.

Gunnar dismounted and led the gelding to a water trough for a drink, then moved into the shade. If Cora was correct and raiders were a problem, there was certainly no sign of it here. The gates stood wide open. The uppity stableman was unarmed and didn't appear as one who could handle a weapon if given one, and there were no other guards. Clearly, this lord wasn't worried about being robbed. Why? If slaves were truly what the raiders were after, why not come to the source and take them all, rather than just a few here and there? Unless...unless this man was behind the thefts.

Gunnar had known a great many slavers, callous, cunning men to a one. The raiders weren't freeing slaves; they were stealing them to be resold. The rumor of rogues building their ranks was a ruse—a ruse that allowed this man to steal from his competitors and customers alike. Gunnar made a mental note to be extra careful in his dealings.

His surety faded at the sight of the portly figure hurrying toward them. A crimson cloak fastened in the front with two gold brooches flowed behind him. His green silk tunic, heavily embroidered at the cuffs and neck with gold and red thread, strained at the seams. His appearance was so contrary to that of a hardened devious mastermind that Gunnar waited mute for him to confirm his identity.

"Greetings, my lords, and I see from your attire *northern* lords. Some of my best customers are northern lords like yourselves." The man's nervous prattle and profuse sweating belied his jovial greeting. He pulled a linen square from his pocket, nervously dabbing the beads of perspiration from his jowls. "I am Tibbot, and I've sold a great many slaves to your brethren bound for Iceland. Is that where you're headed? And did you come recommended by anyone in particular?"

"No," Gunnar replied to both questions, declining to share any further details with him.

"I only ask so that I may reward them for the referral on their next purchase." He paused, waiting for Gunnar to expound on his curt reply. When Gunnar did not, he shrugged and continued. "Well, it matters not. Come. There's no need for us to stand out here in this heat. I swear, I've never felt a spring so hot in all my life." Tibbot turned and began walking. Past the stables. Past the doorway to the storehouse, out in the open towards... nothing. "How is it you came through the front gates?" he asked over his shoulder. "Most of my northern customers come from the river. Don't you have a boat?"

"We came on horseback, and these were the directions we were given. Yes, we have a boat," Gunnar replied, trailing him from a distance. Seeing no evidence of slaves in the direction Tibbot was headed, he was wary of a trap.

"Where is it?"

"Balbriggan," Rask blurted. Gunnar shot him a withering look. He had not intended to reveal the Huntress's location in case Tibbot was behind the thefts, though it seemed increasingly unlikely.

"Ah, Balbriggan," Tibbot murmured, pausing at a low short row of stones while he waited for them to catch up.

Gunnar took a quick glance in all directions, concerned that the stones marked a distance for archers. He saw nothing. Only when he moved closer, could he see the steps leading down into the ground. Tibbot gave them a quick nod before descending to the solid wood door at the bottom. Pulling a large key from a silk cord around his waist, he slipped it into the iron lock and heaved open the door. After retrieving flint and steel from a small shelf just inside, he struck a light to a nearby torch, then motioned for them to follow.

Gunnar stared down into the hole, the hair on the back of his neck raised stiff. It bore an uncanny resemblance to the entrance of a grave. Feeling Rask's curious eyes on him, he took a deep breath and started down the stairs. A wave of cooler air washed over him as he entered the tunnel. Nerves on edge, he stood poised just inside the doorway, ready to pounce if Tibbot made any attempt to escape and trap them there. But the slaver simply closed and locked the door behind them, then led off, pausing only to touch his torch to others that were spaced every twenty feet along the walls.

"What sort of slaves do you seek?" Tibbot asked, his voice echoing in the narrow passageway. "I have many fine females for bed slaves, men for hard labors, even children if it's domestic servants you need. My man mentioned you'd be making a large purchase?"

"We require twenty men. Strong and fit," Gunnar replied, trying to keep his voice steady.

"I've an excellent selection of strong workers. The viewing chamber is right this way." Gunnar heard the smile in Tibbot's voice and knew the cause.

With the exception of an occasional beautiful woman, prime laborers were always the most expensive.

After following the corridor only a short distance, they made a left, then a right, then another left. Gunnar tried to keep track of the turns in his mind, but with no landmarks, he soon lost his bearings. His breaths coming quick and shallow, he reached out to touch the damp, chiseled-stone walls, trying to focus on anything other than the tons of earth and stone threatening to crush them at any moment.

As unsettling as the place was, he couldn't help but appreciate it from a strategic standpoint. It was an underground stone fortress—impossible to breach and easy to defend. One good fighter could hold off a contingent of invaders for hours in the narrow tunnels.

And it was an ideal place to keep slaves. Not only would escape be nigh impossible, but here below the surface, they'd be protected from the elements with a steady temperature maintained year-round. It was ingenious but would have taken many years to excavate. He couldn't imagine the pudgy man waddling in front of him having that sort of fortitude.

"This place is impressive. Did you build it?" Gunnar asked.

"Me? Nay. My great-grandfather discovered these. He believed them to be built by Romans, and I agree. Many say the Romans never had an occupying force here, but these tunnels and other things he discovered are evidence to the contrary. He was just a simple cow lord, but with these tunnels, he amassed considerable wealth. Buying things when they were plentiful and inexpensive—grains, wool, textiles—then safely storing them here without fear of damage from weather or vermin until the price was high. Though no amount of wealth could make him a highborn," he muttered to himself.

"I converted the chambers to hold slaves. There's far more profit to be made from them if you're not squeamish, which I am not. Every year my earnings have exceeded the last with only one exception. That year a twenty-foot spring storm tide flooded the tunnels through the river entrance, and much of my merchandise drowned. That was a bad year."

"How much further is it?" Gunnar asked, feeling his anxiety spike anew with the added image of slaves scratching and clawing at the stone walls in rising floodwaters.

"Not far now. My apologies for the distance. Had you come from the river, the route is much more direct. The viewing chamber is actually under the main house, and I avoid all this walking." He hesitated as if he'd said too much, then added, "Normally, my guards would escort you from the river dock."

Just when Gunnar thought he could bear it no longer, they stepped into a spacious, well-lit cavern. Gunnar wiped the film of cold sweat from his forehead with the back of his hand and quickly scanned the room. There was only one other doorway. The walls were covered with fine tapestries, and the half dozen sturdy wood chairs spaced throughout the room were draped with fine thick furs. A smoldering fire burned in a corner fireplace with a large bed occupying a prominent position nearby. Gunnar wondered if Tibbot occasionally slept there until he noticed the iron rings secured to the four bedposts. The bed was not for rest; it was to sample bed-slaves before purchase.

"Please, take a seat." Tibbot waved Gunnar and Rask to the chairs, but Gunnar shook his head. "As you wish," Tibbot said, turning to the second doorway. "Rearden!" he called out and clapped his hands.

The man who appeared was tall and fit with the sharp eye of a warrior. Gunnar wondered how many more like him were hidden in the maze.

"Rearden, bring thirty of our best male slaves. And only quality stock. We have discerning buyers today." Tibbot smiled at his customers to see how the compliment was received, but the two stood in boorish silence as if they'd not heard. *Damn Northmen, with their insolent, self-important airs.* It grated him to have to grovel to them, but he hadn't been lying when he boasted about them being good customers. They were by far his best, so grovel he would.

"Something to drink while we wait for Rearden?" Tibbot waved to a table lined with an assortment of barrels, bottles, and jugs. "I have a superb ale made by the monks in the Swords Abbey and fine wine from Frankia. Or perhaps our special Irish poteen?"

Gunnar declined them all with a shake of his head as Tibbot poured himself a goblet of deep red wine.

"You've come to the right place," Tibbot said, nodding after he took a sip. "I have the finest stock in Swords or Dublin."

"I actually heard that you and Quillen were the two I should seek, but that Quillen has had a run of the flux in his stock."

"I see you are well informed, but I can assure you that even without the flux, my stock is far superior to that of Quillen," Tibbot said, glancing nervously at something behind them.

Gunnar turned to follow Tibbot's gaze. He'd noted nothing unusual in his original perusal, but Tibbot's odd behavior made him inspect the area again. Still, everything seemed in order. It wasn't until he was about to turn away for the second time, that he noted the two inconspicuous steps at the base of a large tapestry—steps that appeared to lead into solid stone—a secret entrance to the main house, which explained how Tibbot normally avoided walking.

The sound of rattling pulled Gunnar's attention away from the steps and secret door. Slaves shuffled into the room in single file, bound together by short lengths of chain. Their wrists and ankles were fettered and all were barefooted and bare-chested. Some wore trousers, others kilts, and some only loincloths. Of the first thirty men, Gunnar chose sixteen, eliminating the others for various reasons—too small, bad teeth, and a Gaul who looked to be very strong, but whose eyes were hard with pride. A slave like that would be trouble and could incite other slaves to do something reckless.

When he bypassed him, Tibbot seemed disappointed and called his attention back. "This one's a fine specimen. Strong and..."

"He's not to my liking." Gunnar cut him off, sure now that his assessment of the Gaul being trouble was well-founded. Tibbot was too eager to be rid of him. "Have these sixteen stripped all the way."

Gunnar waited while his request was met then walked down the line again, eliminating one more for drainage from his cock. "Do you have others?"

"Aye, of course, but these will have been the best."

"Then those I pick from the next batch should not be as costly."

"I, uh, aye, rightly so. Rearden, bring ten more."

Gunnar picked out the last of the twenty and prepared for the negotiating, hoping Tibbot would not waste too much time by starting with inflated prices. After a surprisingly brief negotiation, a fair price was agreed upon.

"Shall I have them prepared to take with you now?" Tibbot asked. "Or will you be returning with your ship to retrieve them?"

"No. I would avoid the tax I hear they are collecting in the bay."

"Tax," Tibbot swore under his breath. "'Tis nothing but sanctioned extortion," he spat.

"I shall return for them tomorrow at nightfall—with armed men. I've also heard of some difficulties other slave purchasers have run into."

Tibbot scowled again. "I see that you are, in fact, very well informed, my lord. I'd like to say they were only a few isolated incidents and the precaution of armed guards unnecessary, but the scoundrels have yet to be caught, and I would hate for our first dealings to have issue."

"As would I," Gunnar agreed.

"Will you be needing shackles for them? You'll find my prices on accessories very reasonable as well."

"Only neck collars and enough chain to link them together—and warmer clothes," he added. "I'll pay you a quarter now and the rest when we return." He turned to Rask. "See that all are marked with this on the upper arm." Gunnar unclasped a heavy cloak pin with a stippled three-inch ring on the end and nodded toward the assembled line of slaves.

Rask moved toward the fireplace, but Tibbot stepped in front of him, twitching nervously.

"I usually don't allow them to be altered before the sale is final," he said to Gunnar.

"The sale is final, and when I return, I'll be in a hurry and not have time to inspect them all again. If by some chance I were not to return, the quarter you receive now will more than cover any loss in their value from bearing a mark."

Tibbot nodded and stepped aside. After Rask repeatedly heated the pin in the fireplace and seared it into the men's upper arms, Gunnar nodded, satisfied. The mark was clearly visible, yet small enough to not affect their performance.

"Why did you mark them?" Rask asked as they returned to their horses.

"Normally I would not, but I do not wish to return and find inferior slaves in place of the ones we chose."

"Do you think he would dare to swap them?"

"I don't know what he would dare. He seems soft, but do not underestimate him based on how he appears. A man in his position will be cunning."

Rask nodded. "Why did we not take them with us now? The two of us could easily handle twenty chained slaves. Why return at night, and with armed guard?"

"There are rumors of slaves being stolen soon after purchase. From what I was told, the raiders are brazen and attack in broad daylight."

Rask smiled and placed his hand on the hilt of his sword. "Let us hope the rumors are true."

Chapter 4

As Gunnar slogged through the mud, he was thankful for the lull in the driving rain that had plagued them since leaving Tibbot's earlier that night. He tried to imagine the hot, dry days ahead in the East—the red dust clogging his nostrils, the brutally intense sun, the sweat and grime collecting in layers under his hardened leather armor. He would long for this cool Irish damp then. He glanced up at the nearly full moon about to be overtaken by a small cloud, then at the more threatening clouds looming ahead. The rain may have let up for the moment, but it appeared the reprieve was not to last.

"Run!" The unexpected shout and jangle of chains from one of the prisoners jolted Gunnar from his musings. His hand closed on the golden hilt of his sword just as the small cloud that had previously flirted with the moon's perimeter plunged them into total darkness.

Gunnar turned and took a quick assessment of the slaves. All remained securely tethered together by the chains between their neck collars. None seemed poised for escape. He glanced at his men who were also trying to identify the recipient of the slave's sudden warning. Some had weapons drawn. Others had their hands ready on the hilts of their swords. All eyes and ears strained in the darkness, trying to detect any signs of an impending attack.

Gunnar cursed the cloud that prevented him from seeing for whom the warning had been intended. His decision to travel at night, to slip unseen by local raiders if the rumors were true, was working against him. Now it was he and his men who couldn't see, and they had the added disadvantage of not knowing the terrain.

Lightning flashed overhead, giving a split second of sight before submerging them once again in blackness. Another flash. Then another. The unpredictable bursts bathed the countryside in eerie otherworldly light, creating unnerving mysterious shadows without providing enough time to discern what was real. Nerves stretched taut, Gunnar awaited the next flash, half expecting it to reveal a hard-charging assailant closing in on him. He pulled Maid's Dream from its sheath.

The suspense was maddening. If an attack was coming, Gunnar wished they would just bring it. Here, on an open spot in the road, whoever attacked them would lose the advantage of knowing the terrain. Fighting hand-to-hand up close, they would fight on equal terms, and unless they were significantly outnumbered, Gunnar was sure of the outcome.

Unless they had archers. If that were the case, this position, so ideal to take on a foe armed with sword and battle-axe, would provide little protection. Gunnar's gut tightened at the thought of being showered with clouds of winged death from a faceless opponent, then realized it was unlikely. A blanket attack by archers in the darkness could not differentiate between captor and captive; it would kill Viking and slave alike. And if slaves were the goal...

Still, he found himself listening for the distinctive whir of feather fletching in flight, hopefully in time to raise his shield. He hated archers.

Rask moved up beside him. His sword was drawn and his eyes were wary, but a hint of a smile played at the corners of his lips. Gunnar shook his head at his eagerness and returned his full focus to their surroundings, waiting for the cloud to pass. The wind picked up. He felt several drops of rain, though the most ominous clouds were still well off in the distance. With excruciating slowness, the small cloud moved on—moonlight once again turning the impenetrable darkness to near day.

Gunnar saw the woman on the road ahead now. She didn't appear to be aware of them—must not have heard the slave's warning for the wind. She stood slightly stooped, holding up her horse's near front leg while she inspected its hoof. The animal was a common farm steed, thick-legged and coarse, and the woman's hooded brown cloak was plain.

The men looked to him for orders, but Gunnar shook his head for them to wait. Had this been an ambush, he would have expected it to come in the dark woods ahead. Still, his gut told him something wasn't right. Women didn't frequent roads alone at night.

"Run, lass!" One of the prisoners screeched his warning again. This time his men were ready, and the man was quickly silenced with a club to the jaw.

The woman released the horse's leg and turned to face them. At first, she appeared to be relieved at the prospect of aid and even took a half step toward them. But as her eyes took in the group of armed men, their round shields unmistakable, then the smaller group of men huddled and chained together between them, her body stiffened with alarm. She spun away, yanking on the horse's reins in a frantic attempt to flee.

The horse, hobbling on his left front leg, trailed gamely behind her. One of his men chuckled. Another whistled. Then all looked to Gunnar for the order to proceed. He held up his hand, silently signaling them to hold their position while he scoured the surroundings once more for anything he might have missed. Finding nothing but empty countryside, Gunnar sheathed his sword and retook the lead. The group advanced slowly.

The darkest clouds had yet to reach them, but the rain fell harder now, while the wind whipped with occasional stronger gusts. His men maintained a slow march, but still, they gained on her. Every few strides she darted a glance over her shoulder. Each time when she saw they were closer, she would tug on the horse's reins with renewed terror. Mud now caked the bottom of her skirt and shoes, and the extra bulk and weight began to slow her even more. Gunnar was surprised she hadn't abandoned the injured animal by now, but people did foolish things when they panicked. He'd seen it so many times before.

The road disappeared into a section of dark forest ahead, and for a moment she was lost from view. After another signal to his men to remain vigilant, they followed. Saplings and small trees bent and swayed in the wind on either side of them. Nothing else moved. Animals were all bedded down waiting out the foul weather.

Gunnar cast quick, repeated glances at her, just long enough to verify she was still desperately pulling at her steed, before returning his full attention to the sides of the road. They'd trudged on high alert for what seemed an eternity when he saw signs of the next clearing ahead. The bright moonlight in the open area was like a beacon. Gunnar began to relax. The way forward was clear; no obstacle blocked their path. The woman was still frantically laboring in front of them in a futile attempt to escape.

They were quite close to her when she slipped and stumbled to her knees. Only her grip on the horse's reins prevented her from falling headlong into the mud. She scrambled to her feet, using the animal's shoulder to steady herself, then whirled to face them.

"Stay back!" she screamed as she continued to retreat, floundering in the mire, the horse limping obediently beside her.

A great gust of wind blew the hood of her cloak from her head, and for the first time, Gunnar could see her face. Pale Irish skin, huge eyes dark with fear and defiance. His breath hitched in his chest. She was stunning. Without the protection of the hood, the wind soon freed her long dark wavy hair. Red highlights glinted in the moonlight—not the fiery red of some of the Irish, only hints of red like a prized sable fur. Gunnar faltered, shocked by his visceral reaction to her.

"I mean it! You stay away from me!" she screamed again. Another gust threatened to tear the cloak from her completely. She spun away from them, her arms flailing in an effort to pull the errant cloth back around her body.

Gunnar signaled his men to stop. The excitement that had been building in them as they stalked her was physically palpable now. The chase was at an end. Their prey was at hand. All could feel it. Gunnar waited for her to turn back to them. Waited to see her reaction when she realized it, too. He was close enough now, he would be able to see it in her eyes. She began to turn.

His anticipation made her movements seem to come in slow motion. His eyes hungrily took in every detail as it was revealed—the soft curve of her jaw, her high cheekbone, the edges of her thick dark eyelashes. Finally, her eyes—the centers so dilated and dark he was unsure of their true color. Fully expecting to see her terrified cowed expression, it took Gunnar several seconds to comprehend what he actually saw. There was no fear. No resignation. No defeat. In fact, her eyes were quite the opposite—hard and bright with triumph.

The wind whipped at her cloak again, but this time she made no attempt to check it. As it lifted away from her body and blew back over her shoulders, she raised the loaded crossbow and aimed it directly at the center of his chest.

"You'll be releasin' those prisoners now," she called out with no trace of the terror that had seemed to grip her only seconds before. Gunnar reached for his sword, but in that instant, felt as much as heard the forest around them come alive with men. He glanced over his right shoulder at a wall of drawn bows, swords, and axes, and swore under his breath.

"Perhaps you Norse are as hard of hearing as you are ugly. I said release the prisoners. Now," she repeated.

Even with the threat in her words, her lilting accent was like water running over smooth stones—pleasing to his ears. Gunnar stared at a stray lock of wet hair plastered to the base of her throat. Mesmerized, he watched a tiny rivulet of water run from the soaked tress to the point where it disappeared under her dress. His eyes continued to follow its imagined journey downwards until his gaze fell again on the crossbow. The sight of the loaded bolt aimed at his heart snapped him back to the actuality of his situation.

"Rask, release the prisoners," Gunnar commanded under his breath, never taking his eyes from the woman.

"But...," Rask balked. "We can take them. They're nothing more than a bunch of armed peasants. They'll be no match for us. We may not even lose a single man."

"Rask!" This time Gunnar did tear his eyes from the woman, furious at the lost seconds of appraisal his second's insubordination had cost. "Release the prisoners—now," Gunnar seethed through gritted teeth.

Rask opened his mouth as if to argue further, then snapped it closed at the look in Gunnar's eyes. He turned and relayed the order to the other men. Gunnar heard their grumbles, then clinking as the slaves' collars were removed.

"Send them forward," the woman commanded. His men held fast until Gunnar nodded. The prisoners rushed forward in a wave. Even as they swept by her, her crossbow never wavered from his chest.

A young man pushing a rickety hand cart appeared on the road behind her. No one moved or spoke while he forced the cart through the mud. After he positioned it a short distance away from her, she bobbed the crossbow at Gunnar. "One at a time, come forward and put your weapons on the cart. Startin' with you," she said.

Amidst louder grumbling from his men, Gunnar stepped forward and unbuckled the belt that held Maid's Dream. The bejeweled sword was his most prized possession—an incredible, unique trophy from his most recent

Middle Eastern raids. As he laid it on the rough boards of the handcart, he never took his eyes from her. "This is a valuable and honored family heirloom," he lied. "I would have it back."

She smiled a cold hard smile. "Aye, I'm sure that it is. Perhaps one day we can even return it to the family you stole it from."

"I think I've been most obliging in this negotiation," Gunnar said, ignoring her jibe. "You could at least tell me your name."

She looked at him with such utter disdain, Gunnar was taken aback. Her haughtiness was certainly like no peasant girl he'd ever met before. Then again, he'd never met a peasant so bold they would dare to take up arms to attack Northmen—in feeble attempts to defend themselves perhaps, but never to attack.

"You'll be havin' no need of my name," she said. "You will never see me again."

He wanted her to say more—to say anything, so he could hear her voice and watch her eyes flash, but she waved him off with the crossbow. After the last sword was relinquished and he and his men were herded back into a group in the center of the road, the loaded handcart was pulled away by several men. When it was long from sight, she bent down and removed something from her horse's front leg. Tossing it aside, she led the now-sound animal forward a few steps before climbing into the saddle and galloping away.

As the armed men surrounding them melted back into the forest, Gunnar went to search for what she had discarded. He found it just off the side of the road—a simple device made from two leather straps and a small blunt piece of wood. Attached to the inside of the animal's leg, it had been unnoticeable, but every time the horse had taken a step, the wood had harmlessly jabbed it, causing it to limp.

Rask appeared at his side. "Well, I guess that answers the question if the rumors of raiders are true. What now?" he asked.

"Send a small party to retrieve our weapons. Men pulling a loaded handcart in this weather will be easy enough to overtake—if they haven't abandoned it already. The rest of us will continue on to the Huntress. Tomorrow we'll return to Tibbot's to replace the slaves."

"But you just paid good coin for this lot," Rask seethed.

"Who said anything about paying for the next ones?" Gunnar said, his voice grim. "Only one man knew we were moving those slaves tonight. And only one man has much to gain by selling twice their number. I shall have a serious discussion with our friend in Swords and show him what happens to those who double-cross us."

And discover the identity of his beautiful accomplice in the process.

Chapter 5

Fiona leaned her back against the barn door, feeling the wind and rain battering against the other side. Her heart was pounding, but she knew it wasn't from fighting the heavy door, nor the hectic ride home. She had done it! She, a woman, had done what most Irishmen were too terrified to even contemplate. She'd faced an armed party of Vikings and triumphed!

In the warmth and safety of the stable, the thrill, terror, and magnitude of the accomplishment made her legs feel suddenly weak. They'd been even more fiercesome in real life than she'd imagined. And so huge! But she had prevailed! She'd faced them with her wits and a crossbow, and she had won!

Cautiously, Fiona made her way in the darkness to the corner where the lamp was stored. Withdrawing the flint and steel from its nearby pouch, she struck a light, then hung it back on its hook, well away from hay or straw. She looked around the stable. The gray carthorse hadn't gone far when she'd released him to wander while she battled the door. He stood peacefully munching a pile of hay only a few lengths away, water dripping from his flanks. The other horses watched over their stall rails with sleepy, curious eyes. She took a deep, settling breath. Everything was normal. She was home. She was safe.

Fiona reached under her cloak and unbuckled the belt before pulling it out to examine it. The gold and gems on the hilt of the sword winked and sparkled in the soft light. She slid the blade partway from the sheath, half expecting to find it horribly encrusted with dried blood, but the steel was clean and finely polished. She withdrew it the rest of the way. It was an unusual thing—lighter than a broadsword and curved in a sweeping arch. How strange. And what a trophy.

As she returned the sword to its sheath, a shiver rippled through her body. Then another. In all the excitement, she'd barely noticed the wet and cold. She needed to get out of these soaked clothes, hide the sword, and tend to Dobbin.

"I'll return straightaway," she murmured to the gray gelding and gave him a pat before climbing the ladder to the loft. She paused at the top, her eyes unable to see anything in the pitch blackness, but even with the winter hay stores almost gone, she dare not strike a light here. She felt her way along the wall until she reached the far corner. Rummaging through the loose hay with her feet, she found the blanket-wrapped bundle she'd left there hours before.

Fiona quickly stripped out of the wet peasant wool kirtle and pulled her fine linen kirtle over her damp shift. Without taking the time to lace it in the front, she stepped into her outer wool gown and pulled the two wide straps up over her shoulders, securing each of them in the front with a brooch. She gave the side laces of the outer gown a quick cursory yank, then tied them off and donned her dark blue wool fur-trimmed cloak.

Her teeth were chattering now, and even though the new clothes were dry, they held no warmth. She rolled the sword in the empty blanket, then stashed it and the wet dress under the hay before retracing her steps and returning below.

She pulled the gelding's saddle and carried it to the furthest rack in the tack room. On the way back, she grabbed a rag and a bristle brush and paused at the barrel of oats. She put a quick scoop into a bucket. The soft silky rustling of the falling oats drew hopeful nickers from several of the horses, but Fiona only murmured apologies to them as she passed them by and hung the bucket on a hook for Dobbin.

The sound of the gelding's blissful slobbery munching as he enjoyed his extra treat, and the effort of currying him calmed and warmed her. She'd done it, she thought again with less of the exhilaration. She had really done it. She'd saved all those men from the hands of the pagan devils. She thought back to their leader and the predatory intensity in his eyes as he'd boldly stared at her. But, oh, how his expression had changed when he realized the trap!

Though it hadn't changed to fear. Fiona frowned. That was the only regretful aspect of the whole endeavor; not one of them had seemed afraid. She would have liked for them to cower and beg for mercy, but strangely they had not. Their leader even had the audacity to address her—and to ask for her name?! She snorted. Arrogant brute. Perhaps she should have made them all kneel in the mud. Aye, that would have been a sight. But even as she appreciated the image, something in the back of her mind warned her that he would not have complied. Something about him.

"Fiona, what in God's name are you doing here at this hour?" Cahan's voice startled her from her reverie. "And what are you doing with Dobbin?" He paused, taking in her appearance. "Have you been out, lass?" he asked, incredulous. "In this weather? Your hair is soaked and...where have you been? Has this to do with Aiden? I've turned a blind eye to his shenanigans because of what he endured, but if he has dared to involve you...."

"Cahan, I am well," Fiona attempted to reassure him.

"Nay lass, you're not! You look half-drowned. This...," he sputtered and waved at her and the gelding, "is never to happen again; do you understand me?" When she didn't answer right away, his eyes bulged and he puffed out his chest. "I asked you a question, lass!"

Cahan had not addressed her in such a manner since she was a child, and the fact that he did so now, told her how upset he truly was. She could have rebuked him. He was their head stableman after all, but she would never do that. Cahan was like a second father to her, and she knew his harsh words were borne only out of concern for her safety. "Aye, Cahan, I understand."

"Very well, then," he nodded, his tone softening in the face of her acquiescence. "I'll finish that. You get yourself back to the residence and into your warm bed before you catch your death of cold. And for the love of Saint Peter, don't let anyone else see you," he grumbled as he took the brush and rag from her, nudging her towards the door. "If Meirna were to learn of this, she'll have both our heads."

Fiona thought of Meirna and knew he was right. As upset as Cahan was, Meirna would be livid, and she was a force to be reckoned with. Though her title was that of head housekeeper, she was far more than that. After Fiona's mother had died, Meirna was the one to raise her. And even though Fiona was now a woman grown, it was still a responsibility Meirna took very seriously.

On the walk back to Balbriggan, Gunnar reviewed everything that had happened, his thoughts lingering on the details of the woman. Her dark wavy hair whipped free by the wind and highlighted red by the moonlight. Her glistening wet pale skin. Her perfect full kissable lips. Her eyes, the centers so large, he'd been uncertain of their color. Green perhaps? Or maybe violet? And when he thought of the water running down under her soaked dress...

She'd be a hellcat in the furs, he was certain of it. She was bold. And the way she'd looked at him—like he was truly beneath her. Oh, how he would enjoy showing her otherwise. His mind took liberty with the details and ran wild. He imagined subduing her—pinning her arms to his furs, her thick dark red hair spread out in glorious waves around her. She would struggle at first, but that wouldn't last. In his vision, her lips were parted in a willing smile, and her green eyes soft and drowsy with desire. Yes, they'd be green, he decided. So strong was his reaction to the mental picture, he was forced to put the thoughts aside, as walking became physically uncomfortable.

He tried instead to think of how he would deal with the slaver on the morrow, but even that returned to the fiery peasant beauty. How were they connected?

He'd know soon enough, Gunnar thought grimly as he led his men through the outskirts of the sleeping port town in the pre-dawn darkness. He'd catch a few hours of sleep, then return to Tibbot's. The tunnels might be a fortress, but he'd seen nothing to indicate that the residence was.

As they began their descent into the town, Gunnar spotted the torches and commotion ahead. The docks were in chaos. He picked up his pace.

"What's happening?" he asked a man who was sprinting past.

"A ship's been scuttled," the man called over his shoulder without slowing.

Gunnar started to run. Not the Huntress, he prayed silently. *Gods forbid, not the Huntress!* As he ran, he strained his eyes to find the great dragon's head in the darkness but couldn't. He raced down the long dock, past the now countless fishing vessels that were in for the night. His men's boots pounded the planks behind him. *There! The Huntress was there!* His relief was short-lived when he saw how she leaned at a kilter, leaving no doubt which boat the man had been referring to. Though not scuttled completely, he frantically reassured himself. She was still afloat.

When he reached the ship, Gunnar rapidly assessed the situation. A handful of men lined the dock next to her. With hooks set into the ship's far side bulwarks, they strained against ropes to keep her from rolling. He knew they dare not tie it off. A ship the size of the Huntress could take the aged wood with it—if she went down.

More men were on the ship, desperately bailing. Despite their valiant efforts, there was over a foot of rising water in the boat. Bailing wasn't going to be enough. They had to get her out of the water, but how? A solid line of fishing vessels stood between them and the shore.

Gunnar quickly divided his men into thirds. "Olag, take your group and find more ropes and hooks. We can't let her roll." He turned to the next. "You men find anything you can to bail with and help the men on board. Rask, take the rest and move those ships." Gunnar pointed to the fishing boats. "We'll pull the Huntress down the dock to the beach."

"There's no time to move them," Rask disagreed. "We should just cut them free."

Gunnar grimaced—he'd already thought the same, but to cut them loose to drift with no crew would mean the certain loss of many. He couldn't do it—not even for the Huntress.

"No. Secure them somewhere else out of our way."

Thankfully Rask didn't argue. He and the remaining men dashed toward the nearest boats.

Gunnar leapt on board the Huntress, splashing through the water past the line of bailing men—Northmen and Irish working side by side. They were seamen first, and a ship in trouble united them without hesitation. Gunnar recognized a man with a nasty gash on his head as one of the few crewmen he'd left behind to guard the ship. He didn't need to ask what happened. The skeleton crew had been taken by surprise and overwhelmed. They, nor he, had expected the ship to come under attack. He reached the stern and the small group of men who were hunched over, struggling to stanch the flow of black water that roiled up through the hull with a large piece of hide. "Can you patch it?" he shouted to the man closest to the hole.

"Nay, it's too big! We can't stop it," the man yelled back over his shoulder.

"Do what you can to slow it. We need to keep her afloat long enough to get her hauled from the water. They're moving the other ships now." The man nodded, renewed his grip on the hide, and plunged his arms back into the frigid water.

Gunnar grabbed a bucket from an older Irishman who was tiring and started to bail. The muscles in his back and arms were soon burning, but he was glad for the release the repetitive labor provided. The rage inside him threatened to boil over at any moment. The loss of the slaves had been galling, but this—this someone was going to pay dearly for.

The water had reached his mid-calf when he heard Rask calling to him. He glanced up without slowing. Several boats had been moved, and the short section of the dock ahead was clear.

"Olag!" Gunnar shouted. "Have the men start her towards the shore. But go easy!"

The Huntress shuddered beneath his feet but didn't move. Then inch by critical inch, the ship began to scrape along the barnacle-encrusted dock toward shallower water and the safety of land.

The sun had fully crested the horizon when the last of the great ship's hull finally cleared the water. Balanced on logs laid crossways on the sand, it was pulled up beyond the high tide mark, then propped and blocked for repair. Water dripped from along its full length but ran in tiny rivulets from the gaping hole in the stern. Like blood, Gunnar thought as he got down on his hands and knees to survey the damage. Fresh axe marks were clearly visible in the wood, and the iron fittings that supported the rudder were gone.

He ran his fingers gently over the splintered edges as if he were touching a wound. How had she not sunk with such a hole? He stood up and walked toward the bow, his eyes and fingers tracing the full length. He stopped at the base of the dragon's neck, having found no other damage. The perpetrators had known exactly what they were doing, chopping a single hole where the ship rode the lowest in the water. He glanced up at the great beast's lifelike eye.

"Apologies, Huntress," he murmured. "Nothing like this will ever happen again. I swear it. And know that I shall find who did this and make them pay."

He turned to his men who had silently gathered behind him. "Olag, find a shipbuilder if this town has one. If not, find the nearest and tell him we need him to begin repairs immediately. Sven, where are the swords? Rask said you recovered them."

"Apologies, my lord. All were recovered except for yours."

Gunnar ran a hand over the tight braids on his head and grit his teeth. This trip that had started so incredibly well had, in the blink of an eye, turned from one disaster to the next. He rubbed the back of his neck, stiff from bailing. "Someone find me a sword," he muttered.

"Here, take mine, lord." Sven unbuckled his scabbard and offered it to him.

"Rask, you are with me. The rest of you remain here. From now on, the ship is to be heavily guarded at all times." Gunnar buckled the strange scabbard belt around his waist, missing the familiar feel of Maid's Dream.

Chapter 6

The hostler, Larkin, was cleaning stalls when they arrived. They rented the same two horses and spurred them out onto the road to Swords. There was no stopping at the Red Stag tavern this time. No need for directions. Gunnar never slowed the bay gelding as he turned through the open gates and galloped up the short drive. A stately carriage was parked in front, and as Gunnar slid his horse to a stop, oyster shell fragments sprayed from beneath its hooves, hitting the back of it with a clatter.

"His lordship has company," Rask noted. "And highborn from the looks of it."

"That will not save him," Gunnar snarled as he threw a leg over the horse's neck and dropped to the ground. He took the steps two at a time and kicked open the door. A startled manservant ducked for cover just inside.

"Where is he?" Gunnar demanded.

"His lordship has guests," the man stammered.

"Where?" Gunnar walked to the nearest door and pushed it open. It squealed on its hinges, then slammed against the wall inside as he barged through it. Empty.

"My lord. You must stop," the manservant pleaded.

Gunnar covered the distance between them in three strides, pulling his dagger along the way. Slamming the man against the wall, he pressed the razor-sharp tip to the soft skin under the man's chin. "Where...is...he?" he repeated.

"My lord. I am here." Tibbot announced in a hushed voice as he hastened towards them. "Please lower your voice. My wife has an important guest—a noblewoman. T'would not do at all for them to see or hear you. Come, let us retire to my viewing chamber."

Gunnar released the servant and gripped Tibbot by his fleshy throat with one hand. He longed to choke the life out of him then and there—the jagged edges of the ship's torn hull still vivid in his mind. But he also wanted information from him before he killed him, and the underground cavern would be easier for him and Rask to defend than here in the open.

"Yes, that will be better. The stone will muffle your screams if I'm not satisfied with your answers," Gunnar said as he released him, though he could imagine nothing the man could possibly say that would save him from that fate.

"My lord, I assure you I will be most cooperative in every way," Tibbot wheezed through his partially collapsed windpipe and moved to the front door.

Gunnar didn't follow him. "Not that way, Tibbot. There's a faster way somewhere in here."

Tibbot shook his head. "We cannot. That entrance is through the room where my wife is hosting her guest."

Gunnar weighed his options, then nodded. The extra walk would mean a short delay in exacting his revenge but would eliminate having to deal with two hysterical women, their servants, and any guards they might call to their rescue.

When they stepped into the slave-viewing chamber, Gunnar instructed Rask to close and bolt the door to the river entrance, then to stand guard at the doorway they'd come through. Balling his fist, he turned and struck Tibbot squarely in the face with all his pent-up rage from the night. The force of the blow lifted the squat man off his feet. He landed on his back on the stone floor, limp and still.

"Have you killed him already?" Rask asked. "I thought we might draw it out a bit longer than that."

Gunnar shook out his hand as he knelt over the prone body. He held two fingers under Tibbot's nostrils. It had not been his intent to kill him yet. He'd purposely missed the man's nose to prevent it from being driven back into his brain and causing just such a result. A soft exhale swirled around his fingers. "No," he said. "He yet lives."

"That was some shot," Rask chuckled.

"Only a taste of what is to come."

"I'm happy to assist," Rask offered.

"No. This is all mine." *For the Huntress.*

Gunnar stepped over Tibbot's body and walked to the table of spirits. He pulled the cork out of a jug, took a sniff, then a swallow, gasping again at the powerful kick of this drink they called poteen. Returning to Tibbot, he tipped the bottle, trickling a thin stream over the slaver's face. Tibbot sputtered and retched, then cried out as he reached for his split cheek.

"Get up," Gunnar commanded and returned the jug to the table.

Tibbot staggered to his feet, repeatedly touching his face, then staring at the blood on his fingertips as if he could not comprehend it.

"You know why I'm here?" Gunnar asked.

"Aye, my lord, but I swear I had naught to do with it. In fact, I've offered a reward of double your purchase price for the slaves' return. Why would I do that if I was involved?" he whimpered.

"Because as the man behind the theft, you know you'll never have to pay such a reward! Do you take me for an idiot?"

"Nay, my lord," Tibbot stammered. "Feel free to search my entire premises. Your slaves were all marked. You'll not find them here."

Gunnar knew there was no way he could ever search all the underground caverns, and even if he could and the slaves were not here, it wouldn't prove anything. Tibbot could have hidden them somewhere else or taken them straight to a ship in the port and sold them again. Before he could respond, Tibbot continued.

"And why would I steal slaves from my own customer?"

"To make more coin." Gunnar stated the obvious.

"But my reputation would soon be ruined, and I would make no coin at all."

"I have no idea what motivates you, nor do I care. One thing I do not understand, though, is my ship. Why would you attempt to sink it and leave me stranded here? Surely you must know I would seek revenge for that."

"Your ship?" Tibbot blinked at him. "I heard only that you were accosted on the road and the slaves were taken. I heard nothing about your ship."

He looked so surprised that Gunnar almost believed him. And there was also his choice of words. He said *heard* nothing of your ship, not *knew* nothing of your ship. It was a small detail, but he'd found that people under duress often gave themselves away with such small details. But there was no way that the slaves and the Huntress were a coincidence. And if not Tibbot, then who?

"I don't believe you," Gunnar said and pulled his dagger from his belt again, testing the point against one of his fingers to make sure he had Tibbot's full attention. "You must know that we Northmen have ways to make a man talk. Terrible ways. I would like to say that it will be quick because I'm in a hurry, but since my ship is disabled, that's not the case. I'm free to linger here for days if need be—plenty of time to remove enough of your body parts until I'm assured you've told me everything you know."

Tibbot blanched and wobbled. Gunnar wondered if he was going to faint.

"I would never cross you—not a man like you. I'm not a fool."

Gunnar stared silently at him for a long moment. Either Tibbot was truly the best liar he'd ever encountered or he was telling the truth. Even when faced with the terrifying prospect of being dismembered, he showed not the slightest inclination of confessing. It didn't make sense. What was he missing?

Gunnar moved to one of the large fur-draped chairs he'd declined to sit on during his first visit and took a seat. Leaning back, he put his boots up on another. "Pour me a glass of that poteen and then have a meal brought in. It was a long night, and this appears as though it might take a while."

Tibbot handed him a goblet with a trembling hand, then moved towards the doorway where Rask stood guard.

"Nay, Tibbot," Gunnar said and shook his head. "Not that way. Through the door to the house...there." Gunnar nodded to the hidden doorway behind the tapestry.

"But I cannot," Tibbot implored. "My wife and her guest."

"Oh, you can...or I will. My patience is at an end. Though I would caution you not to venture through the door far enough for the fair ladies to see you. Your countenance is a bit gruesome at the moment."

Tibbot reached up again to touch his cheek. The swelling had spread to his left eye; only a slit remained open. His shoulders slumped in resignation as he shuffled toward the secret door.

"And don't do anything foolish," Gunnar warned, "like try to run or call for help. Or it will not only go badly for you, but for your wife and her guest as well."

Tibbot nodded and pushed the tapestry aside. He released the door latch, then began to pull the heavy, well-oiled stone slab inward. As the door opened wider, Tibbot heeded Gunnar's warning to remain hidden and stepped sideways behind it, clearing Gunnar's line of sight into the room. A woman in a burgundy silk gown stood with her back to him, her thick braided hair coiled at her nape.

Tibbot called out to his wife. "Leona, darling. Please have food prepared and delivered to my business chambers. My guests are hungry."

Gunnar heard another unseen woman's sharp gasp at the request, followed by shocked babbling that sounded to be a mix of apologies and outrage. But Gunnar was only vaguely aware of her words. His mind was reeling. The woman he could see had turned and stood facing him with a cup raised to her lips. Her perfect full lips.

She looked nothing like she had the night before. In fact, her appearance was so far removed that Gunnar's mind struggled to accept it. Her green eyes focused on the open doorway with simple curiosity, widening slightly as they probed deeper into the cavern interior. When she discovered him sitting there, her alarmed recognition was unmistakable. It was truly her!

Having made his request, Tibbot pushed the door closed, and the woman was lost from sight. Gunnar stood and rushed across the cavern, reaching Tibbot as the latch clicked into place. The lying foot-licker had nearly fooled him with all his trembling and groveling. Not only did he know about the raid, his accomplice was in the very next room!

"Who is that woman?" Gunnar demanded.

"There would only be my wife, her maid, and her guest," Tibbot mumbled, confused, peering at him with one eye, the other having now swollen completely closed.

Not a maid. And his wife? Impossible. Gunnar quickly discounted both. "Your wife's guest, who is she?"

"Uh, Lady Fiona. Lady Fiona O'Neill."

A highborn lady working with a slaver? Gunnar couldn't conceive it. Though he also couldn't conceive a lady dressing as a peasant to rob armed Vikings—and he'd most certainly seen that with his own eyes.

But Tibbot had given up her name with no hesitation, something he wasn't likely to do if she was his collaborator. Was the man truly innocent as he proclaimed? Was this lady a spy? Pretending to be friends with Tibbot's wife to gain information, then reporting it to someone else? That would explain her unusual friendship with a lowly merchant lord, but not her actual participation in the raid. Gunnar wasn't going to waste another moment attempting to figure it out on his own. The one person who knew the truth was here. She could explain it to him.

"Open the door," he said, grabbing Tibbot by the collar. "You will make introduction."

"Nay, I cannot," Tibbot gasped, trying to squirm free. Unable to break Gunnar's grip, he attempted to throw himself to the floor, but a quick boot to his rump kept him on his feet. "I beg of you," he pleaded. "She's my wife's only highborn friend—the only one who accepts us. If she were to see me with you, that will all be ruined."

"Make introduction now, or I can assure you your social standing will be the least of your worries."

"But...," the man protested.

"Now!" Gunnar roared.

Tibbot gave a quick nod. "God forgive me," he whispered as he lifted the latch and tugged gently on the heavy door.

Exasperated, Gunnar reached around him and grabbed the door himself. Yanking it open, he shoved Tibbot up the two steps and through the doorway. He didn't need the man for an introduction, but not knowing what other security might be summoned, he may very well need him as a hostage to escape.

The room was empty. The door on the other side stood ajar. He could hear an excited female voice coming from beyond. "Move," Gunnar instructed and propelled Tibbot across the floor.

A maid carrying an empty tray came through the doorway as they approached. She dropped the tray at the sight of them, then quickly curtsied to Tibbot. "Apologies, my lord."

"Where are my wife and Lady Fiona?" Tibbot asked.

"Lady Fiona has taken ill and is preparin' to depart," she replied, staring at them wide-eyed.

Gunnar pushed Tibbot past the maid, out into the entry hall. A lone heavyset woman dressed in garish multi-colored silks paced and wrung her hands just inside the closed front door. Her mouth fell open when she saw them. "Tibbot, what do you think you're doin'?"

"I am to make introduction."

The woman stormed towards them. "You most certainly are not!"

"We don't have time for this, Tibbot," Gunnar muttered.

"But she's already gone," Tibbot stuttered. "We're too late."

"We can still catch her at her carriage."

"Nay!" Tibbot's wife screeched. "I'll not allow it. Have you gone mad, Tibbot? You've already humiliated me—interrupting us and summoning me like some servant to deliver food. That's probably why she left; she was appalled by your base-born behavior! She probably isn't ill at all, just too polite to say what she really thinks of us—of you! If you accost her with this... this barbarian, she'll never return here. Then no one else of import will ever come either. I'll be ruined." She sobbed at the thought.

Gunnar attempted to guide Tibbot around her, but she lunged at him, clutching his arm.

"Nay! Stop...you must stop! I'll be ruined," she squalled. Gunnar jerked free from her grasp and side-stepped, sending her plummeting to the floor in a flurry of silks. With Tibbot firmly in tow, Gunnar hastened to the door and pulled it open.

The lady had made it to the bottom of the stairs and was walking briskly toward her carriage.

"Stop her, Tibbot," Gunnar prodded.

"Lady Fiona," Tibbot called out.

She didn't acknowledge him, though Gunnar was sure that she'd heard.

"Louder," Gunnar prompted, accelerating the man down the steps.

"Um, Lady Fiona," Tibbot called louder.

She reached the carriage without looking back and opened the door herself. Thankfully her driver and footman were nowhere to be seen— probably taking refreshment and gossiping with Tibbot's servants, unprepared for her early departure. Only a stable boy held the carriage horses. She had just hoisted herself up inside without the aid of her footman or step box when Gunnar and Tibbot caught up to her.

"Um, Lady Fiona," Tibbot began. "I wish to make introduction of..."

"You advance beyond proper limits, Tibbot. Did your wife not tell you I am ill?" She cut him off mid-sentence with the same haughtiness Gunnar had witnessed the night before, though now it made perfect sense.

"Aye, my lady, apologies," Tibbot murmured and bowed his head.

"Please find my driver and footman and send them at once," she commanded, then reached for the carriage door. Releasing Tibbot and shoving him aside, Gunnar stepped forward to block it.

"I shall introduce myself then—while Tibbot finds your men," he added. He turned to Tibbot who stood frozen with horror. "Go on, man; the lady is not feeling well and needs her driver and footman." After Tibbot had fled, Gunnar turned back to her with a grim smile. "A pleasure to meet you, Lady Fiona," he said, placing heavy accent on her title. "But I believe we've already met."

She glared at him with raw hostility.

"What? No words for me without your crossbow? Lady Fiona O'Neill." He added her family name.

"I have no idea what you're referrin' to."

"Then why the rush to leave so soon after seeing me?"

"As you don't appear to be deaf, you undoubtedly heard that I've suddenly taken ill."

"Well, that is a shame. And you know, until I saw you standing there, Tibbot wasn't feeling too well either—and he was about to feel much worse. Your presence has spared him of that, at least for now."

"Anything you were to do to him is far less than he deserves," she hissed.

She clearly loathed the man, so likely not partners. Gunnar filed the fact away. He didn't have time to make sense of it now. The crunching of boots on shells behind him told him that men were approaching.

"I will have my sword," he demanded.

"I don't know what you're on about. Now take your filthy hands off my carriage and move away. I must go."

"Agree to meet me and return my sword, or I will not allow it."

"You'll not allow?" she scoffed. "Where do you think you are, Northman? Even you would not be so bold as to accost a lady in public—and certainly not without all your men."

"Perhaps not, but you no longer hide safely in anonymity, lady. I now know who you are and will easily find out where you reside. You can either meet me at a time and place of your choosing, or you *will* meet me at a time and place of mine." He paused to let the words sink in. "Choose the first, and I give you my word no harm will come to you, and you'll be allowed to return home. Make me come for you, and not only do I offer no such guarantee, but any who attempt to stand in my way will fare very poorly. Do you want that? Do you want me to come for you in the night and slaughter your guards and servants?"

"You wouldn't dare," she seethed.

"I have dared far worse, I can assure you."

She glared at him, her green eyes flashing, but he could see she believed him.

The footsteps behind him were close now. Her driver and footman would soon be upon them.

"Time is running out, lady. Your decision. Which will it be?"

"Ward's Crossing. Tomorrow. Midday." With that, she yanked on the door, ripping it from his grip.

Gunnar jerked his hand away, narrowly avoiding his fingers being smashed. "Nay, my lady, the pleasure was all mine," he said, nodding deferentially as if in reply to something she'd said, just as her driver and footman arrived.

The two men stared at him bewildered for a moment, before the driver turned and asked through the door, "Are you alright, my lady?"

"Aye, Rafferty. Please return me home at once."

After one last suspicious look at Gunnar, the two men climbed up onto the carriage. With a snap of the whip, the horses sprang forward, whisking the carriage away.

"You see," Gunnar said to Tibbot, who had just returned and now stood with his hands on his hips, gasping for breath. "No harm done. In fact, the lady's endorsement has convinced me that you and your wife are innocent of any involvement in the raid and my ship."

Tibbot wheezed something unintelligible.

"Apologies for the misunderstanding and rough treatment. Fatigue and the events of the night bore heavily upon me. I'll retrieve my man now, and we'll take our leave. And my apologies to your wife," Gunnar added, feeling especially generous.

Tibbot nodded, still struggling to catch his breath.

Rask burst through the doorway at that moment and stood at the top of the steps with sword drawn.

"Rask," Gunnar called to him. "Find the horses. We need to get back to the ship and see to the repairs."

Rask slammed his sword into its sheath, then went in search of their horses that had wandered. He returned with them a few moments later, red-faced but silent. Both men mounted. When they were halfway to the gates and Gunnar had yet to explain, Rask exploded.

"We're just leaving?"

"We are."

"In the middle of an interrogation, you mumble something about a woman, burst from the room, and leave me standing alone with cock in hand. When I finally abandon my post to follow, I find the woman of the house wailing on the floor, the highborn carriage speeding away and you talking with Tibbot as if nothing had happened. What about the slaves? What about the damage to the Huntress?"

"I've discovered one who was involved, and they will lead me to the rest."

"It's not Tibbot?"

"I don't think so."

"So we're going there now?" Rask asked, still angry but slightly placated.

"No. I'm meeting them on the morrow."

"Who is it?"

"It doesn't matter," Gunnar replied, preoccupied with his discovery.

"Doesn't matter? Gunnar, I'm your second, for fuck's sake. I have a right to know what's..."

Gunnar jerked his horse to halt and swiveled to face him. "Your rights as second are what I deem them to be. They include giving me your counsel when I ask for it. When...I...ask...for it. Your *rights* also include obeying my orders without question. Do you understand? It's very simple, but if beyond your grasp, better to know now so that you can be replaced before we head east. I will not have this discussion again. Say the words."

Rask stared at him, his face a mixture of shock and fury. "I understand," he finally muttered through clenched teeth.

"Good." Gunnar nudged the gelding forward, his thoughts immediately returning to the woman and his next move.

It had all happened so fast. Setting up a private meeting with her was the first thing that had come to mind. Though he doubted she would actually be there. And if she were, she would likely not be alone. One carefully laid trap had already been set for him. Whoever was behind this wouldn't hesitate to set another.

He considered taking his men, then decided against it; he would not leave the ship unguarded. But that was only part of the reason. On the off chance that she did come, he wanted her all to himself. He'd go to this Ward's Crossing alone, but he would go very early. And if she had some new treachery in store? He'd meant every word he said about finding her. He hoped she knew that.

Fiona leaned her head back against the cushion, trying to control her shaky breathing. He'd been so close—his face barely a foot away from hers when she'd reached for the door. Close enough to see the steely gray flecks in his fierce blue eyes and the lighter streaks in his blond hair, braided tight against the sides of his head in strange small rows. With furs draped and secured over his shoulders, he appeared more animal than man.

Her heart skipping and thumping in her chest brought back the fear she'd felt the night before while waiting for them alone on the road. Fear that had threatened to grow to outright terror when they'd been closing on her. She'd intentionally chosen the place in the open to give them time to drop their guard before they reached the trap, and it had worked, but the heavy mud caking her shoes and skirts, bogging her down, were details she hadn't accounted for. Details that could have cost her life.

As her fear slowly began to subside, Fiona balled her fists. She wanted to scream and pound them against the seat in frustration. Why had she not been sitting with Tibbot's wife where she wouldn't have been seen? And why had she turned to look into the maw of the sordid cavern when Tibbot opened the door? Had she hoped to see some poor wretch in chains? As if she did not know enough already of how they suffered.

For that matter, why had she gone there at all today? Today of all days? But she knew the answer to that particular question. Because she'd wanted to gloat. To hear first-hand while it was fresh, how raiders had pulled off the impossible—stolen slaves from Norse warriors. Her own hubris had cost her this.

Filthy, black-hearted Viking anyway. How dare he run her down and demand introduction? Who did he think he was? And why had she agreed to meet him? At the remote Ward's Crossing of all places? Everything had happened so fast, she hadn't had time to think. But Fiona knew that wasn't the only reason. She'd been afraid. Last night in the woods he'd been close, but not like this—not face to face, and with her unarmed. In that moment, though she hated to admit it, she would have agreed to anything to get away.

Of course, she'd never meet with him. But she had to do something. Now that he knew her name, he would find Tir na Lionmhar eventually. She could increase the guard around the estate, but how would she explain it? That she'd been threatened by a Viking while socializing with a slave merchant's wife? She groaned. Her father would have her married off in no time. There'd been a lull in that conversation for awhile now, for which she was grateful, but that would surely renew it.

Fiona pushed the underlying marriage problem from her mind. She had a far more imminent catastrophe to worry about right now. Did she dare to meet with him? He'd sworn she would be unharmed. Fiona snorted under her breath—as if the word of a Viking meant anything. But if she didn't, would he come for her some night, slaughtering her servants as he'd threatened? He didn't seem as one who offered idle threats.

This was all because of that damned sword. If only she'd left it in the cart with the others. But she hadn't, and all the lamenting in the world wasn't going to change that now. She had to give it back. She would go to Ward's Crossing, deliver the sword, and be done with this mess. She'd just go very early to make sure he didn't have a trap for her. And she wouldn't be riding the carthorse, Dobbin, this time. She'd be on Barca, her beloved mount and the fastest horse in two kingdoms. No one could catch her on him.

As the carriage bumped its way along the slowly drying roads, she wished she was on Barca now—flying with the wind in her hair instead of being banged and bruised at this snail's pace.

Chapter 7

"Were you able to find a shipbuilder?" Gunnar asked.

"Aye, but he's only just arrived, my lord," Olag replied. "He's inspecting the ship now."

"Does he seem to know what he's about?"

"He came highly recommended, but perhaps you should decide for yourself." Olag seemed eager to be rid of the responsibility.

Gunnar nodded and turned his attention to the gray-haired man who was slowly walking the perimeter of the Treasure Huntress. Short and stocky, his shoulders were stooped from years of hard labor, but Gunnar was relieved to see that he was older. The thought of some novice clumsily chopping away on the ship turned his stomach. The shipbuilder occasionally stopped and examined something on the hull, then moved on. When he reached the bow, he stopped and stared at the dragon's scales. He reached out to touch one, then another.

From his own inspection, Gunnar knew there to be no damage there, but he also understood the impact of seeing the carvings up close for the first time—especially to someone like this man who would recognize the level of skill required. He waited for him to complete his perusal, then approached.

"I'm Gunnar, captain of this vessel," Gunnar introduced himself and held out his hand.

"Parlan," the stocky man replied, taking his hand with a firm grip. His short-trimmed, thick gray beard and bushy sideburns gave his head an almost comical round appearance, but his eyes were serious and direct. "She's a fine vessel. I've never seen such craftsmanship."

"Can you repair her?" Gunnar asked.

The man said nothing for a long time, rubbing and pulling at his beard, leaving Gunnar to wonder if the beard was actually trimmed or rubbed away during such long ponderings. He forced himself to be patient, sure that the man was preparing a detailed answer about the specifics of the repairs, but when the shipbuilder finally spoke, he simply said, "Aye."

"And she will be as seaworthy?" Gunnar asked.

Again a long pause before Parlan nodded. "Aye, she will."

Gunnar prayed the man worked faster than he talked.

"But...," Parlan started, then stopped again.

"But what?"

"I expected your ship to be made of oak but instead, 'tis crafted of larch wood. The closest we have here is birch."

"Can you get larch?"

"Aye, but 'twould have to be brought in...could be a fortnight or more."

Gunnar grimaced. They were well ahead of schedule, but a fortnight plus was out of the question; the fleet was to depart from Aalborg in less than three weeks. "Is the birch as strong?"

"'Tis." Parlan nodded.

"Then go with birch. How long?"

Parlan appeared not to have heard him. "The problem with the birch is that it will cure out lighter than the larch. You'll always be able to see the repair."

"Like a scar," Gunnar mused.

"Aye, just like a scar."

"Only fitting, I suppose. When can you start?"

"Today. Now."

"And how long will it take?" he asked again.

"A day to remove the damaged planks, a day or two to dry, three days to bring in the wood, shape the planks, form the rudder. The mounts that supported the rudder will have to come from the forge in Drogheda, a day's ride there, a day or two for the smith to structure them, a day's ride back. But that could be done while we're working the wood." He mumbled a list, counting on his fingers, before concluding. "Eight days."

"Then a day to launch and reload the ship. So nine days before we could be ready to sail," Gunnar finished for him.

"Aye," Parlan agreed. "If all goes well. Nine days."

If all goes well. All certainly hadn't been going well recently. Gunnar wondered if the streak of bad luck was over or would continue to plague them. "Very well. Can my men be of any service?"

"Nay, my grandson will help me. He's my apprentice."

As Gunnar watched the shipbuilder and his apprentice laying out their tools, he felt the overwhelming need for a drink. The grandson was little more than a child. Gunnar didn't see any way possible the two of them could finish in eight days. After instructing Rask where to set up a temporary camp, Gunnar headed for the Red Dragon.

Cora met him just inside the door. "You've returned," she greeted him, seeming genuinely pleased. "I was worried after what happened to your ship, not to see you again. Dreadful business that. I'll have you know, I've heard not a whisper of the culprits, but I'll keep my ear to the ground for you, love. Sooner or later someone is bound to say somethin' that'll give them away."

"I appreciate that, Cora, but I've already discovered one of those responsible. Tomorrow they shall lead me to the others."

"You have?"

Gunnar nodded. "And I'll have that poteen again today. Bring a jug...and two cups," he added.

She smiled, then bustled towards the bar. Returning with equal speed, she plopped down on the chair next to him. The stout wood creaked loudly beneath the sudden load. Gunnar feared it might collapse beneath her, but Cora seemed unconcerned. Pulling the stopper with her teeth, she filled the mismatched cups halfway and handed him one.

"I need directions to a place called Ward's Crossing," he said before taking a deep breath and downing his in three gulps. He set the empty cup back on the table with a sharp exhale, feeling the liquid burning all the way to his stomach. He waited for the calming effects to follow.

"Ward's Crossing?" Cora asked as she refilled his cup, then took a deep swallow from hers. "There's nothing there but a few sheep."

"Do you know it then?"

"Aye, love, but are you sure they said Ward's Crossing?"

"I am."

She shook her head, troubled. "I can draw you a map, but there's no reason for someone to want to meet so far away from everythin'. Sounds like they're up to no good to me."

Gunnar smiled at her intuitiveness and frankness. "Those were my thoughts, too."

"So you'll be taking your men with you?"

"I'm taking necessary precautions," he answered vaguely. He didn't see any way that the Lady Fiona and Cora could be connected, but he'd have never put Fiona with Tibbot either. Someone had gone to great lengths plotting these raids, and until he knew the extent of their network, there was no sense giving away information.

Cora shrugged and took another sip. "I better find somethin' to draw that map with now before my head gets too addled from the drink."

Gunnar dropped his roll of sleeping furs near one of the fires his men had built in the new camp and glanced up at the clear night sky. No sign of any more rain; he wouldn't take the time to pitch his tent tonight, though many of his men had. Their small single-man structures dotted the area all around him. He kicked a few stones out of the way, then spread out his furs and lay down on top of them. The sharp point of a rock jabbed him in the back; he shifted sideways.

He knew the men were unhappy with the location—out on the tip of the small spit of land that formed the harbor's southern natural breakwater. The wind, rocks, and lack of wood for fires made it far from desirable, but he hadn't relented. The spot had advantages that outweighed the inhospitable ground. Large boulders around the camp provided natural defenses, while the single path leading to the point was devoid of vegetation—impossible for anyone to traverse without being seen. That was not only good for spotting intruders, but also any of his men who might think of slipping off to look for trouble in the coming days.

Most importantly, the location provided clear line of sight to the ship. Gunnar rolled onto his side and looked across the harbor to where the Treasure Huntress was propped. The wood of the hull glowed a rich golden brown from the firelight of the men who were stationed on guard duty there.

Satisfied that nothing was amiss, Gunnar lay back down, lacing his fingers behind his head. Having been awake for two days straight, he expected sleep to come quickly. Instead, he found his mind skimming over the recent tumultuous events. The theft of the slaves. His panic at the near sinking of the ship. The loss of Maid's Dream. His brief interrogation of the slaver.

But of everything that had happened, his thoughts always came back to her—Fiona. Lady Fiona. His reaction to her was unfathomable. Last night had stirred something within him, but today—seeing her so close in the light of day had been nothing short of intoxicating. He shook his head and stared up at the stars, wishing he could clear his mind of this woman as easily as the night sky had cleared itself of clouds.

What is wrong with you? Of all the women you've known since Brigitta, she is the one who moves you? She almost sank the Huntress! Perhaps not by her own hand, but she's involved. And if that weren't enough, she's a worthless noble—not a daring raider as you first thought. It was fine to think of bedding her then, but now that you know the truth, you must put all thoughts of her from your mind. Once you are in her company for more than a few moments, you'll see the truth about her; she'll be shallow and self-centered like all the rest. Whatever she has awakened in your blood will quickly fade.

You must focus on what's important—getting information. You have nine days to punish the men responsible for the slaves and the ship, and she is the key. But first, you need to pull your head together. That's twice now, in her presence you've done something foolish—nay, not foolish, downright witless. First, you gave up the slaves and your sword without a fight—even though you knew Rask to be correct; you probably could have taken them without losing a single man. Then you see her at the slaver's, drop everything, and split from Rask to chase after her. Rask was right to criticize you about that, too, and you know it.

Now you intend to meet with her alone in the middle of nowhere? Even Cora smelled a rat there. Odds are, the only people waiting for you tomorrow will be large, hairy, and well-armed. And if perchance she is there, what is your plan? You cannot afford to make another poor decision while spellbound by her nearness. The next one could cost you your life. Perhaps you should heed your command to the men and not leave camp—just stay put until the Huntress is repaired and then head to the East as planned.

Despite the numerous reasons why he shouldn't, Gunnar knew he would go. Like an addict of the poppy, he was drawn to see her again—regardless of the potentially life-threatening consequences. This time would be different, he assured himself. Both of the previous times he'd seen her, he'd been taken by surprise and had to make split-second decisions. This time he was prepared.

Chapter 8

Gunnar halted his horse and unfolded the primitive map Cora had drawn on a dirty square of linen using a piece of coal from the tavern fireplace. Much of it was smudged and illegible, but the last landmark was clear—a single ancient oak tree. He'd passed it several miles back; he had to be getting close.

The road tracks ahead curved to the right and dipped down into a swale where they were lost from view in dense willows. *A perfect place for an ambush.* Even though he was early, Gunnar decided to take no chances. He turned the bay from the road and gave the animal its head to climb to the top of the nearest low hill.

Upon reaching the crest, he dropped the horse's reins for it to graze, then pulled out his scope to scan the surrounding countryside. The heavy morning mist was lifting, and from his vantage point, he could see quite well—not into every thicket, but well enough to see if there was a force lying in wait. There wasn't. Everything was exactly as Cora had described—a desolate place with windblown meadows, rolling hills, and occasional rocky outcroppings.

About a half-mile ahead, he found the intersection of the two roads that gave the place its name.

Widening his search, he panned back over the area a second time, this time finding the lone rider on a hill on the opposite side of the crossing. He smiled. He was at least four hours early, and she was already here, clearly taking the same precautions.

Reassured by her early presence that she also feared a trap, Gunnar stowed his scope, pulled the gelding's head up from the spring grass, and returned to the road below. He fought the urge to kick the animal into a gallop, chastising himself for the eagerness he felt to see her again. *Keep your mind on the business at hand—retrieving Maid's Dream and discovering the identity of those in charge.* Holding the horse to a steady walk, he proceeded to the middle of the intersection, then stopped.

She remained on the hill, watching. When she finally began her descent, Gunnar's eyes feasted on every detail—his directive from only moments earlier to keep his mind on the business at hand already forgotten. She wore a hooded dark blue cloak trimmed in fox fur. The color signified noble birth, but the shade was subdued enough to not draw attention. Her hair was concealed under the hood, but her face was flushed from the exertion of the ride, the cool morning air, and the dangerousness of the meeting.

Gunnar's mouth went dry. So far he'd seen her three times—once in soaked peasant garb, once in silk finery, and now fully shrouded by a cloak. Yet each time, his reaction to her was the same.

Her horse's hooves sank in the soft soil, sending pebbles rolling ahead of them as the animal slid down the last embankment and onto the road. Gunnar didn't realize he was holding his breath until she stopped about twenty feet away. The horse pranced sideways beneath her, tossing its head, pulling at the bit, resisting her command to be still. She corrected it unconsciously, never taking her eyes from Gunnar.

The animal's antics pulled Gunnar's attention briefly to the horse she rode. It was one of the finest he'd ever seen. A tall powerful animal, its muscles rippled beneath its glossy copper hide. It looked as though it could jump a house and outrun a deer. She seemed so small on its back, but as Gunnar watched, he realized her control of the animal was never in question. With subtle cues—a touch of her heel, the twitch of a rein, a shift in her balance, she controlled the massive beast, moving with it as if they were one.

"You are early," Gunnar called out to her.

"As are you," she countered.

"It appears we trust each other equally not," Gunnar said.

"You expected differently?"

"I've given you no cause not to trust me. You, on the other hand, have shown yourself to be quite adept with the setting of traps." Gunnar dismounted, and took a step toward her, hoping she would do the same. She did not. Instead, she turned her horse away slightly.

"Stay where you are, Northman. I know a man can move more quickly than a horse in close quarters. I'll not allow you any nearer. As far as not trustin' you—if the bloodthirsty ways of your pagan people weren't already well-known, seeing Tibbot's battered face yesterday gave me plenty of cause."

"What happened to Tibbot was a misunderstanding." Gunnar dismissed it with a shrug. "I thought him to be responsible for the theft of the slaves and the attack on my ship. He was the only one I could see who was benefiting."

"Your words prove my point, Northman. You only suspected Tibbot and still beat him mercilessly. You *know* me to be involved so why would I not expect the same treatment?"

Because I would never dream of touching your beautiful face in such a way. As the thought skimmed through his mind, Gunnar knew it was true. For the slaves alone, he could have killed Tibbot. But with her...

"Your sword is over there behind that rock." She pointed to his left. "'Tis a gaudy, ostentatious thing for a man to carry," she added.

Gunnar retrieved it, immediately pulling the sword from its sheath to inspect the curved blade. The steel still gleamed with a perfect edge. "You are not the first to say so, but I quite like it."

She sniffed. "So our business here is concluded?" Fiona held her breath, hoping beyond hope that this would be the end of it.

"Hardly. There is still the matter of the slaves that I lost. Give me the name of who put you up to it. For a lady to risk her life, it must be someone close to you. Your father or husband perhaps?"

"I did it myself," she replied.

"You cannot protect them." Gunnar dismissed her claim. "I won't stop until I find out who they are, so you can save us both a lot of time by telling me now."

"Do you find it inconceivable that a woman would have the intelligence to do such a thing?"

"Not the intelligence, only the ambition. And not because you're a woman. My people have many women who are more than capable of such deeds, but you're a highborn. Highborns don't risk anything—certainly not themselves without something to gain."

"Perhaps your people only act out of personal gain, but decent..."

"Please," Gunnar cut her off. "You sit in your...castle, I presume, while men and women bow down to you. You wear silks and satins while they wear coarse wool. You eat lavish, sumptuous meals while they go home to cabbage and salted meat—enough of it for their entire family only if they're lucky. The sale of that horse you're riding now alone would feed ten families for a year or more. But never mind all that. Just tell me who put you up to it. Who organizes these things? Clearly, you're the spy, gathering information from your friends in Swords."

"They're not my friends."

"Yet you pretend they are to gain information. How like a noble to call commoners to their bosom when it suits their purpose." Gunnar couldn't keep the disdain from his voice—the costs of the recent war in his sister's new homeland were still too fresh.

Stung by his insult and how easily he'd rejected her being behind it, Fiona fumed. He was certainly not the first man she'd ever met to hold a woman's intellect in low regard—far from it. But somehow, coming from him it was worse. To have some ignorant lowly Viking feel superior to her...it was too much.

Before she knew it, she was rattling off details of previous raids. Secret details she had painstakingly organized. It was uplifting to be able to give voice to her accomplishments. She could tell him because he didn't matter. He was no one. "There are even raids that people don't know of," she continued. "Times where I planned it so carefully it was assumed that the slaves escaped on their own." She paused. "But for you, Northman, I chose to be the bait, knowing that a ruttish Viking couldn't resist attacking a helpless woman."

Gunnar didn't know the specifics of other raids to know if she spoke the truth, but she seemed passionate and didn't appear to be lying. Still, her knowledge could be explained if she were close to the plotter.

"Why did you not expose me to Tibbot?" she asked, interrupting his thoughts. "If you knew me to be deceiving them, why not tell them?"

"Things happened rather quickly, as you may recall. When I first saw you, I believed you to be conspiring with him. I'm still not convinced otherwise," he added. "Why else would you risk your life and reputation?"

"To you, slaves are nothing more than simple beasts to be used and discarded. But they are men. Sons. Brothers. Husbands. Fathers. Do you have any idea what happens to their families when the men are taken? They're shattered." Barca reared low beneath her and she steadied him, loosening the reins she had inadvertently tightened during her outburst. She proceeded more calmly. "I'm afraid the loss of the slaves and the coin you paid for them is merely the cost of participating in such an ugly business."

Gunnar shrugged. "On that, I might agree, but there is still the matter of my ship."

"You cannot hold me responsible for the loss of your ship. You know for a fact I was nowhere near there. I was relieving you of your slaves and your weapons—remember?" She smiled. "Northmen still hold the city of Wexford, about a week's ride south of here. You can go there to nurse your wounded pride and find a ship bound for your homeland. But by the time they make space for you and your crew, I'm afraid there'll be little room for slaves."

Was that the reasoning? Gunnar had yet to find a single rational explanation for someone to sink the ship and trap an angry crew of Vikings here. Was it really about the slaves? Was she truly the one behind it? If so, where was the rage towards her he should feel? He conjured the image of the Huntress's torn hull, even imagined her standing with axe in hand, yet still felt nothing. Gunnar shook his head. It defied all reason.

He examined her more closely, trying to determine what it was about her that drew him with such power. She was beautiful, but he'd known many beautiful women. She was confident and bold, yet he'd also known many bold women. So what was it? He'd expected to be bored of her by now, but instead, she was even more of a mystery—even more enticing. How did a highborn lady come to be a rogue for the benefit of commoners? He wanted to know it all—and he wanted to hear it from her lips.

"My ship wasn't lost, lady—or did you not know that?" Gunnar could tell by the sudden stiffening in her spine that she did not. "My men were able to save it. Even as we speak, repairs are being made. But that does bring me to my next matter. If you speak the truth and are solely responsible for the slaves—and my ship, for I know that was no coincidence—then I have naught to do for the nine days while the repairs are completed. Nine days I had thought to fill with finding the culprits and exacting my revenge. *If* I am to take you at your word, do I now sit idle while that time passes?"

"I have not the slightest interest in how you spend your time, Northman," she spat. The horse danced beneath her, eager to be away. "Perhaps you'll take in some of the sights of my beautiful country." She smiled a cold smile. "Though I wouldn't stray too far from Balbriggan and Dublin. They may be more accepting of your kind after Sihtric's long occupation, but you'll not find other Irish nearly so accommodating."

"But what of your role in this? You must know I cannot allow it to go unaddressed. The slaves I could possibly forgive, but the ship? The ship demands retribution. Now, what would be a suitable punishment for you?" he murmured. "The question begs careful consideration. I can hardly thrash you. Well, I could, but I wouldn't enjoy it—marring such perfect skin. Yet it must be something. What shall it be, lady? How are you to pay for your crimes?" Gunnar could think of so many ways and his gut tightened.

She scowled at him, but her eyes grew wider. He rubbed his chin while he deliberated, barely feeling the stubble there. He was in a quandary but not over her punishment as he outwardly pretended. He was desperate not to let her go, not without finding some way to see her again.

He scrambled for something to hold over her. Threaten her family, perhaps? But he didn't even know if she had family; the way she ran wild, suggested not. The slaves? Yes, it had to be the slaves. If she were telling the truth, all of her actions centered around some sense of obligation to the slaves. Gunnar smiled grimly. He knew what he had to do.

"I see you've come up with something, Northman. Give voice to your thoughts and have them considered. Is it gold you seek?"

"Nay, I have enough gold, and more will not spare me the time I'm being forced to waste here. But I do think you've supplied me with the answer. I shall take your advice, lady, and see the sights of your country...." He paused a long, deliberate pause. "And you shall accompany me."

Fiona laughed aloud at the absurdity of the idea. "Don't be ridiculous."

"It was not a request, lady." Gunnar's voice dropped to a menacing tone. "If you refuse me, I'll acquire triple the number of slaves of my original purchase, and I will insist that as many as possible come from this area. Do you want that on your conscience?"

"You're lying. Your ship couldn't hold that many."

"My ship won't need to hold them all. I'll choose the best...and sacrifice the rest. You spoke so passionately only moments ago of their families. How many children would you orphan? How many women would you widow? How many innocents would you send to slaughter?"

"First, Northman, I would be doing no such thing—you would. And second, while I believe you to be more than capable of such a despicable, vile act, I do not believe you would waste the coin. Your kind seems driven for riches far more than any other."

"My lady, I am captain of the Treasure Huntress, a ship destined by the gods to live up to her name. In my time aboard her, even before I was captain, I've amassed more fortune than I could spend in ten lifetimes." It was true. Alone, he had little to spend it on. "Such an expenditure would be a pittance and would matter naught to me. But it would mean everything to you. Everything you've accomplished, every man you've saved, everything you have risked would be wiped away with a single stroke.

"I'll hang their bodies for their families to find and mourn over. Perhaps I'll even do it close enough to your lands for you to hear the cries of their women and children. Or maybe you'll ride out on that fine horse of yours and see them for yourself—see what you cost them. Picture it, Fiona, and know that it is all preventable. All for only a week of your time."

Fiona stared at him in stunned horror. Somewhere, somehow she had lost control. What had started as a simple meeting to return his sword and be done with him, had spiraled into this. This grotesque ultimatum. Her cloak felt as if it were smothering her. She wanted to rip it from her body and run. To give Barca his head and not look back. But run to where? Nowhere was safe now. Even if she could find a place to hide, the poor men in Tibbot's caverns could not.

"You cannot possibly think that I would enter into such an agreement to prove my convictions to you." Her voice was softer now. "Or that I'm so foolish and naive to believe that by sacrificing myself, it would save them."

"No one said anything of sacrificing yourself, Fiona. I seek only your company. During our trip, I will guarantee your safety and not to lay a hand on you. And let me remind you, I have other options to spend time with you—options that do not require your consent. I'm offering you an easy and safe solution. The question now is simple—will you save those men's lives or not?"

"Even if I wanted to, I could not. I can't simply leave for a week unescorted."

"Says the woman who rides wild at night with armed men. Clearly, you're a resourceful liar; I'm sure you can come up with a suitable excuse."

She sat motionless, staring at him. Gunnar was shocked and thrilled to see she was actually considering it. He found himself desperate for her to agree, knowing he had little recourse if she did not. Contrary to what he'd told her, he couldn't abduct her. With nowhere to hide and no way to escape without a ship, the risk of being discovered with a missing noblewoman was too high. And once the Huntress was repaired, he was committed to sail for the East, a grueling trip even for experienced crew—certainly no place for a highborn beauty.

Fiona's mind was racing. She couldn't possibly agree—couldn't possibly go with him. But if she refused, would he truly murder the slaves for spite? The countless tales of Viking atrocities that she'd heard ever since she was a child, suggested so. Assuming they were true, what would he do to her? Rape her? Kill her? Both?

Though if his intent was to molest and murder her, why did he need her to agree to go with him? She pondered that for a long moment. He didn't. He could simply come and take her in the night as he'd threatened to before. Her mind flew back to the horrifyingly vivid scene he had suggested—of men slaughtered and hung like butchered animals. Could she live with the murder of innocents on her conscience?

Nay.

She tried to imagine what it would be like driving around the countryside with him in some filthy oxcart. But he could not expect her to travel so.... Her mind worked furiously through an alternative.

"I will accept your proposal, Northman, but only if you accept my additional conditions."

"Which are?"

"First, in exchange for my agreement, you will leave this place as soon as your ship is repaired, taking *no* slaves with you and harming no others. Second, I can make an excuse to be absent, but I will have to say I am visiting friends. To make the lie believable, at some point I would have to meet with my noble friends and transfer my belongings.

"On the southern road out of Kilcock are the remains of a burnt church. Fearing the location was cursed, the site was abandoned and the church rebuilt on the other side of town. It will be private. I will be there tomorrow at midday. You must be there with suitable transportation—and by suitable, I mean a nobleman's carriage so that my servants will not be suspicious. You will not alight from the carriage nor show yourself to anyone. If you are, in fact, able to do this, when I arrive I will have my footman transfer my trunks onto your carriage. We will then proceed with this arrangement. If you are not able to comply, for any reason, I'll have my driver return me home. My obligations of this deal will be considered fulfilled, and you will agree to honor yours. I will never see nor hear from you again."

"I accept your conditions and shall see you on the morrow at midday," Gunnar said without giving it a moment's thought. Before he could say another word, she gave her horse its head and they galloped away.

Gunnar remounted the bay but remained in the middle of the crossing, stunned at the turn of events and unsure of which direction to ride. It was impossible. She knew it was impossible. Maybe if he had a few days, but by tomorrow? Yet again, befuddled by her presence, he'd considered nothing beyond the astonishing fact that she had agreed. Before he made things worse now by running off with no plan, he needed to gather his wits and think.

He began by reviewing every unusual thing that had happened so far. The abnormal winds had put him well ahead of schedule so the delay was not affecting his trip to the East. He'd lost his sword. He'd retrieved his sword. The Huntress, by all reckoning, should be sunk, but instead would soon be ready to sail again. In the middle of interrogating Tibbot, he'd demanded food that he didn't really want, which caused the slaver to open the door and reveal her. Coincidences? They couldn't be—not all of them. Everything was ultimately working out in his favor. He just needed to make a decision now and go with it.

"So to Dublin in hopes of finding a suitable carriage to rent? Or..." The normally placid bay gelding tugged at the reins and tossed his head, pivoting to face the way they had come. Gunnar smiled and nudged him with his heel. "Of course. We'll ask Cora."

Chapter 9

"**Y**ou're back again, and so soon? Did you find Ward's Crossing?" Cora asked as she set down a handful of empty mugs and moved to meet Gunnar at the doorway.

"I did," he replied.

"And yet here you stand, fit as a butcher's dog with no harm done to you. I was more than a bit concerned, I must say. So what'll it be this time, love? A toss upstairs, perhaps? I'll not charge you for it. Although I suppose you've already paid me enough, it wouldn't exactly be for free." She winked.

"You've already earned every bit I paid you," Gunnar declined as he made his way back to the quiet corner table. "But I do require more information. Important information," he added. "Join me and bring us each an ale."

Cora returned in a flash with two tankards and took the chair next to him. "What is it you be needin' to know now?" she asked.

"I'm in need of a carriage." He held up his hand before she could recommend her hostler friend. He'd seen nothing in Larkin's stables close to what he needed now. "A fine carriage. A nobleman's carriage," he elaborated.

Cora chuckled. "Well, I'm flattered that you think I keep such company, love. And as much as I'd like to take your silver—and to help you, of course, that particular request may be a bit beyond me. Lords are a scarce sight in here."

Gunnar rubbed his temple. Cora was of no help, and he hadn't even mentioned that he needed it by morning.

"Unless." Cora's fingertips moved unconsciously to her mouth; she tapped on her front teeth, her brow furrowing as she gave great consideration to some thought. "But nay." She shook her head.

"What is it?" Gunnar asked.

Cora glanced furtively around the room, then leaned in close to him. "Well, there is a lord who visits the tavern now and then," she whispered, "not here in the front with the common folk, mind you, but in a private room in the back. He's the son of a very prestigious Dublin family, but rumor has it, they've banished him to one of their lesser estates in Drogheda to limit their embarrassment from his drinkin' and gamblin'. He's good at neither, so they keep his losses in check with a monthly stipend.

"Rather than travel all the way to Drogheda, other nobles from Dublin will sometimes meet with him here to gamble, but occasionally he'll wager with a commoner. And when his funds are low, he's been known to play for unusual things." She leaned even closer. "I hear his losses this month have been quite significant—and since you seek only the use of his carriage and not coin..."

"How do I find him?" Gunnar asked.

"He's here now. The other lords left not long ago."

Gunnar slid back his chair. Cora grabbed his arm and held him down in his seat.

"Nay, you can't just approach him," she whispered fiercely and looked over her shoulder. "The barkeep makes all the arrangements. Whether or not you gain introduction is for him to decide. I'm not even supposed to know his name, but of course, I do, and I'll tell you if you'd like."

"His name matters naught to me."

Cora shrugged. "I suppose it wouldn't." She glanced around the room again. "I'm not to speak of him. He's a very valuable customer, and if that were jeopardized because of something I said, it would go very badly for me." Cora looked at him, her eyes filled with concerned question.

"I seek only an honest wager, and I have silver," Gunnar reassured her. "There will be a substantial sum for you and the barkeep if introduction were to be made."

Cora's eye's brightened again. "I'll be back." She pushed away from the table and heaved her considerable form to its feet. "But when I return, we never had this conversation—only that you mentioned you had silver and wished to find someone to wager with. It'll be better for me—for the both of us, if the barkeep thinks 'twas his own idea."

She returned directly with the elfin barkeep. "Cora says you wish to gamble?" he asked as he eyed Gunnar suspiciously.

Gunnar nodded.

"And that you have silver?"

"I do," Gunnar confirmed.

"I may be able to arrange something...for a small fee."

"I'm listening," Gunnar said, trying not to appear eager.

"I have a distinguished guest who occasionally likes to wager. I can perhaps introduce you, but only if you can be discreet."

"And you have verified that he also has coin?" Gunnar asked, pretending not to know the circumstances.

"He is a lord," the barkeep blustered. "He has far more coin than you'll ever..." The man bit off the rest of his sentence, spying the pouch on the table behind Gunnar's tankard.

Knowing he had the man's full attention, Gunnar pulled the pouch in front of him and opened the drawstrings with deliberate slowness. He shook out a piece of silver and handed it to the barkeep. "For your trouble. The rest, you can see, is plenty to cover my gambling with his lordship, and I don't even wish to know his name. Is that discreet enough for you?"

The man clamped his fingers closed on the silver before Gunnar could change his mind, then nodded. "Follow me."

Gunnar slipped another piece to Cora as he stood, then followed the small man through a low doorway behind the bar. While the barkeep secured the door behind them, Gunnar glanced around the smoke-filled room. A lone man sat at a table in the center. His head was tipped back watching rings of smoke rise to the ceiling. Gunnar immediately recognized the exotic scent of hashish, something he'd only ever smelled in the East. A fired red clay flask with a seal stamped in the neck was open on the table. Wine from the Mediterranean. Clearly, the man's limited budget did not preclude him from enjoying the finer things in life.

"My lord, I have a man here who wishes to gamble." The barkeep stopped two paces away from the table and bowed his head. "And I've verified that he does have coin."

"I'm sure you were well compensated for your effort," the man drawled without looking at them, then took another long, slow pull from his pipe.

Gunnar resisted the urge to cross the room and stuff the pipe down the man's insolent long neck, reminding himself what was at stake.

When he deemed they'd waited long enough, the nobleman turned to evaluate the newcomer. "A Northman," he said, surprised. "And you wish to gamble?"

"I have a specific wager in mind." Gunnar went straight to the point. If the arrogant bastard wasn't interested, he'd not waste another moment here. "I seek the use of your carriage for ten days. To come with a driver and footman. In exchange, I wager this." Gunnar stepped to the table and dropped the pouch in front of him. "Silver." He answered the unasked question. The bulge and size of the pouch were clear indication of its value.

The nobleman's eyes flicked to it greedily before he hooded them with feigned disinterest. "My carriage? And my servants?" He laughed, then looked Gunnar over more closely. "And your sword—will it be included in the wager?"

Gunnar shook his head.

"May I see it at least?"

Gunnar pulled the sword and handed it to him. The nobleman first examined the jewel-encrusted hilt, then the polished blade.

"Does it have a name?" he asked.

"Maid's Dream."

He chuckled. "If it were me, I'd have given that name to my *other* sword."

Gunnar had heard the reference more than once. With friends, he would joke about it, but not with this pig-nut.

"It's a fine sword; I can understand why you wouldn't risk it," the nobleman said as he handed it back. "My driver is good, but I must confess, my footmen barely pass for noble servants. What is your purpose?"

"Private, but suffice to say I need it to impress someone."

"Well, and take no offense by this...," He raised his eyebrows and gave Gunnar another prolonged disparaging once-over, "but even with my fine carriage, you could never pass for a lord. Highborns can sniff out noble blood better than hounds, and I can't imagine that you have even a trace." He paused again, considering. "But if I were to agree, what would be the game?"

"Your choice."

The man stared at him, unblinking. His prominent lower eyelids stretched to cover his odd bulging eyes, reminding Gunnar of lizards he'd seen in the deserts of the East.

"You must want this very badly," he murmured. "Very well, Northman, take a seat. I will play you for the use of my carriage, my driver, and my two footmen for ten days. And because I'm in a generous mood, I will add to the wager two changes of nobleman's clothes. We are of similar height, and I have some older clothes that are cut large enough they might fit you."

Noting Gunnar's dubious glance at his thin frame, he added. "When I was first exiled, I was quite a bit heavier. Oh, I'm sure you know of my circumstances, for you to be so bold as to approach me with this request. And I think..." He nodded subtly. "Aye, in exchange for my offerings, you will put up your bag of silver and—your sword." He leaned back in his chair and took a delicate sip of the blood-red wine. "Those are my terms."

Gunnar seethed at the inclusion of the sword he'd already said was not in the bargain. He wanted nothing more than to smash the lizard-eyed worm to a pulp, and hated that he could not—though it was not the man's noble blood that stayed his fists. The scut was right; he did want something from him very badly.

Gunnar stood for a moment, thinking of what he stood to gain. The sword he would miss. The coin he could easily replace. The risk was worth it. And what were the odds that such an opportunity would present itself—that every impossible thing he needed would be set in his path so easily? Surely the gods had a hand in it. And if so, then there was no risk at all.

"Very well. I accept your terms." Gunnar unbuckled his belt, placed the sword and sheath on the table next to the pouch, then took a seat across from him. "And the game?" he asked.

"Simple high dice. One roll. Winner take all."

Gunnar watched carefully when the man rolled. If the dice were loaded to turn up a certain number, he would mimic the technique. *There.* Lizard-eyes tossed them high with a subtle flick of his wrist at the end to set them spinning in the air—the height and revolutions allowing any added weight to have effect.

The first di stuck flat showing a six. The second bounced and spun, then landed with a five. The nobleman clapped his hands with glee, unable to contain his excitement. "It appears you have your work cut out for you, Northman. Only one roll can beat me. And if you match me, we'll go again."

Gunnar picked up the dice, shook them in his hand, then tossed them high with a last-minute twist. The first landed with a dull flop showing six. The second bounced once, then twice before finally landing, showing...six. Gunnar heard the barkeep's sharp inhale. He held his own breath, waiting for his opponent's reaction.

As the smile slowly faded from his face, the nobleman rocked back in his chair and took a long draw from his hashish pipe, his eyes never leaving the dice. He shook his head and exhaled the aromatic smoke. "This has not been my month," he murmured to himself. "I must admit, I am intrigued as to your purpose, Northman. Will you at least reveal the identity of who it is you seek to impress? Rest assured, I'll not breathe a word of it."

Gunnar shook his head.

"Ah, pity. I shall leave it to my imagination then. When do you require the carriage? I assume I'll not be forced to walk home this evening?"

"Tomorrow morning at dawn. Here at the tavern."

"I'll make the arrangements. You may leave now."

Gunnar stood and retrieved his sword and pouch from the table. Not even the man's insolent dismissal could foul his high spirits. He held his grin in check until he'd ducked back out through the low door into the main tavern. Giving a quick nod to Cora, he returned to the seat he'd vacated only moments before.

"So you got what you were after?" Cora asked quietly as she approached. Gunnar nodded.

"Then we must celebrate." She went to the counter and returned with two cups of poteen. "To your victory." She smiled and raised her glass. "Skol."

"Skol." Gunnar smiled back and took a sip. It felt off to suddenly have time to spare. Doubts that his success could all be for naught began to worm their way into his mind. Once she had time to think, the lovely Fiona would likely come up with a different plan. But if she double-crossed him on this, she'd regret it. He would find her when the Huntress was ready to sail and take her with him to the East, her comfort be damned.

"If you'd like, I can be available in the morning to help you...dress," Cora interrupted his thoughts.

Gunnar had given little thought to the nobleman's clothes, but it didn't matter; he had no intention of wearing them.

"I could even have a bath drawn for you," she offered.

"Not necessary," Gunnar declined. "The person I'm meeting tomorrow is already fully aware of how I look."

"May I be blunt, love?"

Her tone gave Gunnar pause. "Of course. Speak freely."

"Well, I don't know how to say it delicately, so I'll just say it. Mayhaps whoever you're trying to impress doesn't care how you look—or smell, but if you step out of that carriage looking like you do among strangers, well... at best, they'll think you stole it, and at worst, that you murdered a lord and then stole it. Folk from here to Dublin are more accepting of your kind, but you don't have to go too far for that not to be the case. There are a great many who've lost things at the point of a Northman's sword. And more than a few, I'm sure, who would relish the chance to return the favor."

Gunnar considered her words. Fiona had said much the same.

"My words were only meant to keep you safe, not to offer offense," Cora added.

"No offense taken, Cora." He took a deep breath and nodded. "Your aid with the clothes would be much appreciated."

"And the bath?" she asked tentatively.

He smiled wryly. "Arrange whatever you feel is necessary. Tomorrow morning I shall be raw clay in your hands."

She grinned at him. "Grand! And have no fears, love, when I'm through with you, your appearance will rival that of the finest Irish lord."

Gunnar rolled his eyes and drained his glass. "I can hardly wait."

Chapter 10

Gunnar stepped from the dark street into the tavern. Cora was waiting for him with a single oil lamp. "They're already here, love," she said, noting the concern on his face. "Out back. That's where his lordship always has them park, so that's where they came."

Gunnar felt like a load of stones had been lifted from his chest. Only then did he realize how much he'd doubted this would actually come to pass. He smiled with relief, and she smiled back. "Now for the hard part," she teased. "I have his lordship's clothes and a bath drawn for you in my room."

"I would have a quick word with them first."

She nodded and led him to the back entrance.

The men eyed him dubiously as he described their upcoming roles, concluding with the bonus each would receive at the successful completion of the week. He then informed them of what would happen, if, by their actions, things were to go awry, the loss of the bonus being the least of their concerns. As the men gaped at him, Gunnar was glad he had yet to change. His appearance made the threat that much more convincing.

"Do you understand?" Gunnar asked.

They nodded.

"Then repeat it back to me. The first stage is critical."

The driver, Garrett, began with their arrival at the church ruins in Kilcock. The two footmen, Bryen and Orin, took over when it came time for their roles. Gunnar nodded as the men finished recounting the last detail of their upcoming performance. "Very good," he acknowledged. "I'll return shortly, and then we'll get under way." He paused. "Are you hungry?"

The men glanced at each other, looked away and shuffled their feet.

"Have you eaten yet this morning?" Gunnar rephrased his question, perplexed by their odd response.

"Cora brought us something to eat and drink," Garrett admitted.

The way he said it, it must not have been something allowed by Lord Lizard Eyes. Gunnar turned to Cora. "It seems you have everything well in hand. I suppose I'm ready for you as well."

Cora nodded and led him up the stairs to her room just as a young woman was leaving with two still-steaming, empty pails. The woman's brow was damp with sweat. This was clearly not her first trip, though her eyes were still drowsy.

"It's ready, mum," she mumbled.

"Gratitude, Taney. Go back to bed now. I've no further need of you."

Gunnar followed Cora into her room, closing the door behind him.

Fiona awoke with a start, her breath coming in gasps, her heart pounding in her chest. She lay perfectly still, trying to reassure herself the horrifying images that she could still see in her mind were not real. Men's bodies hung upside down like a row of hogs, their throats slit. Women and children keening and wailing all around them. The last image to fade was a small lad clutching his father's lifeless, bloody fingers, sobbing, "Why, Papa?" over and over.

Fiona rolled onto her back on the soft down mattress and twisted her head in the deep pillow, trying to relieve the knots in her neck as her heart slowed to a dull thud. It was only a nightmare. She had nothing to fear. None of it would come to pass.

"Ah, you're awake," her maid, Siara, murmured as she entered with a tray. "I brought your breakfast and to wake you, but I see the hardest part 'tis already done." She smiled and set the tray on the table, then went to the window to pull the curtains open wide. "Big day for you today," she said as she approached the bed, and arranged the pillows for Fiona to sit up, before returning to the table to retrieve the tray.

If you only knew.

"How exciting for Lady Abiageal to have invited you to her uncle's estate," Siara continued, oblivious to the fact that the conversation was not being returned. "You'll have such an adventure."

I surely hope not.

"How I so wish I could attend you."

"And I, too, but there will be no room in the carriage; Lady Abiageal is bringing two maids. Apologies."

"'Tis not your fault, my lady," Siara said as she arranged the tray. "I'll pray every day while you're away that you'll meet a handsome lord and fall in love. Then you can become betrothed and be married in the most beautiful wedding." As Siara concluded her fantasy with a sigh, Fiona thought of the actual man she'd arranged to meet and scowled.

"Honestly, Fiona, what have I told you about making that expression?" Meirna asked from the doorway. "You'll end up with a permanently wrinkled sour face if you're not careful. What do you have against marriage, lass? You used to be eager to meet eligible young lords. Now you have to be practically pried from the house. Unless it's to ride," Meirna frowned. "And you'll never find a husband that way. It does my heart good that you're taking this trip."

It wouldn't if you knew the truth. Fiona turned her attention to her breakfast. Still shaken by the nightmare, she had no appetite but knew she'd never hear the end of it from Meirna if she didn't eat something. She bypassed the runny egg and took a spoonful of the honeyed oat porridge. Normally her favorite, today it sat on her tongue like a gummy blob. She chewed, grimaced, and swallowed. When her stomach threatened to reject even that bland offering, she took a sip of cool milk. The milk was good. She took another swallow.

Fiona looked back at the plate of salted ham, porridge, a thick slice of fresh currant bread, and the egg. She couldn't do it. When Meirna's attention was diverted to her gowns, Fiona stirred the contents of her plate around with her fork, sliding as much as would fit underneath the bread. Satisfied that it looked like she'd eaten something, she slipped from the bed and carried the tray to the table.

Meirna looked up and frowned.

"I ate some oats. I'm just too wrought up to eat the rest." That part was true and must have shown in her face because Meirna nodded.

"Very well. I'll have Haisley pack a light meal for you to take with you. Come sit down and I'll start on your hair," Meirna said. "But first, put on your chambergown, there's a nip in the air this morning. It's too cool for just your shift."

Fiona quickly stuffed her bare arms into the long sleeves of the chambergown. It was a unique oversized, shapeless garment that covered her from neck to toes, securing in the front with multiple ties. Meirna had patterned the first one for her when she was a child. Fiona had loved it so that Meirna had made her a new one every year since. This latest was her finest, though. Two layers of teal-colored silk quilted together with a thin layer of ultra-fine goose down between them.

This morning Fiona skipped the ties, overlapping it snuggly across her chest instead. Satisfied, Meirna patted the stool in front of her and asked, "How would you like to wear your hair today?"

"Just something simple for travel," Fiona replied as she sat.

"You look tired, lass," Meirna said, examining her reflection in the polished tin plate mirror. She tightened Fiona's skin at her temples, then pinched her cheeks. "And you're so pale. You need to calm yourself."

Aye, Fiona, calm yourself. This will all be over soon. The murdering Northman scum will not be there and this will all be behind you.

Meirna braided her hair into two long braids, then coiled and secured them behind her head with a single pearl-inlaid silver comb. "Not like that." Meirna turned and chided Siara, who had started packing Fiona's trunk. "If you pack it like that, she'll need fifteen trunks just for the week. Every inch must be used." Siara started again. "Nay, not like that, either," Meirna said, exasperated. "If you fold a gown like that, it will be naught but a wrinkled mess when she pulls it out." Giving Fiona's hair a final pat, she went to take over the packing.

Fiona felt a surge of guilt at the work she was putting them through— only to have it undone in a few hours. *God willing.*

No one had questioned it when she'd returned from her ride yesterday claiming to have run into Lady Abiageal's messenger on the road. Nor had they doubted the last-minute invitation to accompany Abiageal to her uncle's coastal estate in Bray.

"Are you ready to dress?" Siara held up her new light green silk gown. "This one is so beautiful."

"I really think I should save that one and wear the blue for travel." Fiona referred again to the older gown that Meirna had firmly rejected.

"I'll not have you arriving there in a three-year-old gown, lass," Meirna reiterated. "People will think your father's fallen on hard times."

And we couldn't have anyone think that. Not at my age. Even though she knew Meirna meant well, it was hard to hold her tongue. *People will think… people will think…* How many times she'd heard those words and how she hated them. As a child, she'd delighted in retorting something cheeky, but that rebellion had oft caused more grief than it was worth. She'd learned that it was sometimes better to keep silent.

Which is exactly what she did now as she slipped out of the chambergown and stood in her thin linen shift waiting for Siara to lift the ivory silk kirtle over her head. Long-sleeved and full-skirted, the kirtle could have been worn alone, but Meirna would never allow her to go out dressed in a single layer like a peasant. Not that anyone could ever mistake this kirtle for a peasant's dress—not with the fine brocade silk or the light silver and gold embroidery at the neckline, hem, and cuffs.

After lacing the front and smoothing the skirt, Siara retrieved the short-sleeved outer gown. It was a beautiful thing—pale green silk, heavily embroidered with gold, silver, and multiple darker shades of green across the bodice and in a wide band along the skirt hem. The gown skirt was shorter than the kirtle's by about six inches and cut narrower with high slits on both sides. Designed to allow her free movement, the side openings also displayed the cream-colored kirtle whenever she took a step.

Most of her outer gowns laced on the sides with wide shoulder straps that attached to the bodice in the front with brooches, leaving the top of her kirtle to show. This new gown laced in the back and covered the entire upper kirtle except for the sleeves. For this trip, Meirna insisted that she take all three of her newer style gowns. She was convinced they showed she was a lady of means because the back laces clearly required a maid to dress her. Fiona found it a silly notion; the silk and intricate detail of the embroidery would indicate her status long before anyone could see her back. But again, she didn't argue.

While Siara laced the gown, Fiona clasped her silver link belt around her waist and attached the small matching pouch purse to it with a silk cord. Siara moved on to her stockings and had just finished tying the garter of the second below her knee when a knock sounded at the door.

"Are Lady Fiona's trunks ready?" her footman called out. "I'm here to take them to the carriage."

"Aye, Dorrel. Come in," Meirna replied as she closed and latched the second trunk.

Fiona felt her confidence rising. Even with all this help, it had been difficult for her to be ready in time. The Northman faced an impossible task, and she'd not allow him a single extra moment. When the Kilcock midday Sext bells rang for prayer and there was no fine carriage, she would write a quick note for Dorrel to post somewhere in plain sight for Lady Abiageal—a message stating she'd taken ill at the last moment and would be unable to accompany her after all.

Of course, Lady Abiageal would never receive it, but that didn't matter. The message was for her own servants. Just another detail to make the lie convincing. Details were everything. Then she would instruct Rafferty to return her home with all haste—perhaps even summon the healer for good measure. That would be a nice touch. With everything she'd been through these past days, a sleeping draught from the healer might even be welcome.

She smiled inwardly at the thought of being sedated and resting comfortably back in her own bed this very afternoon, rid of this Northman who'd become a dark cloud hanging over her. He had his sword. They had a deal. He should just go away. To be safe, she'd give him no opportunity to confront her again. She'd not leave Tir Na Lionmhar for several weeks— enough time to ensure his ship was repaired and he was gone. She took a deep breath. Everything would work out grand.

Chapter 11

As the carriage rolled through Kilcock, Fiona caught herself chewing the tattered edge of her thumbnail, a childhood habit she'd worked hard to break. Angrily she balled her hands into fists and held them in her lap. *He will not be there. Will not. Will not.*

She longed to look out the window to catch a glimpse of the church ruins before they arrived but resisted the urge. She would not be seen gawking through the curtains like a child. She had to be patient. It was almost over. They were close now.

The carriage slowed. Fiona heard Rafferty check the horses and felt the carriage lurch slightly as they pulled off the road. She held her breath—waiting and praying for his next words to be, "*No sign of Lady Abiageal yet, my lady. Will you be waiting in the carriage or will you step out to stretch your legs?*"

Instead, Rafferty called something to the horses, and the carriage changed course slightly back to the left—as if he were maneuvering them in tight quarters. Fiona swallowed hard and lifted the curtain, no longer worried about appearances. She had to see. She had to know.

Four matching black horses hitched in pairs were the first thing to come into her view. They were only about ten paces away, and her knowledgeable horseman's eye quickly took in every detail. Well-bred animals wearing clean harness with high-polished brass buckles. Next, the front of a large carriage appeared, its driver perched upon the high bench. Then the side—the curved dark-stained wood shouted quality workmanship. The foul weather shutters were latched open and brass lanterns, secured for travel, hung from both upper corners. When the rear of the carriage with the two footmen standing on the back platform came into view, the curtain fell from Fiona's slack fingers. *Four horses and two footmen?* Either was pure extravagance.

Fiona's mind replayed and scrutinized every detail, looking for anything to free herself from her commitment—anything that shouted impostor. But what she'd seen actually made her own carriage look plain. The only detail that didn't fit with her story was the lack of luggage that Lady Abiageal would surely have had on the roof.

Rafferty called a final halt to the horses bringing her carriage to a stop. Fiona sat frozen, her pulse and mind both racing to a frenetic beat. In no scenario she'd imagined had this been a possibility. She wanted to scream to Rafferty to leave at once and take her home. But she couldn't; she'd never be safe there now. If she reneged on their agreement, he'd surely come for her.

Fiona heard boots approaching the carriage but was afraid to look. What if it was him? Or one of his loathsome men? But either would nullify the deal! She'd stipulated that he not show his face so her servants wouldn't be suspicious.

The boots stopped just outside her door.

"Shall I help you with Lady Fiona's luggage?" A strange male voice with an Irish brogue no foreigner could ever master, called up to Dorrel. Fiona's fledgling hope plummeted. It was one of his footmen—and he was Irish, not Norse. She felt the carriage shift as Dorrel untied her trunks.

"That would be most appreciated," Dorrel responded.

"My lady sent her luggage ahead so we've plenty of space; they'll be easy to load," the strange footman added.

The Northman not only had the man use her name, he'd even thought of an excuse for the lack of luggage. She had sorely underestimated him!

"Have you been here long?" Dorrel asked, making conversation as he slid her first trunk to the edge and prepared to hand it down to him.

"Aye, we were early. Almost an hour now, I would suspect. I believe her ladyship is napping," came the man's reply.

"Oh, very good, then I'll keep quiet."

The scraping sounds of her trunks sliding over the edge raked across Fiona's raw nerves.

"I'll give you a hand with those," Dorrel said as he jumped down.

"Gratitude," the strange footman replied without a hint of deception. Their footsteps faded away as the two men carried her first trunk to the other carriage, then grew louder as they returned for the second.

Fiona sat with both of her palms pressed to her forehead. What had she done? She couldn't possibly go through with this. But what of her countrymen? If she ran now, would he really kill them? Could she take the risk? But what of the risk to herself? The voracious base appetites of Vikings for young Irish women were well known—so many had been snatched, never to be seen again!

A single pair of footsteps returned and stopped just outside the door. That would be Dorrel—waiting for her. It was too much! She could not be expected to do this alone. The tiny lad from her nightmare clutching his father's lifeless hand came unbidden to her mind. He was an innocent. They were all innocents. How could she live with herself if she was such a hypocrite that she did not even try to save them?

"Lady Fiona?" Dorrel called out curiously.

Frantically she glanced around the carriage for a weapon, her eyes landing on the bundle of food Haisley had packed for her. Fiona ripped open the carefully folded linen, revealing two apples, a piece of the currant bread... and a knife. *Praise God!* Sliding the blade up inside the sleeve of her kirtle, she took a steadying breath, pulled her cloak tight around her, then answered him. "Aye, Dorrel."

"We've arrived, my lady. Your trunks have already been transferred, and I have the step in place if you're ready?"

"Aye, Dorrel," she murmured. *Nay, Dorrel! Nay! Nay! Nay!*

When he opened the door, she took his offered hand, then stepped down. Her knees wobbled.

"Are you well, my lady?" Dorrel asked. "You look..."

"I didn't sleep well last night. Gratitude for your concern, Dorrel." Fiona patted his hand.

He nodded and smiled. "The excitement of the trip, I'm sure."

Fiona doubted her ability to walk, to even take that first step, but then somehow she was moving—dutifully going through the motions of what was expected of her as she so often did. But never in a situation like this—like walking to her own execution. While her mind screamed for her to flee back to the safety of her carriage, her body continued to move forward of its own accord.

The foul weather shutters of the larger carriage were open, but the weighted curtains were tightly drawn, befitting a lady sleeping. One of the Northman's footmen was waiting for her at the door while the other finished lashing down her trunks to the roof.

"My lady." The strange footman held out his hand. She took it. He opened the door and stepped slightly behind her, blocking Dorrel's view inside. *The Northman had considered every minuscule detail.* Fiona stepped up onto the box step and grasped the brass handrail with her other hand. She faltered. Then, bracing herself to pass through the very gates of Hell itself, she climbed inside. The door closed quickly behind her, snuffing any thought she had of escape.

Her eyes sped over the plush gray interior to where the Northman sat in the opposite corner. But it wasn't him. Gone were the rows of ratty, tight braids. His now seemingly lighter blond hair was pulled back into a nobleman's tie. Gone too were his animal-like clothes, the leather jerkin, and shaggy furs.

He wore a fine rust-colored wool cloak, the cloth interwoven with varying shades of red and streaks of gold. The cloak clasped at his right shoulder with a single large brooch, and the full length of it was edged with heavy gold braid. The parting revealed the front of an amber and rust silk tunic over dark trousers and boots. At first glance, he would have passed for a noble. Until you looked closer and saw the wind and sun-baked toughness of his skin—the piercing predatory alertness of his blue eyes.

The carriage was large, but his presence filled it, stifling her. She'd never been this close to him. Well, she had when he'd forced introduction to her at Tibbot's, but this was different. This time they were together in a confined space. Her heart stuttered wildly in her chest. The carriage tipped as the second footman climbed up to the platform on the back. Without uttering a word, the Northman raised his right arm. His cloak fell away, revealing the long sleeve of his white fine linen undertunic shirt. In his hand was a cane—a unique piece made from polished knurled wood adorned with a silver lion's-head handle. He tapped on the roof. The carriage lurched forward. They were away.

DAY ONE

"I see you're admiring it—so you like the carriage then?" Gunnar asked.

"I'm just surprised. I was fully expecting an oxcart filled with straw," Fiona responded, trying to project some semblance of composure.

"My instructions were clear; an oxcart would never do. Though I'm sure you were hoping for that—any excuse to tell your driver not to stop." Her eyes flashed at his perceptiveness and he chuckled.

"Where are you taking me?" she asked.

"Taking you? I'm not *taking* you anywhere. We made a deal, and you are here of your own accord, remember?"

"You forced me to agree to it; I had no choice."

"Nay, that's not true, and you know it. You agreed because you thought I'd be unable to meet your demands and you would win, getting something for nothing." He paused. "But that's all behind us now. Are there any places you'd like to see?"

Was he mad? Did he really expect they would have a sightseeing tour together? "The only thing I wish to see are the gates of my estate and the back of this carriage disappearing in the distance."

"You'll get that soon enough—in seven days to be exact. It's already on the list but as the last attraction, of course. Anything else?"

Fiona ignored him.

"I thought you might be less than amicable, so I took the liberty of making a list of my own. But feel free to offer suggestions at any time."

He smiled at her—a taunting smile. He was toying with her! He knew she was afraid and was enjoying it. How funny would he think it was if she leapt across this carriage right now and stabbed him? She imagined his smirk turning to bewildered disbelief as he looked down at her paring knife sticking from his chest. Now that would be funny.

The image bolstered her. She wasn't defenseless. She had bested him before. She had to stay calm and think. Clearly, with the carriage and the clothes, he was planning to honor this farce of a bargain, at least initially. He hadn't lunged across the carriage and ripped at her dress or stopped the carriage and dragged her out into the bushes. Not yet. Perhaps he was less like the bird of prey that she'd first imagined and more like a cat, playing with its food before devouring it.

Well, she was no simple peasant girl. She could take him in a battle of wits. And surely wits would triumph over brawn. Wouldn't they?

She pushed aside that last fleeting doubt and turned her attention to the carriage, trying to find some clue as to its owner. How had he convinced a noble to lend it to him? Or had he stolen it? If so, then maybe someone was looking for it, and, once located, the brute would be captured and hanged. At first, the thought appealed to her—until she thought it through. Until she thought of the repercussions to herself of being discovered inside a stolen carriage with a Viking.

Her reputation would be ruined and with it, any chance of a respectable marriage. Not that she'd been thrilled with the prospects thus far, but it would devastate her father. And there'd be no way around her lies about the trip. She had to pray they remained undiscovered and pray the Northman kept his word.

"My given name is Gunnar," he said out of the blue.

"I've no intention of ever being that familiar with you."

"I only thought you should know it in case we are in public and you need to address me. 'Twould probably not fare well for either of us if you were to refer to me as Northman. Though I suppose, if you prefer not to be so familiar, you can always address me as *my lord*."

"If the need arises to address you in public—for which I shudder to think—it will certainly not be as *my lord*. You can rest assured of that," she snapped and looked away.

Gunnar found it difficult to take his eyes from her when she was this close. Her pale green cloak, trimmed in white ermine fur, brought out lighter flecks in her deep emerald eyes that were wide and dark with fear and anger when she looked at him. She had to be terrified, yet here she sat, so stoic and so beautiful. He still could not believe she'd come and recognized how much courage it had taken for her to do so. Gunnar was impressed by few people, but he was impressed by her yet again.

He noticed she repeatedly touched something inside the cuff of her right sleeve. Clearly, it was something she thought would protect her, but it had to be small. Likely a weapon or a cross. He'd seen people cling to both before when they were desperate. He glanced back at the set of her jaw and remembered her with the crossbow. It would be a weapon. He'd allow her to keep it since it brought her comfort, but he'd be sure to watch for it.

The sudden rapping of the cane on the roof startled her. Fiona had no idea how much time had passed. It felt like an eternity but could've been less than an hour. With her senses so heightened taking in every tiny detail, it was difficult to tell. Renewing her grip on the knife handle in her sleeve, she watched the Northman pull the curtain and call outside, "Garrett, this looks like a suitable spot to rest and water the horses. We'll stop here."

"Aye, my lord," the driver called back.

Fiona's pulse resumed a staccato beat. This would be it. Here, far from any dwellings, is where he would reveal his true intent. The carriage stopped. The Northman disembarked, leaving the door open behind him. Fiona remained seated, suddenly reluctant to leave the carriage she'd been terrified to enter before.

He reappeared in the doorway holding something heavy in his left hand. She couldn't see what it was; the carriage wall blocked it from her view, but she could see the weight of it pulling down on his left shoulder. *An axe?*

"Come," he said.

"Why? What are you planning to do to me?" Fiona bit her tongue too late and was furious to hear the last words slip from her mouth. She'd only meant to ask why, not to voice her inner fear.

"Do to you?" he asked with his eyebrows raised, pretending to be confused, but she could see that infuriating amusement in his eyes again.

"I'm going to feed you, Fiona." He lifted the basket he was carrying so she could see it. "I gave my word to allow no harm to come to you. Do you still not trust me?" He stepped back and waited.

Fiona stood and moved to the doorway, then looked down. The carriage was quite a bit higher than hers, and neither of the footmen were anywhere to be seen with the box step. That would likely be the Northman's doing, so she would have to ask him for help.

"I would offer you assistance," he said as if reading her mind, "but I've also promised not to lay hand. Unless, of course, you wish to release me from it?"

"There's no need for you to pretend havin' manners I know you do not possess. I can manage quite well on my own." Fiona eyed the distance to the ground again. Holding the knife tight in her sleeve with one hand and gathering her skirts with the other, she jumped from the carriage.

"If we're speaking of manners, that wasn't the most ladylike exit."

Fiona glowered at him.

"And that scowl." Gunnar shook his head as he turned away. "I've seen friendlier countenances on some very rough tavern wenches."

Fiona bit back a retort and took a deep breath. *Get ahold of yourself, Fiona. With every barb and insult that you allow to rile you, he's beating you at your own game—using his wits and not his brawn. He's an inferior cretin. Do not let him provoke you.*

As the Northman walked away with the basket, Fiona hesitated. Did she dare follow him when she was safe here? She wondered what was in the basket and her stomach rumbled. She'd eaten very little the night before and virtually nothing that morning. The driver had unhitched the last pair of horses and was leading them to the stream to drink. The footmen were carrying a cloth sack, which she assumed was their meal, to a shady spot under some trees. All seemed ordinary and tranquil. But what if he was luring her away from the other men to...

"Are you hungry or not?" The Northman called back without slowing.

After another brief moment of indecision, Fiona followed him. Who knew when they would eat again, and she had to keep her strength up. Besides, she hated giving him the satisfaction of thinking she was afraid.

Gunnar stopped on a grassy knoll just out of sight of the carriage. Satisfied with the view of the surrounding countryside, he placed the basket down on the grass and sat next to it, stretching his legs in front of him. When Fiona arrived but didn't sit, he cocked his head to look up at her.

"I shall remain standing to eat," she replied to his unasked question.

"Do you fear I'll take advantage if you were to sit?"

"Nay, the grass will soil my dress," she lied.

"I suppose I should have brought a blanket from the carriage to sit on, but as you pointed out, manners are not my forte. Here..." He unclasped his cloak, leaned over as far as he could reach without standing, and shook it out over the ground with the lining facing down. "Sit on this. If it stains, it will be on the inside and will not show when I'm wearing it. I'd hate for you to stain yours."

"That's not necessary," Fiona sputtered. What she really wanted to say was for him to put it back on immediately. She hadn't been worried about the grass at all, and, with his cloak removed, his full form was revealed. The amber and rust tunic belted at his waist and went to mid-thigh with short sleeves that extended only a few inches below his shoulders. It fit snug across his broad chest, but it was the sleeves of the white linen shirt that were most appalling. Instead of being loose down their full length as they should be, they stretched obscenely tight over his upper arms. So tight, she swore she could see shadows on his skin underneath. *Some hideous barbaric tattoo?* She shuddered and tore her gaze away.

"'Tis already done," Gunnar said and shrugged. "Sit if you want—or stand. I don't care. I'm hungry and I'm going to eat." He turned his focus to the basket.

"It may ruin your cloak," Fiona said in a last attempt to get him to cover himself.

Gunnar paused again and looked up at her. "We both know that it's not my cloak, and I do not see the true owner ever wearing it again after I return it. More likely he'll burn it," he said with a grin. He turned back to the basket and heard the rustling of silk as she sat and settled her skirt around her.

"Who is this *he* you refer to?" she asked.

"A dear friend, of course. I know many nobles."

Fiona snorted. "Keep it a secret if you will. I only worry that the carriage is stolen."

"It's not," he said as he pulled out a small un-dyed linen cloth from inside the basket, unfolded it, and spread it on the ground between them. He hadn't thought much of it when Cora had handed the footmen the basket and sack to stow, but now he realized how important they were. How important her insight about everything had been.

He reached inside, withdrawing each item and placing it on the cloth between them. A fresh loaf of bread, a block of cheese, small cooked sausages wrapped in wax cloth to trap their juices, and a jug. Gunnar pulled the cork and took a sniff. Ale.

He looked into the bottom of the basket. No utensils. The bread he could tear and the sausages were small enough to eat by hand, but the hard cheese required cutting. He reached for his dagger, remembering too late he didn't have it. He did have his sword but was not about to use Maid's Dream for that. He gripped the block with both hands and attempted to break it in half, but it was too hard. He turned to her. "Hand me your dagger so I can cut this," he said.

"What?"

"Your knife—the one you keep hidden in your sleeve."

"I don't know what you're on about."

"Would you like me to show you?"

"You swore not to lay a hand on me," she warned.

"I did. And trust me, that oath will keep you far safer than your little blade ever will." He held out his hand. "Your knife so we can eat. Please," he added.

Fiona considered refusing but realized it was only the element of surprise that made the small weapon effective. If he already knew... She carefully shook the blade from her sleeve and handed it to him.

Gunnar sliced the cheese in half, wiped the blade on the grass, and held it out towards her.

"Here, you can have it back—to keep you safe from me," he added with a chuckle, letting her know how ridiculous the thought was to him.

Fiona took the blade with two fingers and laid it on the ground next to her. Visible bits of cheese still clung to it; she could hardly slide it back inside her sleeve that way. He was so disgusting.

"Not the quality of fare you're accustomed to, I'm sure, but..." Before he finished, Fiona picked up the loaf of bread and ripped off a piece with her teeth.

"There, is this more what you're used to, Northman?" she asked with her mouth full.

"Nay, but feel free to act however you wish. I won't judge if you let your manners slip. And I'm hungry enough now, the sounds of a pig at its trough wouldn't spoil my appetite. So, by all means, continue to scowl and jump from carriages with your skirts halfway up your legs, stuff food in your mouth. Whatever you desire."

Had he just called her a pig at a trough? Fiona wanted to fire back with insults of her own, but the dry bread had lodged halfway down her throat. "Is there any water in that basket?" she croaked.

"Only ale. Do you want some?" Before she could answer, he tipped the jug and took several long swallows. After wiping his mouth on the back of his hand, he offered her the jug. "There are no cups either, so we'll have to share."

Repulsed by the idea of their lips touching the same surface, she shook her head and took a small bite of one of the moist sausages instead, hoping it would dislodge the bread. It did not—only added to the food backed up in her throat. She motioned for the jug, and Gunnar handed it to her. Even in her desperation, she took the time to make a cursory wipe of the rim with the hem of her skirt before lifting the jug and gulping down the ale.

Gunnar smiled as he took another bite.

Chapter 12

When they returned to the carriage, Fiona was relieved to see one of the footmen waiting with the box step already in place; she wouldn't be forced to climb back in on her own. Not an impossible feat, but one that would require some unladylike maneuvering if she were to refuse the Northman's assistance, which she absolutely would. He seemed oddly bound by his oath not to touch her, and though she'd not rely on it, she was not about to release him, just in case.

As the footman offered her his hand, she examined the man closer. She'd been too terrified the first time to pay any attention to him at all. He was average height but stocky. His broad nose was crooked in the middle, and a short, thin hairless scar ran through one of his thick eyebrows. Things you might expect to see in a peasant farmer who enjoyed his drink a bit too much, not a noble's footman. But his dark hair was neatly trimmed, and he did look down appropriately when she took his hand.

Fiona took her seat while the Northman climbed in behind her, and once again they were underway. She let out a long, slow exhale. The food and stout ale had done wonders to quiet her nerves. She'd been alone with the

Northman, out of view of everyone, and nothing untoward had happened to her—other than being repeatedly annoyed. She wondered where they were going but would not ask him again. Was he really only planning to see sights? Of course not. Her mind drifted through the possibilities but without the earlier biting edge of fear.

She refused to look at him, sure that he was staring at her. He was always staring at her. Sometimes he seemed to be puzzled, other times he was clearly admiring her. She recognized those looks because men had looked at her in both ways before. But other times he looked at her with something else. Something deeper. Something raw. A wild hunger of sorts. And he was never embarrassed to be caught staring—never looked away. He had no manners at all—like it was his right to look at her however he pleased.

As the hours passed, the combination of little sleep, a full stomach, and the effects of the ale began to pull at her eyelids. Even with the rough road, Fiona felt her body sinking into the thick cushions. She sat up straighter and stretched her eyes open wide. She dare not let her guard down around him, and she wanted to try to keep track in her head where they were going. So far, they'd stayed on smaller roads and had passed through no towns, but she was relatively certain they had started out going east and were now traveling south. Her eyelids drooped, only to be ripped open by the sound of his cane pounding on the roof.

"Garrett, we'll stop for the night at the next inn we come across."

"Aye, my lord," the driver replied.

An inn. Other people…Other people?! Her first thought had been one of relief; an inn would be far safer than if he'd simply told the driver to pull over for the night. But a public place harbored dangers of its own. What if someone recognized her? Or worse, what if they recognized him for what he truly was? How could they not? This charade of fancy carriage and fine clothes would never fool anyone. And assuming by some grace of God that they made it past the initial prying eyes, what then?

Did he think that she would share a room with him as she had the jug of ale? She'd only done that because she'd been practically choking to death. Granted, she'd drunk more later, but then only as a precaution not to choke again. How far did he think she would go? How far *would* she go?

Was she to walk with him and pretend...what? That they were together? But under what other circumstances would a lord and lady be traveling unescorted if they were not together? And if together, of course they would share a room. Nay. She'd not do it. She'd draw the line and face the consequences. Surely he wouldn't force the issue and do something rash. Her life might be figuratively over if they were discovered, but his would be *over* over.

And he would know that. He wasn't stupid. He wouldn't drag her off to a shared room like the true barbarian that he was. Nay, far more likely he'd only secure one room and then watch with amusement as she struggled to come up with a dignified response.

Well, she was ready for him. She would simply demand a second room. Let the inn folk think they were together but having a tiff of some sort. It would even explain why she was distant and cold toward him. It was a good plan—assuming they didn't immediately recognize him for the Viking scum that he was.

She glanced over at him, looking for any indication that he shared her fears, but he'd pulled open his curtain and sat calmly looking out the window. Did he truly have no idea of the risk he was taking? Did he have no idea what an angry mob would do to him?

"Aren't you afraid of what will happen when the people at the inn see you?" she finally asked.

"No," he said. "Why would I be?"

"Because they despise Northmen."

"But I'm not a Northman today, remember?"

"You can't possibly think that you'll fool anyone. It takes far more than a nice carriage and fine clothes to make a nobleman."

He didn't reply, only rolled his eyes.

How dare he dismiss her concerns so readily? Her life was at risk, too. "You know," she posed, "there's a fruit vendor in Dublin who dresses a monkey in fine robes and a crown. He's even trained it to bow and shake hands. 'Tis entertaining, but no one thinks for a second that it's really a king. Fine clothes do little to hide the filthy animal underneath when it's screeching and scratching itself."

The Northman's sea-blue eyes narrowed and his jaw tightened at the obvious comparison she was making. Fiona's feelings were split by his reaction. On the one hand, she was happy to have been able to rile him as he did her seemingly so easily, but on the other, she was more than a bit apprehensive as to what his response might be.

He stared at her for a moment, then grunted and shook his head. "People will see what they want to see, Fiona. With few exceptions, people are always that way—unable to see beyond an individual's circumstances to the real person beneath. When we arrive at the inn, the people will see the coin they are about to earn and think of the tales they can tell their friends of the highborns who stayed there. They'll see the fine carriage, the servants, and the elegant clothes...and they'll see you and the imperious way you carry yourself. They will never, for a moment, doubt me."

"But you can barely even speak; your accent is atrocious."

"It doesn't matter. They'll still believe it. And not because it's such a great disguise, as you've pointed out. They're expecting something that they want to believe, so they won't examine it too closely. You're no different."

"Me? How can you say that? I see right through you."

"To see what you want to see. You hold fast to the details that support what you think you know and reject those that contradict your preconceived notions. You've decided that I'm a brutal, ruthless savage." His mouth quirked as he gave a half-shrug. "Of which I'm more than capable of being—but I'm more than that. My people are more than that, and it's your people's inability to recognize that simple fact that's leading to your demise.

"You consider yourselves superior and in that arrogance you underestimate us. You may win a few battles and drive us back a few times, but we'll keep returning, and each time we'll be stronger until all of this land is ours. At least as much of it as we want—and from what I've seen so far, that *will* be all of it. " He paused and fixed her with a stare. "Because when we're not raiding, Fiona, we don't spend our time *screeching and scratching ourselves*. We're learning from our failures. Plotting. Improving."

Before Fiona could think of a suitably scathing response, the carriage swayed as the wheels bumped out of the road tracks and slowed to a stop. Her thoughts jerked back to the immediate dilemma of their being discovered.

"Shall I see to your rooms, my lord?" one of the footmen called down.

Gunnar had been reaching for the door but stopped short at the footman's words. Contrary to what he'd just told her, he knew he needed to be mindful of first impressions. "Aye, Bryen," he replied.

Bryen cleared his throat. "Um, will you be needing one room or two, my lord?"

Gunnar looked at Fiona, who remained peering through a slit in her curtain as if she'd not heard. He waited.

Fiona held her breath. *Why did he not answer? If he thought for one moment that...* Unable to stand it any longer, she turned to face him. He sat with one eyebrow raised in suggestion, a wicked smile playing at the corners of his mouth. She shot him a withering look of disgust and returned her gaze out the window.

Gunnar laughed out loud. "Two rooms, Bryen," he said, still chuckling. "And arrange for appropriate lodgings for you men."

"Aye, my lord." The carriage tipped and rocked as Bryen left for the inn.

Fiona wanted desperately to chew a fingernail. Surely this ruse would soon be at an end. No one could possibly believe him to be a nobleman when they saw him up close. He was too tall, too broad, too hard. Though thankfully his bulging upper body was once again concealed under his cloak. Maybe if he had the sense to skulk off to his room without speaking, but he seemed neither aware nor concerned of the danger.

Her heart began to race again. Her fear of being discovered now equaled the fear she'd felt when she first approached the carriage. Who would be the first to recognize him for what he was? The innkeeper? Another traveler? A servant? Who would be the first to point their finger at him, and whisper to the person next to them. Whisper the one word that so many dreaded. "*Northman.*"

Fiona heard the step box being placed outside the door.

"'Tis done, my lord," Bryen said as he opened the door and stepped aside. The Northman climbed out, his shoulders briefly filling the doorway before he dropped down. He moved off to one side and stood stretching while Bryen helped her out. Fiona glanced up and down the road. There were no structures for as far as she could see. Nothing looked familiar.

She took a deep breath and walked around the back of the carriage to face the inn. It was a small quaint place with old wood timbers and a thatched roof. A handful of people were gathered outside the door to welcome them, and movement from curtains told her they were being watched from every available spot. Her feet rooted to the ground. This would never work.

Chapter 13

"Greetings, my lord, my lady," a short middle-aged woman said as she stepped forward and did her best curtsy. "Welcome to our humble inn. My husband is out but shall soon return." She looked to Gunnar. "I've prepared our two finest rooms for you and..." She glanced at Fiona.

"My sister." Gunnar filled in for her without hesitation.

His sister? Even as she balked, Fiona appreciated how he'd subtly covered the need for two rooms. But his sister? The lie was so glaringly obvious, she expected the woman to break into uproarious laughter.

But she did not. Instead, she murmured, "Aye, my lord," her voice filled with reverence, as if she were in the company of a high king. "This way."

Without looking at his face and the satisfied smirk she knew would be there, Fiona followed the woman through the door and up the creaking wood stairs.

"This one 'ere is for you, my lady." The woman opened the door to the first room on the right. She did another small curtsy as Fiona brushed past her, then turned back to Gunnar. "Your room is just 'ere, my lord." She stepped across the hall. "Will you be joining us below for supper? I've made a fine shepherd's pie."

"I'll take my meal in my room," Fiona said, annoyed that the woman seemed to have forgotten her presence entirely.

"Aye, my lady. I'll send it up straightaway," the innkeeper's wife said over her shoulder. "And you, my lord?"

"I'll be down shortly. Shepherd's pie is one of my favorites, and I have a feeling yours will be delicious." He smiled at her, and she stifled a giggle.

Fiona couldn't tear her eyes from the appalling scene. He was flirting with the innkeeper's wife? And the woman had giggled?

"Hopefully, you serve it in large portions," Gunnar added, "for I have a hearty appetite."

"Aye, I'm certain that you do, my lord. Your bowl will be as if bottomless, I assure you."

Gunnar heard Fiona's door slam and smiled. It was good for her to see that other women did not view him as the ogre that she did.

The innkeeper's wife turned to the closed door, her face filled with sudden concern.

"Don't mind her," Gunnar reassured her. "She's a nervous sort—easily flustered. Truth be told, she's only my half-sister, and her mother—my father's second wife, tends to be that way, too." He shrugged.

"Aye, my lord," the woman exhaled with relief and the honor of a shared confidence with a nobleman.

Fiona stood at the door, listening to their lowered voices with bated breath, fully expecting to hear the woman shriek in sudden terror when she finally came to her senses. When the creaking of the stairs indicated her departure, Fiona rested her forehead against the door in relief, then turned to survey her room. Though sparsely furnished with only a small bed, a table, and two chairs, it appeared to be clean.

A knock sounded on her door. Fiona yanked it open, sure that it was the Northman come to gloat. Bryen stood alone in the hall with one of her trunks balanced on his shoulder. His eyes widened at her dour expression.

"Apologies for the intrusion, my lady," he stammered. "I've brought your trunk. Shall I come back?"

"Nay, of course not, Bryen." Fiona did her best to smile. "Come in. You may set it over there."

"Aye, my lady." He did as she instructed, then returned to the door without looking at her.

"Gratitude, Bryen. And there's no need for you to bring the second. This one will suffice."

He stopped, nodded, and was gone.

Twenty minutes later when another knock sounded on her door, Fiona tempered her response and opened the door slowly, even though she was sure it had to be the Northman this time. A young lass with mousy brown hair stood with her head bowed, holding a tray with her meal. The resemblance to the innkeeper's wife was unmistakable, and, judging the girl's terrified expression, Fiona was sure the woman had warned her she was taking food to a troll. Seeing Bryen's hasty retreat probably hadn't helped.

Fiona smiled as sweetly as she could through her exasperation. "Come in. You may set the tray on the table," she instructed and stepped back.

"Aye, my lady." She did as she was bade then scurried back, stopping inside the doorway, but giving Fiona a wide berth. "Apologies, my lady, but we have no wine. I brought you cool milk, but if you'd prefer ale or mead...or water, I can bring those, too."

"Milk is my favorite. Gratitude, um, what is your name?"

"'Tis Ashleen, my lady. Will there be anythin' else?" she asked without raising her eyes from the floor.

"Nay, that will be all," Fiona said, unable to think of anything to say that might convince the lass she was nice. When Ashleen spun on her heel and fled, Fiona sighed. "Oh well. 'Tis not as if it's a contest," she muttered to herself as she latched the door.

Good thing it's not, because he's winning, her subconscious goaded.

Fiona took a moment to consider it. How was that even possible? How was it possible that the first impression of the inn folk was so horribly backwards? She was the nice one. He, the dangerous impostor. Savory smells from the tray interrupted her thoughts, and she moved to the table. She'd think on it later after she'd eaten. Meirna always said problems seemed trifling on a full stomach.

She removed each item from the tray, carefully positioning them around her wooden plate. Since there would be no one to serve her, she had to be able to reach everything from her seat. The tureen of shepherd's pie and the small loaf of bread wrapped in a warm cloth she placed to her right. The bowl of sweet cream butter and apple tart to her left. After making one last adjustment, she sat and arranged her skirt.

She lifted the lid to the tureen and served a small portion of the shepherd's pie onto her plate, pleased by the numerous plump portions of tender lamb and thick brown gravy. Next, she broke open the still-warm loaf of bread, pausing to inhale the heavenly smell of yeast. She spread a thick layer of sweet cream butter on one piece, then placed it on the edge of her plate.

Even though she was famished and the food delicious, she limited herself to small bites, dabbing her mouth gently with a square of linen after every partial spoonful as if she were dining in fine company. Here alone in her quiet room, she could pretend she was far away from the detestable Northman and misguided common folk, and she intended to take full advantage of it. She drew out the meal as long as possible, finishing by nibbling the apple tart until only crumbs remained.

With the exception of the additional servings she'd consumed, she was satisfied her behavior had been very ladylike and appropriate. She vowed to do it again the following night if given the opportunity. This was who she was.

Identity firmly reasserted and some semblance of her life restored, Fiona pushed her chair back from the table, just as a burst of raucous laughter rose from the small common room below. The noise had grown steadily louder throughout her meal as the diners gave way to drinking patrons. Surely the Northman wasn't still among them. He'd told the innkeeper's wife he intended to go down to eat, but surely he hadn't lingered. Even he was not that bold. Was he?

With anxiety threatening the calm she'd achieved during the meal, Fiona tried to think of something else. Her thoughts soon landed on another predicament—how was she to undress? Meirna's insistence that she wear a newer gown that laced up the back now posed quite the challenge. She reached up behind her neck, untied the top bow, then began unlacing the top few inches that were within her reach. She'd just begun the contortions required to reach the next section when there was a rap on the door.

"Who is it?" she called out without opening it this time.

"It's Ashleen again, my lady."

Fiona opened the door a crack and peered around it to make sure the girl was alone before opening it the rest of the way. "Come in, Ashleen. Have you come to take the tray?"

"Um, your brother sent me, my lady. Told me how your maid had taken ill suddenly and that you had no one to aid you."

Was there no end to his ability to lie?

"Now, I'm no lady's maid to be sure, but if you'll tell me what to do, I'll try my very best."

"Gratitude, Ashleen. Your timing is perfect. I actually do have need of assistance with this dress. Would you unlace it for me?"

"Of course, my lady. And perhaps I could draw you a bath?" Ashleen offered.

"Nay, that won't be necessary." Fiona declined as she turned her back for Ashleen to reach the laces.

"Are you sure you won't have a bath?" Ashleen asked.

"Aye. I'm sure."

"Then, perhaps there's somethin' else I could do for you?" Her voice was distracted as she tentatively reached up and grasped the silk cord laces.

Fiona turned to face this new Ashleen who suddenly wished to linger when earlier she couldn't wait to flee. "What is it, Ashleen?" Fiona demanded.

Ashleen looked at the floor. "Well, my lady. 'Tis just that your brother paid me good coin, very good coin, in fact, to see you well attended. If I go back now...well, if I go back now, so soon, I fear he'll want it back," she blurted. "And rightly so, I suppose." Her voice trailed off.

Fiona studied the girl, recognizing the opportunity to redeem her image. "We can't have that now, can we?" She smiled and patted her hand. "He paid you enough to draw me a bath?"

"Ten baths, my lady, to be truthful."

"Very well, Ashleen. I'll have a bath, and afterward, you can help me with my hair."

The girl beamed. "I'll be back with the tub quick as a flash."

"Nay, wait. There's something else I need you to do for me first."

"Anythin'?"

"Is the Nor..., my brother downstairs?"

"He is."

Fiona groaned inwardly at the image of him drinking with the other inn folk, then shook it off. "I need you to fetch our driver, Garrett, and bring him to me, but it's important that my brother doesn't see him. Is there a rear entrance?"

Ashleen nodded but seemed troubled by the request.

"I'm plannin' a surprise for...my brother...for...his birthday." It was the first thing that came to mind to explain the secrecy. "Garrett is helping me and I'd prefer...my brother," she coughed out the offensive word for the third time, "did not see him."

Ashleen bobbed her head and smiled, happy to be included in the secret. "I'll fetch him straightaway." She practically skipped to the door and was gone.

Fiona paced as she waited. What if Garrett refused to come? What if the Northman had given him orders not to speak to her? She couldn't go to him—a lady moving about in this small place would never go unnoticed, no matter how careful she was.

Finally, there was a light knock on the door and Ashleen's voice. "My lady?"

"Come in. 'Tis not latched."

Ashleen entered with a large wood half-barrel balanced on her hip. Garrett remained in the hallway twisting his cap in his hands.

"Come in, Garrett." Fiona smiled and addressed him by name, though he'd never actually been presented to her.

Garrett hesitated.

"Well, come on, silly. Don't keep her ladyship waitin," Ashleen chided as she set the tub down.

Garrett nodded and stepped over the threshold, remaining close to the door.

"Ashleen, will you give us a moment?" Fiona asked.

"Aye, my lady. I'll start fetchin' the water."

As soon as she was gone, Fiona turned to the driver. "Garrett, I need you to answer a few questions truthfully."

"Aye, my lady, but perhaps they would be better directed to his lordship." Garrett averted his eyes.

"You and I both know what he is, Garrett, and he is no lord."

Garrett said nothing, only stared at the floor.

"How did he come by you and the carriage?" Fiona asked.

"All I know, my lady, is that he and my lord made an agreement, and I... we are to serve him as we would his lordship for ten days, then return home."

"And who is your lord?"

"Apologies, my lady, I'm not at liberty to say."

That order could have come from the Northman or the noble. "Does he mean to do me harm?" Fiona asked the question that was foremost on her mind.

"What?" Garrett looked up at her, startled. "Why would you think that? You met him and came...I thought..."

Dear God, the men thought this was a love tryst!

"He tricked me into coming, Garrett, and I must know if I should fear for my safety." Her eyes bore into him.

"My lady, I do not claim to know his mind, but if he wished to harm you, I see no reason for him to have gone to such lengths as needin' the carriage or..." He struggled for words. "What I'm tryin' to say is, knowin' what...I mean who, he really is, if his intent were to harm you...well, I'm sure he had easier ways to do so without all this," he stammered his conclusion.

"And the footmen, can I trust them?"

"Aye, my lady. Bryen and Orin may seem a bit rough at times, but they're both good lads."

"If you were ever to learn of something regarding my safety, I would hope you would tell me."

"I would."

"Will you give me your word?"

"Aye." He nodded. " You have it."

"Gratitude, Garrett. And if you would please not mention our conversation to...his lordship." The words still stuck in her mouth when referring to him, but she had to be mindful of being overheard.

Garrett nodded. "Of course, my lady."

Ashleen arrived with the first two pails of steaming water. After holding the door open wide for her to pass, Garrett took his leave.

Gunnar watched over the rim of his tankard as Garrett descended the last few stairs, then turned and disappeared from view out the back. He'd carefully chosen this seat tonight, to be able to see both the entrance and the stairway in case Fiona attempted to flee. He'd not been expecting this—for her to be plotting already. He set his ale down on the table, then stood and asked for the privy. Once outside, he headed straight for the stables. If she was cooking up some scheme with Garrett and the other two, he'd rather know it sooner than later.

The two footmen were nowhere to be seen, but he found Garrett watering the horses. He watched him for a moment without announcing himself. Garrett's behavior seemed normal. After approaching each horse with a bucket and allowing the animal to drink its fill, he gave them an affectionate pat and murmured something before moving to the next. Gunnar waited for him to finish before stepping from the shadows.

"Garrett."

Garrett jumped. "Apologies. You startled me, my lord," he said, refusing to meet Gunnar's eyes.

"I saw you inside the inn. What was your business there?"

Garrett squirmed but did not answer.

"Your duty is to serve me during this time, is it not?"

"Aye, my lord."

"You have no such arrangement with her ladyship, correct?"

"Aye, that's correct, my lord."

"So why did she summon you?"

"She asked that our conversation be private," he mumbled.

"Garrett!" Gunnar barked, sure now that Fiona had somehow convinced the man to aid her—but in what?

Garrett took a deep breath and nodded. "She asked who my lordship was and how you came by his carriage; I did not tell her."

"And?"

"She asked if your intent was to harm her." He looked up at Gunnar then, his eyes filled with concern. "She does not have to worry on that count, does she, my lord?"

Gunnar studied the man. He appeared to be telling the truth. "No, Garrett, she does not."

"That's what I told her," he said, but was clearly relieved to hear it.

"What else did she say?"

"Only that you tricked her to be here."

Gunnar chuckled. "She came willingly, Garrett. You saw that with your own eyes. Is that all?"

Garrett nodded.

"Very well. Get some rest. I will not tell her we spoke; your confidence with her will remain intact. But Garrett?"

"Aye, my lord?"

"If you should become aware of any plan of her ladyship's to do me harm, I expect you to inform me, no matter what she makes you agree to. Is that clear?"

Garrett's brow furrowed at the similar odd requests from two people, who until moments ago, he'd assumed wanted to be together. "Aye, my lord."

Gunnar returned to his seat in the inn's common room. He wondered how she would be the next day and hoped that her talk and secret alliance with Garrett would alleviate some of her fears.

All in all, today had gone very well, but tomorrow he had to do better. He had only a week to win her trust. A week to convince her that with him, she was safe to shed propriety and be the woman he'd seen that night, unrestricted and free. To do that, he needed to emphasize what they had in common instead of antagonizing her.

After the last bucket was emptied, Ashleen wiped her brow and turned to Fiona. "Shall I finish your dress now, my lady?" she asked. Even after the labor, she was still eager. The Northman must have paid her a great deal indeed.

"Aye, Ashleen."

The girl's nimble fingers made short work of the laces down her back. She lifted the green gown over Fiona's head and laid it carefully on the bed, before repeating the process with the silk kirtle. Fiona removed her shoes and stockings, stepped out of her thin shift and underdrawers, then lowered herself into the tub. She had to fold her knees to her chest to fit in the small space, but still, she sighed as the heat magically melted the tension from her muscles.

Ashleen chatted away as she neatly folded the green gown and hung the cream-colored kirtle to air for Fiona to wear again the next day. It wasn't dirty and she only had four kirtles for the trip—all basically the same and able to be worn with any gown.

"Is this the one, my lady?" Ashleen held up an older style blue gown from the trunk.

"Aye." Fiona nodded, watching the lass hang the gown next to the kirtle. She knew she'd been extremely fortunate to have Ashleen's help tonight and wasn't about to put herself in the same predicament tomorrow. The newer style gowns would remain safely stowed for the remainder of this trip. Ashleen layed out a fresh shift, pausing to admire the chambergown. "This is so beautiful – what is it?"

"It's a chambergown—to be worn when my room has a chill and I do not wish to dress."

The chambergown seemed to intrigue the lass more than her day gowns; Fiona realized it might not be the garment so much as the idea of relaxing in a private bedchamber. Ashleen likely shared a sleeping space with her entire family, and there was never time between work and sleep for lounging.

Lost in the glorious feel of the soothing bath, Fiona closed her eyes and attempted to block out Ashleen's quiet chatter. But with no discouragement from Fiona, the girl's tongue became loosened.

"And I'd have never pegged the two of you as brother and sister, that's for sure. You with your dark hair and him so fair. And he talks so strange." She stopped abruptly. "Apologies. I shouldn't have said that."

"Nay, it's alright, Ashleen. He does talk strange." *Because he's a murdering pagan.*

"And you're such a proper lady, and him, well..."

So they could see through him. Fiona felt vindicated even as she recognized it put them in jeopardy.

"I mean, he's a proper lord, to be sure, but..., well, I feel almost sad for him. To have spent so much of his life in foreign lands that he's nearly lost his own tongue. 'Twould be a terrible thing for an Irishman to bear. On the other hand, 'tis quite amazin'. Did you know he can order ale in five different tongues? And he said some places don't even have ale, and they drink something made from the roots of trees. He said it tastes most awful. Which I imagine it would. How could it not? And 'tis so good of you to be accompanying him on this trip to reacquaint himself with his homeland and his people. He's very fortunate to have such a kind sister."

Fiona went rigid in the tub. *That was his story? He—an Irishman? Who had traveled for so long he forgot how to speak? How ridiculous!* Yet as she listened to the girl babble on about him, she realized his prediction in the carriage had been correct; people saw what they wanted to see.

"Me oldest sister dreams of marryin' him," Ashleen confided. "Me mum threatened to send her to clean the stables if she didn't quit gushin' over him like a ninny, and I hope she does it. 'Twould serve her right to muck out a few stalls," she laughed.

"Can you please not talk about my *brother* anymore," Fiona cut her off.

"Of course, my lady. Apologies if I said somethin' out of turn; I'm forever doin' that."

Her tone had come out harsher than intended, and Fiona attempted to salvage it. "Ashleen, do you have a brother?"

"Aye, my lady, three in fact," the now subdued girl mumbled.

"And do they ever annoy you?"

"Oh, aye, nearly all the time," she said with some of her earlier liveliness.

"Well, that's how it is with me and my *brother*. Often I find him annoying and would prefer not to talk about him."

"His lordship? 'Tis hard to imagine him so—as someone's scamp brother, but I do understand it. Me little brother, Tommy, is nothin' but pure rascal, but does me mum see it? Nay. She spoils him then tells him what a good lad he is. He's rotten to the core, that one, but me mum sees only the face of an angel."

"Then you understand me well."

"Aye, that I do, and you'll hear not another word about his lordship from me."

With Ashleen gone and the door safely latched behind her, Fiona blew out the candle and crawled onto the low bed. Bathed, fed, and relaxed, she snuggled into the thin straw tick, and began to think back over the entire day.

"God gave you three important gifts, Fiona. Clear eyes, a sharp mind, and a good heart. Do not squander any of them by being lazy and taking other

people's thoughts for your own. Always see things fresh with your own eyes, then measure what you see with your heart and mind."

It was one of her father's favorite things to say, and she'd tried to live by those words her entire life.

As for her current situation, Fiona realized she had a lot to be thankful for. One day of her commitment was successfully completed. She was safe, and had it not been for her fears—none of which had come to pass—the day would not have been altogether unpleasant. The Northman was grating, but far more civilized than she thought he could be. And the inn folk had not reacted to him as she'd expected them to, which was to her benefit, so why did it vex her so?

Because it made him right and her wrong. If she conceded that, then it opened the door for him to be right and her wrong about other things. He was obviously far more intelligent and resourceful than she'd given him credit for. And though he was surely uneducated, his worldly experiences did give him a well of knowledge to draw from. In that respect, she supposed one could consider him educated in his own way.

Was she wrong about him? About Vikings in general? Was she looking at him through the eyes of another, her mind filled with preconceived notions as he'd accused?

Nay. She'd seen him that night with the slaves chained and huddled together in the road. Even if she hadn't, he'd confirmed her beliefs with his own words when he threatened to slaughter innocent men and hang them like butchered animals. Those were not the acts of a decent man.

But he didn't deny being a ruthless savage. In fact, he'd admitted it, but claimed he was more. Was he? Could someone be both?

She thought back over his behavior throughout the day. He'd not touched her once. That he understood what an oath meant, alone went contrary to what she believed Northmen capable of. Taking off his cloak for her to sit on was a trivial thing, and he hadn't even stood up to do it. Still, it was a courteous act.

But it was his sending Ashleen to tend to her that was the incongruity she wrestled with the most. Not so much that he would spend the coin—he clearly had an excess. It was the fact that he'd thought of her comfort at all and then cared to act on it once he did. Especially after she'd insulted him. Why did she behave that way around him? She'd been in unpleasant company before but had never allowed herself to be reduced to such ill-bred conduct. She was a lady.

Uncomfortable with the examination of herself, she turned her thoughts back to him. His excuse of being an Irish nobleman who had traveled for most of his life, was genius really, if she were to give credit where it was due. It covered any improprieties and excused his blunders in advance. It would never stand up in noble company, of course, but for these folk, it hadn't raised the slightest doubt. And he'd called her an accomplished liar. She snorted. He put her to shame there.

Her thoughts moved on to her conversation with Garrett. He'd come to the same conclusion that she had earlier. If the Northman truly intended to harm her, he didn't need to go to all this trouble. Then why was he doing this? What did he want from her?

What he wanted didn't matter. Her only concern needed to be surviving six more days. Starting tomorrow, she would stop allowing him to manipulate and provoke her. No matter what he said or did, she would remain calm and comport herself with proper dignity. It would be difficult; the man was irksome enough to provoke a saint, but she could do it. Satisfied with her plan, Fiona closed her eyes.

No sooner had she drifted off to sleep when loud voices startled her awake. Her first terrified thoughts were that they'd been discovered. She strained her ears for any sounds of an altercation. Jovial laughter filtered up from below. Fiona closed her eyes again and tried to slow her racing heart. Surely he wasn't still among them.

She dozed, only to be awakened once more by the revel-makers. What if he *was* still among them? What if, in a drunken stupor, he revealed himself? Anxious and frustrated, but powerless to do anything about it, Fiona pulled the thin straw pillow over her head to block out the sounds and her fears.

Chapter 14

DAY TWO

"**S**leep well?" Gunnar asked as she approached the carriage.

"Hardly," she answered curtly, blaming him for the seemingly endless night of fitful naps. Starting the day fatigued and testy would make her decision to remain ladylike in his company even more of a trial. Thankfully, Bryen already had the carriage door open and the box step in place. At least she wouldn't have to stand outside, exchanging tedious false pleasantries with him in front of the inn folk, whom she knew would still be watching them.

Without waiting for Bryen's assistance, she stepped up onto the box, reached for the brass handle, and pulled herself inside. The Northman followed, taking the same seat he'd occupied the previous day, diagonal from her.

"And you?" she asked. "Did you enjoy your time with your new friends 'til the wee hours of the mornin'?"

"I did. You should have joined us."

"Nay, I should not have, and you shouldn't have been there either," she snapped. "You managed to fool them initially, but with every additional moment you spent in their company, you risked discovery. Need I remind you, Northman, my neck is on the line as well? All night, I kept waitin' to be dragged from my bed once your lie, now *our* lie, was discovered. I know you're only pretendin' to be a nobleman so this is difficult for you, but for your information, and hopefully your use in the future, noblemen do not sit and swill ale with commoners."

"And noble ladies don't run wild with commoners on stormy nights, yet there you were with your crossbow. But not to worry. Last night, no one seemed to mind. In fact, they seemed to enjoy my company as much as I did theirs."

They were interrupted by a female voice outside. "My lord. Your midday meal, as promised." A buxom girl labored toward the carriage with their replenished basket. She had Ashleen's eyes and mousy brown hair, though hers was carefully curled and adorned with several bows. "I prepared it special myself," she said as she lifted it to him through the open door, her cheeks flushed.

Ashleen's sister—still tryin' to earn time in the stables from the looks of it.

"I shall savor every bite," the Northman said with a genuine smile as he lifted the heavy basket effortlessly with one hand. Today he wore a dark blue cloak with the same thick gold braid trim and a royal blue silk tunic embroidered with green and gold. Thankfully the lighter blue and gold brocade silk sleeve of his shirt was cut a little fuller, and while still snug on his upper arm, did not appear as if the seams were about to burst. She wondered briefly how many changes of clothes he had, with no trunk.

The girl flushed a deeper pink and bobbed her head. "I put in our two best cups. Apologies, my lord. I'm sure they're quite plain compared to what you're accustomed to, but they're freshly scrubbed and will serve you well since your servants forgot to pack yours."

"Gratitude for the extra effort. Was that all?"

The girl only nodded, dreamy-eyed and suddenly mute.

After Bryen closed the door, Gunnar rapped on the ceiling with the silver lion's-head cane.

"Are you sure you've said farewell to *all* your friends?" Fiona asked as the carriage pulled away.

"I am," he replied as he unbuckled his sword and leaned it against the wall farthest from her reach.

Seeing him take that precaution pleased her. At least he feared her a little, too. "And were they sad to see you go?"

"Aye. Some more than others—as you just saw."

Fiona scowled and looked out the window.

"If you were nicer, they might have been sad to see you go, too."

Her head spun back around like an owl.

"Me? Nicer? The difference, Northman, is that I truly *am* nice and you are only pretending to be."

"Is it?"

"Of course it is!" she sputtered. "You and your kind...murder them, steal from them, make slaves of them. I risk my life to save them—to help them."

"Do you really?" he asked dubiously.

"What kind of question is that? You've seen me!"

"I was not questioning your physical presence there, only your motives."

"What is that supposed to mean?"

"That means, I don't think you do it for them at all. I think you do it for yourself. I think you have a wild heart."

Fiona missed the next few things he said, her mind reeling from his words. They were the exact words her father had said to her so many times. Well, not the exact words. Her father always said, *"You have your mother's wild heart."*

"I think you do it because you crave adventure and excitement," he continued. "You can't stand your dull sedentary life with all its rules and restrictions, so you've created a cause to champion for an excuse to run wild. Your actions are not out of some love for your countrymen as you profess. You serve yourself. And if my words are not true, then explain it to me. Since when does a highborn consider a commoner's life of equal value to their own? Why would you risk your life to save men you don't even know? And how does a young highborn *lady* even know of such things, much less give them thought?"

"My father is a scholar. He's taught me a great many things about the world and its injustices."

Gunnar stifled a laugh. Here she sat in a luxurious carriage, dressed in the finest clothes, yet spoke of the world's injustices with righteous indignation. "Why would a man do that?" he asked. "Has he no son?" He saw by her expression his words had hit the mark. "Ah, he does not. He's a fool. Such teachings are wasted on a daughter." He turned and pulled his curtain aside to look out.

Fiona felt the heat creeping up her neck. The intensity of the fury she felt made it difficult to form words. He was like all the other men, thinking education was wasted on a woman. How many times had she been forced to swallow her words in mixed company because they were not proper. But just as when he'd criticized her manners, or her scowl, or anything else, it was somehow far, far worse coming from him.

"Do you really think a woman is incapable of understanding or having valuable thought on worldly subjects?" she asked through clenched teeth.

"Nay, you mistook my intent. I think what your father has done is cruel— careless at best. He's given you a mind in a world where you cannot have a voice. To have thoughts on a subject and never be able to share them, would be like being locked in a prison cell in your own mind. I would think it would be enough to drive one mad." He paused. "Though in your case, it does explain a lot. And I stand by my earlier assertion that you do it for yourself."

"It's not like that," Fiona denied.

"Really? Tell me, do the noblemen who come to court you, appreciate your opinions on worldly subjects? Or is that, in fact, why you are as yet unmarried at your age? How old are you, anyway? Eighteen? Nineteen?" He didn't wait for her to answer. "Too bad for you, you weren't born a Viking. We're far more advanced when it comes to women."

Before she could open her mouth to object, he continued.

"It's true. Women are equals in our culture. Not comely ornaments kept to produce heirs. We value our women. Respect them."

"Our men respect us," she said, indignant.

"As what? As possessions? As they respect another man's fine carriage like this one?" He motioned to the interior. "Did you know that some of our first raids to settle your land were actually led by a woman?"

"This land was already settled! Your people have done nothing more than pillage and plunder!"

He shrugged. "That's irrelevant to this discussion. My point was, a woman led one of the first fleets to your shores. I believe your people called her Inghen Ruaidh—Red Girl. Fighting men *and women* were willing to risk their lives for her vision. But with you...All of your knowledge must be kept hidden as if you did not have it. Because of that, you'd be better served to know only woman things—raising children and managing a household," he said more gently. "Then you'd never know what you were missing and would not be driven to find escape as you are now."

Fiona sat stunned. How could he sum up her whole life after being in her company for less than a day? How could he see so clearly what those who had known her for years, could not? And unlike others, this Northman accepted that she had a mind and was not shocked or appalled by it. Instead, he pitied her.

"You don't know me," she said.

"I think I do better than you care to admit. But I also know this, Fiona. For the next week, you are free. I said it yesterday in jest regarding your manners, but I meant it. Think as you wish. Speak as you wish. Act as you wish. Who are you really? Some nobleman's future mindless brood-stock? A raider? Something in between? Perhaps you don't even know. In that case, take this time to explore the possibilities. Unless you're afraid of what you might discover. Afraid that once you acknowledge your true self, you won't be able to suppress it again. But think on it soon. You have only a week before you return to your gilded prison."

"Six days," she corrected him.

He smiled. "Ah, yes, six days. You have six days left to be free."

Fiona stared out the window, trying unsuccessfully to put his astute observations from her mind. *Be free?* She was free! And pity her? Pity from him was even worse than criticism. His words could not possibly be true, yet try as she might, she could find no fault in them.

"Are you going to sulk the entire trip?" he asked. "The agreement was for a sightseeing companion, not a pouting child—and you don't see me sulking."

"I'm not sulking," she answered truthfully. "And you? What could you possibly have to sulk about? You're not a prisoner being forced to bear odious company."

"My lady, I've far more cause than you. Had you not attempted to sink my ship, I'd be well into a journey I've waited four years to complete. There's also the considerable coin I lost with the slaves you stole. Which, because of my word to you, I'll now have to capture replacements elsewhere—an additional delay, not to mention the risk of injury or death to me and my crew."

"Oh, that the world could be so fortunate," she muttered.

"All by your hands. Yet, unlike you, I've chosen to make the best of it. As for odious company? Well, I prefer not to speak ill of people—and the inn folk were quite nice. You, on the other hand, have lost only a week of your time. Time that you would probably have spent bored to death anyway."

"Must you always be so harassing?" she hissed.

"Unfortunately, it's the only thing you respond to. And I would remind you that most people, as you've seen with your own eyes, do not find me harassing at all."

"Because you're pretendin' to be something you are not. I see through you."

"I think we had this conversation before." He smiled. "What do you see? What in my actions has given you the thought that you know me? I've graciously given in to all your demands and honored my word at every turn."

Fiona would have liked to put him in his place but could come up with nothing suitable, probably from the lack of sleep for two nights in a row—also his fault.

"So where are we going, Northman? You may not understand it, but sightseeing means to stop and see sights, not bounce down the smallest rutted tracks, catching glimpses through the curtains."

"I'm well aware of the definition of sightseeing, my lady. Apologies for the first long day of travel on poorer roads." He paused. "I thought it best that we see more remote things."

"So that I would not be recognized," she murmured.

"That was the plan."

"I see," she said. Nothing he did was without purpose. She thought of her resolution the night before to remain civil. Once again, he'd managed to draw out this childish harpy, and she didn't like it. She was not this way. She was a friendly, agreeable person. To everyone. "Very well, Northman. You wish for pleasant conversation?"

"It would be a welcome change."

Fiona suppressed her temper at his latest dig. "Then tell me of your ship, The Gold Seeker or whatever you called it."

Gunnar eyed her carefully, not sure how to take this new Fiona, then proceeded with caution. "She is the Treasure Huntress."

"She?"

"Aye, she."

"And what makes this Treasure Huntress so special?"

He loved to hear her speak. Her words and phrases flowing in her musical brogue. "The Treasure Huntress was built for my predecessor, Jarl, by the great shipbuilder, Sigurd, and his ailing wife, Leila. Leila died before the ship was complete, and some say she blessed it from the afterlife." He glanced at her, saw she was actually listening, and continued.

"Many of our ships have a dragon's head on the bow, but Leila had a vision for the Huntress that far surpassed any ship before or since. She had Sigurd carve an entire dragon's chest coming up from the waterline, and from a distance, that's all you can see. But up close, the individual dragon's scales, each about the size of a man's palm, become clear. Within each scale are finer carvings of every beast of the land, wind, and sea. Many believe the Huntress channels the spirit and strength of each of these animals."

"And do you believe that?"

Gunnar turned away and looked out the window. He didn't know what he believed and wasn't sure how to answer her. "I believe it is something, yes. I don't know if she was blessed by the gods, or by Leila when she left this world, or by all the animals within the carvings, but it is something. When you step onboard her..., nay, when you are even close to her, you can feel it. You feel almost as if...," his voice trailed off, the sentence unfinished.

"As if what?"

"As if she is alive," he finished with a lame grin and a shrug, knowing how it sounded.

Fiona looked at him curiously. His words were ridiculous, of course, and he clearly knew that, so why would he share them with her? Why share that he had such feelings about a boat when they conveyed weakness? Why leave himself vulnerable to her ridicule?

"Why do you tell me these things? Why don't you lie?"

"I'll not lie to you."

She laughed. "Are you tryin' to tell me that you don't lie? I've seen the evidence to the contrary, and you're quite good at it, I might add."

"No—I only said I won't lie to you."

"Why?"

Gunnar was quiet for a moment. "Because I don't want to."

Fiona was uncomfortable with the intimacy of his words, and he was looking at her in that way again. She returned them to the safe subject of the ship.

"So how did *she* come to be yours? Did this Jarl die? Or did you kill him to have his ship?"

"No. Jarl fell in love with a woman and chose to stay with her."

Fiona took a long moment to digest that. He seemed sincere, but it was too impossible. First that a Northman could feel something akin to love, much less feel it so strongly that he would relinquish something of such value to be with her. She put it from her mind. She'd have to think on that later. "So you purchased the boat from him?"

"No. The Huntress can never be bought or sold. That is the rule. When her captain loses the desire to sail with her, he must give her away."

Fiona smiled, sure now that he was teasing her.

"It's true," Gunnar defended. "If her captain falls in battle, then she goes to his second, but all believe that if the Huntress doesn't accept him, his position will be brief. I was actually Jarl's third-in-command, but his second chose to remain with him in the East, so she came to me instead."

"Who made this rule?" Fiona asked. "It seems a very convenient superstition to prevent a crew from mutiny."

"Sigurd assigned that single condition when he first released her to Jarl."

"So it's never been tested? What do you think would happen if you sold her? It sounds to me, that there's no risk to the seller, only the new captain who would need to fear."

"Perhaps someday a captain will risk the wrath of the Huntress and sell her, but it will not be I."

"You find it acceptable to buy and sell a man, but not a ship?"

Gunnar pondered the significance of her question then nodded. "Yes. Not this ship."

"Tell me more of this Jarl and his woman."

"We are nearly there, my lord," Garrett called down, interrupting them.

"Gratitude, Garrett." Gunnar turned his attention back to Fiona. "Perhaps another time. It's a good story. But now, it's your turn. I told you something of myself that you asked, but you never answered my question of how it is you came to do what you do...in your spare time."

She hesitated, then surprised him by taking a deep breath and answering. "Years ago, a fever swept across the land. For weeks my mother and our priest tended to the sick, but many died. My housekeeper's nephew, Aiden, was among the orphaned, and my mother insisted that he come to live with us." She paused, her face clouding. "The fever had all but passed when it took her. My father was inconsolable. He blamed the priest and sent him away, then became a recluse—remaining a victim to his grief for many years. During that time, Aiden and I were raised together by my housekeeper, Meirna, and our head stableman, Cahan.

"Summer two years ago, Cahan sent Aiden to Dublin to deliver a colt. When he never returned, Cahan traced his steps only to find that after delivering the colt, Aiden had simply disappeared. By the time my father discovered that he'd been snatched off the street and accused of false charges, Aiden had already been sold into servitude for his *crimes*."

"To Tibbot," Gunnar murmured.

"Aye, to Tibbot. Of course, we went straightaway to purchase Aiden's paper from him."

"Your father took you into the tunnels?" Gunnar interrupted, incredulous.

"Nay, I stayed in the house with Tibbot's wife and sipped honeyed wine. In the very room where you later saw me. My father went with Tibbot to conduct the business, only to learn that even though Aiden had not yet arrived there, his paper had already been promised to a Northman. He was bound for five years of hard labor in Iceland. Aiden was gentle and kind and dreamed of becoming a skilled carpenter. He would never have survived it."

Gunnar had to agree. From what he'd heard, the life of a slave in Iceland was harsh—and brief.

"Even though my father offered more coin, Tibbot refused to sell. He cared naught that Aiden was innocent. He said he needed him to fill the quota—that a Northman was already waiting. When Aiden arrived on the prisoner transport the following day, he was to be shipped out immediately.

"That night, our house was like a tomb. No one could eat. Meirna could not stop crying. The next morning my father rose early and set out for Tibbot's again. He swore he'd not take nay for an answer this time, even barter with the Northmen when they came to collect Aiden, if necessary.

"I also rose early, but instead of returning to Tibbot's, I waited on the road outside of Swords to intercept the transport. I didn't doubt my father's intentions or his resolve, but there was too much at stake, and Tibbot had already refused him once. The driver of the prisoner transport was not nearly so concerned with a quota of men bound for Iceland, as he was my emerald brooch. For it, he was willing to report that he'd been set upon by bandits, which gave me the idea for later."

"So you freed him."

"I did."

"And why continue? After Aiden."

"After his dreadful experience, Aiden was determined to help others in any way that he could. When I heard his stories of how many other innocent men suffered the same fate, and saw how my one action had so immeasurably changed the life of someone I cared for, I wanted to help, too."

"He was there, that night?"

"Aye, he pushed the cart."

"He allows you to risk your life?" Gunnar could not keep the disapproval from his voice.

"Nay. That was the first raid I actually took part in. Normally, my role is to consort with Tibbot's wife and devise a plan from the information I gain. But you knew of the previous raids and were taking precautions. I needed a plan that would have you drop your guard. A blockade on the road would have had the opposite effect, but a defenseless woman... Well, as we saw, your kind could not resist that—blindly stalking me like slathering dogs to a meal."

"But why you?"

"Why not me? I was to remain cloaked and would have, had it not been for the wind."

"But there was wind. Did you not fear being recognized?"

Fiona laughed. "By whom? Aiden's lads? They were far too terrified to take their eyes from you."

"It would only take a glance."

"With a glance, all they would've seen is a poor, soaked peasant lass."

"I recognized you."

"Because you did not glance; you stared in your obscenely rude manner, much as you have continued to do."

He shook his head. "I still cannot believe this Aiden would allow you to be put in harm's way."

Fiona sighed. "He didn't. When I first revealed my role, Aiden adamantly refused, but I forced him to concede. It caused a great rift between us. I intended to make it right later, but never had the opportunity."

"Does anyone else know—your father, Meirna or Cahan?"

"Only Cahan. And he only just recently. He discovered me in the stables the night we robbed you and swore to put an end to it. The next day when I returned from Tibbot's, I sought Aiden out to make amends, but he was gone—to a carpenter apprenticeship that had suddenly become available in Kilkenny. I'm sure Cahan arranged it to prevent any future plotting between us. I didn't get to bid Aiden farewell or make things right with him."

Gunnar silently applauded the stableman. He cringed at the thought of her out on another raid—of what would've happened to her had anyone but he been leading the group of men that night.

"We've arrived, my lord." Garrett interrupted them.

"Very good, Garrett. We'll walk from here."

"Am I allowed to know what we're about to see, or is it a surprise?" Fiona asked.

"No surprise. In honor of how we met, and ironically a fitting punctuation to this conversation, today we shall see a great abandoned quarry. They say it's so vast you can barely see across it, and so deep it struck the ocean at the bottom. It's supposed to be a marvel of human achievement, though I suspect the slaves who lost their lives excavating it would disagree. Slaves who were sacrificed by your people for the stone to build your castles. For whatever you might believe, Fiona, Northmen aren't the root of slavery here. Your people had put many a Scot, Welsh, Pict, and even fellow Irishman under the yoke long before we arrived. I thought it an appropriate first sight for us. Then afterward, you can tell me again how different we are."

They stood at the edge of the precipice in awestruck silence. It was as described. An immense hole gouged from the earth so deep, it was easy to believe that the blue pool of water in the bottom was, in fact, the sea.

"It is incomprehensible to me," Fiona murmured.

"What is?" he asked.

"That men could achieve such a thing with simple tools and bare hands. And how would they have ever got the stone up?"

"There." Gunnar pointed to a ramp that sloped down into the pit about a quarter of the way around. "They must have brought the wagons there to load them."

"But it doesn't go all the way to the bottom," Fiona disagreed.

She was right. At most, it only went a third of the way down; the steep wall commenced from there.

"Come. We'll take the carriage around to have a look," Gunnar said, carefully backing away from the edge. "From there we'll be able to see the walls better without risking our necks hanging over."

"I dare not take us any closer, my lord," Garrett called out as he turned the carriage sideways on the sloping ramp and set the brake. Fiona and Gunnar disembarked, but instead of proceeding straight to the cliff edge, Gunnar walked to the nearest side wall. Fiona followed, watching as he ran his hands over the sharp, angled edges of the stone. They weren't at all smooth as they'd appeared from a distance.

"These grooves here." He pointed to the long narrow semicircle indentations. "Each one is where a rod was driven down into solid stone. It's a dangerous job and requires two men. One to steady the rod and rotate it between strikes to ensure it doesn't become wedged. The other to wield a sledgehammer.

"For the one holding the rod, every blow is life-threatening. If the man wielding the hammer were to miss, it could shatter his hands. Or worse, if a glancing blow was struck and the hammer deflected, his skull." Gunnar didn't tell her that children would have been most often used to hold the rod. They were cheaper to purchase, ate less, and could stay bent over for longer periods of time. He didn't need to. He could see she was suitably horrified, imagining it with a grown man. "Each one of these grooves would have taken hundreds of blows, and when you factor in exhaustion and poor food..." Gunnar shook his head and moved away.

Fiona stood looking at the grooves she'd barely noticed before. They were everywhere. How many men had been maimed or died in that small area alone? The Northman was walking slowly towards the drop-off, studying the walls and the ground along the way. Occasionally he bent over, picked up an item to examine it, then discarded it and moved on to something else. He seemed to have forgotten all about her. She looked closer at the things on the ground but saw only rubbish—a rusty neck collar, a broken piece of wagon wheel, certainly nothing to explain his fascination.

He made it to the rim and stood staring out. When he showed no indication of returning, she joined him, stopping a few feet away. He glanced over at her, briefly acknowledging her presence, then returned his gaze out over the abyss.

"What are you looking at?" she asked.

"I was just trying to picture how it worked when it was in full production. I think I've figured it out." He leaned over and picked up a large iron ring with a channeled edge. "This was part of a pulley system. That's how they brought the slabs up to be loaded onto the wagons here. There are even some of the ballast stones left." He pointed to a scattered pile of rocks as evidence. When she looked blank, he explained. "For counterbalance. Though they probably wouldn't have needed them much of the time. They'd have also been sending things down: fresh slaves, supplies, tools, and food, because I'm sure they kept the slaves down there and never let them out."

"How could you know that?" Fiona peered over the edge looking for remnants of slave shelters in the bottom, but saw nothing.

"Because this place is a natural prison. With the hoist being the only way out, even if slaves were to gain control of it, a single well-placed archer could wreak havoc on them while they were suspended and exposed in the open. A handful of men could safely guard hundreds, perhaps even thousands of slaves."

Fiona wondered if he thought of everything in terms of strategy. She tried to imagine what he described. Terrified men being forced out onto a swaying platform, or perhaps into a net, before being lowered to countless other men moving like ants below. Hammers clinking. The creaking of ropes straining under the loads going up and down. Those sounds perhaps underscored by an occasional scream as a man's hand was shattered or he suffered some other unimaginable fate. All the while, lines of wagons waited at the top to be loaded—their drivers engaged in casual conversation, heedless to the suffering going on all around them.

"We should go," Gunnar said, breaking into her thoughts. "It may be awhile before we find another inn."

Fiona nodded and followed him.

When they arrived at the next inn that evening, Fiona felt her anxiety spike again, but soon realized she had nothing to fear. Their arrival and greeting were just as the night before. Not a single person looked at him askance.

As he made small talk with the innkeeper, she scrutinized the Northman, trying to understand what it was these people saw. It was still difficult for her to see past the image of him that was seared into her mind—to not see him in his leather and furs with his strange braided hair. But she tried.

He did have an easy smile, and the occasional hint of dimples made it more engaging. He held their gaze while they spoke, as if their words were of import—really listening to them. She made a mental note to tell him it was inappropriate for a nobleman to speak to common folk that way, but then realized that even with that simple gesture of respect, they didn't speak as equals. Something still set him apart—set him above them.

It wasn't arrogance or condescension, it was something else. It was confidence. The Northman was confident without being overbearing. Casually, comfortably confident, like being obeyed was never in question, so he didn't need to prove anything. It had to be from his position as a ship's captain, but in this setting, it came across as the natural air of a lord.

"Will you join me for supper tonight?" he asked, interrupting her perusal.

"Nay, I shall take it in my room again."

"As you wish, my lady," he said with a deep exaggerated bow.

Fiona shook her head, but found herself fighting back a smile at how absurd he was.

Chapter 15

DAY THREE

The next morning, their departure routine was also repeated. The Northman was waiting for her at the carriage and once again he asked if she'd slept well—which this time she had. He wore the same amber and rust tunic from the first day, suggesting that the answer to her question of how many changes of clothes he had was two. After waiting for her to climb inside and get settled, he followed. Again, he unbuckled his sword and set it out of her reach. There was even another late arrival of their freshly stocked basket, though this time the innkeeper brought it himself. Fiona wondered if he did it to keep his womenfolk removed from the Northman's charms, but wasn't sure as even he seemed to enjoy his company.

Once again, they were underway.

Later, when Garrett announced they'd reached their next destination and they alighted from the carriage, Fiona knew exactly where they were. The earthen mounds and single obelisk stone were renowned throughout all of Ireland. *Tara.*

"Today we shall see a mystical Irish stone," the Northman began.

"The Stone of Destiny," Fiona finished for him.

"You know it?"

"Every Irishman knows of this place. Since days of old, men have come here to be crowned, in hopes that the stone will declare them to be the high king of all Ireland. Legends say that if the man is such a king, the stone will roar with joy three times."

"Have you heard it roar?" Gunnar asked with a smile.

"Nay. The stone hasn't roared since Cuchulainn cleaved it with his sword in anger when it remained silent for his candidate. That was many, many years ago and since then, Ireland has remained divided."

"So your people—Christians—still believe in a pagan stone?"

"Oh, aye," she nodded. "And every new king still journeys here, just in case. Were it to roar again...I can assure you, no one would ever hear the end of it, Christian or no."

————————◆————————

"You never told me how old you are," Gunnar said after they'd viewed the stone up close and returned to the carriage.

"I'm twenty," she replied.

"Twenty? How have you not been sent to a convent at twenty? Does any man take a wife so old? I suppose a widower who already has heirs might not care that you are perhaps past childbearing age." Gunnar pretended to consider aloud, trying to keep the grin from his face. When he felt himself being unsuccessful, he looked out the window so she wouldn't see it. He heard her sharp intake of breath and imagined her face. Her jaw tight. Her green eyes flashing. Her cheeks tinged with pink.

"I am twenty, not thirty!" she sputtered. "And there are plenty who would have me."

"I don't know," he said, shaking his head, trying to be serious. "If it were so, why are you not yet married? Have you not found even one man suitable?"

"I have not," she replied tersely.

"And why is that? What were their flaws? Not rich enough? Well-bred enough? Tall enough? Educated enough?" He paused and smiled. "Perhaps they were just not man enough."

The carriage slowed, then stopped. Fiona found that odd. Garrett had said they'd a lot of ground to cover to reach the next sight on the Northman's list.

"Why are we stopping, Garrett?" Gunnar called out.

"There's a man in the road, my lord," Garrett answered, unconcerned.

Gunnar immediately reached for his sword. Just as his fingertips neared the hilt, the carriage door was ripped open and a blade thrust inside. He stopped just short of impaling himself—the tip of the strange blade wavering precariously close to his throat. Fiona shrieked, but the sound was lost in the chaos that erupted all around them. The carriage lurched sideways as men climbed up onto the driver's seat and the footmen's platform. Boots scraped and scuffled. Men yelled and grunted. The carriage rocked to and fro. Then sudden stillness.

"Out you come, now. Real slow and easy like," the stranger holding the sword said softly as he backed away.

"You stay put," Gunnar said to Fiona under his breath as he moved to the doorway. He stepped down, pushed the door closed behind him, then stood in front of it, quickly evaluating the men who faced him, ranking them in order of threat in his mind. The man who had nearly ripped the door from its hinges stood to his right, single sword in hand, dagger in his belt. He was enormous, with a bulging forehead and small beady eyes. He could likely crush a man's spine with a bear hug, but he would not be nimble or quick.

Gunnar shifted his attention to the man on his left. Small and wiry, he would be much faster. The man grinned at him, revealing a single rotten tooth. His lips seemed too big for his mouth, likely from missing teeth, and even grinning widely, they hung slightly slack. He also had his sword drawn, but his eyes twitched nervously to a third man who stood a few paces away.

That man would be the leader. Gunnar studied him the closest. A wicked scar ran the length of his jaw and another along his hairline. The man was no stranger to violence. But it was his eyes, vicious and calculating, that told Gunnar the most. He knew the type. A man of limited intelligence in charge of even lower men. Dangerous. No honor. There would be no negotiating.

Gunnar made a quick sweep of the surrounding bushes, finding no evidence of any other men. That left the two or three guarding the footmen and driver on the carriage behind him. With their attention on their charges, they'd be slower to react. If he moved with haste, he should have enough time.

"Now what's a fine lord doing 'ere in our parts?" the leader asked.

Gunnar didn't answer, pleased that the man had not examined him as closely as he should have. It was one thing for inn folk to not look beyond the finery, but a fighter should know better. He smiled grimly to himself. It would soon be a very costly mistake.

"There's a woman still inside," the giant reported.

"Is there now?" The scar-faced leader raised his voice and directed it toward the carriage. "Her ladyship will come out now, so we can greet her properly, as well." The skinny man giggled and wiped the drool from his oversized lips onto the back of his dirty, free hand.

"She will not." While keeping his eyes on the ringleader, Gunnar turned his head slightly and spoke loud enough so that Fiona would know the words were for her. That was where the command to attack would come from, he was certain. The other men wouldn't move without it, and by watching him, he'd know which one to deal with first.

"She will not, he says." The leader mimicked, then spat. "Now ain't he somet'in'. It seems we have a right gallant one 'ere today, lads."

The other men laughed.

"I think 'tis time we showed his lordship 'ere that he's not at home—and we're not his lackeys." He turned back to Gunnar and spoke, his voice low and menacing. "Get your woman out 'ere now and produce all of her jewels and your coin. If you don't, we'll still take them, mind you, but only after we sample her other valuables first. Then we'll kill you both." The slack-lipped man to his left giggled again, and another one Gunnar couldn't see on the carriage whistled.

Fiona pressed her body as far back as she could into her seat to remain unseen through the gap in the curtains. Heart thudding in her chest, she pressed her cheek against the wall and lifted the curtain edge slightly with one finger. She could see the Northman's back and part of his profile. The enormous man who had ripped open the door stood slightly to his right with sword poised. She couldn't see the giggling man but judged him to be just on the other side of the wall from her.

From the earlier scuffling sounds, there was another one with Garrett and at least one more covering the footmen, possibly two. Counting the voice that had hailed her to come out, that meant there were five or six armed men! She scrunched down in an attempt to see the man who was giving the commands, but he was too far away. She could only see the toes of his dusty, worn boots.

She glanced around the carriage interior. The Northman's golden sword still leaned against the opposite wall. She slid down in the seat and reached across the space with her legs, keeping her body below the level of the window. Moving carefully, so as not to rock the carriage, she balanced her feet on the opposite cushion, then slid further until she could reach the sword with her toes. After pinning the scabbard between her two feet, she laid it over onto the cushion, then pulled it to the edge of the seat. She paused briefly to renew her grip; she dare not drop it and have the noise alert those outside to her actions. Ever so slowly, she lowered it to the floor. Keeping it rested on top of one shoe, she slid it toward her until it was close enough to reach with her hand.

Silently she withdrew the sword, then stared at the curved, polished blade with disappointment. Even if she were an accomplished swordsman, which she was not, it was too long to wield in such a small space. But perhaps she could find a way to get it to the Northman.

To what end? What do you expect he can do against six of them?

She pushed that doubt from her mind and hid the sword in the folds of her skirt, then covered the scabbard with her cloak on the seat beside her. She retrieved the paring knife from the niche between the cushion and carriage wall where she'd kept it stored since the Northman had discovered it in her sleeve. Holding it with a firm grip in front of her, she took a deep breath. That the Northman intended to take a stand against them was obvious, but if and when he fell, the first rogue through that door would pay dearly.

"Did you not hear me, pigeon?" The leader of the brigands called to her again. "Come out now, or else I'll have to hurt his lordship 'ere. I'm giving you one last chance."

"She's not coming out," Gunnar cut him off. "And I'll give you one last chance. If you wish to live to see another day, you and your men will walk away. Now."

The disrespect goaded the man to action. He gave a quick nod to the giant. The burly man raised his sword. Fiona screamed a warning, but Gunnar feigned ignorance as it slashed down toward him. At the last second, he stepped back against the carriage and grabbed the man's wrist and forearm with both hands. Using the man's momentum and his own full strength, Gunnar lifted a leg and drove the man's wrist down hard upon his raised knee.

Gunnar fully expected to hear and feel bones breaking, but the man had the bones of an ox. Still, the giant roared with pain and the sword fell from his limp grasp. As he clutched his lower arm with his free hand, Gunnar rocked back and lunged forward, head-butting him in the forehead, sending him reeling to the ground in a daze.

Crouching beside him, Gunnar grabbed the dagger from his belt. He palmed the blade without standing, rotated on his heel, and sent it winging through the air towards the drooler he knew would be the next to attack. He watched the man's stupid grin change to slack-jawed wonder as he stared at the hilt sticking from his chest and dropped to his knees.

Gunnar picked up the giant's sword and stood. He spun it once in his grip to get a feel for the weight and balance, then advanced on the leader. All the while, his ears remained keyed for any sounds of movement from the men on the carriage behind him.

"That was a huge mistake, you stupid shite," the leader grunted. "I'll take my time with your woman now. You can rest assured of that. Maybe even keep you alive long enough to watch. Or maybe not." He pulled his own sword and lunged.

Gunnar blocked the man's first savage attack, then stepped into him. Raising his free arm, he drove the point of his elbow into the side of the man's head just above his ear. The leader staggered a few steps, then recovered. As he raised his sword again, Gunnar saw the first seed of doubt in his eyes. He would have liked to prolong it, to toy with him and watch that doubt blossom into full-blown fear, but he didn't have the time. Commotion on the carriage told him that at least one of the men guarding it had left his post and was coming for him.

Gunnar closed the distance between him and the leader, feinted to the right, but stepped to the left. The man struck hard where he thought Gunnar would be. Realizing his mistake, but unable to change the direction of his sword, he reached for his dagger with his other hand. The knife had no sooner cleared his belt when Gunnar severed his still-outstretched sword arm just above the wrist. He screamed—a bloodcurdling desperate sound of shock, terror, and agony as he watched his sword, fingers still gripping the hilt, fall to the ground. Gunnar brought his own sword up and around in a back-handed slash across the man's throat, silencing him in mid-shriek.

Boots tromped close behind him. Gunnar pivoted and ducked. There were two. Sidestepping the first man's attack, he raked his sword deep across the man's lower torso. Assured by the appearance of glistening pale pink intestines in the gash that the man was done for, Gunnar advanced on the second without slowing. His blade flashed red as it swept up in a full arc over his head, gaining speed and power. He buried it in the second man's neck with a solid thunk, nearly decapitating him. Warm blood spattered his face and hands as he yanked it free.

The final raider abandoned his post, jumping from the front of the carriage and sprinting toward the willows. Gunnar returned to the giggler's body and kicked it over. Plucking the dagger from the dead man's chest, he took aim and flung it hard. The blade sank deep into the runner's back, and he staggered forward, disappearing into the bushes.

Bryen and Orin had jumped from the carriage and stood poised over the giant who remained on the ground, dazed and groaning. "What do you want us to do with this one, my lord?" Bryen asked eagerly.

"Finish him. Then find the one who ran and finish him, too, if need be. When you're done, drag all the bodies away from the road. But take care not to get blood on your clothes," he added as he glanced down at his own blood-spattered tunic.

"Aye, my lord," they said in unison.

"After you've finished with the bodies, search the area for horses and release any you find, but be careful; they may have left a man or two behind to guard them. Here, take this. You might need it." Gunnar tossed his blood-soaked sword to Bryen. "There's another one over there," he said calmly to Orin and pointed to the ringleader's sword on the ground, hand still attached.

"Aye, my lord."

"Are you alright?" Gunnar called up to Garrett as he heard the giant gurgle his last breath behind him.

"I'm grand, my lord. Not a mark on me. But you're bleeding; you should have the lady tend to you."

Have the lady tend to you. That was rich. Gunnar could only imagine her expression when he opened the door covered in blood. Any progress he'd made with her was surely lost. "It's not my blood, Garrett."

"Not there, my lord. On your forehead," Garrett clarified.

Gunnar reached up and felt the small split in his skin and the rapidly-forming knot. The oaf's skull had been as thick as his arm bones. "'Tis nothing." He turned to the carriage door but hesitated, pulse still racing from the fight. Taking a deep breath, he opened the door and climbed inside. He sat, closing his eyes briefly while stretching the knots from his neck, then looked at her—fully prepared for her horror and disgust.

"You *are* bleeding," Fiona confirmed. Still holding the knife, she moved to sit next to him. His sword, forgotten in her skirt folds, clattered to the floor. She reached up to touch his forehead, but he turned his head away.

"'Tis but a scratch."

"Let me see it," she demanded.

He turned back. After a few seconds of inspection, Fiona bent over and cut a piece of material from the hem of her shift with the paring knife, dampened it with ale from their basket, then gently began to wipe his blood-spattered face.

The cool cloth felt good, but not near as good as her body so close to him. Gunnar sat still as a stone.

"That was very foolish; you were sorely outnumbered," she chastised him as she cleaned.

"Not really," he murmured.

"When I first met you, Northman, I might have believed you couldn't count, but now I know better."

"Fiona, there are few men in this world whom I'd not be confident matching myself against."

"But there were five of them. Six, if you count the one who tried to run away."

"And yet six did not equal half of one skilled fighter," he said as his eyes scanned her face, elated to see true concern there. In the face of a bigger threat, he had ceased to be the enemy, at least for the moment.

"You could not have known that," she disagreed. "You should have given them our valuables."

"I did know that, Fiona. A life of raiding has taught me a great many things, and one of the most important is how to measure a man—and how to do it quickly. Those men would not have been satisfied with our coin and jewels. That was only a ploy. They would have killed us all—you, after they... did other things."

Her nearness had his nerves stretched taut as bowstrings. Having been in the carriage with her for two days had been bad enough, but she was so close now, he could actually feel the heat of her body and smell her scent, warm and so enticing. He breathed it in deep, filling his lungs and holding it. With the battle fever still running molten in his veins, the urge to turn and take her in his arms was nearly overpowering. To press her back into the cushions and kiss her mouth with no constraints. To have her right then and there in the carriage. No one could stop him. Not the driver. Not the footmen. And after what they'd just seen, he doubted they would even try.

Not like this. Not—like—this! His subconscious interjected its warning a second time with more emphasis. Gunnar closed his eyes and summoned every bit of restraint he possessed, unsure for a moment if it would be enough. *Thor, it was agony!*

"But you had no weapon," she chided, oblivious to his inner turmoil.

"That's not true. I had my choice of weapons—all of theirs." He tried to smile but managed only a grimace.

She reached up to dab at his wound this time, the motion taking her unwittingly even closer. As the damp cloth touched his skin, her breast inadvertently brushed against his upper arm. Gunnar flinched and groaned at the exquisite torture.

Fiona jerked her hand away. "Apologies. Did that hurt?" She searched his face, unaware of what had caused his reaction.

Gunnar exhaled. "Nay. I wish only to have been wounded in other places to warrant more of your gentle touch. Had I known it would be so, I would have delayed in dispatching them so quickly." He managed a tight smile this time.

"You jest of being wounded," she said disapprovingly.

"I do not jest. I speak only the truth to you, as I said I would, and always have."

Fiona didn't know what to say. She had moved to tend to him without thinking, her concern only for the wound and blood. Only now did she realize how close they were. How charged the air was between them. His eyes were the color of the deepest sea on a sunny day, and he was looking at her in that way again. But this time it was something more. Something raw. Something primal. She couldn't look away. Her pulse raced. Her throat constricted. Her lips tingled.

"'Tis done, my lord," Bryen reported giddily from outside. "There were no horses and no more of them."

Bryen's voice snapped Fiona from her trance. She sat up straight and slid away, then returned to her seat on the opposite side. Gunnar exhaled and ran his hand through his hair before bending to pick up his sword and return it to its sheath.

"Where to now, my lord?" Garrett called. "Do we need to find a healer?"

"Nay, Garrett. Our trip continues." Gunnar leaned back in the seat and stared at the ceiling, thinking of the many ways he'd like to make Bryen pay for the interruption, though he doubted it was the footman's fault. This had all the markings of Loki. The trickster god was having great sport with him today.

Fiona sat silent for a long time. Several times he caught her looking at him with a puzzled frown. She hadn't seemed upset by the killing for which he was beyond grateful, so he wasn't sure what troubled her. Perhaps she'd sensed how close he'd been to breaking his oath.

"Do all of your men fight as you do?" she finally asked.

"In a similar manner, yes. I have more experience than many, but we are all trained to fight."

"Why did you kill the one who would run away? He was no threat."

"Had it not been for you, I may have let him live," he admitted.

"I don't understand."

"If he'd been allowed to alert their families and friends, they might have come after us again, and they'd have been more prepared—possibly with archers. I may not have been able to protect you a second time."

"Your concern was only for me?" she asked dubiously with one eyebrow raised.

"Aye," he said softly. Seeing she was uncomfortable with the intimacy of his response, he added, "I gave my word to guarantee your safety, remember?"

"Do you truly not fear death?"

"No." *In fact, there was a time when it held much appeal to me...before I met you.* "To die with my sword in hand assures me a place in Valhalla—feasting at Odin's table and fighting with the greatest warriors for all of eternity. I fear only a poor death."

She seemed to be wrestling with another question. "Northman, that night when we took the slaves from you, why did you not fight? After what I just witnessed and what you say—is it because we had archers?"

He hesitated. "No. Your archers were too close to be effective. We'd have raised shield walls, then split and charged both sides of the road. Being untrained slaves and peasants, half of them, perhaps more, would have broken ranks and run. The other half...well, the other half would've been no match for us, as you just saw. Though had you just ambushed us in the road and not given advanced warning, it might have been a different story."

"Then why?"

He looked at her, deliberating how to answer. But there was only one answer, and he knew it. "Because of you. Because during the fighting I wouldn't have been able to keep track of you, and my men would not have seen you as I did. We've fought many forces with women warriors, and they'd have thought naught of injuring or killing you. I could not have that."

"But you didn't know me."

He shook his head and exhaled softly. "I cannot explain it. Seeing you there that night, so brave, so beautiful—it did something to me. Got inside my head. To this moment, if I close my eyes, I can still picture it as clearly as if it were just happening."

Fiona didn't ask anything more. Didn't want to know anything more. His stark honesty about his feelings—his admitted weakness for her was too much to take in. Nothing about him fit. And again, why did he not lie to her?

"My lord? There's a brook ahead. Permission to stop and water the horses?" Garrett called down.

"Yes, Garrett."

When the carriage came to a stop, Gunnar opened the door and stepped out while Fiona waited for Bryen and the step box. Once she was safely down, Bryen turned to Gunnar. "Perhaps Orin and I should check the bushes, my lord, to make sure 'tis safe?"

"As you wish. Then help Garrett with the horses."

"Aye, my lord."

"My lord. If you wish to change your clothes, I'll soak the ones you're wearing in the water to keep the blood from setting," Garrett offered.

Gunnar smiled. "I didn't know you were so domestic, Garrett."

Garrett chuckled, embarrassed. "I've learned a few things from my wife, my lord. Mostly how not to rile her. Coming home with blood set in my clothes is a sure way to do that."

"A wise man," Gunnar agreed. " Yes, I'll change now."

Fiona couldn't help but notice the new way the men behaved around him. They'd been respectful and dutiful before, but it had always seemed just that, that they were doing their duty. Now there was something else. An ease, a respect, a strange bond, as if they all *wanted* to serve him.

That night their greeting at the next inn was the same as the previous two, and Fiona finally accepted it would always be so. Garrett and the footmen had been instructed to breathe not a word of what had transpired, and they'd arrived as if nothing were amiss. She wondered what excuse the Northman would come up with to explain the cut and knot on his forehead, but didn't ask. It was late, she was exhausted, and she had no doubt whatever he said would be believable.

He asked if she wished to dine with him. Again, she refused. Alone in her room, she ate her meal in silence. Lost in thoughts of the day's tumultuous events, she barely tasted anything. She bathed, but the water did little to relax her this time. She worried as she climbed into bed that she'd be unable to sleep, but her mind went dark soon after her head touched the pillow.

Chapter 16

DAY FOUR

"**M**y lady? Your brother wishes to know if you'll be breakin' your fast with him below this mornin', or in your room," Gleana, her most recent maid, asked.

Fiona hesitated.

"He's there now, but did not want us to bring his meal until he knew if you were joinin' him."

Fiona nodded. "Tell him I shall be there shortly."

"Aye, my lady," Gleana curtsied and left the room, closing the door behind her.

Fiona glanced at herself in the polished tin hand mirror and reached up to tuck a stray wisp of hair behind her ear. The outer gown she wore today was another of the older style that laced on the sides. It was one of her favorites. Made of pale peach silk, its ivory and gold embroidered shoulder straps attached to the bodice in the front with two gold brooches. The color brought out the highlights in her hair and the pale flecks in her green eyes.

What are you doing? Your appearance doesn't matter! He may have saved you yesterday, but you'd never have been in danger in the first place had it not been for him. Don't forget that.

Fiona scowled at her reflection and turned for the door.

"Shall I bring another poultice for your head, my lord?" the serving girl asked him as Fiona approached the table. The lass was petite, and Fiona mistook her for being quite young until she drew nearer and noticed her curves.

"Nay, the one your mother provided last night has worked wonders," the Northman replied. "The bump is much smaller and there's no pain. Extend my gratitude to her once again for me."

"The secret's in the goat's milk, should you ever be needin' another one. But truly, my lord, you must be more careful," the girl admonished him.

Fiona's mind skipped back to how he had received the injury—the savagery and speed, the strength and brutality. She wondered how he'd explained it that he could be sitting here now discussing it so casually.

The girl curtsied as Fiona approached. "My lady. May I bring you something to drink—a light morning ale or water or goat's milk?"

"Milk, please," Fiona replied as she sat down across from him. He wore the amber and rust garments that he'd started the previous day with, and even though she looked carefully, she found no traces of bloodstain. She glanced at the considerably smaller knot on his head. "It does look much better," she agreed after the girl had left. "But more careful? How, pray tell, did you tell the lass you came by your injury?"

"Being the clumsy nobleman that I am, I tripped and fell headfirst into the carriage wheel, of course."

Clumsy? She could never imagine that word paired with him in any circumstance. "Of course," she murmured. "Aye, you must be more careful."

"Sleep well?" he asked as he had every morning, but today his eyes probed her face.

"Aye." She nodded.

"I was worried you might have nightmares," he admitted, still scrutinizing her, trying to discern the truth.

Fiona raised her eyes to meet his. "Nay. No dreams of any sort. Seeing you fall into that wheel must not have been as disturbing as you thought."

He nodded and smiled.

The serving girl returned with a leather cup of milk, then took their requests: oat porridge, toasted bread and butter with a side of honey-preserved pears for her; three duck eggs, toasted bread, and fried salt pork for him. They ate their meal in relative silence, the serving girl hovering nearby.

In between her delicate bites, Fiona surreptitiously watched him eat. It was a serious business, one large mouthful quickly following the last. She glanced around the room to see if his manners were drawing undue attention, but no one paid him any mind.

"Is that good?" she finally asked him.

He paused in the middle of a bite, instantly recognizing the innuendo in her question. He set his fork back on the plate and finished chewing, then ran his tongue over his front teeth with his mouth closed, before responding. With a hint of a wry smile, he slowly wiped his lips on a linen square cloth and looked up at her, clearly prepared for verbal combat.

"Yes, it is," he replied. "And yours?"

"Aye, mine is quite good also."

"But?"

"But what?" she asked innocently.

"Clearly, there is more you wish to say."

"I was only curious if the food was that delicious or if the bump on your head made you skip supper last night. You seem rather ravenous." She took a small bite of bread.

"Do my table manners offend you?" he asked.

She doubted that any answer would truly bother him, but still, she pressed her rare advantage. "Nay, they are better than I expected—and quite adequate for a starving man. I'm actually very relieved to see you use utensils."

"Yes, I'm quite well-trained. Far better than the vendor's monkey in Dublin, I imagine. Though I don't see why, if a man is hungry, he should pretend that he is not. It seems your people spend most of their lives pretending." He took another bite, but Fiona noted with satisfaction it was a smaller one.

She refused to let him turn the tables on her. "Then why use the utensils at all? Surely they must be slowing you down. Why not grab the food with your fists or press your face down in the plate and satisfy your hunger all at once?"

His response was immediate. "For the same reason I'm wearing these ridiculous clothes. During the brief periods of time on this trip that we must spend in the company of others, I'm also forced to be a pretender. But don't worry, my lady. Soon we'll be back to the freedom of the carriage."

The serving girl was back. "Is there anything else I can bring you, my lord, my lady?"

Gunnar glanced at Fiona and raised his eyebrows, waiting for her to respond first.

"Nothing for me. It was very good and the service exceptional," Fiona added.

The girl beamed and curtsied. "Gratitude, my lady. I'll take your plates then." After stacking their wood dishes and bowls and returning them to the kitchen, she was back in a flash with a pitcher. "So do you think you'll find the falls today?" she asked him as she topped off his mug of morning ale. "You'll be glad for it if you do."

Fiona was unsure what the lass referred to, but the Northman seemed to know—likely a continuation of an earlier conversation.

"Do you swim there?" he asked her.

"Aye, I do. Sometimes bare." She covered her mouth with her hand, aghast that the words had slipped out in front of them.

"It's not too cold to swim?" he asked, ignoring her embarrassment.

"'Tis a chill at first, but you soon become accustomed."

"I should like to try it, but we don't have time today, and my sister doesn't swim." He leaned toward the girl and lowered his voice conspiratorially. "She's a timid, unadventurous thing."

Fiona started to protest but bit her tongue when she saw his smile. He was quite enjoying himself. His blue eyes danced with mischievousness. A small section of his blond hair had come loose from its tie, adding a softness to his rugged features. In that moment, she could almost see what the other women were admiring.

"How I wish I could accompany you," the girl said wistfully, then turned bright red and rushed back to the kitchen.

"I see you've managed to fill yet another simple girl's head with foolish infatuation. This one to the point of having the poor creature openly speak of removing her clothes," Fiona observed.

"Yes, it's a curse I must bear—having women always wishing to disrobe in my presence. But what is one to do?" He smiled and shrugged.

"I can see it causes you great distress."

"It's a terrible thing really, if you think about it," he said with mock seriousness. "It's a wonder I ever get anything done."

"You're shameless." Fiona shook her head, pursing her lips to hold back a smile, unable to continue down the line of conversation any further, even though she had started it.

"Perhaps that's what I find so intriguing about you. Your insistence to remain fully clothed at all times—without ever even a hint of otherwise. It's a puzzle. You seem to be immune to my..."

"Curse?" she finished for him. "And I do not *seem* to be immune. I am *quite* immune, I assure you. If anything, your presence makes me wish to cover myself with a thick blanket."

"Here is your midday meal, my lord, my lady." The girl returned and heaved their heavy basket onto the table.

The Northman didn't respond, his eyes remaining locked on hers. Fiona flushed but didn't feel the need to rebuke him. She wasn't sure why. Perhaps it was that she'd slept soundly for the second night in a row and was well-rested. Or perhaps it was how he'd saved her life the previous day. Or perhaps it was just that his relaxed, playful nature today was contagious.

"Apologies, my lord," the girl said, after receiving no response. "Shall I take it to the carriage for you?"

"That won't be necessary," Gunnar declined. "My lady?" he said to Fiona. "Are you ready?"

She nodded and stood, then proceeded to the carriage with him following close behind.

They alighted from the carriage on a hillside. In the distance below was a winding river and a huge turf-covered mound rimmed with boulders.

"This is it? Bru Na Boinnes?" the Northman asked, clearly disappointed. "I thought Bru meant palace?"

"It does," Fiona confirmed.

"But it looks like a burial mound. Granted, it's huge..."

"My father has explored it and says there are no bones, only a labyrinth of stone passageways—even a great chamber."

"Who built it?"

"An ancient race of people who worshiped the goddess Danu. They were actually mythical beings themselves, but when the Celts invaded these lands, they were so fierce that the ancient ones moved underground to escape them. They are said to have built a whole world below, and they use the faerie knolls and mounds to go between our world and theirs. Sometimes they snatch unsuspecting human folk and take them down to live with them."

"I should like to see it closer."

Overhearing his last comment, Garrett stuttered. "Apologies, my lord. I cannot take the carriage any nearer. The beasts fear this place," he added sheepishly.

"Then the lady and I shall walk. And if we should happen to be sucked underground by the faeries..." Seeing the three men's stricken expressions, Gunnar didn't finish. "Apologies...'twas only a poor jest. You men go ahead and eat your midday meal. We'll take the basket and eat by the river."

After finding a trail down, they walked the perimeter of the enormous structure. It was far larger than it had appeared from the hill; Gunnar counted over one hundred paces along one side. The massive stones that made up the outer walls were covered with unusual symbols, and each stood well over his head. He was familiar with runes so he understood the painstaking work required to create the chiseled patterns, but the raised ones were unlike anything he'd ever seen. The entire stone face had been removed except for the designs, so the symbols protruded from the surface.

They paused at what appeared to be an entrance. "Do you think there's treasure inside?" he asked.

"My father says not, but I'll wait here if you wish to see for yourself."

"I would not leave you unescorted." He shook his head.

"Do not deny yourself for me, Northman." Fiona smiled, sensing his reluctance to enter had nothing to do with her safety. "I can easily find my way home if the faeries were to take you."

"If there's no treasure, it's not worth the time," he declined. "And I'm hungry. Shall we eat?"

Still smiling, Fiona nodded, then followed him down to the river's edge. She waited while he unfolded and spread a blanket on the ground; then both of them sat. After he unpacked the food, the Northman filled their cups with ale. There was always only ale to drink, which she suspected was intentional. Ale was not her favorite, but with food it wasn't so bad, and the relaxing effects, so often needed in his company, were agreeable. At least after the first inn, they each had a cup and didn't have to share it from the jug. They ate in silence, then sat sipping ale, watching the subtle swirling eddies and gentle ripples of the slow-moving current.

"This place is beautiful," she murmured.

"Aye," he agreed and lay back on one elbow, looking out over the water. After a few minutes, he stood. "I think I shall swim. It's been on my mind ever since the girl mentioned it this morning," he announced.

"Do you think it's safe? Spring currents can run swift."

"Are you worried for me?"

"Hardly. And I didn't mean you specifically. I meant if anyone were to swim."

"Are you considering joining me then? You don't have to do it bare like she does. You could wear your shift."

"Which would become sheer once wet,—hiding nothing from your eyes. Gratitude, but nay," Fiona declined.

"I could promise not to look," he offered, trying not to smile. "I've yet to break my word to you."

Fiona shook her head. "Go and enjoy yourself. I'll be fine here. I'm a timid, unadventurous thing, remember?"

Gunnar laughed, knowing that his earlier remark would have ruffled her. "You are anything but that. But if you choose not to join me, know that you are free to look as much as you wish," he said with a devilish grin before turning to walk down to the water.

"I do not wish for that," she called after his retreating back.

"If you change your mind, you have my permission," he answered over his shoulder without slowing.

Fiona shook her head. He always had to have the last word. She refrained from looking in even the remote direction of the water until she heard a splash, then sputtering as he came up for air.

"There may not be falls here, but this is wondrous. You should try it." His voice, a full pitch higher, verified his claim.

"I can't," she declined.

"You can't swim?"

"Of course I can swim," she retorted.

"Then what's stopping you? How many times must we have this conversation, Fiona? You shall return to your life of *can't* soon enough. Don't deny yourself this experience for the sake of rules that do not exist here. You are free. No one will see you. No one will know." He turned and swam toward the center, leaving his words to echo in her mind rather than pleading further.

What's stopping you? You are free, Fiona. No one will know. She tried to ignore his words and the splashing sounds of his enjoyment. She did want to—wanted to very badly. So what *was* stopping her? Even the serving lass from the inn was free to swim. Did she have less freedom than a serving lass? She was a strong swimmer, and the water looked so inviting.

Her heart began to race at the scandalousness of it as she considered it—really considered it. Did she dare? She stood and walked down to the water's edge, stopping next to his clothes and sword—stark reminders that the Northman was bare. "You will not look?" she called out to him.

"I will not," he reaffirmed

"Swear it to me."

"I swear." Gunnar turned away, treading water.

Before she could change her mind, Fiona's fingers raced through the side laces on her gown. She paused. Was she mad? Was she really about to swim with a Northman? How, in just a few short days, had her entire perspective shifted to where this could be acceptable?

She wasn't swimming with a Northman, she told herself firmly as she unclasped the brooches and stepped out of the gown. She was just swimming, she reaffirmed while unlacing her kirtle, stripping off her shoes and stockings, and wading out over the smooth stones in her shift.

The temperature of the water near the shore was quite cool and dropped significantly with every step. Goosebumps raised on her skin. It made her wonder if the Northman's tone had actually been raised in merriment or had simply been an uncontrollable reaction to the chill.

"It's too cold," she called to where he remained treading water facing away from her as promised.

"You must jump all at once. It's truly not so bad then," he replied.

She waded another few feet, the cool water creeping ever higher, prickling more of her skin with each step. She stopped, gasping when it reached her sensitive stomach. It was unbearable. "I cannot."

"Yes, you can. Just leap."

"I don't wish to wet my hair."

"What's that you say? It's safe for me to turn around?"

"Nay. Northman, I did not say that and you know it."

"Very well. If you are safely out of sight beneath the water, I shall turn around now."

"Don't you dare!"

He started to turn. Fiona looked back to the bank and her clothes. She would never make it. Even if she rushed through the water, soaking herself in the process, he would have many seconds with full view of her rear.

"Northman! I command you! Do not turn around."

"Yes. I heard you. You are safely covered underwater. I'm turning now."

She could see his ear and now the tip of his nose and chin. He really was turning around! Holding her fingers to her nose, Fiona sank beneath the surface. He was right; all at once was much better, and the shock was not near as bad as she was expecting. She kicked off the bottom and swam a few lengths underwater, the thin shift clinging to her body. When she surfaced, blinking the water from her eyes, she was only about ten feet away from him. He was grinning, and she splashed water at his face.

"You're a cad. You said you wouldn't turn around and you lied."

"You were losing your nerve, and I did not lie, I never actually turned around."

"You were about to."

"Was I?" he shrugged, still grinning. "We'll never know. Besides, I was right, was I not? The water is incredible."

She didn't answer.

"Was I not right?" he repeated his question.

"Aye. You were right. Are you so happy to hear it?"

"I am."

"A lord does not gloat over a lady."

"Lucky for you there are no lords here, or you would still be sitting on the bank only wishing to swim."

She splashed water at his face again then turned to swim away. When she felt water droplets on her hair, she assumed the Northman had splashed her back until she saw the distinctive cupping pattern on the smooth surface of the water all around her. Rain? But that was impossible; they were in full sun—the closest clouds miles away. Before she could turn to him, the very heavens seemed to open with raindrops that were so large, when they hit the surface of the river, the back-splash made it seem to be raining up as much as down.

"Are you alright?" the Northman shouted through the blinding sheets of water.

"Aye," she shouted back, laughing, while using a hand to shield her mouth and nose in an attempt to keep from inhaling water that came from all directions.

Then, as quickly as it began, it was over, the only evidence there'd been rain at all was a low rainbow and a cool breeze.

"We should probably get back before Garrett panics that the faeries have taken us," Gunnar said.

After Fiona nodded, they swam the short distance back upriver that they'd drifted during the downpour. Remaining submerged, Fiona surveyed their soggy clothes with dismay. "Our clothes are soaked," she said.

"Go and wrap up in the blanket. It's wool, and even wet, it will be warmer than a dress. I'll bring your clothes."

"Only after you look away, Northman."

Gunnar smiled and turned his back. When she called to him that she was safely covered, he waded out, quickly pulled on his wet clothes, then grabbed her drenched dresses, shoes, and stockings. He carried them to where she stood wrapped in the blanket facing away. It was still sunny, but the breeze was stiff now and cut through his wet tunic. She had to be freezing.

Gunnar cursed himself for his carelessness. The weather had been so pleasant, they'd left their cloaks in the carriage. He knew better; he knew spring storms. But she'd been so at ease with him today, he'd been distracted and had given thought to nothing else.

"Turn around, please, so I can dress." Her teeth started to chatter.

"There's no time. We need to get you back to the carriage and into dry clothes. Here are your shoes. Put them on."

Walk back wearing just her shift under a blanket? The idea was daring and brazen, though no more so than what she'd just done, she supposed. And the blanket was starting to warm; she dreaded the thought of shedding it for a cold dress. "Very well," she agreed and slipped her bare muddy feet into her shoes.

The Northman nodded for her to lead the way then followed, carrying her clothes and the basket. When they neared the top, he stepped up beside her. "I'll go ahead now and have Bryen place your trunk in the carriage."

She nodded, but as he started to walk away, she called out to him. "Wait. Hand me my gowns." When he started to decline, she added, "As it stands, Northman, they'll believe I'm wet from the rain, but if you're carrying my clothes for all to see, they'll know I disrobed in your presence. Then who knows what they'll assume we were doing; I highly doubt it would be swimming. Hand them to me, please."

Gunnar held out the dresses and waited for her to pin them to her chest with a blanket-clad arm. "Don't dally," he said, then looked at her and smiled. "Though your color is much better now—much less like a corpse." Before she could respond, he was moving up the hill again.

Like a corpse? What a horribly grotesque and vivid image. No decent person would ever use such a word to describe a lady and certainly not in her company. He said the most inappropriate things—just whatever popped into his head without any censoring. She watched his long strides eating up the distance, then began to follow, though she no longer felt the need to rush. After the brisk pace uphill inside the blanket cocoon, her teeth had quit chattering, and she actually felt comfortable.

He reached the carriage and spoke with the footmen. One of them, she could not tell which from the distance, stowed her trunk inside and adjusted the box step for her. Then all the men retreated out of view behind the carriage—all except for him. His fair hair gave him away. Only when she was close, did he join the men on the other side.

Fiona climbed inside, laid her wet clothes on the seat, and closed the door behind her. After making sure the curtains were drawn tight, she dropped the blanket from her shoulders and opened her trunk, pulling out a clean, dry shift, kirtle, and gown. She reached down and gripped the wet shift at her hips preparing to lift it over her head, then hesitated. Even though the thin damp material was moulded to her body and provided virtually no cover, it was still an alarming feeling of taboo to remove it—the last vestige of propriety—to stand fully bare when four men stood only feet away.

Not that she feared the three. Certainly, not with the Northman around. And she didn't really fear him anymore under normal circumstances. Though something deep in her mind warned her that if she were naked, he might not be the same. She lifted the damp shift over her head and dropped it to the floor in a soggy pile.

She glanced down at her body, seeing nothing overly exciting—breasts smaller than some, legs and stomach far too lean and muscular from riding. She wondered daringly what the Northman would think of it. Would it rank favorably amongst all the others he'd seen? If the way that women, young and old, threw themselves at him was any indication, he should be a veritable expert. Not that she wanted him to enjoy it, of course, only to know his unbiased opinion.

What a shameless hussy you are—harboring thoughts of a brazen harlot! Clothe yourself immediately! So loud and clear were the thoughts, it was as if Meirna were standing in the very carriage with her. Fiona pulled the clean, dry shift over her head, trying to ignore the soft material brushing against her tight, sensitive nipples. Keeping her mind far from its earlier divergence, she stepped into her kirtle, quickly jerking the front laces tight, then her dark green gown—another older style that laced on the sides. She wrapped herself in her cloak, opened the door, and called outside, "I'm finished."

Bryen removed her trunk, and the Northman climbed inside. He was barely seated when the carriage jerked forward, bouncing down the road. Eager to put distance between them and the ancient faerie mounds, Garrett had set the horses to a brisk pace without waiting for his signal.

After verifying she was warm, the Northman didn't speak to her, but the air between them held no tension. She studied him as he looked out the window. His straight blond hair was mostly dry, and he'd swept it back but not tied it. He'd removed his amber tunic and spread it on the seat next to him to dry. The bottom of his damp white linen shirt was untucked and draped over his trousers, and the sleeves were rolled up to just below his elbows. Fiona's eyes were drawn to a green mark on his skin that disappeared underneath the sleeve on one arm.

"Why do you have those?"

When he looked at her with eyebrows raised in question to what she was referring to, she pointed to the tattoo.

He glanced down at his forearm. "They are to remind me of things that were important to me."

"Are they painful?" she asked.

"The receiving is painful, and some pain remains for a few days while it heals," he admitted, "but then, no. I have many of them. Would you like to see a few?" He reached down and gripped the shirt bottom as if to lift it.

"Nay, I would not," she said with a mixture of alarm and indignation before turning to look out the window.

"You would not? Or think you should not?"

She turned back to him.

"You just swam with me when I was fully bare, Fiona. It seems odd to fall back on propriety now."

"But I did not look. I only enjoyed the water."

"Would your peers find it acceptable, since you did not look?"

"You know they would not."

"Yet no harm was done. I thought you'd finally accepted that for these few days you are free to shed the restrictions of your title—the restrictions that smother who you really are." He could see she was wavering. "Be the reasonable, open-minded woman that you so pride yourself to be. It would only be looking. You will not be scarred from it, and no one else will ever know. And if it offends, simply say the word, and I will cover myself immediately." He paused. "So I ask you again, Fiona, would you like to see my tattoos?"

She stared at him, her mind rocking and lurching far more than the rushing carriage. He was like the snake charmer she'd seen once as a child in a group of traveling entertainers, mesmerizing her. Turning her thoughts and world upside down and somehow making it seem like it made perfect sense. How did he always seem to know her innermost thoughts, fears, and frustrations? Truthfully she did want to see his tattoos. She wanted to be shocked by them. And it would only be looking...

"Aye," she murmured. "I would like to see them."

Gunnar pulled the shirt over his head. Fiona squirmed in her seat, averted her gaze momentarily, and then looked back. Gunnar's gut wrenched. She was so incredibly beautiful. Her thick hair hung loose and damp, the curls and waves cascading over her shoulders. Her eyes, framed by thick dark lashes were wide and unsure—pools of green so deep, he could easily drown in them. As they raced over his chest and torso taking in the designs and symbols, Gunnar felt as much as saw her gaze. The sensation was extremely sensual—almost as if she were physically touching him. He swallowed hard.

Fiona barely saw the tattoos, so shocked was she by his bare form. She'd seen Aiden shirtless before, but nothing prepared her for this. His muscles were so sculpted, so defined...so large. *He* was so large. She'd assumed garments exaggerated his size, yet bare, he somehow seemed even bigger. The smooth, raised planes of his chest were covered with light brown and golden hairs, and his stomach rippled in multiple thick short bands. But his arms...his arms were magnificent. Gracefully curved arcs of muscle smoothly tying into the next in sleek lines, like the finest horse. Like Barca. She thought of running her hands over Barca's strong forelegs and shoulders while she groomed him and wondered if the Northman's would feel the same. Heat engulfed her face.

Realizing she teetered on the edge of turning back, Gunnar began to explain the significance of each mark, keeping his voice low and matter of fact. "This one here," he traced the top of the green symbol she had pointed to. It began on his bicep and trailed down across his elbow to the top of his forearm, "is Thor's hammer. And this one." He glanced up to make sure she was still watching, then continued, her eyes raptly following his fingers as they outlined the next. And the next.

"And that one?" She pointed to the last when he stopped with no explanation.

Gunnar braced himself. He knew what she pointed to. He gave the tattoo a quick cursory glance, waiting for the familiar pain—ready to avert his eyes when he felt it. There was nothing. He examined it more closely, taking in every oh-so-familiar detail of the fox—the symbol of his wife, Brigitta's Baltic tribe. He exhaled with a soft snort at the lack of reaction. "That one was for my wife." *Who has haunted me every day since she died, until now.*

"You are married?" she asked, shocked.

"I was married. She is dead."

"How did she die?" Fiona shook her head. "Apologies, that was an insensitive and improper question."

"It's alright. You are not bound by propriety here, remember? Satisfy your curiosities. She was killed by Germanian raiders."

"Did you love her?" she asked quietly.

"Very much."

The carriage hit a large stone in the road, throwing them both out of their seats.

"Apologies, my lord," Garrett called down from the driver's seat. "'Twas unavoidable. And my lord, we're nearing the ford to cross the river. There's an inn on this side. Do you wish to stop there? I know it's early, but I doubt we'll come upon another without going into Drogheda."

Garrett didn't explain the significance of Drogheda, but Gunnar understood. The banished lizard-eyed lord's home was somewhere near, and the carriage might be recognized.

"Yes, Garrett, we'll stop," Gunnar said as he slipped his shirt and tunic back over his head, frustrated again by the loss of another shared moment.

Fiona had looked away at the interruption. At the mention of the inn, she frantically began finger-combing her long hair. "I must look a fright," she said, attempting to twist it into a makeshift bun behind her head. "They can't see me like this."

"You are beautiful," he said.

Their eyes met, and she flushed again.

"If you're concerned, wear the hood up on your cloak. No one will see anything out of the ordinary. You can go straight to your room, and I'll have them bring you a bath and supper."

"Gratitude, Northman."

"It's my pleasure." *More than you know.*

Gunnar took his meal alone in his room that night along with a bottle of poteen. He'd limited himself to ale so far on their trip, but tonight he needed something stronger. He sat sprawled in a chair in front of the small fire he'd had the chambermaid light, ostensibly to take the chill from the room, but in reality, he just found fire soothing. He took another sip of poteen, enjoying the burn in his throat as he stared into the flickering flames.

What are you doing, Gunnar? Do you truly see a future with her? Do you see her giving up everything she knows to be with you? And what of your word to Jarl and Tryggr? Would you go back on that now after all this time? If you could live with yourself, how do you see this ending? She's a noble. Has riding in a fine carriage and having people bow and scrape to you for a few days, gone to your head? Do you fancy yourself a highborn now? Don't be a fool. Her people will never accept you.

That's assuming you can even win her in the short time you have left. If you cannot, would you take her away against her will? To where? To the East?

She couldn't make that trip. She's strong in many ways, but she's not hardened. Or perhaps you would leave her somewhere safe while you travel—like you did with Brigitta.

You're playing with fire, and she's the one who's going to get burned. If you care about her at all, you'll stop this now—before it goes too far. There is no way this ends well—for either of you.

Chapter 17

Fiona was up with the sun the next morning, feeling more anticipation than she could remember in a long time. She was dressed in the second of her newer gowns and she admired it while she waited for the maid to finish her hair. Made from dark burgundy brocade silk, the style and cut were almost identical to the pale green she'd worn the first day, with heavy embroidery on the bodice, short sleeves, and skirt edges. Accentuated by the darker color, the ivory, silver, and gold embroidery were even more striking, and the deepness of the red was further emphasized by the cream-colored kirtle where it showed in the sleeves, the side slits, and the bottom of the skirt.

"How is that, my lady?" the maid asked.

Fiona held up the polished tin hand mirror and examined the long loose braid laced with spring wildflowers. She smiled. "'Tis perfect, Kera."

The girl beamed. "Shall I bring your breakfast now, my lady?"

"Is my brother eating below?"

"Nay, his lordship took his meal in his room early and has gone out."

Fiona frowned, not wanting to admit she was disappointed. "Aye, bring me something light—perhaps just a slice of bread with honey."

After devouring the bread, she made her way outside. The Northman was leaned against the front of the carriage having a discussion with Garrett. He'd alternated his garments again and wore the blue today.

"Shall I retrieve your trunk, my lady?" Bryen stood up from placing the box step, spying her in the doorway.

"Aye, Bryen," she replied.

Their interchange alerted the Northman to her presence. He dismissed Garrett and moved toward her.

"Sleep well?" he asked, his eyes unable to refrain from making their usual admiring sweep of her. His gaze lingered on her hair and he smiled.

Though inappropriate, Fiona was pleased he'd noticed and found it oddly reassuring. "Aye," she said.

"Very well then." He waved towards the carriage.

"What is next on your list?" she asked after they'd taken their seats and the carriage pulled away.

"I would have liked to see the Cliffs of Moher or Slieve Liege or Giant's Causeway, but our short time precludes us from traveling that far. Instead, we're going to Dundalk. There are supposed to be magical stacked boulders there. It is said if you toss three pebbles up and they remain on the top stone without rolling off, you'll be granted a wish within a year."

Fiona had never seen Proleek Dolman, but her cook, Haisley, hailed from Dundalk, and she'd told Fiona many times of the ancient boulders. Though in Haisley's version, if you cast three stones and they stayed, you'd be married within a year. Fiona wondered if Haisley had altered it for her, assuming that would be her wish. Not wanting to think of that now, she remembered an unfinished conversation with the Northman.

"You promised to tell me of your predecessor, Jarl."

"What do you wish to know about him? Where he was born? How important his family was? How much land they owned?" he teased.

She shook her head. "Tell me of the woman and why he gave up the ship."

Gunnar described the East, the tribes, the fierceness of the warrior Teclans, how they'd skirted their lands to avoid them, and the battle that resulted in Nena's capture after she'd cut off part of Tryggr's ear. "Jarl had never met a woman who moved him as Nena did. She was very beautiful, though like a wild animal in many ways. To be honest, every morning when I awoke, I half expected to hear that she'd killed him. Eventually, Jarl was able to win her over, and they seemed quite happy together. So when she escaped, it was a shock to all."

"She left him?"

"Aye."

"Why?"

"I don't know for sure. My best guess is she felt she had obligations to her family and her people. Her father was a chieftain so she was like royalty—a princess of sorts."

"But she loved Jarl?"

"I believe so, but perhaps she didn't know it yet. Or perhaps she did but felt she didn't have a choice. Perhaps because their peoples were enemies, she thought they could never be happy together." He frowned, not relishing the similarities to his current situation. "We were soon to return home as far richer men, but none of that mattered to Jarl. When Nena escaped, we followed her south all the way to the Teclan stronghold. When we could find no weakness in their defenses, Jarl took off his armor, left his weapons, and rode in alone."

"Were they so fierce that you could not defeat them? Even fighting as you do?" Fiona's eyes were serious as she hung on his words.

"They fought like no others we'd ever encountered. And they had the added advantage of the lay of the land. Their mountain home is like an impregnable fortress. *If* we were able to defeat them, and that is far from assured, the cost in lives would have been very high. Jarl would not ask that." He paused. "And I believe if he were to discover she didn't love him as he loved her, I think he didn't wish to go on living."

"What happened?"

"They captured him and beat him."

"Did she save him? Beg her father for his life? If he was a king he could..."

"I'm getting to that," he chided, and she flushed. "Her father, the chief, sentenced him to die by combat against the fiercest warrior in all the land, Nena's older brother. But Jarl prevailed."

"He killed her brother?"

"Nay...there's more to it, but their culture would take forever to explain. Nena chose him to be her husband and, by doing so, made Jarl a part of the tribe. That allowed her brother to yield to him with honor."

"The woman chooses the man?"

He nodded.

"So he stayed with them," she murmured. "But if her brother will be chief, Jarl will one day have to answer to him."

Gunnar smiled that she recognized the friction of such an arrangement. "Her brother will be chief, but Jarl and Nena did not stay. Jarl chose instead to build a settlement on the north shore of the Caspian Sea—a fresh start in a new place for both of them."

"He did that for her—and gave you the ship?"

Gunnar nodded. "I was to return the following year with the wealth he and Tryggr had left behind in Norway, but I've been delayed and it's been four."

The carriage slowed. "My lord, there appears to be an overlook that might provide views of the sea in both directions. Would you like to stop here?" Garrett asked.

Gunnar glanced out the window at the ocean beyond. "Aye, Garrett."

The walk to the point was rough going—a field of jutting slanted rocks separated by patches of green grass; they had to pick their way carefully. When they reached the overlook, Gunnar walked to the furthermost tip and stood staring out over the water. It was a strange thing. When he was away, he didn't necessarily miss it, but when he was near the sea, he felt invigorated—stronger. The salted mists seemed to breathe life into him.

Fiona was looking further up the coast to the north, and Gunnar joined her.

"That sand begs to be ridden upon," she said, pointing to a wide strip of beach exposed by the low tide. "Nay, such smooth firm surface begs to be raced upon," she amended, her voice filled with longing.

Gunnar evaluated the site's potential. There were occasional rocky outcroppings where the beach met the grassy dunes, but nearest to the water's edge the sand was clear. It would be good for racing. "Too bad we only have carriage horses," he said.

"That would not deter me, Northman, if I'm being my true free self," she challenged.

"They're carriage horses," he pointed out again. "We don't even know if they're broke to ride."

"Nay, we don't. That would add to the adventure. We can lead them out to the soft sand and find out there. Less risk that way."

"We have no saddles."

"You're coming up with a lot of excuses." She smiled. "If you're afraid, just admit it. Just say...I'm afraid and I wish to concede, Fiona. You are the victor. Is that what you wish? To concede?"

Gunnar shook his head at her manipulation. "I never concede, my lady. It's not in my nature. And they weren't excuses. I was only making sure you knew what you were getting into. I did guarantee your safety after all."

"And I release you from that responsibility—for this one act only," she clarified.

"Did you pack any clothes more suitable for riding?" he asked as they began the trek back to the carriage.

Fiona glanced down at the beautiful burgundy gown. "I did not."

"So what would you wear?"

"What I wear is not your concern, Northman. Your only concern is to try to win. I will even let you choose your horse first since it will have the additional handicap of your weight. I want you to have no excuses when you lose."

"Very well, I accept your challenge, and I choose the near-side, rear horse."

Fiona grinned.

"What? He's by far the biggest and strongest of the four." Gunnar defended his selection.

"Aye, he is. That's why he's a wheel horse. Bigger and stronger and content to follow other horses all day—as he will be content to follow my horse as I race to victory. I choose the off-side front horse. He's lighter, faster, and bolder."

"My lady, this competitive side of you is quite shocking. I rather like it," he murmured as they reached the carriage. "Garrett, please unharness the horses. The lady and I shall go for a ride."

"Aye, my lord. But I don't know that they've been ridden before," Garrett cautioned, echoing Gunnar's earlier concern.

"Understood, Garrett."

They led the two horses by their bridles up the road until they found a trail leading through the grassy dunes to the beach.

"The footing is perfect," Fiona shouted giddily over the surf. "But before I ruin my dress, see if you're able to stay on your horse, Northman," she instructed.

After unclasping his cloak and laying it on the sand, Gunnar grabbed a handful of his horse's black mane and swung up on its back, clamping his legs tight against the horse's thick sides. Unaccustomed to carrying weight, the horse leaped sideways in the air, landed, and launched again. The battle was brief. The animal had been pulling the carriage for days and was not fresh with excess energy. After steering it in a few practice circles with only some head tossing and prancing, Gunnar stopped in front of her.

"Your turn, my lady. My horse is ready. It appears you will have to back up your bold claims and earn your victory today. You shall not win by default."

"Good. Do try to stay on long enough to at least start the race. Now please turn away while I adjust my dress."

"Oh, I would, but this horse...well, he has his own mind."

"He does not. He's a wheel horse. They are chosen for the very reason that they do not have a willful mind." Fiona waited for him to comply.

He did not.

Exasperated, Fiona glared at him, then pulled her horse up so that it stood between them. She removed her cloak and tossed it aside, then studied her dresses. The side slits in her outer gown should allow her to ride if she hiked it a bit and twisted them to the front and back, and the full-skirted kirtle would cover her legs. But her shift... She reached under her skirts and grabbed the hem of the thin shift with both hands.

Gunnar heard the sound of material ripping. There was a brief pause, then more tearing. *What was she doing back there?* When she reappeared with no evidence of torn cloth, his curiosity was piqued even more.

Fiona stood at her horse's side, stroking it gently while she contemplated her next move. The skirts were too heavy and cumbersome for her to swing aboard as he had. She snugged both reins, grabbed a handful of mane with one hand, then vaulted up onto her belly across the horse's back. Before she could swing her leg over, the animal snorted and pivoted its hindquarters out from under her. It stood facing her with bulging eyes and flared nostrils.

"Do you need a leg up?" Gunnar asked

"I do not."

"Can I at least hold him steady for you?"

"If I need your assistance, Northman, I will ask for it."

"As long as you are not so stubborn that you would do so before your neck is broken."

"Not your concern. I've released you from the responsibility of my safety for this," she reminded him.

Gunnar watched, curious but more than a little nervous. She murmured to the horse, soothing it, stroking its forehead and rubbing beneath its eyes. When it was calm, she once again moved to the side, still stroking its neck and talking softly. Gently she pulled on the farthest rein until the animal's nose was almost touching its opposite shoulder. She hopped up on its back on her belly again. The horse started to spin, but this time, because of the tight rein, it turned in controlled circles, each step taking its body further underneath her instead of away. Her voice never changed pitch as she murmured constant soft reassurances. She remained on her belly until it slowed, then sat up and swung her leg over in one swift practiced move.

The animal stood perfectly still. Only its ears, flicking rapidly back and forth, conveyed its nervousness. Fiona continued to talk to it, soothing it, then gave it a gentle nudge with her heels. At the same time, she uttered the low clucking sound Garrett used when he wanted the team to move out. The horse stepped forward tentatively, familiar with the command, then gave a little buck and tried to squirt out from under her.

Gunnar's eyes combed the vicinity for any rocks that might injure her if she were to fall. The sand was clear. Satisfied, he returned his focus to Fiona. Her face was determined but very calm, her full attention on the signals the horse transmitted through its ears, the reins, and her legs. No matter how quickly the animal moved, it couldn't unseat her, and all the while, she never stopped her smooth singsong brogue. Within moments the horse was relaxed and obeying her commands. Gunnar had never seen anyone, man or woman, so naturally gifted with a beast. It was a wonder to watch. She looked up at him and smiled.

"I believe we are ready," she said.

"How far?" Gunnar asked.

Fiona looked down the beach through her horse's pricked ears. "To that driftwood log, the one with the large burl." She nodded far ahead, unwilling to remove either hand from the reins to point.

"Very well then," Gunnar accepted. "Are you ready?"

"I am."

"Then start us at your leisure, my lady," Gunnar said as he brought his horse up next to hers.

"On my mark. And...go!" Fiona shouted.

Both horses jumped forward, then stopped, plunging stiff-legged at the sudden excited urging. Fiona was the first to get her horse in hand, and the pair bounded away to a several-length lead. Gunnar's horse leaped after them, not wanting to be left behind.

Though his horse was running all out, they weren't gaining on her. To make matters worse, the wet sand kicked up by her horse's hooves was a constant barrage, stinging his face and blinding him. He wondered how his horse could see at all and had just tucked his head and closed his eyes in an attempt to clear them of sand, when the bombardment suddenly ceased. He squinted ahead. Her horse had spooked at a breaking wave and swerved up into the drier, deeper sand.

Seizing the opportunity, Gunnar lashed his horse's hindquarters with the ends of the long driving reins, keeping the animal on course in the firmest sand at the water's edge. They surged past. For a moment, Gunnar heard nothing other than the wind and his horse's hooves pounding the wet sand with dull solid smacks. He was about to look back to make sure she was alright when he heard her coming. Heard her yelling—urging her mount. He leaned lower on his horse's neck and yelled, too. His horse responded by lengthening its stride and flattening out even more—its rock-hard muscles straining, driving, flexing beneath him.

Her horse's outstretched nose appeared at his knee, nostrils flared wide. Slowly it inched up beside him. He could see its eye now, wild with excitement and determination. Then Fiona's hands tangled in its black mane. Her face leaned low over its neck. Her hair had come loose from its braid and the dark red of it mingled with the horse's black, making the animal's mane appear to be tipped with fire.

She didn't look over at him, only continued to call to her horse, asking it for more. Gunnar glanced ahead. The driftwood log was close. If they could just hold her off a little longer! Side by side, they raced. Stride for stride. Then, whether it was his extra weight or her horse's desire, Gunnar didn't know, but she began to pull ahead. At the driftwood, she led by a neck.

Gunnar sat up, his horse dropping almost immediately to a trot, then a walk, its sides heaving. It took Fiona another hundred yards to slow her mount enough to turn it back.

"What a good brave lad you are. Well done, my boy," she praised the animal as they returned to him. Her horse tossed its head proudly, prancing sideways beneath her, nostrils still flared and blowing hard.

Gunnar stared at her, awestruck. She was a vision. Her cheeks were spattered with sand, but her face glowed with the rush of victory, and her smile was pure and uncensored. Her windblown hair fell about her shoulders and down her back, and her skirts, plastered with wet sand, showed clear outline of her legs. Gunnar knew he was gawking but couldn't help himself.

"Oh, how I've missed that," she exclaimed. "I haven't done anything like that since I was a child."

"You raced with Northmen on the beach?" he finally recovered enough to ask, trying to sound nonchalant, trying not to reveal how much she moved him.

"You know that's not what I meant. I used to race with Aiden." She paused and looked at him—really looked at him. "Gratitude, Northman."

"It's Gunnar," he said, holding her gaze.

She considered the significance and the request in his words, then nodded. "Gratitude, Gunnar. For this. For all of this. I shall never forget it."

They relived every aspect of the race as they walked side by side back towards the starting line and their cloaks. "When your horse spooked, I thought I had you for certain," Gunnar laughed.

"As did I," she agreed. "But he ran like the wind after that." She patted her horse's neck again just in front of his withers.

Gunnar retrieved their cloaks then remounted, and they rode back through the grassy dunes to the road. There, they paused for one last look at the beach. Gunnar's smile faded. "We need to get back to the carriage. A storm's coming."

Fiona followed his gaze but saw only blue skies and a calm sea. The weather was beautiful. Even the wind had died. She was about to accuse him of trying to change the subject from his loss, but his face was serious as he continued to scan the horizon.

"We need to go," he said again. "It's going to be a bad one."

"Give him an extra ration of oats tonight, Garrett," Fiona said as she handed him the reins. "He's a champion."

"Aye, my lady." Garrett smiled at her enthusiasm. The horse pranced beside him as he led it back to its position in the team. "He does seem to be quite proud of himself," Garrett said as he struggled to hold the dancing horse in place long enough to get him hitched. "Whoa now, lad. Have you completely lost your senses?" He chastised the animal, losing his patience.

"'Tis my fault, Garrett." Fiona moved to take the horse by the bridle, stroking him and holding him steady while Garrett attached the harness. "I've given him a taste of freedom that lies beyond his station."

"Well, he better put such thoughts from his mind because this is the life he was born to," Garrett responded as he tightened the last harness strap and moved to take Gunnar's horse.

Fiona felt a sudden kinship to the animal. It had not asked to be freed. Not asked to experience great adventure. It had been content with the life it was born to until she had shown it freedoms it could not have.

Just as the Northman—Gunnar, has done with you.

Troubled by the thought, Fiona climbed into the carriage. Seeing the animal resist being returned to its life of restrictions—a life of walking and trotting sedately in close confines with its mates when its heart yearned to race free, took much of the joy from her victory. *This is the life he was born to.* Garrett's words echoed in her mind. And so it was. Just as the life she was born to awaited her two short days from now. Would she be like the horse? Would this taste of freedom leave her forever discontent?

"We need to change our plans and head inland," the Northman instructed Garrett. "Get as far away from the coast as we can. A storm's coming."

"Aye, my lord."

"Apologies, but we'll have to forgo the opportunity to win a wish," he said to Fiona as he joined her inside.

"'Tis of no concern. It couldn't possibly equal today's experience," she said truthfully, still troubled by the horse's reaction at being returned to harness. Gunnar nodded but thankfully didn't notice her pensive mood. He was too preoccupied looking outside. As the carriage turned west at the next crossroad heading inland per his instruction, Fiona glanced one last time towards the sea. The skies were still beautiful and clear, the air still calm. She couldn't help but think he was a bit mad.

While she plaited her hair in a long thick braid, the Northman—Gunnar—
fidgeted in his seat, looking repeatedly out the window. After nearly an hour
of such uncharacteristic behavior, he began running his hands between the
cushions and along the edges of the walls.

"What are you looking for?" she asked.

"Something to drink. Something stronger than ale," he added before she
could suggest the jug in their basket. "Surely his lordship kept something in
here for emergencies."

"Check under your seat. Most carriages have compartments there for
storage of small things. They will have sliding doors."

Gunnar reached between his legs and felt along the base of the seat just
above the floor. Finding a groove in the smooth wood, he slid it to one side,
then reached his hand inside. He withdrew a pair of thin lambskin gloves
that he tossed on the seat beside him with disdain. He reached in again,
and after more rummaging, withdrew a silver flask. The initials, *AMT,* were
boldly engraved in flowery print on one side.

He uncorked the top and took a brief sniff, expecting wine. "Poteen," he
announced before tipping back his head and taking a deep swallow. "And
quite good," he added after he caught his breath. He held the flask out to her.

Fiona hesitated, then took it. She'd oft heard Meirna grumbling that
Cahan enjoyed his poteen a bit too much, and though her father drank it
occasionally, she'd never tried it. She passed the top under her nose and
inhaled. It smelled rich and sweet. Tipping her head back as he had done, she
took a swallow.

Fire scorched her mouth and throat. There was no flavor of sweetness—
no flavor of anything other than burn! It was vile! For a moment, she feared
her ability to taste may have been forever scalded away.

"Are you alright?" he asked with a smile. "You should probably just sip it."

"I think I'll not have anymore," she gasped, her eyes still watering as she
handed it back to him.

He took several more swigs, then offered it back to her. "Try again. But only a small sip this time."

Fiona hesitated, then took the flask again. The burning had subsided, and the warmth that remained in her throat and stomach was pleasant. She took a small sip. This time she tasted a fleeting hint of sweetness before it was overpowered again by the harsh burn. Better, but still far from what she would call good. She shook her head and handed it back to him. "I don't care for it."

She declined his next offer, but he continued to drink until his fidgeting ceased. Once again he sat quietly in his seat.

"Is the temporary release from my oath over now?" he asked. "Am I once again bound to keep you safe?"

"What?" Fiona asked, her mind back on the carriage horse.

"You released me from my vow to keep you safe for the race. I was verifying that I was once again so bound." He smiled a rakish smile.

"You are. Yet I no longer believe it is your word that binds you. I think you would keep me safe regardless."

"Perhaps." He shrugged.

"In fact, I even believe I would be safe to release you from your word not to lay hand," she mused out loud, emboldened by the poteen. "Tell me, Northman—Gunnar, am I wrong? Were I to release you from that oath, what would you do?"

Gunnar stared at her for a long moment. He'd imagined just such a scenario too many times to count, yet wasn't sure she was ready to hear it. The liquor freed his tongue. "First, I would take a lock of your hair and run it between my fingers, over and over. I imagine it to feel softer than the softest silk. Then I would touch the furrow on your brow that appears when you're unsure, as you are now, so I know it would be there, and I would massage it away. I would trail my fingertips in a caress down the side of your cheek to your chin before I tipped it up to position your perfect lips to be kissed.

Not an awkward peck that you may have received from one of your previous suitors, but a slow, deep kiss." He drew the last words out with relish, clearly imagining the experience as he described it. "Then..."

"That's enough," she said shakily. "I should've known better. You've no comprehension of boundaries or decency." Fiona looked out the window, unable to look at him. Her cheeks were flaming; she'd felt the heat creeping up her neck at his words. She hoped he wouldn't see it, but knew that he would. He saw everything. Every tiny little detail. Even the line in her forehead that Meirna had warned would leave a wrinkle when she was older—the line no one else had ever noticed. The Northman—Gunnar saw everything.

"What did you see to make you think there's a storm coming?" Fiona tried to steer the conversation away from her recent lapse in judgment.

"I don't *think* there's a storm coming, I *know* there is. It's not so much what I see, as what I *feel*." He searched for the right words to explain. "The air feels...heavy. Not so much as heavy on my skin, it's heavy here—inside." He placed his hand over his chest. "Can you not feel it?"

Feel air? Fiona closed her eyes and concentrated on her breathing. "Nay," she concluded. "There's nothing to feel. It's air. Isn't that air by definition? Light as air, we say. No one quantifies it and says a pound of air."

"That's not true. You feel it when it's wind. And you do quantify it then—a light breeze, a strong gust."

Fiona gave that serious consideration. It was a very interesting thought. He was right; everyone could feel wind. At what point when wind slowed did the air within it cease to be felt?

"Animals can feel it, too," he added. "Have you never noticed how they will buck and play before a storm?"

She had, but Cahan had explained that animals just somehow knew. Were they simply feeling a change in the air as he said he could? Fiona closed her eyes and tried again with the same results.

"It takes practice," he said.

She nodded.

"What if we don't come across another inn?" she asked as they rolled by open expanses of uninhabited land.

"We'll keep going until we do. Though when we do stop, I'm not sure what they'll think of my *sister* this time. You look rather unkempt," he said with a smile.

"I shall wear my cloak again. It worked well before."

"That will do nothing to hide the dirt on your face."

Fiona reached up and felt the gritty salt and sand on her cheeks. She brushed it away and looked to him for approval.

"Better, but there's still your dress."

She brushed the sand splatters from her bodice, then glanced down at the dried horse sweat and dirt on her skirt—a perfect outline of every part of her that had made contact with the animal. There was nothing she could do about those. "I guess I'll have to wrap my cloak around me very tightly," she said with a smile.

"Yes," he agreed. "I guess you will."

Chapter 18

DAY 6

"**F**iona, it's time."

A man's voice in the darkness. Gunnar's voice. Why was she hearing Gunnar's voice? Fiona rolled over. Straw crunched beneath her. She groaned as the previous day began to come back to her. Arriving at the small cottage in the middle of the night—the only structure they'd seen in many miles. Gunnar convincing the man to allow them to stay.

"Fiona?" Gunnar called again.

"Aye, I'm awake," she replied softly.

"We need to be going as soon as you're ready. Do you need a light?"

"Nay, I'll be just a moment."

She sat up, feeling the stiffness in her shoulders and back. The thin layer of straw covered with a blanket from the carriage had provided little cushion from the hard earthen floor. She remembered it all now. The man hanging two soiled blankets near the hearth for her privacy, all the while apologizing for the squalid conditions, explaining he was a recent widower. Gunnar retrieving two blankets from the carriage for her to sleep on after seeing the conditions inside.

Fiona had been so exhausted she'd barely noticed. She had welcomed any place to stretch out and close her eyes—any place that wasn't jerking and jouncing. She remembered very little after lying down fully clothed—only Gunnar's reminder that they would be leaving early—still so paranoid about *the storm* that had yet to materialize.

Something itched deep inside her bodice. She prayed it was only salt and sand from the race, and tried not to dwell on what else it could be—what tiny vermin she might have picked up in their few hours here. The thought made her anxious to be away. Her braid was loose, but she didn't waste the time to replait it. Instead, she twisted and tied it in a loose knot behind her head, then stood and shook the straw from the two blankets. Tucking them under one arm, she gingerly pushed aside the dirty curtain and stepped into the main room.

Gunnar was waiting for her with a worried frown. "Sleep well?" he asked wryly.

She didn't reply, only looked at him, but her answer must have been obvious in her expression because he took the blankets from her without another word and held open the door.

As Fiona stepped out into the crisp gray dawn light, she glanced at the sky with trepidation. She didn't know what she expected to see, but it wasn't the normal-looking voluminous white clouds. Other than a steady stiff breeze that was unusual for this early in the day, there was no sign of a killer storm—nothing to justify them traveling this way. Fighting back her resentment, Fiona climbed inside the waiting carriage.

Gunnar followed, and after setting the blankets and his sword on the seat beside him, immediately tapped on the roof with the cane. They rode in silence, for which Fiona was grateful. She was itching all over now, imagining tiny unwanted traveling companions crawling across her skin. All because of his mad need to "*get far from the coast.*"

When they stopped a few hours later to break their fast, Gunnar divided what remained in their basket from the previous day among the five of them. The man in the cottage had no food to offer them—quite literally nothing. Sitting on a rock with her back to the increasing wind, Fiona devoured her crust of bread and small rind of cheese. She knew he'd given her the largest portion, but still, her stomach growled. There was no sense complaining when there was nothing to be done about it, and when he suggested they all drink their fill from the stream to help to keep the hunger pangs at bay, she did.

As she was climbing back into the carriage, distant thunder rumbled. Fiona caught her first glimpse of the solid wall of black roiling clouds.

"Do you men have oilskins?" Gunnar asked the men.

"Aye, my lord."

"You should don them now. And Garrett, don't spare the horses. We'll stop at the next inn we come across even though it's early."

"Aye, my lord."

The thought of an inn and a hot bath bolstered Fiona's spirits. Surely they would come across one soon. They'd passed not a single one the entire day before.

Intermittent light rain began to fall, small drops carried on occasional stronger gusts of wind. When the rain grew heavier, they pushed the heavily-weighted bottoms of the curtains to the outside of the window openings to keep the water from running inside.

Fiona glanced at Gunnar. He was looking out through a slit in his curtains, his jaw set in a firm line. Lightning cracked close, followed immediately by a booming clap of thunder. Fiona jumped in her seat. The storm was upon them. Bigger raindrops pelted the roof, sounding like small stones. As the rain increased, the roar inside became deafening.

Gunnar slid across his seat and reached out through the curtains on her side to release the wood foul-weather shutters. After pulling them closed, he latched them firmly, then repeated the process on his side.

It took a few moments for Fiona's eyes to adjust to the reduced light. She couldn't imagine what it was like for the men and horses outside and prayed for another inn. With the wave of heavy rain, the temperature dropped dramatically. She pulled her cloak tight around her, then reached for the two blankets, not caring if they were possibly infested.

The carriage rocked forward as they crested a small hill and dropped down into a swale. Water and mud accumulating in the bottom sucked at the wheels. The carriage bogged and slid sideways.

"Hold on," Gunnar warned, his face grim.

Fiona wedged herself in the corner just as the wheels hit something solid in the mire. The carriage wall slammed painfully against her shoulder. She moved back toward the center and used her legs against the opposite seat to brace herself, spreading her hands and arms wide on the seat beside her for stability. She knew the position was extremely unladylike, but pretenses seemed ridiculous in this dire situation.

On and on it went, the carriage rumbling faster on higher ground, then slowing to a crawl in the rapidly rising water in the lowland dips. All the while, the wind screamed its horrible wrath like a hungry mythical beast. It buffeted the carriage, sometimes threatening to tip it, other times twisting the wood until it squealed and groaned from the strain. Somehow—miraculously it didn't splinter.

Cold and battered, her nerves stretched to their limits, Fiona wanted to scream and cover her ears to block out the roar of the rain pounding on the roof, the twisting screeching wood, and the wraith-like howl of the wind. But there was no escaping it, and she knew it was far worse outside. The carriage tipped forward and began to pick up speed—they were approaching another swale. She pressed her feet against the opposite bench and braced her entire body.

The carriage crashed to a near-halt as the horses plowed into a wall of water. She could feel them lunging against their harnesses, the carriage jerking and sliding behind them. One of her feet slipped from the opposite seat and splashed into water that had seeped up through the floor. She held her breath, praying they would soon be through it, but this time the water and mud proved to be too much. The carriage sucked to a halt.

"Fuck!" Gunnar swore under his breath.

Fiona realized she'd never heard him swear before—not when she'd taken the slaves, not when the bandits had attacked them. That he did so now told her how grim their situation truly was. Though even knowing that, having the carriage still for a moment was a guilty relief to her battered body and nerves.

The two footmen climbed down to push, adding their brawn to the straining horses. Finally, they were once again underway. The next time they became stuck, Gunnar joined them.

Alone in the carriage, she prayed to feel it move again. For if it did not, she knew they'd have no choice but to abandon it in the rising water. She could not imagine stepping out that door. She'd never experienced anything close to such a storm. But he must have; that's why he'd been so concerned. And she had doubted him.

The carriage twitched and shuddered but remained still. Fiona held her breath, adding sheer will to the three men and four horses straining outside. It twitched again, this time continuing to inch forward until it once again reached solid ground. Gunnar opened the door and climbed back inside. Water poured from his hair and mud fell in slick clumps from his boots. She offered him one of her blankets, but he took only a corner to wipe his face. "Keep it," he said.

"But it's freezing and you're wet."

"I'm not cold. The labor of pushing kept me quite warm, and I fear I'll get another taste of it soon enough. You keep it," he insisted and waved her off. He was right. Within minutes the carriage ground to a halt again. Over and over it was repeated. Fiona lost all sense of time. Whenever he opened the door, she could see it was darker outside, but she had no idea if it was truly late or if the storm made the day appear as night. When the carriage lurched free of the most recent bog, she heard him shout, "How much more do the horses have in them, Garrett?"

"I don't know, my lord. Not much, I'm afraid."

"Understood. Keep your eyes open for a shelter of any kind...a cave, anything. We've got to get out of this weather."

"Aye, my lord."

Gunnar opened the door and stepped inside. The water pouring from him formed quick pools on the floor before draining through the cracks between the floorboards. Fiona offered him the corner of the blanket again. He took it and dried his face. "Gratitude," he said and smiled a wry smile. "Not exactly how I was expecting to spend our last full day together."

The reminder of this being the last full day of their trip brought an unexpected pang to her stomach. It had nothing to do with it being the last day with him, of course, only that it was the last day of her new freedom. Her mind sped through the many unforgettable experiences of the past days. The quarry. The attack. The swim. The race. His tattoos. His teasing.

"Praise God, my lord! I see a light ahead," Garrett shouted down through the wind.

"Thank the gods," Gunnar said. "Take us there with all haste, Garrett. If there's light, then there's shelter. They'll not turn us away. I'll see to that," he added under his breath.

When the carriage came to a halt, Bryen yelled down over the wind. "It's an inn, my lord. Shall I see to your rooms?"

"Nay, Bryen, not this time," Gunnar shouted back as he stepped out into the wind and rain. His eyes swept over the building, gauging its sturdiness. He breathed a sigh of relief at the solid stone construction. A thick wooden sign above the door strained sideways against its two chains. Without warning, it skittered and twisted, plunging downward before blowing straight out again. Gunnar eyed it warily as he approached, then ducked underneath through the doorway.

The innkeeper met him just inside. "I require two rooms and lodgings for three servants," Gunnar stated, making sure the man knew it was not a request as he glanced around the crowded common room.

"Apologies, my lord, we are full, with the rooms already double and triple filled. We're the strongest structure for miles, and many have come seeking shelter," he explained. Under Gunnar's steely stare, he added, "I will, of course, vacate a room for you, but would one possibly suffice?" he stuttered. "There's a place for your servants in the stables—they are also of stone."

Gunnar held out a pouch of silver. "One room then, and the rest to cover hot meals for every man, woman, and child here, for as long as the storm lasts."

"Gratitude, my lord. That is most generous. I'll see to it."

"I would also request that a meal be sent to our room and then later a hot bath for my wife if that is possible?"

"Of course, my lord."

Gunnar turned back, hesitating in the doorway. He wasn't sure which storm would be more fierce, the weather, or the one he would likely face with Fiona when she learned of the sleeping arrangements.

"There is only one room," he announced as he opened the carriage door.

"What?" Fiona said as she processed the implication.

"The inn is full of refugees from the storm and there is only one room," he repeated. "Actually not even that, but the innkeeper is going to make it so."

"But..."

"I don't have time to argue with you, Fiona. I need to help Garrett with the horses and get everyone out of this weather. Bryen will escort you inside. I only wanted you to know so that if anyone asks, tonight we are man and wife." Then he was gone into the swirling black night.

Man and wife?

"Are you ready, my lady?" Bryen shouted from the doorway. "I'll do my best to shield you with my oilskin, but with these conditions..."

"Aye, Bryen." Fiona pulled her cloak and the blankets tight around her and stepped out. Her feet had no sooner reached the ground when the wind ripped both blankets from her body. Her cloak threatened to follow them. Fiona clutched the clasp at her neck to keep it from choking her as icy water shot through the layers of her gowns straight to her skin as if she wore nothing. Bryen's oilskin offered no protection, slapping wet against them, then lifting away in the shifting, whipping wind.

"Apologies, my lady," he shouted. "I cannot hold it. Take my hand."

Fiona did and was immediately thankful when a gust almost knocked her off her feet. Bits of debris stung her face. She leaned forward trying to take a step, but the wind held her still. Bryen's grip tightened on her hand, pulling her through the sheets of rain toward the beacon of light coming from the doorway.

The wind shifted again, shoving them both sideways several steps. Through it all, Bryen remained a constant force, pulling her forward until finally, they stumbled over the threshold into the light and warmth of the inn.

At the sound of a thunderous crack behind them, Fiona turned in the doorway. A huge branch, carried on the wind like a twig, slammed to the ground beside the carriage. One of the horses reared in its harness. "Bryen, you must go help them," she pleaded.

"Aye, my lady." He rushed back outside. Fiona chewed a fingernail as she watched the men struggle with the panicked, exhausted animals.

"God bless you, my lady." A woman with a small child on her hip curtsied and bowed her head. Fiona looked at her, confused. Before she could ask the woman what she referred to, boots clattered over the threshold behind her. Fiona turned. It was Gunnar, his tall form filling the doorway. After securing the door behind him, he turned and wiped his wet hair back from his face. The woman dropped to her knees in front of him, reaching out to kiss his hand.

"May God bless you for your kindness, my lord. Gratitude for the meals."

"None required," Gunnar replied, gently extricating his hand and nodding Fiona toward the base of the stairs where the innkeeper was waiting. Others met them along the way.

"Gratitude, my lord, my lady," they all murmured, pressing close.

"You bought them meals?" she asked after the innkeeper departed, pulling the door to their room closed behind him.

"Yes."

"All of them?"

"It's only coin, Fiona. Some of these people will lose everything tonight. They'll need their strength to face that when the storm is over. It was the least I could do." He seemed embarrassed and moved to the fireplace to stand in front of the roaring fire, leaving Fiona to do a quick inventory of the room—a single large hide chair by the fireplace, a simple three-fold privacy screen constructed of woven reeds, a table with two smaller wood chairs and... Her eyes locked on the large bed.

"Don't fret, Fiona. I'm well aware that the arrangement of being husband and wife is pretense only. You shall have the bed and I'll sleep on the floor— or perhaps in this chair. It's large and appears to be comfortable."

He was reading her mind again.

"Come stand by the fire," he added. "You're soaked."

She hung her cloak on a peg by the door, then moved to stand beside him, but soon had to take a step back and rotate her body as the fire turned the cold wet to hot steam. They stood in awkward silence.

"Will the men be alright?" she asked.

"Aye, the barn is solid and quite warm; it's filled with other people and animals."

After another lengthy awkward pause, Gunnar commented, "I'm surprised to see glass windows in an inn. Of all the places I've traveled, few without strong Roman ties had glass windows, and those were usually limited to noblemen's estates."

Fiona didn't ask him under what circumstances he'd visited noblemen's estates, sure that it was not as a guest. She was thankful to speak of anything other than the bed. "We are very fortunate in this area. Most places in Ireland are as you describe and also do not have glass, but there's a family near Drogheda whose ancestor was enslaved by the Romans. While serving a Roman glasier, he learned the craft, and his family continues it to this day. But 'tis a secret they keep closely guarded."

There was a knock on the door. It was Bryen and Orin with her two trunks. She couldn't look at them, sure of what they must be thinking. Gunnar instructed them to place the trunks on the floor near the bed. As they were leaving the innkeeper arrived, carrying a small carved wooden cask and two heavy pewter goblets.

"This was left long ago by a traveling vendor to pay for his rooms." He set the cask on the table. "He said it was made from the finest grapes in Gaul, and I'd like for you to have it; it's far too expensive for local folk."

"Gratitude," Gunnar replied. "After today, wine is much appreciated."

"My lads will be up to fill the bath and bring your meal very soon. Apologies, unlike the wine, the food 'tis only simple fare."

"Any warm meal will be well received, I assure you."

The innkeeper nodded and left. Gunnar pulled the bung from the cask and filled each of the goblets. He brought her one by the fire. Fiona glanced at the deep red wine, then took a tentative sip, still scarred from the poteen experience. The wine caressed her tongue with a velvet-smooth warmth. Hints of cherry and oak were quickly replaced by other flavors too fleeting to discern. It was delicious and unlike anything she'd ever tasted.

There was another tap on the door. This time two boys entered, one with their meal, the other carrying pails of steaming water. The first set their tray on the table while the second disappeared behind the privacy screen, splashing water into an unseen tub. Both quickly retreated without saying a word. With the sounds of the storm dulled by the thick stone walls and the soothing fire crackling pleasantly in the corner, Fiona and Gunnar sat down to eat.

She barely noticed the lads delivering more water as she gulped down her first bowl of the lovage soup. Though there was only an occasional scrap of chicken, the thick creamy broth was filled with lovage, leeks, onions, peas, and even pieces of boiled egg. She washed down every spoonful with a swallow of the delicious wine and soaked up the broth with a piece of dark rye bread.

After only a moment's hesitation, she filled her bowl with a second large serving from the tureen. She was hungry, and with him there was no need to pretend otherwise. She wondered how much she'd had to drink. It was difficult to tell because Gunnar kept their glasses topped, but she thought it might be quite a lot. Her hunger sated after the second bowl, she leaned back in her chair and continued to sip the wine.

When the boys announced the tub was full and took their leave, Fiona didn't venture behind the screen to see. Although she would have liked for nothing more than to soak away the sand and salt—and whatever else she might have picked up at their previous lodgings—she could hardly bathe with him in the same room. And as bad as her day had been, his had been far worse; the bath would not go to waste.

"I'll help you with your dress," Gunnar said, his voice startling her.

"Nay, you cannot."

"Don't be ridiculous, Fiona. I'll see nothing more than the back of your neck. For that matter, after the first knot, I could probably complete the task with my eyes closed."

"Because you've removed so many women's clothes before?"

"A few," he admitted with a smile.

It was tempting. He would only need to help with her outer gown; he wouldn't see anything inappropriate. Still, she hesitated. The idea of him standing so close behind her, his fingers brushing against her...

Something itched on her upper arm. As she scratched through her sleeve, the decision was made. "Very well," she said. "Let me get dry clothes from my trunk."

She returned with a clean shift and her heavy chambergown. Then, not knowing what to say, she turned her back and lifted her hair out of the way for him to reach the top laces. She held her breath, worried that he would linger over the task, mortified that he would take the opportunity to tease her, but he did neither. Instead, his fingers raced swiftly through the laces as if he were in even a bigger hurry than she for it to be over.

"Please don't tarry," he said after she disappeared behind the changing wall. "I would use the water when you've finished, before it's cold."

Fiona rushed through her bath, scrubbing her skin and scalp with the harsh soap. The hot water felt good, but she didn't linger—fearing that any second he would realize it would break neither of his oaths if he came around the corner to watch her. After twisting her hair in a tight knot to squeeze the excess water from it, she cast a last quick glance at the changing wall, then stood and stepped from the tub. Hastily drying her body with a linen square, she slipped into a clean shift and underdrawers before donning her chambergown.

She tied the individual ties in the front in quick bows then glanced down to make one final inspection before she faced him. Satisfied that the bulky shapeless garment revealed less than her day dresses, she stepped from behind the wall.

"I'm finished. It's ready for you," she murmured and moved to her trunk to retrieve a comb.

Gunnar wasted no time. As Fiona sat in the chair in front of the fire to comb out her hair, she heard small waves lap against the sides of the tub. "Ah, this feels good," he groaned.

She concentrated on working through the tangles, trying not to think about his tattooed, muscular body occupying the same water and space that she just had. But when her hair was smooth, there was nothing to distract her from the sounds coming from behind the wall. The thin woven reed mats did nothing to muffle the little splashes as he moved or poured water over himself to rinse. Or the final cascade of water when he stood. Or the water droplets spattering the floor when he stepped from the tub. She imagined the linen cloth on his skin, sliding over the smooth muscles of his chest.

Fiona stood and went to the window. Once dressed, he would surely return to the fire, and she didn't want to be near him for fear he would somehow read her most recent shameful thoughts. He seemed to read her mind so easily other times. She stared out into the blackness, trying to lose herself in the fury of the storm, trying to focus on anything other than the image of his bare painted torso that refused to leave her mind.

A sudden hard gust of wind and rain pounded against the thick warped glass. Startled, Fiona stepped back. It was followed by another even harder blast. She watched horrified as the glass flexed inward towards her. Bowed and bulging from the force of the wind and water pounding against the other side, she was sure it would shatter. Glass did not bend like that! She stumbled backwards, raising a hand to shield her face, but the wind shifted suddenly again—the glass returning to normal as if nothing had ever happened.

Fiona whirled to face him, having completely forgotten all about her inappropriate thoughts. "Did you see that?" she asked in shocked awe. "Did you see the window? I was sure the glass would shatter! How it did not...I..."

He stood near the table, rolling up one of the sleeves of the white linen shirt. The same shirt that fit too snug on his upper arms and showed clear outline of his muscles. Muscles she'd found so repulsive until she'd seen the sculpted magnificence of them bare.

He didn't answer her. Only stared.

Not at the window.

Not at the storm outside.

At her.

He padded barefoot toward her, then stopped, inches away. He was standing so close now she could smell the harsh soap on his skin—could feel the heat emanating from his body. She looked up into his blue eyes, intense with longing and desire. She could not look away. He reached up to caress her cheek.

Fiona closed her eyes. She wanted this—to finally feel his touch. But it didn't come. When she opened her eyes again, his arm was back at his side, his face strained.

"Release me, Fiona. Release me of my vow to not lay hand," he murmured.

Her mouth formed the words, but she could not speak them.

"If you still fear me after all this, then hold me to my word to do you no harm, but release me of not laying hand," he repeated, his voice filled with urgent need.

"I release you," she whispered.

Chapter 19

Her three simple words obliterated every mental constraint he'd managed to maintain these past days. Lust surged within him like a wild beast suddenly freed. He wanted to pull her head back by her hair and run his teeth along her neck. To rip the odd garment and shift from her body and carry her to the bed. Nay, to press her up against the wall and take her standing. Caught off guard by the intensity of the urges, Gunnar struggled to check them.

Oblivious to his dangerous internal conflict, her beautiful green eyes gazed back at him, soft with longing, desire, and—trust. Something else welled within his chest. Something even stronger than the beast. She trusted him. She—trusted—him. He would not betray that. Not now. Not ever. In the face of that blazing certainty, the beast reluctantly began to retreat. His desire for her was in no way lessened, but her faith in him allowed him to control it.

He cupped the sides of her face and gently kissed her. The feel of her soft lips further tormented the beast and it howled its frustration but remained safely restrained deep within. Gunnar lifted her silken hair with one hand and moved to the sensitive area at the base of her ear.

When his lips left hers and kissed her jawline, Fiona thought to have a moment to collect her scattered wits, but the sensation of his breath on her neck and ear were even more dizzying. She placed the palms of her hands flat against his chest to steady herself, feeling the rippling strength of his muscles beneath the shirt.

After one last suckle of her earlobe, he kissed down the side of her neck. Fiona closed her eyes, losing herself in the warm softness of his lips, heightened by the occasional light scrape of his beard stubble on her skin. So focused was she on his mouth, she never felt his fingers on the silk ties of her chambergown—or his hand when it reached inside.

Not until it cupped one of her breasts.

Even through her shift, the callouses on his palm were distinct and well-defined. He brushed his thumb once over her nipple, then slowly brought it back and forth, stroking the sensitive surface through the thin material. Fiona gasped. Though he barely touched her and only in one place, the exquisite sensation shot through her entire body like gossamer bolts of summer lightning.

He pushed the chambergown from her shoulders. It slid down her back, the sleeves hanging up at the bend in her elbows. After untying the single tie at the top of her shift, he pulled it off one shoulder, exposing her other breast, his hand still cupping and teasing the first through the thin linen. He bent his head to suckle the nipple before taking more inside his mouth and running his tongue over the soft, smooth surface. Fiona tangled her fingers in his fair hair to keep herself upright.

He straightened and returned his attention to her face. Weaving the fingers of one hand through her thick tresses, he tightened his grip, pulling her head back. He kissed her lips again. Deeper this time, exploring, probing, tasting her. He tugged at her shift with his other hand, attempting to pull the remaining side from her shoulder, but it was too tight. A soft quick rip enlarged the neck opening and the thin shift joined the chambergown at her elbows.

But that wasn't enough for him. Taking both of her hands in his, he gently pulled them down until her arms were straight at her sides. The chambergown and shift dropped further, stalled now only by the connection at their wrists. He released one hand. Then the other. The chambergown and shift drifted to the floor. When the cool draft falling from the window panes nipped at her bare buttocks, Fiona realized he'd also somehow untied the single tie of her underdrawers and the light loose garment had fallen away with the others.

He kissed the length of her jawline to her second ear and nuzzled it. Continuing his kisses in a trail of fire down her neck, he reached the breast that had yet to experience the magic of his mouth. After teasing it for a moment, he lifted both of her breasts, pushing them closer together, then took turns suckling one and then the other.

Fiona's knees went weak. Before they gave way completely, his strong arms were around her, scooping her up and cradling her against his chest. "Hold on to me," he murmured as he moved toward the bed. She nodded and tightened her arms around his neck.

Supporting her body with one arm, he reached down and yanked the covers back, opening the bed wide before leaning over and laying her gently on the feather tick with her head on a pillow. He stood up, snatched his shirt over his head, and reached for the drawstring at the top of his trousers.

Embarrassed, Fiona looked away. Suddenly deprived of the strength and support of his body, she felt awkward and exposed, lying there naked and alone watching him—waiting for him to...what? Subconsciously she pulled an arm across her breasts.

Gunnar froze and swore at himself under his breath. She'd responded so strongly to his touch, it had been easy to lose himself in the moment, easy to forget he was her first. Still wearing his trousers, he lay down on the bed beside her. Reaching for her chin, he gently turned her face back to him. Her eyes were wide and uncertain, but still willing. *Thank the gods!* He kissed her again, reassuring her. Starting over, he nuzzled her neck and nibbled her earlobes, rekindling and stoking her desire.

Fiona inched closer to him until the full length of his body was solid and warm against her side. She attempted to roll toward him, to feel his chest against hers and conceal her bareness at the same time, but he pushed her furthest shoulder back to the bed and held it there.

When she ceased resisting, he pressed a light kiss to her lips, then looked to his hand that still held her shoulder. One at a time, he slowly folded each of his fingers into a fist, until only one remained touching her. Using that single fingertip, he began to draw an imaginary line—from the point of her shoulder, along the full length of her collarbone, to the bounding pulse on both sides of her neck. Moving with unhurried concentration as if he were mapping her, he followed the soft ridges of her windpipe to the hollow at the base of her throat, then continued down between her breasts, circling but not touching them.

He traced each of her ribs, carefully avoiding the peaks that strained towards him. Only when her body arched and twisted toward his hand, presenting her breasts for his touch, did he oblige—lazily spiraling his finger up their soft rounded contours in small tight rings. At the top, he skimmed the pebbled surfaces with the back edge of his fingernail before trapping the centers lightly between his thumb and forefinger, rolling them into distinct hard points. Fiona's sharp inhale tapered to a soft moan.

He ducked his head for a quick suckle of each, then resumed his fingertip's slow trail down over her flat stomach, her skin quivering at his touch. After pausing briefly at her belly button, he began to draw slow ever-widening circles. Without stopping his finger's leisurely procession, he looked deep into her eyes and kissed her.

Her skin tingled in anticipation of his touch, and the trail it left behind was like a light burn. Each wider circle took his finger ever lower, toward a pulsing ache she'd never experienced before. His finger grazed the top edge of her curly mound. Her breath caught in her throat. He paused. She held her breath, willing him to continue.

When his finger finally resumed its journey, she took a ragged pensive breath. No longer moving in a circle, it forged lower, parting her downy curls in a straight line. Fiona gasped as her senses were flooded by thousands of new stimuli. Every tiny hair, even those that his hand barely brushed, joined her skin in a clamoring report of his progress.

He paused again at the top of her cleft and kissed her once more. But she didn't want his kiss, didn't want any delay in what was to come next. Everything he'd done—the trail of his kisses, the burn of his touch, the tingling tightness he'd left in her breasts, had been building to this. She bit his lower lip and tugged it to one side as her hips tilted up to meet him—needing him to not tease anymore, needing him to...

His finger slid between her soft folds, then pressed upwards, finding the source of the throbbing ache. Fiona moaned. He rubbed gently, the rough skin of his finger now suddenly slick—satisfying a need, but at the same time awakening another. She moaned again.

Gunnar kicked off his trousers and moved over her, spreading her knees apart slightly with his own. She uttered a low inarticulate whimper of disapproval when he withdrew his finger, but he needed both arms to support himself as he began the exploration of her body again—this time with his mouth. Beginning with her lips, he made his way back down her neck, to each of her breasts, teasing them with warm suckling and alternating cool flicks with the tip of his tongue.

He knew she was ready; her body rose to meet him wherever he touched it, yet still, he teased—taking more care than he'd ever taken before. He wanted her to be sure, needed her to be sure, needed her surrender to be complete—and not just of her body, but her mind and spirit as well.

He paused, looking up at her face before proceeding lower. Her eyes were closed, her breath coming in fast shallow gasps. "Fiona. Look at me." She opened her eyes. They were drunk with desire. No trepidation, no trace of uncertainty remained. "Do you trust me?" She nodded a quick short nod. "Then I want you to watch." Keeping his eyes locked on hers, he kissed down the middle of her stomach. Her eyes widened as his lips paused at her belly button, then passed.

"Spread your legs for me, Fiona," he murmured, his voice so husky it was barely recognizable. His eyes burned with an intensity she'd never seen in them before—a fervent combination of need and control. She wanted to do as he directed but managed only a slight parting, unable to open herself wide.

The subtle movement was apparently compliance enough. He shifted his body lower, gazing upon her virgin rima with the rapt anticipation of a man looking upon the wealth of the world. He leaned forward.

Surely he wasn't going to...

She started to reach for him, to pull his face away, but his fingers touched her opening, immobilizing her. She held her breath as they began probing, spreading, seeking. Then his tongue. Her back arched and her head pressed into the pillow, her body a slave to the ecstasy created by his touch and kiss. She opened her legs wider for him, and he responded. His lips suckling, his tongue flicking. It was too much. She couldn't take anything more. Her pounding heart exploded in her ears. Her body began to shudder and convulse. She wondered briefly if she were dying—and didn't care.

Gunnar moved on top of her, spreading her legs further with his knees. She could feel his hardness there, just outside her, solid and hot against her still-pulsing node. He kissed her lips and looked deep into her eyes, his face strained, his body hard as stone.

"The first time is painful for a woman," he murmured, his voice tight with withheld desire.

Fiona didn't know what to say. She knew he was asking her but didn't know how to properly agree. She reached up with both of her hands and pulled his face to hers, giving him her answer with a kiss.

Gunnar groaned, keeping his lips locked to hers as he reached down with one hand and guided himself between her soft folds. He pressed inside, pushing past resistance. Her body stiffened but there was no turning back now. He continued to push deeper until his full shaft was locked inside. He paused, feeling her shift and squirm as she adjusted to taking all of him. He released her lips.

"That's the worst," he whispered. "Are you alright?"

Fiona didn't know what she was. Her pulse still roared in her ears. The area of her body that had brought her unimaginable pleasure now felt stretched beyond limits. He had warned her of pain, and she'd expected something sharp and piercing, not this dull, continuous ache like her very bones were being driven apart. She wanted to tell him to stop, but as she looked into his eyes, so torn between the strain of holding back his desire and his genuine concern for her, she knew she could not.

"Aye," she murmured. Seeing the overwhelming relief wash over his face, Fiona didn't care how bad it got. She would not deny him. Slowly, he began to move within her, pulling out slightly, then sliding back inside. Each time taking him a little further. Each stroke a little deeper. At first, she clenched her teeth, determined not to cry out, but then she didn't need to. With every thrust, her body melded to him, accepted him. Her hips began to move with his, and when he strained inside her, his body shuddering as he called her name, she wanted him never to stop.

He went limp on top of her, briefly pressing her down into the soft feather tick. She luxuriated in the feel of his weight. He lifted himself onto his elbows and stroked the hair from her face. "Fiona," he whispered. "My beautiful, Fiona. Apologies if I hurt you. The next time will be better."

The next time. Fiona's stomach fluttered at the thought of it. The pain had subsided, leaving a dull numbness in some areas, while the indescribable pleasure remained vivid in her mind. He withdrew from inside her, then rolled onto his side. His shaft against her thigh was so soft now she could barely feel it. Such an unbelievable difference, but like him in so many other ways—hard and ruthless, yet soft and gentle.

She twisted her body with her back to his chest, wanting as much of their skin as possible to remain touching. He wrapped his arms around her and pulled her tighter, kissing her hair.

Fiona had never felt as content as she did in that moment. She wanted never to forget a single detail. The feel of his breath on her hair. His strong arms around her waist. His chest hair tickling her back. But it was the simple feeling of his warm bare skin pressed against hers—a feeling more satisfying than anything she'd ever imagined, that she hoped to remember the most.

Chapter 20

DAY SEVEN

Fiona awoke disoriented but feeling oddly secure. Her sleepy eyes focused on the masculine arm draped across her waist and the end of... *Thor's hammer?* The events of the previous night came back in a rush. Her cheeks grew hot and her heart began to race. Ever so slowly, she turned her head to look up at his face, hoping not to wake him, but his deep blue eyes were calmly studying her. She flushed even deeper, wondering how long he'd been awake—wondering what he must think of her after how she'd behaved. He leaned over and kissed her gently on the forehead.

"Sleep well?" he asked softly. The same question he'd asked her every morning, but the circumstances of this morning being so different

"Aye," she said with a shy smile. "And you?"

"That was the best night of my life," he said sincerely.

She wasn't sure how to respond and returned her cheek to the pillow, snuggling her back closer to him, reveling again in the feel of his warm skin against hers. Tightness in her bladder intruded upon her bliss. She tried to ignore it, but the need grew more urgent. She scrambled to think of some excuse to leave the bed and his embrace—something other than her base need; she could hardly reference that to him, but came up with nothing suitable. Her chambergown and shift lying in a heap by the window only complicated her dilemma. She knew it was silly, but she dreaded the thought of walking naked across the cold room in front of him.

"What's wrong?" he asked.

She bit her lip. "I need to use the chamberpot, and I have no clothes."

"You're worried I'll see your body?" He chuckled. "It's a bit late for that. I've already memorized every inch of it."

Fiona couldn't wait a moment longer. She slid to the edge of the bed and swung her legs over the side, sitting up with a quilt draped over her. After taking a deep breath, she stood, dropped the quilt, and ran on her tiptoes across the cold floor to the privacy behind the reed changing wall.

Crouched over the chamberpot relieving herself, she felt the unusual dull ache inside. It was similar to the ache she felt when she rode hard after not riding for awhile, but not the same; this soreness was in different muscles—muscles she didn't even know she had.

After wiping with one of the soft dock leaves from the small box next to the chamberpot, she stood and peered through a crack in the reed panels. He was sitting up in the bed now, covers around his waist, eyes fixed on the privacy screen. *Of course.* Fiona fretted. What if the stark morning light revealed the flaws he'd missed the night before in soft firelight? What if he was disappointed? Running away from the bed, he'd only been able to see her rear, but now he would truly see everything.

"I'm coming back now; you should look away," she called out.

"Why would I do such a thing?"

"Because it's proper."

"Apologies, but I will not." When she didn't reappear, he added, "It must be cold back there. It's quite warm here in the bed; you should hurry back."

Fiona glanced down. Goosebumps were forming all over her body, making her look even worse—like she had chicken skin. "Oooh." Covering her breasts with one arm and her womanhood with the other, she scurried across the room and slipped under the covers. He reached across the bed and pulled her to him.

"Why would you ever want to cover such a perfect body?" he murmured into her neck.

"Is it truly...good?" she asked.

"Good? Is what good?"

"My body. I know you've seen many women unclothed, and I wondered about it before."

"You wondered before what I thought of your body?" he asked, incredulous.

She nodded, embarrassed.

"And when, pray tell, was this? I had no idea you harbored such thoughts."

"When I was changing into dry clothes after we swam."

Gunnar exhaled, whistling lightly through his teeth. "Knowing you were stripped bare only a few feet away tested me to my limits that day. And had I known you were thinking such thoughts...well, probably better that I did not."

"I didn't want you to see it to enjoy it," she defended. "I only wished to know your expert opinion—because of your experiences."

"In my expert opinion, your body is perfection and would rival that of the goddess Freya."

"Do not jest. I know that's not true, and I sought a serious answer."

"I was serious. Shall I describe to you what I see?" He didn't wait for her to respond. "Your hair is like the most glorious silk. The waves and curls ensure that some part of it is always at the perfect angle to capture light, making it shine like golden thread. Your eyes are the most beautiful color I've ever seen—like the precious emeralds on my sword, with an occasional fleck of the paler jade stone from the far, far East. And your lips. Your lips are full and soft and shaped in a way that is pure invitation to be kissed." He paused. "But I could see all those things without your clothes removed, and that's not what you wished to know—is it?"

Her pulse had increased at the intimacy of his words and the admiration in his voice. She didn't dare encourage him to continue; it was too brazen. "Nay, it's not," she whispered, shocked by her own audacity.

He smiled. "The smell of you when I'm close, kissing you here," he nuzzled her neck, "is beyond sweet. Not sweet like perfume or flower. It's a unique warm sweet scent. It is your scent. It is you. I do not have words adequate to describe how it makes me feel, but it's exhilarating and steadying at the same time, and I long to breathe it in." He pressed his nose against her neck and inhaled deeply. "Your skin is so smooth everywhere, but here," he traced the side of her breast with the back of his hand, "and the inside of your thighs, the softness is unimaginable—and it begs my touch and my lips.

"Your breasts fill my palm—the perfect size. Too large, and a woman's breasts are more like a milk cow's, sagging and ponderous. Too small...well, too small leaves a man hungry for more. And yours are high and firm and evenly shaped—with pink nipples, which happen to be my favorite color." He slid a hand up from her waist and brushed one with his thumb before bending his head down to suckle it.

Fiona gasped, but didn't move or speak. He continued. "Your small waist makes the flare of your hips even more appealing, and the curve of your buttocks is just right for gripping." He paused, and she could tell he had smiled. "And your cunny fits me like a glove," he whispered.

"Stop! Do not say anything more."

"Your body is perfection to me, Fiona. That is my expert opinion."

A knock sounded on the door. Fiona jerked one way, then the other, not sure of where to go, only of the need to hide. Gunnar chuckled at her response and held her tight.

"Who is it?" he called out.

"'Tis Garrett, my lord."

"You must not let him in," Fiona whispered frantically.

"Pull the covers up over your head. He'll not see you."

"Nay! He will know."

"Fiona, they'll already know. We shared a room."

"They may suspect, but they haven't seen. 'Tis different. Please," she pleaded. "I'll never be able to face them."

"Very well." He kissed her cheek. "One moment, Garrett. I'll be right there." Gunnar stood and walked around the bed to his trousers, pulled them on, and tied them. Grabbing his shirt next, he turned it right side out, slipping it over his head as he walked to the door. After one last smile at her, he opened it, stepped out into the hallway, and closed it behind him.

Fiona lay with the covers pulled tight to her chin. She wondered briefly what they were talking about, then found her thoughts returning to his words describing her. Once again, he'd just voiced whatever was in his head, with no censoring for decency. But she had asked. And he'd given an honest answer—was that such a bad thing? But he'd actually described her breasts, and her... Oh, it was too much to even think about.

"What did he want?" she asked as Gunnar climbed back into bed. A gust of wind and rain rattled against the window.

"He asked when he should harness the horses. He knows we are to return you home today."

"What did you tell him?"

"That we still needed to eat so it would be at least an hour."

Distant thunder rumbled outside.

"We can't go back out in that."

"I gave my word to return you home after seven days. Your father will be expecting you."

"Not to travel in weather like this. He would much prefer I stay an extra day and be safe, no matter where I was coming from."

"So you wish to stay?" he asked.

"I think it's the only responsible thing to do."

"But your seven days are up. You are free to go."

Fiona noted the quirk in the side of his mouth and realized he was lying—about all of it. He hadn't told Garrett to ready the horses. He just wanted to hear her say she wished to remain with him. Which she did. The idea of returning home now was painful, but that was beside the point. He was toying with her again. Two could play that game.

She took a deep breath and nodded, pretending to consider his words. "That's true. I'm finally free. You know, I thought this week would never end. Very well then." She slid to the edge of the bed. "No sense wasting another whole hour. I can be ready sooner. I shall call for Garrett and tell him to begin preparin' the horses now." She glanced back over her shoulder coyly and laughed at his stunned expression.

"Will you now?" he said and lunged for her.

Fiona squealed and tried to stand, but his hands grasped her hips and pulled her back. "You should have seen your face." She laughed as she struggled to escape him.

"You mock me now?" he grunted as he maneuvered unsuccessfully to capture her wrists.

"You deserved it. You lied to me about what you said to Garrett," she said, managing to bring a knee up between them. She pushed hard with her leg, strengthened by years of riding. The move and her strength took him by surprise; he barely caught himself before rolling off onto the floor.

Fiona scrambled for the opposite edge of the bed, almost making it. Almost. He dragged her back to him, straddled her lower body with his knees, and pinned both of her wrists next to her shoulders.

"You should know better than to try to fight me." He shook his head and grinned at her. "You've seen how skilled I am."

"What about your word to not lay hand? What if I were to invoke that again?" She giggled and continued to squirm.

"It's far too late for that. And that's not how it works anyway. You don't get to *invoke* it. You've released me, and I can assure you I'll never agree to be bound by such a thing again."

Fiona smiled and let her head sink into the pillow. She'd made her point, having done far better than she'd thought to against him. Further resistance was futile. His grin faded to a loving smile as he looked at her. His eyes suddenly filled with the look she'd seen so many times before. The look she'd mistaken early on for predatory hunger, but now understood exactly what it was. Desire. Pure unadulterated desire—for her.

Her body began to tingle in response. Nothing had changed. Their positions remained the same, yet in that instant everything was different. Gone was the playfulness. Longing had taken its place.

"Fiona," he said her name as if it pained him. The raw need in his voice sent her pulse pounding. Seeing the effect she had on him was a heady experience, and so shocking to her. Shocking that such a man—a man who could take whatever he wanted, whenever he wanted, was weak for her. He bent to kiss her lips, releasing her hands. She tangled them in his blond hair, pulling him to her, kissing him back.

Fiona lay on the bed beside him, her hair damp with perspiration, waiting for the roaring in her ears and the pounding in her chest to subside. His arm remained carelessly flung across her bare stomach. He'd been right. The second time was better. There'd been a little tenderness at first, but then it was gone, and only pleasure remained. How had she never known of this? She knew that men and women shared a bed after they were married, but she'd oft heard it referred to as a woman's duty and had been under the distinct impression it was something unpleasant to be endured. Certainly never that it was like this.

Did everyone else know? Is that why women, young and old, made moon-eyes at him? It was no wonder. And why did it not feel wrong? She was defiled—unsuitable for proper marriage. She should feel shame, but the thought bothered her not at all. In fact, she felt like nothing had ever been more right.

"You never answered me when I asked you if you wanted to stay," he said.

"I did."

"No, you said it was the responsible thing to do."

"But you knew."

"I want to hear you say it."

She smiled. "I wish to stay here with you. In fact, I hope the storm rages on and never lets up."

He pulled her into a tight embrace and they lay in silence. "Whatever shall we do for a whole day?" he murmured into her hair. "Cooped up in this room, unable to go outside..."

"Perhaps we could eat. I'm famished."

Gunnar laughed out loud, her response not at all the one he'd hinted at. "I'll see to a meal; I'm quite hungry as well. And we do have to keep your strength up. What would you like?"

"Anything. Eggs, bread, cheese, salted pork—or any kind of meat, honeyed oat porridge...and if they have any dried fruit left from last year, wild berries or apples. Oh, and a cup of milk," she added. Focused on her list, she didn't notice his grin.

"It seems you worked up an appetite."

"I did," she agreed, matching his smile.

"With so many folk here, I don't know what they'll have left for food stores," he warned.

"I'll be content with anything, so long as there is much of it."

"Before we go to the trouble of getting you dressed, let me see if there's a woman who can tend to us today. If there is, your shift and...what do you call that thing?"

"My chambergown."

"...your shift and chambergown should suffice. They're appropriate for a married lady with her husband and less to remove later. Otherwise, I suppose I can bumble through the laces of one of your gowns in reverse, though it would likely take considerable time. I've had far less practice. Putting clothes *on* a woman goes against my nature."

"And therein lies the truth," she accused.

He brushed her temple with a kiss, dressed and left, returning quickly with good news. A woman would be up shortly.

Fiona slipped from the bed and picked up her torn shift from the floor. Embarrassed, she rolled it up and pulled a new shift from her trunk. She'd just finished tying the last bow on her chambergown when there was a muffled rap on the door that sounded more like a kick than a knock. Gunnar opened it, and a woman entered carrying a huge tray heaped with food—a feast. There was another tureen of soup—this time cabbage and salted pork, a loaf of bread, a large bowl of oat porridge, a small pitcher of milk, separate small crocks of honey and butter, a block of cheese, and a leg of roasted lamb. Fiona looked to Gunnar in disbelief.

"In case you get hungry later," he said and stepped behind her. "I'd prefer not to be interrupted again, and you've been eating like a horse," he whispered in her ear and squeezed her buttocks, moving away before she could respond.

Not that she could acknowledge his wicked, intimate action in front of the maid.

While they ate, the woman laid a fire, straightened the bed, and emptied the chamber pot. After verifying that they needed nothing further, she curtsied and left them alone.

When they'd eaten their fill, Gunnar stood and moved to the large chair in front of the fireplace. He removed his tunic and shirt, sat down, and patted his legs. "Come."

After only a moment's hesitation, Fiona removed her chambergown, then sat sideways across his lap in her shift with her head nestled in the crook of his shoulder. His one arm supported her back and held her to his chest, while his other rested on her knees. "Are you comfortable?" he asked.

"Aye," she murmured, staring at the flames. "And you? I'm not too heavy?"

He chuckled. "No."

"What shall become of us? When the storm passes?" She voiced the dilemma that had plagued him for days.

Gunnar took a deep breath, then exhaled long and slow. "You know I've sworn to return to the East, and I must go. But I will return for you as soon as my trip is complete. I would be apart from you not a single moment longer than is absolutely necessary." He rested his chin on the top of her head. "I even gave thought to taking you with me, but the trip is far too grueling and miserable. And I have no idea what we'll find there—if anything even remains of Jarl's settlement."

"How long will it take? Your journey?"

"If all goes well, seven months."

Seven months? She had lived a lifetime in seven days. "So long?"

He nodded. "But know that I will return to you as quickly as I can. Then I shall find a way for us to be together. And not like this—stolen moments— pretending and hiding. When I return, I will find a way for us to truly be together—as man and wife." He kissed her hair.

As man and wife. Fiona snuggled deeper against his chest, wanting to believe him, not wanting to examine at that moment all the reasons why his words could never happen. Pushing all thoughts from her mind, she focused on the slow, steady thudding of his heartbeat against her cheek.

They spent the rest of the day learning of each others' minds and exploring each others' bodies. Insulated from the outside world, they shared everything. With the last of all doubt and pretense stripped away, no subject or act was too bold or taboo. Alone, there was no one to judge them, and they did not judge each other.

Fiona was curious about everything about him. His life. His people and how they lived. His beliefs. His gods. He was attentive, relaxed, and affectionate, answering all of her questions with none of his earlier sarcasm. Being with him was so...easy. She gave not a moment's worry to her appearance, how she acted or what she said. She didn't have to conceal things she didn't want him to see. He saw everything. He listened to everything. And none of it affected his opinion of her.

Gunnar couldn't get enough of her questions. Seeing his world through her eyes as she absorbed the things he told her, moved him deeply. Even when he confessed things he knew would disturb her, she tried to view and understand them in the context of the different rules of his culture. She was so inquisitive, so open-minded and so...good.

She restored his faith in...everything. She knew of cruelty and death but had been mostly sheltered from it, and she still believed in a future where anything was possible. He felt a surge of fierce protectiveness to keep it that way—to stand between her and anything that would jade her to life. As much as his body thrilled to join with hers, it paled in comparison to what she restored in his heart.

"How did you meet your wife?"

"I raided her village."

"Did you force her?"

Gunnar considered her question for a long while before answering. He knew how the truth would sound to her, but he would not lie. He watched her eyes closely, then nodded. "It was something I deeply regretted later."

"She was able to forgive you?"

He nodded again. "I had a lot to overcome, but we were married the following year."

"Why did you not force me?"

"Let's just say I learned a great many things about women in the brief time I was married." He smiled a small rueful smile. "My people have a saying that marriage seasons a man, like the sea seasons a mighty tree into driftwood."

"But you've admitted to lying with female prisoners in the East."

His brow furrowed slightly. "That's different. They're slaves; it's acceptable. Just as with your people, it's acceptable to work a slave to death." She didn't criticize or scold, only nodded, but her unvoiced disapproval burned like a hot iron. Gunnar had never given a second thought to slavery. It was the way of the entire world, not just his people. But that she would be disappointed in him by association suddenly tainted the idea of it. He didn't want her to be disappointed by anything he did.

Later that evening, Gunnar cut thin slices from the cold leg of lamb, then pulled the table to within easy reach of the large chair in front of the fire. They sat down together, his arm once again behind her back, supporting her crosswise on his lap. Using a long stick he'd sharpened from the kindling, he skewered meat slices one at a time, held them over the flames until they sizzled, then offered her each piece after it had cooled slightly.

Since he had only one free arm, and it was warming their supper, Fiona alternated eating a piece with feeding him the next. They shared a smile when he sucked her fingertips clean after every bite, and after she held her goblet of wine for him to drink.

When they could eat no more, they remained sitting in mellow silence. The muscles of his chest were soft against her cheek now that he was relaxed, and Fiona absently examined his skin—the golden-brown hair, the green and black exotic symbols...the scars.

"I've never known anyone with so many scars. Are they painful?"

He shook his head. "Men who receive wounds to the bone sometimes complain of pain that lingers, but mine have all been wounds of the flesh. After they heal, I'm unaware of them."

Her fingers traced a scar beneath his left collarbone, then moved down the side of his ribcage and trailed over another. He twitched, air whistling between his clenched teeth in a short gasp. She jerked her hand away.

"Did that hurt? You said..."

"No."

"Then why..." she lifted her head to look at his face.

"It's not a pain you inflict, but a pleasure so intense it borders somewhere between the two."

She frowned, not understanding.

"I would say it is similar to when I kiss you behind your ear."

Fiona's eyes widened with comprehension. His breath alone on her ear was enough to make her insides melt and her knees weak. "So if I were to do this..." She leaned forward and kissed the scar under his collarbone. "Or this." She trailed the tip of her tongue along the rough scar on his ribs. He held his breath, his body rigid. She smiled at his obvious response. "How have you withstood such grievous injuries when your skin is so sensitive? I would think to be cut would have been unbearable."

"My skin is not always so."

"Only when being touched by a woman?"

"Not even that. Sometimes between a man and a woman there's a... special spark. It's not something you can make; it's either there or it's not. I've only felt it once before."

"Even with all the women you have known?"

"Even with all the women."

"And when did you first feel it—with me?"

Gunnar smiled. "When you stood ankle-deep in mud with a crossbow pointed at my chest. When the wind pulled your glorious hair loose and danced with it in the rain and moonlight. When your eyes blazed with triumph—and loathing, and I knew you would pull the trigger."

"You found those things a spark?" she laughed.

"I told you, one cannot choose it. And yes, those images are forever burned into my mind—and my heart."

In that moment, Fiona understood what it was about him that set him so far above any man she'd ever known. It wasn't his strength or impressive form, though she treasured those things, too. It was something far more profound. Something poignant and pure. Gunnar didn't show his affection by giving her baubles or trinkets. He gave her the rarest gift of all. Himself—his true self. He shared everything: his insecurities, his faults, his fears, his feelings. He peeled away every protective layer of deception and guile, revealing to her the vulnerable man within.

Not that she felt he was in any way less dangerous than when she'd first met him. If anything, she knew now that he was more so, but she understood him, understood the code he lived by. And she knew beyond a shadow of a doubt, she had nothing to fear.

Chapter 21

DAY EIGHT

Fiona stood staring out the window at the blue sky. The inn courtyard below was clear, but not far off, entire trees lay uprooted, and broken branches littered the ground. Gunnar, Garrett, Bryen, and Orin had left on foot at first light to inspect the roads and were just returning.

"The gods favor us yet again," Gunnar reported with a smile as he closed the door behind him and hung his cloak on a hook. "The roads are impassable. Men are clearing them, but we have another day." He glanced at the untouched food he'd had delivered after he left. "You haven't eaten?"

"I was waiting for you." It was partly true. She'd been unable to eat, dreading that he would return and say they were leaving today.

He frowned. "I didn't mean for you to wait. Come, let's eat."

Fiona joined him at the table and, after a quick meal, they retired to their chair. As she took her position on his lap, she felt the hard bulge in his trousers even though he'd made love to her before he left that morning. She smiled. It was such a strange appendage, but one that fascinated her after her initial embarrassment. Sheathed in skin so soft, it rivaled her own even when it was rock hard. And it loved her, standing at full jubilant attention whenever she was near, reaching for her, waving to her, oftentimes much to his chagrin. Her smile faded as her thoughts moved to more serious ones.

"Must you really go—back to the East?" she asked.

"You know I must."

"Why can't someone else deliver your friends' belongings?"

"Because I gave my word."

"Must we leave tomorrow then? The longer we stay, the roads will only get better. I could send word to my father that I am well and that my return will be delayed because of the storm. He'll not question it."

"I would like for nothing more than to remain here with you, but I dare not if I wish to be assured of making it back before winter. I will not gamble with something so important as that. And because of the promise I made to you in exchange for your agreement to accompany me, I'll have an additional delay acquiring the necessary slaves to make the journey."

"You will keep our initial bargain?"

"Of course. You've more than held up your end," he teased and traced a finger across her lips.

"Will there be other women?" Fiona held her breath. She knew there would be. Women were drawn to him. And now she understood why. After seven months, would he even remember her as anything special?

"Does that worry you?"

"Aye," she murmured. "In truth, the thought of you with someone else... like this. It makes my chest ache."

"Sshh. Sshh," he murmured into her hair. "Think no more of that. There can be no other woman for me now. You have ruined me for anyone else."

She looked up at him, unconvinced. He took her chin in one palm and looked deep into her eyes. "I swear to you, so long as you will have me, I'll take no other woman to my furs."

"Not even a slave?" she asked, knowing he didn't consider them the same.

He chuckled softly; she already knew him so well. "Not even a slave. The ache in my groin will be a constant reminder of what awaits me here with you and shall speed my return. But I also have a vow to extract from you."

"I shall not lay with another man," she offered.

Gunnar coughed. "I'd not thought to have to worry about that," he said with a frown.

"Then what?"

"Promise me you'll not involve yourself in freeing slaves in any role while I'm away. The thought of what could happen to you..." He did not share what those thoughts were, but the terrible nature of them was evident in the sudden stiffness of his body.

"I promise," she said, thinking of nothing other than to ease his distress.

"I ask it only until I return. I know it's important to you, and we shall address it together when I'm here to keep you safe."

Chapter 22

DAY NINE

"The gates are just around the next bend," Fiona murmured into his chest, hating to voice the words, but she'd already waited to the last possible moment for them not to be seen.

Gunnar reached for the cane and tapped the silver lion's head on the ceiling. The carriage immediately slowed, and after a few soothing words to the horses from Garrett, came to a complete stop.

Gunnar remained sitting with his back angled into a plush rear corner, his long legs stretched diagonally across the carriage, boots resting on the opposite cushion. Fiona lay lengthwise alongside him, her head on his chest, her upper body safely wedged between his and the thick cushioned seat back. His arm was wrapped protectively behind her shoulder, his large palm resting intimately on her hip. Neither spoke; both remained perfectly still. The only sounds were the clinking of the horses' bridles and an occasional stomping hoof as they shifted in their harnesses.

"You must go," Gunnar whispered into her hair before folding his legs to the floor and gently easing his arm from behind her as he sat them both upright.

Fiona nodded and rearranged her skirt, keeping her gaze fixed on her hands. Her eyes welled with tears at the realization this could possibly be the last time she ever saw him. She couldn't look at him.

"Fiona," he said gently.

She did not look up.

"Fiona," he repeated.

When still she didn't acknowledge him, Gunnar reached for her chin. He tipped it towards him, leaning forward to better see her face. She remained looking down at first, then took a deep breath, and slowly raised her eyes to meet his. Tears clung to her thick dark lashes but did not fall. The pain in her green eyes wounded him more deeply than any sword ever had. He hated to see it for any reason, and to be the cause...

"Please don't cry," he murmured and pulled her tight, his heart feeling as if it were being torn from his chest. "I could not bear it."

Fiona nodded against his tunic, unable to speak for fear her voice would betray her, and she would, in fact, burst into tears.

Taking her face in both of his hands, he kissed her tenderly, then held his forehead pressed to hers. "I will return for you. I swear it. As soon as I am physically able, I will return."

They sat with their foreheads pressed together for another long moment, then Gunnar took a deep breath and brushed her temple with his lips. Without another word, he turned for the door, opened it, and stepped outside into the falling evening light, closing it behind him.

Fiona squeezed her eyes tight and leaned her head back against the cushion, her fists clenched at her sides. The carriage felt desolately empty without him. His presence, his warmth, his strength—gone. The lump in her throat was so large she couldn't swallow, and her eyes burned as she fought the overwhelming urge to fling open the door and call him back. To beg him not to go—beg him not to leave her.

She heard his deep voice say something quietly to the footmen on the back, then his footsteps to the front and another few words to Garrett. Her heart was beating so hard, the rushing of blood through her ears made it impossible to make out his words. She was sure he was reiterating the instructions he'd given them that morning about when they dropped her off—a last reminder for them to make haste and not speak to any of her servants. She stared at the door, holding her breath, willing for it to open again, unsure of her resolve if it did.

With a soft whistle from Garrett, the carriage lurched forward. Fiona closed her eyes and pressed the back of one hand to her mouth, the other to her stomach, trying to physically hold back the sobs that threatened. She would not cry. She could not. She dare not. She would be home in a matter of minutes. The key to the continued success of her lie was for her return to not arouse suspicion. If she alighted from the carriage a tearful wreck, it would do nothing less, and pressing probing questions would surely follow.

She sat up straighter as the carriage made the turn through the gates of Tir na Lionmhar. "Get hold of yourself, Fiona," she whispered fiercely. She took several deep breaths, gently dabbing the tears from her eyes, careful not to rub or apply too much pressure that might leave red marks. A few more deep breaths. She summoned a fake smile, trying to imagine how she'd be after spending a week with friends.

She'd be tired from the journey home, especially with the roads still rough from the storm. She could say she was exhausted and groggy from a long day of fitful dozing in a moving carriage. It would explain her slightly disheveled appearance and any redness in her face. She'd ask for a bath straightaway and perhaps, if she were very lucky, she could take to her bed without talking in any detail about her trip. Aye, that would do it. It had to.

The carriage slowed, then shifted and rocked as Bryen jumped down before it came to a complete stop. Orin was already sliding her trunks to the edge. He quickly handed them down to Bryen, who set them gently on the ground.

"My lady?" Bryen called out to her as he set the box step outside the door.

"Aye, Bryen, I'm ready," she replied and plastered a false, weary smile on her face. The door opened, and she reached for Bryen's hand.

"How very improper for them to leave you so—a lady standing alone amidst her luggage." Meirna voiced her disapproval as she watched the carriage speed away.

"They fear for their families in the storm and are eager to return to them."

"That's hardly an excuse. A few moments to see you properly sorted would make little difference in their families' fates," Meirna muttered.

"It was at my insistence, Meirna. I don't know how it was here, but in some places the destruction from the storm was terrible. I pray for them and their families."

"That's because you have such a good heart." Meirna patted her hand before casting one last frown at the departing carriage.

"Perhaps Siara could draw me a bath as soon as possible. The roads were frightful; my body feels as though 'tis tied in a thousand knots." It was not a lie; the only untruth was the cause.

"Of course, my dear," Meirna agreed, happy to fuss over her, the rude footmen forgotten. "Are you hungry?"

"Very," Fiona lied. "But only something light to start with, please. At least until my stomach has recovered from all the bouncing. You cannot believe the poor condition of the roads." Fiona did her best to make small talk as she led the way inside and up the stairs to her room.

Gunnar paced on the side of the road, counting the minutes. He alternated between hoping for things to go well and hoping for things to go wrong—so horribly wrong that it would give him no choice but to... What? If there'd been another option, he would've already taken it. And unless he came up with a plan, he'd face this same dilemma when he returned. His oath to Jarl and Tryggr would be fulfilled, but his circumstances with Fiona would remain unchanged.

He needed to consider it as a tactical problem. Take a full accounting of the obstacles, measure them against the things in his favor, then decide upon the best strategy to achieve his goal. It was no different than planning a raid. He could do this; it was his strength.

Ireland was her home, and the land more to his liking than any other place he'd ever been, so it had to be here. But with no free land to claim, that left only three options: take land from the Irish, join an existing Viking settlement, or take land from other Vikings. He quickly eliminated the first. As the wife of a Viking conqueror, Fiona would be a pariah—never to be accepted by her peers as he wished.

The second option would be the easiest, and there would be other Irish nobles—those who'd agreed to pay tribute to the Northern invaders rather than abandon their lands. But it would require that he pledge his allegiance to another man, something he was loathe to do. Not only because he'd find it difficult to follow someone else's orders now, but also because he knew those orders would eventually lead to expansion deeper into Ireland. The peace they experienced now was temporary. The Irish didn't want to see it, and the Northmen there denied it, but Gunnar knew it was the truth. The current Viking settlements were merely footholds—places to build their strength in numbers and wealth until they were ready to strike again.

That left option three. Wresting land away from another Viking—a Norse or Dane warlord with his own battle-tested army. It would require a sizable force, but Gunnar knew he could raise one. After this next campaign to the East, there would be plenty of newly-rich men desiring to settle—men who would follow him. He could return with a fleet of ships filled with veteran fighters whose abilities would be more than up to the task.

Gunnar scowled and ran a hand through his hair. Was he really considering killing his own people for personal gain? To what end? To be named a king? The very thought made bile rise in the back of his throat. He'd be no different than the Dane kings whose quest for land and riches had cost him the last four years of his life.

There had to be another way—something he was missing.

His thoughts were interrupted by the sound of horses' hooves and the rumbling of carriage wheels on the road. Hope surged unbidden in his chest that somehow she was returning to him. When the carriage came into view and her trunks were no longer on the roof, that hope withered to a hollow pit that settled deep in his gut.

"All go well?" he asked curtly, waving off Bryen before he could step down to open the door.

"Aye, my lord," Garrett replied.

"Take me back to the Red Dragon." Gunnar glanced around the carriage interior as he climbed inside and closed the door. He hated everything about it now. Hated that it was empty. Hated that even knowing better, he'd still looked for her inside. Hated the crushing disappointment he felt when she wasn't there. Hated the gods for forcing him to make such a decision. Hated himself for having done it. But most of all, he hated the nagging fear that this was a test and that he was making a mistake—that he'd return to find something had happened to her—as he had with Brigitta.

Chapter 23

Gunnar opened the door and stepped lightly to the ground as the carriage came to a halt behind the tavern. They'd driven through the night, stopping only for a few hours to rest and graze the horses. The first sliver of sun was just peeking over the horizon. He withdrew three small pouches of silver from inside his tunic, tossing one to each of the men. "For exceptional services rendered," he said in answer to their shocked expressions. "Your obligations to me are complete, but I'm still owed this day of your service. Spend it as you wish."

"Gratitude, my lord," Garrett said. "but if his lordship were to find out that we did not return immediately...," he shook his head without finishing.

"On second thought then, I may yet require your services—though it is *highly* unlikely," Gunnar added with a small smile. "Tend to the horses and then to yourselves in whatever manner you choose. You can return to his lordship in the morning." Avoiding an awkward farewell, he turned and strode through the back door.

"Well, aren't you a vision," Cora said, "standing there with the sunlight streaming in around you. Like an angel from above."

"I've no need of your flattery, Cora."

"Have you need of anythin' else, then?" she asked and moved closer, ignoring his curtness.

He took a deep breath and shook his head. "Only my clothes," he said in a resigned, softer tone.

"Alas." She feigned disappointment. "Follow me. They're in my room."

Gunnar followed her up the steep stairs and waited while she pulled his folded clothes from a well-worn trunk and laid them on the bed. "I cleaned them for you. Well, as best I could. I didn't wash the fur or leather for fear of ruining them, but they're wiped, well-aired, and brushed."

"Gratitude," he said as he pulled the blue tunic and shirt over his head and dropped them on the table. Cora sat down on a stool to watch unabashed as he reached for his trousers.

After shaking his head, Gunnar ignored her, stripping out of the nobleman's trousers and into his own. When he draped the final garment, his wolf cape, over his shoulders, he almost groaned at the familiar comfort. He handed Cora a pouch of silver. "With my deepest gratitude for all of your assistance."

She nodded and lifted her skirts to stow the pouch on a cord around her waist. All the while her keen eyes studied him. She cocked her head. "You're different now; there's a hard air about you. Were you not successful?"

"I was."

"And all this for a woman, I take it?"

He glanced at her before nodding. "Yes."

She pursed her lips. "Good for you, but pity for me, I suppose. Though if a fancy carriage were required, then she must be a noble. Watch your heart with a highborn, love. They're fickle creatures, and I'd hate to see you suffer."

"Gratitude, Cora, but your worry is unfounded; I'll soon be leaving these lands. If you could do me one last favor and see that his lordship's clothes are returned to him? I doubt he'll want them back, but that was the wager, and I've no further use for them."

"Consider it done. Fare thee well, Northman," she said as he moved toward the door.

"And you," he said sincerely, pausing to give her a brief nod before returning to the tavern below.

Bypassing the few morning patrons who bore uncanny resemblances to those he'd seen there before, he stepped out into the road. Expecting to find it empty, he was surprised by the crowd of people setting up temporary stalls for market day. He turned toward the harbor, stepping over piles of storm debris that had been hastily swept aside. He'd only gone a few paces when he saw the Treasure Huntress still propped on the beach near the docks below— or what was left of the docks.

The long pier they'd originally tied off to had been reduced to bare pilings with occasional pieces of splintered wood jutting from them at odd angles. Only two fishing boats still floated, and the beach was littered with flotsam and jetsam. Women and children scoured the shore for anything of value brought in by the tides.

"Gunnar!" He followed the direction of the voice. Rask was making his way through the crowd toward him. He was easy to spot, being a full head taller than anyone else. "You've returned safe," he said as they clasped forearms. The relief was evident in his tone, and though his eyes were full of questions, he didn't voice them.

Gunnar nodded. "How fared the Huntress in the storm?" he asked as they walked.

"She is unscathed. We lashed her down in every possible direction to anything of substance. It was a web of ropes to have made a spider envious. I thought it excessive at the time but am glad to have done it. That storm was the worst I've ever seen. Other ships did not fare so well."

Gunnar wondered if Rask had known to make the web or if one of the other men had instructed him. It didn't matter. He'd done well. He either already had the knowledge or had the sense to accept someone else's counsel. Both were equally important. Gunnar had seen many ships lost when men used extra ropes but tied them in the normal fashion. In bad squalls, where raging winds shifted direction with little notice, ropes tied in criss-crossing web-like patterns were the only way to effectively secure one.

"And the men?"

"A few cuts and bruises from flying debris. No serious injuries."

"Are the repairs complete?"

Rask nodded. "Finished last night. They were well ahead of schedule until the storm caused delay."

They reached the ship. Starting at the bow, Gunnar inspected both sides for any new damage, then got down on his hands and knees to inspect the full length of the keel. He paused at the stern, giving extra scrutiny to the repair. Pale white wood met seasoned golden brown in smooth, even lines. He ran his hands along the seams, feeling for any raised areas that might create drag in the water and affect the ship's handling, but found none. The joinings were smooth and flush, the workmanship superb. Other than the difference in the color of the planks, the Huntress was returned to original form. Satisfied, Gunnar crawled back out, stood, and brushed the sand and bits of seashells from his hands and trousers.

"It is good—very good. Has the shipbuilder been paid?"

"Not yet. He is to return today."

"When he does, pay him what he asks and see to launching her. In the meantime, go to the market and purchase supplies and trade goods. You'll find the silver you need in my chest onboard. I have one more thing I must do."

"You would leave all that to me?"

"Are you not my second?"

"Yes, but..."

"Then have the men and ship ready to sail on tonight's tide."

"Praise the gods. But what about slaves?"

"It seems you'll get your wish to wet your sword early after all. We'll capture them on the way."

Gunnar felt a surge of relief as he stepped into Tibbot's viewing chamber. Even knowing what to expect, the tons of crushing earth and narrow corridors had still left him unsettled. He knew the fear was irrational; the passages had likely stood for hundreds of years, but that did little to alleviate it. Man was not meant to be underground, he concluded, not until he entered his grave.

The guard, Rearden, had escorted him this time. Tibbot stood waiting on the other side of the cavern with two powerfully built men who could have been Rearden's brothers positioned carefully between them. After their last encounter, Tibbot clearly didn't trust him, but still had not refused his business. Greed was such a powerful motivator.

"You are in need of another purchase?" Tibbot asked.

Gunnar nodded. "I am."

"You were unsuccessful then in recovering your previous ones?"

"That matter was settled to my satisfaction," Gunnar replied evasively, ignoring Tibbot's raised questioning eyebrows. "This time I seek something special."

"Ah, so you've changed your mind on a woman." Tibbot smiled and nodded. "I have many fine women to choose from. Any one would do well to keep your bed warm. Do you have preferences? Short? Tall? Full or slender? Young?" He grinned slyly. "I'll even permit you to sample the wares first," he waved toward the bed and shackles near the fire, "to make sure she is to your liking."

"No, not a woman."

"What then?"

"A nobleman."

"A what?" Tibbot coughed.

"A nobleman," Gunnar repeated.

"Apologies...I just assumed..." Tibbot stuttered.

"I know you must get them—a black sheep, a drunkard, a gambler, a habituate—a family embarrassment," Gunnar continued, oblivious to the true nature of Tibbot's shock. "Don't pretend you know not of what I speak. Problems a family pays for you to take care of when they're too squeamish to do it themselves."

Tibbot shifted uncomfortably. "What you are suggestin' would be unlawful."

"I'm not talking about a prince, Tibbot, simply a highborn from a—lesser family."

Tibbot glanced around, a nervous habit Gunnar found ridiculous in their current location. It certainly wasn't like anyone could sneak up and overhear them here, and his men already knew his business.

"Well, it's not like that...mostly," Tibbot began. "More often 'tis the people they've wronged who bring them to me, seekin' money owed as you suggested, or compensation for other transgressions..." His voice trailed off. "If I think I can successfully return them to their families..."

Gunnar cut him off. "You mean if you think their families will pay a ransom."

"Ransom is an ugly word. I look at myself as more of a facilitator. If I think I can facilitate their return to their families, I pay their debts. If the families agree to compensate me for my troubles and expenses, I return them safe and sound. And if not," he shrugged. "Depending on the individual's age and condition, they all have some value, as you know." He waved his hand in the air. "But 'tis moot; I don't have any here now. It's not like I get them all the time."

"It was just a thought. Perhaps your competitor, Quillen." Gunnar turned to leave.

"Wait, wait. Couldn't another man do? Why does he have to be a noble? I would think another man could..." Tibbot struggled for words that would not offend. "...service you just as well. You could dress him however you like and, with a little training, he could pretend to be noble for you, I'm sure."

Gunnar scowled, finally realizing what Tibbot thought he wanted the slave for. "I don't want him for buggering, man," Gunnar snapped. "I need one to teach me. I wish to learn their ways."

"For what purpose?" Tibbot asked, no less shocked than when he thought the slave was for debauchery.

"My purpose is not your concern. But the man must be a highborn."

"Of course." Tibbot's face went smooth as he mentally whirled through his inventory. He held up a finger. "Perhaps I can still help you."

"Then you do have someone? I'll pay handsomely—more than his debt."

"Nay, it's not like that. But I do have a man. He's a...a nobleman's man. A manservant."

"A commoner?" Gunnar scoffed. "I've no need of a commoner. I can go to any tavern and learn the ways of commoners for the cost of a few pints."

"He may be of common blood, but he's far from what I'd describe as common. I think he even fancies himself a noble with all his high talk. And who better to know their ways? How they dress, how they talk, how they dine." Tibbot's face clouded. "I was paid quite well to ensure that he be sent far away. If we were to reach an accord, you would take him far?"

"I would. To the East."

Tibbot pondered then nodded, seeming satisfied. "My patron expected that he would go to Iceland, and I must admit, I did, too. Your people's quest to colonize that god-forsaken land seems to require an unending supply of laborers. But Iceland was never specified, and the East would be even farther. Aye, it would satisfy my obligation," he concluded, though Gunnar knew Tibbot had been less concerned with his obligation and more with the likelihood of being caught. "Let me at least present him to you. You can speak to him and judge for yourself. You're already here. What's the harm in another few moments?"

Gunnar gave a curt nod.

Tibbot turned quickly to his guards. "Rearden, go and fetch the manservant."

Rearden scowled. "The mouthy one?"

"The healthy, strapping manservant," Tibbot corrected him with an urgent edge to his voice.

"T'would be naught but good riddance," Rearden muttered, still scowling as he left the cavern.

Rearden's response almost changed Gunnar's mind about staying. Of all the slaves who passed through this place, what was so offensive about this one to make the man react so?

Recognizing Gunnar's fading interest, Tibbot poured two goblets of deep red wine and offered him one. Gunnar tossed it back, ignoring Tibbot's perturbed pucker that it was not properly savored, then turned to the doorway at the sound of approaching chains. A tall, broad-shouldered man shuffled through the doorway with Rearden following close behind.

"This is him?" Gunnar asked.

Tibbot nodded.

"Why was he not offered the first time I was here? He looks strong."

"He's only just arrived, my lord. Very unexpectedly."

Gunnar approached the slave and stood before him, eyeing him, perplexed. "You're big for an Irishman." He said it as a statement, but there was clear question in his voice.

"My mother was a whore near the Dublin docks, so perhaps we are kin." The slave tipped his head with a half-grin. "Aye, now that I'm looking for it, I swear I can see a family resemblance."

Tibbot blanched and nodded to Rearden who gave the chain attached to the man's neck collar a vicious yank. "Watch your tongue, slave," Rearden growled. "There's no way you're kin to anything but a mongrel."

Tibbot turned to Gunnar. "Apologies, my lord. I assure you, his mouth is truly his only flaw, though I'm sure *you* could quickly teach him to hold his tongue." Tibbot glared at the slave.

Ignoring Tibbot, Gunnar continued to size up the man. He didn't mind the swagger, but his size and the tattered rags he wore made it difficult to believe he was a nobleman's manservant.

"My proper clothes bore my lordship's crest," the slave offered, sensing the trail of Gunnar's thoughts. "They were taken from me to ensure no connection was ever made to him."

"I need someone to teach me highborn ways. Is that something you could do?"

"Better than they could, I would expect."

Gunnar studied him for a long moment. "Very well," he said and turned back to Tibbot. "How much for this one?"

Tibbot named a low price, and Gunnar wondered as he nodded his agreement, if he was somehow being duped.

"I've already been paid quite well to dispose of him," Tibbot reminded him. "Would you like to place your mark on him then?" Tibbot waved eagerly toward the fire.

"No, not this one," Gunnar declined. "But I'll need a horse to return him with me to Balbriggan. I'll leave it there with the hostler, Larkin, for you to retrieve at your leisure."

Tibbot pretended to consider. "I can do that, but it will cost extra."

Gunnar shook his head. "I've already paid you plenty, and I'll have you throw in some decent clothes for him."

Tibbot didn't quibble. "Done."

"What are you called?" Gunnar asked as he pulled the lead rope of the second horse to walk alongside his. The man still wore wrist cuffs, but the neck collar and leg shackles had been removed at Tibbot's.

"My name is Eamon."

"Eamon, I am Gunnar, and I'm embarking on a trip that I intend to have completed within seven months. During that time, it will be your duty to teach me everything you know of being a highborn. How they talk, how they dress, their manners, customs...everything." Gunnar paused, then mused aloud. "Perhaps even to read and write. Can you read?"

"Aye." Eamon nodded. "And my other duties? What will they be consistin' of?"

"That is all."

"That's it?" he asked. "No other...services...required?"

Gunnar scowled, disturbed that two men would assume that about him in one day. "Did your previous lord insist on other *services*, from you?"

"Nay," Eamon shook his head vehemently.

"Then why would you ask me that?"

"Because before we left, Rearden told me my arsehole would soon be as big as my mouth."

Gunnar laughed out loud and shook his head. "Rearden was having sport with you. He didn't much care for you, did he?"

"Rearden *is* an arsehole," Eamon spat.

"I assure you, Eamon, I only have need of your mind and what's inside it, nothing more. At the end of this journey, it is my intent to return here. If you are still with us at that time, you'll be rewarded with silver."

"You're comin' back here and you would bring me? What of your deal with Tibbot?"

"I agreed to take you far away. And I will. Nothing was said about not bringing you back."

Eamon smiled. "Aye, I suppose that's true. And where are we journeyin' to?"

"Does it matter?"

"Nay, I'm only curious."

"The deserts and plains of the East."

"Praise God."

"That's a strange response. You know of it?"

"'Tis far removed from Iceland, and that's all that matters to me."

They crested the top of the hill overlooking Balbriggan. Gunnar pulled both horses to a halt. "There is one more thing. Once you step aboard my ship, you'll be a free man."

"What does that mean?" Eamon asked cautiously.

"It means just that. You will no longer be a slave. It's important to me that you know that."

Eamon looked at him blankly.

"It means that you can jump into the sea and swim for shore, or get off at our next landing if you so desire. You will be free. But only if you make the entire journey will you be paid."

"Why would you free me after just spendin' good coin to buy me?"

"I gave my word to someone that I would take no slaves from this place. I realize this is probably splitting hairs, but I can live with it."

"So how am I to act toward you, then, in front of them? As your manservant? Friend? I assume this man will be there?"

"You will be my...adviser. And no, you shall never see the person I made the vow to," Gunnar said under his breath, his voice pained.

Eamon sat silent, his brow furrowed. "If you don't mind my askin'—why would you do that? Honor your word to someone who will never know if you do?"

"Because that's what giving my word means. Hold out your hands," Gunnar directed. Eamon offered up his wrists and Gunnar removed the shackles.

"And if I were to flee now?" Eamon asked as he rubbed the red marks left by the cuffs.

"I'll run you down and thrash you to within an inch of your life. Believe me, I'm aware of the temptation and fully understand it. That's why I waited to tell you until just now. You're not free until you step aboard the ship."

"Fair enough," Eamon said, then nodded solemnly. "I give you my word, Northman; I'll teach you to the best of my ability, and I'll not run. If you're willin' to keep your word to someone who'll never know, that tells me somethin' about you." He shrugged. "Though if I'm bein' entirely truthful, I've nowhere else to go—to remain here, I fear, might pose significant risk to my health."

"This is our ship?" Eamon asked, his face filled with wonder as he stared at the Treasure Huntress floating regally near the water's edge.

"My ship," Gunnar corrected him with a frown before striding toward the group of men gathered on the beach.

"Listen up, men. That is Eamon." Gunnar pointed, raising his voice loud enough for all of them to hear. "He's coming with us, and he's not to be harmed."

"Coming with us as what exactly?" Rask asked.

Gunnar surveyed the stacked cargo. "Why isn't the ship loaded? It should have been completed an hour ago."

"There was a delay in getting her launched," Rask began.

"Then why are these men sitting? The tide is already slack high." Gunnar motioned to men lounging amongst the crates and bags of trade goods. Without waiting for Rask to reply, he shouted, "Get off your arses and get this cargo loaded. Now, before we lose the tide!"

Men scurried to do as he commanded.

Eamon couldn't tear himself away from the great golden beast. He stepped into the shallow water to better see the intricate carvings within the scales. His gaze moved up the dragon's neck to its head. The open mouth displayed sharp fangs carved in a level of detail he'd never before seen. Growing up in Dublin, he'd seen plenty of Viking ships, many of them even adorned with a dragon, but they'd all been crude, blunt things. Nothing like this. The eye was so lifelike, he swore the beast was looking back at him.

"Don't be a fool. 'Tis nothin' more than wood," Eamon chided himself under his breath, disturbed that even as he said the words, he still felt a beast.

When the first of the crew splashed past him carrying cargo, Eamon wasn't sure what to do. He'd never been on a ship other than to briefly step aboard one in the Dublin harbor. He had no idea how they were loaded. He looked to the other men for guidance, but they all averted their eyes.

He had his work cut out for him. Even with Gunnar's command that he not be harmed, Eamon knew very well that these rough men could still make his life a living hell—and Gunnar wouldn't always be around. He didn't take it personally. It was to be expected. He was an outsider. And sitting idle now while they worked would do nothing to help him in that regard. Spying a younger lad working alone on the ship, Eamon picked up a sack of grain, tossed it over his shoulder, and waded out to him.

"I don't know how things are stowed, so I'll bring them to you, and you can do it."

Uncomfortable at having been singled out, the boy cast a quick glance at Gunnar who was watching the interchange. "Very well," he muttered, unwilling to refuse him under Gunnar's scrutiny. "Alternate bringing me sacks with barrels."

Chapter 24

"**F**irst time at sea, Irish?" Rask taunted.

Eamon lifted his head from over the side and wiped the last traces of bile from his lips with one hand while maintaining a death grip on the top of the ship's bulwark with the other. He turned in time to see Rask rip a bite of chicken from a cold, greasy drumstick. The sight of the tattered flesh dangling from the bone brought a fresh round of dry heaves.

Rask laughed. "You haven't seen anything; it's not even rough yet."

Eamon would have liked to respond, but he didn't have the strength. When the heaves subsided again, he closed his eyes and turned, slowly sliding his back down the cool curved wood until he was safely on the deck. Only then did he release his hand from the top to cross both arms over his stomach.

Why did he bother to hang on? Why prolong the torture? Perhaps it would be better if he tumbled headlong into the sea. Drowning couldn't possibly feel any worse. And if it did, at least it would be brief.

"Here, Irish, have a drink."

Eamon cracked open one eye. The lad, Anders, whom he'd handed cargo to, offered him a waterskin. He waved it off weakly. "'Twould only be a waste of good water," he croaked. "Might as well pour it over the side than give it to me. That's all I'll do with it anyway."

The boy grinned. "It will pass. And once it does, you'll never get it again. They laugh at you now, but every man here has felt it to some extent. Njord is testing you. But you need to drink." He held out the waterskin again.

Eamon glanced at the other men. Not a one was even mildly afflicted by the curse that seemed hellbent on turning him inside out.

"Drink," the youth insisted, snapping him from his reverie.

Eamon accepted the waterskin, took a small sip, then handed back the bag.

"One more," the boy urged.

Eamon groaned and snatched the bag, not relishing the thought of having more in his stomach to evacuate over the side, but needing the lad to leave him to die in peace.

———————————◆———————————

When he awoke, Eamon wasn't sure how much time had passed, but for the first time since leaving Balbriggan's harbor, he didn't feel the need to vomit. He remained curled on the deck, afraid that any movement would change that. His entire body from neck to groin ached from the retching. His throat was raw, his lips cracked, and his tongue seemed swollen too big for his mouth. As miserable as all that was, it was a vast improvement over how he'd felt before.

He carefully straightened his legs, then rolled onto his back, staring up at the sail. It was odd; the sail was stretched taut by the strong west wind, yet here on the deck he felt little. His feet were even quite warm, hot actually. He turned his head to glance down at his too-tight boots roasting in the sun, then slowly widened the scope of his perusal. The dragon's head and neck cast a shadow from his mid-calf upwards, protecting the rest of his body. He sat up tentatively.

"Irish has decided to live," Rask announced. "You'll owe me that coin, after all, Olag."

A man with thick-ridged burn scars on his right cheek and chin stepped closer and peered into his eyes. "Is it true? Has the goddess, Hel, refused your Irish arse in Niflheim?"

When Eamon didn't respond, Olag moved off toward Rask, handing him something Eamon assumed was coin. They'd actually wagered on whether or not he would die. So much for the lad's assurances that it would pass. He spied the waterskin on top of a small barrel only a few paces away and attempted to stand, but his legs were too unsteady and weak. He dropped back to his hands and knees. No one offered to retrieve it for him. Even Gunnar, watching him from the bow, looked amused.

Eamon knew better than to ask. He was not some lord to be served. He needed to prove himself to these men if he ever hoped to be accepted. He began to crawl toward the water, ignoring the laughter and jeers. When he reached it, he gulped down half of the tepid fluid before leaning back against a sack of grain with the waterskin clutched in his grasp. His thirst was far from quenched, but he wanted to be sure the first would stay down before adding more.

Tipping his head back, he closed his eyes, feeling the warmth of the sun on his face. He was thrilled to be able to enjoy it—to be able to enjoy anything. The laughter around him gradually subsided. When he opened his eyes again, no one paid him any attention. For the first time, Eamon began to have hope. Maybe he would live after all.

Fiona pressed her forehead against the thick cool glass in her bedchamber and stared out through the drizzling rain. It seemed an eternity since the carriage had dropped her off. An eternity since she'd felt his touch and looked into his deep blue eyes. Well, that wasn't exactly true, she felt and saw them every night; in her dreams, he never left her.

Her first days home, the weather had been bright and clear with a steady bracing wind that rolled across the land from the west. She'd taken Barca and galloped to the point of exhaustion every day. It was the only way to keep her mind clear; all of her focus and physical strength were required to stay with the horse's leaps and bounds.

Escaping her thoughts of Gunnar had been difficult enough then, but now with this rain, stuck indoors and unable to ride, it was impossible. She couldn't help but relive every moment of their time together. Every precious moment. Not that it had all been good, but from the instant she'd climbed into his carriage, every second had been lived to the absolute fullest.

Such a sharp contrast to this, where everything was slow and safe, and properly scheduled. With every passing hour, she swore the walls were constricting around her, squeezing the very life from her bones. If only she could be the one on a journey, seeing new things and facing new challenges, rather than the one left behind. Sitting. Waiting. Trapped.

At times, she actually felt imprisoned. She knew it was ridiculous. With the privileges of her station, she could demand the carriage to take her anywhere, regardless of the weather—and she would have, if she thought it might help. But she could think of nowhere to go that would make her feel any better. There was no geographical cure. She was truly—how had Gunnar put it? *Like a prisoner in her own mind?*

How ironic though, that her current predicament was not at all because of her being educated, as he'd asserted that day in the carriage. This was his fault. Not that it mattered. The result was the same. Her life hadn't been perfect before, but every day had at least felt full. Not like this. Never like this.

She thought again of the young carriage horse she'd raced to victory. The poor beast had never been able to properly resume its role with the others. Much to Garrett's exasperation, the animal had pranced and sometimes even cantered in place next to its mates—often working itself into a lather. Garrett said the horse might be ruined—at best would need to be retrained. Was that what she faced? Did she need to be retrained, her spirit subdued to accept and carry on with the duties of her true life? And this was her true life. Wasn't it?

As she watched a trickle of water run a crooked path down the outside of the thick warped pane, she wondered if Gunnar could also predict a storm's end. In all of their conversations, he'd never mentioned it. She would be sure to ask him when next she saw him.

Assuming he returned.

And if he did? What then? He was no lord returning to ask for her hand. Would they secretly while away afternoons in love trysts until they were caught? Or until her father insisted that she marry? He was certain to do so eventually. And it could never be to Gunnar—a pagan. There was no way this ended well. She knew that. So why did she continue to pray for the seven months to pass?

"My lady?" Siara called from the doorway. "Supper is about to be served. Your father awaits you."

Fiona nodded and stood, thankful for the interruption. Perhaps her father knew of someone in a similar situation where it had worked out. He was wise. Open-minded. She respected him. So long as she worded her questions carefully, he should not suspect anything.

"It seems as if this rain will never stop," Fiona grumbled as she pushed food around on her plate with her fork.

Her father looked up at her with raised eyebrows. "After the last storm, this one does not seem bad at all."

Fiona bit her tongue. Lost in his books and letters, her father probably hadn't even noticed the rain. And before her time with Gunnar, that would have been her, too—enjoying being outdoors when the weather was fair but happily content to be inside reading when it was not.

"Papa, what if I were to fall in love with a man who was...unsuitable?" She broached the subject and took a bite of roasted venison as if her question was nothing more than a casual surmise and his reply were of no importance to her whatsoever.

"Unsuitable how?" Her father frowned.

"Oh, I don't know." She shrugged. "Just someone unsuitable."

Her not having something specific put him at ease, and he resumed eating. "Well, there are many levels of unsuitable, of course. There is unsuitable as in already married...." He glanced at her to gauge her response as he began a hypothetical exploration of her question.

She pretended to consider it, careful not to rush, then shook her head. "Nay, of course not married," she concluded, then added, "but perhaps widowed."

"Widowed is acceptable. Those things happen. 'Tis apparently God's will," he muttered.

"What about unsuitable in another way—say, of lower class?"

"Like a merchant lord?" he offered.

Fiona smiled to herself, that a merchant was the lowest class he could imagine in their mock scenario, then nodded.

"Living on a limited income is not what I would choose for you, but there will be the fortune you will inherit, so I suppose you would still live comfortably enough." He nodded. "If you loved him, I would not oppose it."

"What of a foreigner?" She carelessly took another bite.

"Honestly, Fiona, I would hate to have you live far removed. Though I can't imagine I ever have to worry about that; you are a child of Eire. You could never leave here; 'tis in your blood." Their eyes met, and she smiled, nodding in agreement.

They both resumed eating, quietly contemplating their own thoughts. "If only Lord Nevyn had a son who yet lived. You could marry him and remain close."

"If Lord Nevyn had a son, he'd be older than you." Fiona pointed out.

He nodded. "I've heard he's quite ill. If an heir cannot be found..." his voice trailed away. "Well, 'tis just a shame for a family to end that way. Tir na Laoch lies in shambles now, but 'twas a grand place once."

Fiona tried to lighten his mood and hopefully steer him back to her topic. "'Tis my understanding that his search for an heir is still ongoing. He may yet find one," she offered, though she doubted her words were true. Such a man would have already come forward.

"Aye, we must pray that he does. Now, what were we discussing?"

"My marriage to someone unsuitable. What of a commoner?" She raised her eyebrows and cocked her head at him as if the idea had just come to her.

"Fiona," he admonished. "Do not even say such a thing in jest. What has brought about this sudden line of questioning? Is there someone...?"

"Nay, Papa," Fiona reassured him with a quick smile. "My questions are purely whimsical. I've been so bored of late that my thoughts have wandered quite far."

"'Tis good that you have a vivid imagination, but pray to God that your heart never takes you in such a direction. You could never be happy. You're sure there's not..."

"Nay, Papa, of course not," she chided. *It's far, far worse than that.*

After searching her face, he smiled, too. "As much as I may disagree with it on a scholarly level, this is the world we live in, and common folk and us...

well, we might as well be from two different worlds." He changed the subject. "You know Davin will be visiting soon."

Fiona nodded, preoccupied.

"It will be good to see him again, to see the man he's become. He always had great affection for you," he hinted.

Fiona frowned, regretting having brought up the topic of marriage and suitors.

"I know he wasn't the most physically impressive lad," he chuckled, "but he's well-educated, and since we are on the topic."

Physically unimpressive was being generous. Fiona thought back to the diminutive, near-sighted Davin whose squinting was oft so severe, it was difficult to see his eyes. He'd been her father's pupil, and she'd sat in on many of his lessons, making him one of the few people in whose presence she could speak her mind.

Though, if Davin harbored thoughts against a woman being educated, she doubted he'd have voiced them. He was too fearful of reproach to engage in confrontation. Her mind drifted to Gunnar, who had countered and challenged her at every turn—their intense lively banter and his constant probing and questioning of her thoughts and beliefs.

Davin couldn't be more opposite. And to consider him as a husband as her father suggested? To share a bedchamber with him? She thought back to his timid squinting glances and compared them to Gunnar's confident roving stares. Surely they hadn't been having the same lustful thoughts. Davin was so...fastidious, so mousy, so correct. She couldn't imagine him capable of even a pale version of the act that Gunnar performed with such skillful abandon.

Fiona flushed at the thought. What was wrong with her? Would she now measure men by how competent she thought they'd be in the bedchamber? She stood and pushed back her chair.

"Apologies, Papa. I didn't sleep well last night and shall retire early."

"Of course, my dear, would you like Haisley to prepare you a sleeping tea?"

"Nay, it won't be necessary. I'm quite drowsy now."

"You could never be happy." The conviction in her father's words haunted her as she climbed the stairs. But Gunnar had sworn he would find a way—like his friend Jarl had with the native woman, Nena—though their solution required Nena to leave her people.

If Gunnar asked that of her, could she do it? Her father was right when he called her a child of Eire; this land was in her blood. Could she forsake it? Could she disgrace herself, her father, her family name, and run off with him? To where? To live in some dirt-floored hovel in Norway or Daneland? Would she braid her hair in knots and wear leather and furs like an animal? Raise dirty little heathen children? Anywhere Gunnar would be accepted, would mean to live as a pagan. Could she do that? Could she watch him sacrifice animals and smear their blood on his face in barbaric rituals? She shuddered.

It all seemed so impossible after seeing him as a lord on their trip. In fact, it was difficult now for her to even remember his appearance when she'd first encountered him with his ratty braided hair and furs. But that was who he truly was—she had to accept it. He'd freely admitted during their travels that he was pretending to be something he was not, and that he found the act to be uncomfortable and pretentious. If they were to have any chance, one of them would have to change.

If it were her, what would become of her father? She and Tir na Lionmhar were all he had. If she left, he'd be exactly like Lord Nevyn with no heir—a situation that clearly caused him great distress. Could she do that to him?

Fiona closed her bedroom door behind her and returned to the window to stare out at the rain. What if she was worrying for nothing? What if Gunnar never came back? What if something befell him on his journey? Her thoughts took an even darker turn. What if he had no intention of returning? What if he never had? What if she'd simply been a way for him to pass the time while his ship was being repaired—something, though she'd never admitted it to him, he clearly knew had been her doing. What if this had been his way to exact revenge for that? To take her virtue and leave her pining for him.

Fiona angrily pushed the thoughts from her mind. Why was she torturing herself this way? Gunnar had never been false with her. She recalled his face when he held his forehead pressed to hers before they parted for the last time. The intensity of his goodbye and his words, *"I will return for you. I swear it."* He hadn't been lying. She'd felt the strength of his conviction.

Fiona prayed for a break in the rain. This weather was driving her mad.

Chapter 25

"What do you think they're on about, always sitting off to the side talking like that?" Olag asked under his breath, nodding towards Gunnar and Eamon.

"I have no idea," Rask muttered, "but I'm going to find out."

"Nay, it's caaaaaariage. Not crrrrge." Rask overheard Eamon correcting Gunnar as he approached.

"You're learning more of their language?" Rask asked.

Gunnar nodded.

"I thought you spoke it very well already."

"There's always room for improvement."

"Seems like a waste. Even I speak Irish well enough to get what I want, and you speak it much better."

"Do you speak it well enough to negotiate a treaty?" Gunnar asked.

"I speak it well enough to demand their possessions and kill them if they refuse me. I have no desire to make treaties and deals."

"That's fine for a soldier, but as a leader, you'll need to be able to do more. Men who follow you will not always share your desires; some will wish to settle and raise families. You'll be expected to negotiate for them."

Rask shrugged.

"Let's say you had to negotiate something else—something important, say a ransom. If you couldn't speak a local tongue, you'd have to trust your words and ears to someone else. Perhaps someone like Eamon here," Gunnar added, knowing Rask's dislike for the Irishman; it was no secret. "If it was something important to you, would you trust him?"

"You know I would not. If it were something important to me, I'd only trust my own."

"Someone like Hrut, perhaps?" Gunnar named the Dane who'd betrayed Rask's family during the recent war. "He was your people."

"Hrut was a lying scut."

"You know that now, but you won't always be able to choose the company in which you find yourself. Any way you can limit your reliance on others and make them reliant on you increases your control and power."

"My sword gives me all the control I need," Rask disagreed as he sat down cross-legged next to them. "Changing the subject, how long do you think it will take us to reach Aalborg tomorrow?"

"I believe we've landed about a half-day south of the Skagerrak Strait; we should make Aalborg by mid-afternoon."

"And how long will we be staying after we arrive?"

"One night, two at most. We'll depart ahead of the others to capture slaves, then rejoin the fleet in Visby."

"If I may also change the subject," Eamon interrupted. "The men have told me more of this mission in the East. I would like to become a member of the crew for a share. I'm good with a blade."

Rask snorted while Gunnar shook his head.

"I can hold my own," Eamon maintained.

"Your cock doesn't count," Rask laughed.

Eamon ignored him and kept his attention on Gunnar. "Allow me to prove myself."

Gunnar had no intention of letting Eamon fight. If fighting were done with words, Eamon would be a champion like no other, but with sword? Gunnar wouldn't risk it. In the short time he'd been his student, Gunnar had come to realize the enormity of what he didn't know. Eamon was a wealth of information. He felt his hopeful gaze still upon him and searched for the best words to soften his refusal. "How is it you come to handle a sword?" he asked, pretending to be considering.

"My lordship maintained a sword master. I was often his sparring partner."

"Was your lord good with a blade?"

Eamon shook his head. "Fair, at best. Handling a sword did not come easily to him."

"But it did to you?"

"It seemed to, aye."

"There's a vast difference between sparring and fighting for your life."

"I was born in the back of a brothel in Dublin, not raised in privilege under the stairs in a lord's manor. My mother, God rest her soul, died a whore's death when I was eleven, strangled by a patron. After I killed that man, I survived on the streets by my wits and my fists. I'm well aware of the difference in sparrin' and brawlin', and I assure you I'm prepared for both."

Gunnar nodded as an idea suddenly came to him—one that would address two issues. "Very well then," he paused and looked to Rask. "If Rask is willing—a demonstration of your skill."

A slow, grim smile split Rask's face as he realized what Gunnar was suggesting. "Oh, I am willing."

Gunnar nodded, satisfied that he'd come up with the perfect solution. Rask would make short work of Eamon and, in doing so, put an end to his

dreams of becoming crew. At the same time, it provided Rask the opportunity
to give Eamon a thrashing—something he'd clearly been itching to do since
day one. And, since it would all take place under his own watchful eye, he
could prevent Eamon from getting killed.

"Make the square," Gunnar called out.

"Weapons, lord?" Olag asked.

"Sword and shield. But with Ander's wooden practice swords," Gunnar
added. "They can beat each other all they want, but I'll not have serious
injury today."

Men scurried to do as he asked, and Gunnar heard the words 'make the
square' eagerly repeated multiple times. Wagers were hastily made as a square
was formed on the ground with pieces of driftwood.

"Do you know this?" he asked Eamon.

Eamon shook his head.

"You will fight inside the square. There are no rules other than that—the
fight can be in any manner that will gain advantage. Fists, swords, teeth. Any
manner," he repeated. "Fighting will cease only when a man steps out."

"What if I'm intentionally pushed out?"

"Willingly steps out," Gunnar clarified, "though I doubt that will be a
concern. Rask will wish to prolong this as long as possible."

As Gunnar watched Eamon repeatedly adjust his grip on the shield, he
realized he'd unwittingly given Rask an even greater advantage. By including
shields, he'd thought to offer Eamon some protection, but instead had
inadvertently given Rask two weapons to Eamon's one. Irish shields were
heavy and cumbersome, used primarily for defense, while their Viking
counterparts were a weapon in their own right. Lighter and more easily
wielded, they were often used to batter an opponent—something Rask would
have practiced from a young age.

There was nothing to be done about it now, and it didn't really matter. He intended to stop the fight as soon as Eamon appeared to be in danger.

After a few practice slashes through the air to get a feel for the crude wooden sword, Eamon took up a crouched fighting stance and tapped it against the front of his shield, signaling he was ready. The men laughed at his bent pose, but he paid them no heed and waited for Rask to make the first move. He didn't have to wait long.

Rask lunged. Eamon dodged, light on his feet, deftly blocking Rask's blade. Rask came again in a rush, but Eamon nimbly side-stepped him and made a stab at his back. Channeling a sixth sense, Rask raised his sword behind him, deflecting the blow, and forcing it off to one side so fast that Eamon had difficulty bringing it back around in time to ward off Rask's next vicious strike.

Their swords locked. Rask swung his shield around in a smashing blow to Eamon's shoulder. Eamon reeled and staggered sideways, stumbling to his knees. Rask didn't pursue him. Instead, he raised his sword and shield and roared in a circle to the cheers of the other men.

Eamon raised himself to one knee but didn't rise. Supporting himself with the edge of his shield and sword, he remained with his head bowed.

"If you've had enough Irish, step from the square," Rask called to him.

When Eamon didn't respond, Gunnar wondered if the shield had hit, not only his shoulder as it appeared, but his head as well, leaving him stunned.

"Very well then." Rask smiled and stepped towards him.

Rask was two paces away when he raised his wooden sword. Eamon had still yet to move. Gunnar was about to call a halt, but something in Eamon's demeanor stayed his hand. Rask took another step. Eamon sprang to life. Dropping his sword, he grabbed a handful of sand and flung it in Rask's face as he lunged to his feet. He tossed his shield from the square as he launched his body like a spear into Rask's midsection. The force of his charge drove

Rask backwards. They hit the ground as one with Eamon raining punches on Rask's face, head, and upper body.

Unable to bring his sword or shield up between them, Rask abandoned them, wrapping Eamon in a bear hug. Twisting and arching his back, he flipped them both, breaking his grip in the process. Both men leapt to their feet.

Eamon kicked Rask's shield from the square as he scrambled back for the sword he'd dropped. Rask retreated to a corner, retrieving his own sword on the way. He stood there for a moment, slowly twisting his head and neck, trying to clear his head after the unexpected attack. While the other men whooped at the surprising turn of events, Rask smiled and nodded. Then he charged again.

Their wooden swords struck with such force, Gunnar expected several times they would break. When neither man could gain advantage with sword, those too were abandoned, and the fight deteriorated to an all-out brawl of kicking, tripping, and bludgeoning with elbows and fists.

Rask landed several staggering punches, but shockingly Eamon shook them off and fought on. Gunnar noted the murmurs and growing respect on the faces of the men who were watching. To them, the ability to take a blow was almost equally as respected as being able to give one. Eamon was not only taking brutal blows, he was giving as good as he got. Amidst catcalls and cheers, the two men pummeled each other, panting, growling, and grunting. Neither stepping from the square. Neither holding anything back.

"That's enough." Gunnar raised a closed fist, calling an end to the fight. "I must say, Eamon, I'm impressed," he said, though his tone conveyed far more frustration than praise.

"As am I," Rask panted as he spat out a mouthful of blood and grinned. "I didn't think you had it in you, Irish."

Eamon stood bent over with his elbows on his knees, sides heaving, looking up at Gunnar expectantly.

"Very well," Gunnar muttered, exasperated that the contest had not gone at all as he'd planned. "I will agree to this. When we land in Germania to take slaves, prove yourself there, and I will make you an equal member of the crew. But for Odin's sake, do not get yourself killed. I have need of your mind far more than your sword."

Eamon grinned. "My lord, you shall have both."

"So we're to hunt men for slaves in Germania?" Eamon asked as Olag cleaned a gash on his brow, then packed it with a paste made from chewed leaves. He glanced over at Rask being similarly doctored and smiled to himself.

"Aye, that's where we always get them," Olag replied, then bit off a piece of dried moss and pressed it into the paste. "Until this year. Purchasing them in Dublin was unusual. Even our previous captain, Jarl, always captured Germanians to honor Gunnar's wishes; his hatred of them has never been secret."

"Why?" Eamon asked.

"Why does he hate them?"

"Aye."

"They killed his wife."

"Hmm."

"It was many years ago, before I knew him."

"So that's why he's so gruff."

Olag took a quick glance around. "Nay. If anything, other than when it comes to Germanians, he's always been more of an easygoing sort. But ever since Ireland, he's been different. Perhaps it's because he almost lost the Huntress, or that he was unable to retrieve the slaves even after searching for them all that time. Whatever it is, he's pushing the crew like he never has before."

Chapter 26

Fiona threw back her coverlet and ran to the window. The sky was clear—not a cloud in sight. She could ride today! It would be too muddy to gallop, but she'd be free of these walls and safely away from Meirna's probing eyes and prying questions. Questions, she'd managed to answer so far with vague altered recollections of previous trips, but she could tell Meirna wasn't wholly satisfied.

After dressing quickly in an old kirtle and gown, Fiona jotted a note to Meirna, then snuck down the back stairs to the kitchen. Intending only to grab bread and cheese from the larder, she was surprised to find Haisley already there with an iron cauldron simmering over the fire.

"Good mornin', Haisley."

Haisley shrieked, nearly dropping the wooden bowl she was carrying. After much juggling, she managed to renew her grip and set it on the table. "Fiona," she scolded, holding a hand to her chest. "You gave me near a death of fright, lass, sneakin' up on me that way. What are you doin' up so early?"

"The weather has finally cleared, and I can escape this house. I intend to ride all day."

Haisley nodded, still flustered. "Then you'll need a hearty breakfast. Sit down. I'll dish you a bowl of porridge."

Fiona wanted to refuse, but the delectable smells in the kitchen were making her mouth water.

"Would you like apple in it?" Haisley asked as she resumed bustling about. "I'm sorting through the last of them today. Most will have to go to the hogs, but there's still some good to be had from a few."

Fiona glanced at the basket of shriveled, mostly-brown apples from last fall's harvest and nodded. Stifling her impatience, she took a seat at the heavy wooden preparation table and picked up a paring knife to clean apples while she waited. Having spent much of her childhood here with Aiden, she was as comfortable in this place as the dining hall.

"The porridge'll be a few moments more; here's a piece of warm bread to tide you over." Haisley handed her a slice of dense brown bread slathered with sweet cream butter.

"Why are you up so early?" Fiona asked as she bit into the thick crust. "And what is in the cauldron? It smells delicious."

"That pot's not what you smell, lass. That's only the bones for tonight's oxtail soup. What you smell is my special tonic." Haisley nodded to a smaller copper pot cooling on a side table as she filled a bowl with porridge. She topped the bowl with cream and honey, then rooted through the basket of apples. Finding one that still had some red to its skin, Haisley peeled away the bad spots, cutting the remainder into small pieces. "There you go, lass. Just the way you like it."

Drizzled with honey and covered with apple chunks, the mountain of brown porridge rose like an island from a sea of sweet cream. Fiona's stomach rumbled with approval.

"Who's the tonic for?" Fiona asked as she stirred all the ingredients into a lumpy brown mash before taking the first bite.

"Several of the tenant children have a nasty cough. It's no wonder with this foul weather. But my tonic will fix them up, right as rain." Haisley paused and chuckled. "Right as rain—when likely 'tis the rain that made them sick in the first place." Still chuckling, she walked over and gave the copper pot a cursory stir, peering in at the contents.

She raised her head and turned to Fiona. "Would you take it to them on your ride? I was goin' to have Finnian deliver it, but I swear the lad's as scatterbrained as a hen. He starts off with good intentions, but before he's gone twenty paces, he's sidetracked—chasin' a squirrel with his sling, or lord knows what else," she muttered. "He seems to find it impossible to keep his mind to purpose."

"I'll take it," Fiona said between mouthfuls. "I've no destination in mind today."

"Grand. As soon as it cools, I'll bundle it careful so it won't leak."

Fiona finished the porridge and squirmed in her seat.

"Alright, alright. I suppose 'tis cool enough. I can see you're chompin' at the bit to go ride." She grinned a half-toothless grin. "How do you like that? I did it again. Chompin' at the bit to go ride. Right as rain. I could be a bard."

Fiona shook her head and smiled at how pleased Haisley was with her wordplay.

"And while you're there, do stop in and see old Maive. She'll appreciate a visitor."

"But..."

"Fiona, don't tell me you believe any of that nonsense about her being a witch."

"Nay, 'tis not that. I haven't believed those stories since I was a child, but I've been trapped indoors for so long..."

"Then just imagine how she must feel, stuck in that cottage all alone. You'll be like a breath of fresh air."

"Aye." Fiona agreed reluctantly as Haisley placed a tightly stoppered jug on the center of a large square of coarse linen, then folded up the corners, forming a pouch. Before Haisley could burden her with any more requests, Fiona took the makeshift sack and moved quickly to the door. Without slowing her stride, she tied the ends of the cloth together in a loop and slung it over one shoulder on her way to the stables.

The barn doors stood open wide. The horses were fed, the stalls mucked, but no stable boys were about. She knew she should find someone to saddle Barca for her but hated to waste the time when she could easily do it herself. There'd be a resulting lecture from Cahan about it not being ladylike, but that wouldn't be until she returned. She set down the sack and ran for Barca's bridle and saddle.

———————◆———————

Barca pranced sideways beneath her, necked bowed, occasionally pulling at the bit, asking for more rein. As much as she would have liked to oblige him, the mud was deeper than she'd expected, and even walking, he was slipping and sliding.

"Maybe tomorrow, lad," she murmured, stroking his neck.

Barca tossed his head, snorting his frustration as if in response to her words, and she laughed. Her spirits were high. She was free and outdoors. The rain-cleansed morning air was crisp and fresh—filled with the smells of saturated soil and drenched spring plants. Gunnar would appreciate such a beautiful day.

Gunnar. She'd hoped riding would keep him from her mind. Yet her first thought was wishing to share with him how wondrous the world appeared today. She missed him so desperately. Missed his voice, his thoughts, his touch. Missed how she felt just being with him. How was that possible? How, after spending little more than a week with him, could her entire previous life seem trivial and meaningless while the time with him became what was genuine and true?

Granted, the countless hours they'd spent alone together in the carriage equaled months of stolen moments in proper courting. By that standard, what she felt was validated—and she knew what she felt. She loved him. She loved a Northman.

With that realization, her mind became as clear to purpose as the day was beautiful. She would not live without him. When he returned, she'd not be parted from him again, no matter the sacrifice required. She had months to find some way to present it to her father that he could accept. Excited by the decision and new goal, her spirits soared, and even that she longed to share with him.

The smell of burning peat intruded on her thoughts. She was nearing the tenant village. The thought of sitting idle with Old Maive now, so early in her ride, was unbearable. She couldn't do it. She'd drop the tonic today and return to visit Maive tomorrow. Maive wasn't expecting her; she wouldn't be disappointed. Feeling more than a little guilty with the decision, Fiona rode through the village looking for someone to hand off the tonic to, but she found no adults, only children playing. She stopped a small lad running by. "Are your parents about?"

"Nay, my lady. This last rain has loosened the soil, and everyone is busy preparin' it for plantin'. 'Tis there anythin' I can do for you?"

"Gratitude, but nay." Fiona shook her head; she didn't dare leave the tonic with a child. She glanced toward the small daub and wattle cottage half covered in vines. Old Maive's cottage. No one knew exactly how old she was, only that she was ancient—so ancient that she still believed in the old gods. Gods, who some whispered fearfully were the same as the Northmen's.

Fiona would like to ask her about them, but not today. She'd deliver the tonic, then make an excuse to leave. After dismounting and tying Barca to a sturdy sapling, she took one last look around for anyone else, then walked up the short stepping-stone path to the door. She held her breath as she knocked, half hoping for no answer.

"Come in," a woman's voice rattled from within.

Fiona opened the door and stepped inside. She remained in the doorway, looking around the cramped, dark space, her nose assailed by unfamiliar smells and stale, smoky air.

"Who's there?" the woman asked.

"'Tis Fiona."

"Fiona? Come in, child, and close the door behind you."

Fiona did as she was instructed but remained near the door.

"Closer now, so I can get a good look at you. My eyes are not as sharp as they once were."

Fiona moved toward the old crone, who sat in a chair with a thick blanket over her lap. "I brought Haisley's tonic for the sick. Do you need any?"

"Nay, lass. Sickness can get nothing from these old bones. It prefers the tenderness of youthful flesh. But I would have something warm to drink. Would you heat some water?"

"Aye." Fiona set the tonic on the table.

"There are some dried wildflowers in the faded yellow crock that make a nice brew when steeped."

Fiona could feel the woman's eyes studying her every move as she added a peat brick to the banked fire and filled the kettle with water from a small barrel.

Just one cup, then you can go, she told herself as she crumbled a handful of the dried flower mixture into the boiling water. Some of the flowers she recognized—meadowsweet, hawthorn, gorse, and wild cherry, but there were others that she did not.

After handing a cup to Maive, Fiona sat on a stool in front of her and sipped the tea. It had quite a pleasant taste. There was no need to hurry; she had plenty of time to ride. The more she drank, the more comfortable she became. The cabin was actually quite cozy, not dark and strange as it had first seemed. Fiona wondered briefly if her sudden relaxation had anything to do with the unknown flowers in the tea, but the idea didn't alarm her, and she didn't dwell on it.

"You're the image of your mother," Maive said.

"Did you know her?"

"Aye. A fine lady, she was—always riding that huge bay horse your father gave her as a wedding gift. She loved to ride. Do you?"

"Aye, 'tis my greatest passion. I could hardly bear being cooped up this past week."

Maive nodded knowingly. "An anxious spirit always finds being confined more unbearable than a content one. What troubles you?"

"Oh, I was not troubled—only bored," Fiona murmured and shook her head.

"You don't have to share it with Old Maive if you don't wish to, lass, but don't lie to me. Your spirit is restless. I can feel it from here."

It seemed a rather witch-like observation, but oddly Fiona wasn't troubled by that either. She wondered again about the contents of the tea. "Would you tell me more of my mother?" She changed the subject. "No one in the house will speak of her for fear of reawakening my father's grief."

Maive nodded and closed her eyes as her thoughts went far away. "I first saw your mother on a spring day, much like this one. She and your father were riding together. I knew right away that he was courting her—and that she was special."

"How?"

Maive grinned a toothless grin. "There's no magic to that. Your father was astride a horse for pleasure. Riding never came easily to him; he was always more comfortable traveling in a carriage or remaining indoors and not traveling at all. But for your mother, he'd do anything." She paused, her cloudy eyes seeing the past. "They were as opposite as two people could possibly be, yet somehow they completed each other. Much like the night completes the day, I suppose."

Hours flew by unnoticed as Maive shared recollections of her parents—stories Fiona had never heard before. Occasionally her thoughts wandered, but Fiona easily directed her back with specific questions. Questions she'd longed to have answered for as long as she could remember.

"I'm hungry," Maive suddenly announced. "There's some leftover stew in that small covered pot; not much but 'twill be enough for the two of us."

Fiona replaced the kettle of water with the small pot and added two more peat bricks to the dwindling fire. She lifted the lid and glanced dubiously inside at the unappetizing congealed fat on the surface, wondering how old it was. She took a sniff. It didn't smell rancid, and as the fat slowly melted back into the broth, it began to look more appealing. When it was hot, she ladled it into two wooden bowls and took the fullest one to Maive.

As she watched each trembling spoonful journey to Maive's mouth—half the contents falling back into the bowl along the way despite her concentration, Fiona didn't dare distract her with more discussion. Instead, she sat quietly, pacing her sips to match.

When Maive finished, Fiona rinsed and wiped both bowls, then resumed her seat on the stool. "Maive, can you see the future?" She asked the question that was foremost on her mind.

Maive eyed her thoughtfully. "Sometimes—if the gods choose to reveal it to me. Is there something you wish to ask them, child?"

"That's the problem, Maive; I'm far from a child," Fiona murmured, very aware that the woman's reference had been to the old gods, and not God. "Will I ever marry?" she finally whispered.

"Are you sure you wish to know? Knowledge of the future can be a heavy burden—too heavy for some to bear, and the frettin' over it drives them mad."

Fiona considered that, then dismissed it. It could be no worse than the fretting she was doing now. She nodded.

"Very well. Come closer."

Fiona slid her stool to the foot of Maive's chair. Maive leaned forward and reached out with both of her hands. Her long skeletal fingers skimmed over Fiona's face as if she were seeing through her fingertips. Fiona had seen a blind man do such a thing once, but Maive could see. Was she channeling her features to someone or something that could not? Fiona shivered at the thought.

"Now give me your hands."

The woman's shriveled fingers moved over her palms, tracing lines, real and imaginary. As Fiona awaited her verdict, she watched her face closely, waiting to see shock and disgust as she somehow discovered her secret. But Maive's face remained focused and calm.

"Aye," she finally said and nodded. "You will marry."

"Who?" Fiona whispered, barely able to ask.

Maive glanced back at her hand before releasing it. "You will marry a powerful Irish lord and by your marriage that power will grow. Your children will shape the future of these lands."

Fiona's heart plummeted in her chest. She suddenly felt it difficult to breathe. *A powerful Irish lord?* Not Gunnar? But who? And why? Would Gunnar not return? Would he be killed? Would she ever know his fate? Would she eventually give up waiting or be forced to marry another? She wanted to ask it all, to confess everything to this woman and know the truth, but she dared not.

"Are you certain?" she asked instead. "You said before sometimes you cannot tell."

"Aye, my dear, that is ofttimes true, but with you the signs are absolutely clear. You will marry, and it will be soon...before the year is out."

They were interrupted by a soft knock at the door. Without waiting for Maive's response, the door opened and a young woman, heavy with child, entered carrying another pot.

"Apologies, Maive. I didn't know you had company. I brought your meal," the woman said as she reached up with the back of one hand and brushed a section of curly hair from her flushed face.

"You can set it there, lass." Maive directed without inviting her to stay. "And there's a jug of tonic on the cupboard that Lady Fiona brought with her. Take it and give a spoonful to each of the children who has a cough."

"Aye, mum," the young woman murmured, then curtsied and nodded shyly at Fiona before leaving.

"I don't recognize her," Fiona said, surprised that no introductions had been made.

"She is Alma. Only recently moved here from Tir na Torc after marrying Bayne." Maive lowered her voice. "One day, when you're married and share a bedchamber with your husband, your belly will swell like that. Though me thinks Alma is a bit too large to have conceived on her wedding night. Far more likely is that the early sharing of her fruit with young Bayne is what led to that special day." The old crag shook her head. "A young woman must guard herself against the honeyed words of a man before marriage."

Fiona felt suddenly sick. What else had Maive seen in her vision? Were her words about Alma's indiscretions coincidence? "*Guard against the honeyed words of a man before marriage? Share a bedchamber and your belly will swell?*" Was she with child? Is that why she would marry so soon—before the end of the year? Would her father arrange a marriage when he found out? But who could he convince to have her if she carried another man's bastard? *Davin?* He'd mentioned Davin was coming soon to visit. Davin carried the title of lord, and while his father was known for his attempts to gain favor from the king at every opportunity, their family wasn't overly powerful.

Fiona chewed on a fingernail, wondering desperately what Maive knew. By the time she built up the courage to ask, Maive had dozed off. Sitting there with her head lolled to one side, she looked so innocent and frail when earlier she'd seemed so shrewd and insightful.

"Apologies, Maive," she murmured so as not to startle her. "But I must return home. I've already stayed far longer than intended, and Meirna will be worried," she lied.

"Of course, lass," Maive replied, her eyelids fluttering open.

Fiona hesitated. "But I should like to return to talk more, if that's alright?"

"Aye, that would please me greatly."

Fiona walked through the quiet village toward Barca, unaware of anything beyond her tumultuous thoughts—thoughts that were split evenly between trying to feel anything unusual inside her belly, and the consequences if it were true. When would she know if she was with child? She knew it usually took nine months for a baby to come after a wedding but wasn't sure how long it took to see the first signs.

The village midwife would have the answers, but she dare not ask her, not even with feigned interest. If Meirna were to hear of it, it would lead to a barrage of direct questioning that her fabricated story about the trip would not withstand.

And how would she explain it, if it turned out to be true? She couldn't, of course. No one would ever understand how she'd gone from being a proper lady to a Viking's...what? Mistress? Concubine? And all in a single week?

Chapter 27

The men stood gathered on the dark gravel beach in front of the Treasure Huntress.

"Just so we are all clear," Gunnar began. "This is a hunt, not a raid. Our goal is to capture able-bodied men with as little injury to them as possible. Once a man is captured, he is to be bound and gagged, then left to be retrieved later. Do not be too hasty with that. Make sure they are secure before leaving them. If one were to escape and warn the rest of the village, our advantage is lost. Understood?"

When the men murmured assent, Gunnar continued.

"We'll divide into groups and spread out in a wide perimeter to catch men working alone in the forest or fields first, then move in from there. The village will come last, but the primary goal is men, able-bodied and uninjured," he repeated for emphasis.

"What of women?" someone asked.

"We're not taking any women; I'll need all of your strength for the trip, but secure any who might raise a warning." He paused, singling out the new man. "And Eamon."

"Aye, my lord?"

"Try to not get yourself killed today."

The other men laughed.

"That goes for all of you. There will be plenty of opportunities to join our brothers in Valhalla in the rich lands of the East. I would see you all wealthy men before you make that final journey."

Swords were raised amidst muted hurrahs.

Eamon glanced at the huddled prisoners securely chained together, their forms barely discernible in the darkness at the edge of the firelight. There was no guard on them. There didn't need to be; they would not escape. These Northmen were extremely skilled at handling and binding men. And even if one were to get free, there was nowhere for him to go. After the raid, they'd loaded the new slaves onto the Treasure Huntress and sailed to a small desolate isle off the coast.

Little more than a long pile of rocks jutting from the water, it was ideal for their purpose. There was plenty of driftwood for fire, and they needed nothing else from the inhospitable strip of land; they'd seized enough food and drink from the Germanian village to eat like kings for a week.

As Eamon half-listened to the conversations going on around him, he adjusted the hood of his new sheepskin cape to keep the light drizzle blowing in off the Baltic from reaching his face. This kind of weather normally chilled a man to the bone, yet tonight he sat, warm and dry under the soft thick fleece. His stomach stuffed full of sausages, cheese, and as much stout, dark Germanian ale as he could stand, Eamon's body was relaxed, but his mind still raced through the day's events. Everything had gone exactly according to plan, and he would never forget any part of it.

Never forget the sounds of blades scraping bone, parting sinew, and piercing flesh. Never forget the shrieks of terror, agony, and death—each with its own distinct pitch that he could now easily recognize. Never forget the near-deafening roar of flames, as one by one the huts in the Germanian village were consumed.

Almost as powerful as the sounds had been the smells—acrid smells of smoke, sweat, and blood. So much blood. His sword had been covered in it, and the stickiness as it dried had actually melded his hand to the hilt, making it an extension of him—an extra appendage. So strong was the bond that he'd had difficulty peeling his fingers free when it was all over. He'd held a sword countless times before, but never had one felt like that.

The one thing he knew he would remember long after the sights, sounds, and smells faded from his memory—the most shocking thing of all, was what he'd felt. How facing another man who looked back at him with murderous intent, had awakened something inside him—a primal combination of fear and rage from somewhere deep and previously unknown. Fear and rage that drove him to act and move as he'd never moved before—pushing his body beyond its limits and heightening his senses to a level he didn't know they were capable. All the while, his heart pounding so hard in his chest, he feared it might burst.

Today he'd been animal, not man. Men had rules, restrictions, codes, basic decency. In battle all that was stripped away, leaving only a basic animal core. A core with only one goal—to survive—at all costs.

Like a wolf slaying a stag, he'd been vicious—efficient—merciless. It wasn't that he'd enjoyed the killing, but there was no denying he'd been excited by it. Though whether that excitement stemmed from his enemy's death or his own survival, he couldn't be sure—because in that moment they were one and the same. The blood, the screams, the smoke, were all horribly gruesome, yet he'd reveled in them because each signified that he was still alive and might yet continue to live.

Even tonight, when he celebrated as he drank their ale, wore their clothes, and ate their food, it wasn't a celebration of their deaths so much as a celebration of his own life—of the lives of every single man around this fire. It had come at the Germanians' expense, but for fate, could have easily gone the other way. And they all knew it.

He'd assumed before that Northmen were inherently different—that while they appeared as ordinary men on the surface, deep down they were simply savages who enjoyed killing. Now he understood that it was within every man—no matter what land he hailed from, his lineage, or his upbringing. Compassion and mercy were virtues and values that men cloaked themselves in when times were good to falsely set themselves apart from, and above simple beasts. But when faced with death, men quickly shed that shell of decency and reverted to the resilient raw animal inside.

Specific scenes of the fighting flitted and flashed through Eamon's mind, like lightning flashes in a storm. The Germanian with the battle-axe raised over the back of the unsuspecting Sven. His own hand pulling a smaller axe, a weapon he'd never used before, from his belt, and throwing it with all his might. Seeing it miraculously find its mark in the base of the Germanian's neck. Watching the man fall, without Sven ever being aware of how close to death he'd come. Elated, turning to find another Germanian collapsing at his feet, a knife slipping harmlessly from his grip as Rask withdrew his sword from the man's back. Rask giving him a quick nod and a half-grin before moving on.

Rask had saved his life, as he had done for Sven. But there was no expressing of effusive gratitude—no congratulating or talking up the magnitude and importance of what they'd just done. It was expected, and all the acknowledgment they required was a nod and a grin. Eamon had felt a sudden surging kinship to these men—a bond that he could only assume was like brotherhood, having never had a brother. A sense of belonging. A sense of unity. And he'd reveled in that, too.

He pulled the thick fleece cape tighter, the cape that Rask had pulled from one of the Germanian huts and tossed to him before they torched it. A cape of such quality he would have never dared hope to own its like before. After the cape, he'd joined the others in the looting, seizing anything he wanted—a curved bone-handled dagger and a pair of lace-up, deer-hide boots that seemed to have been made for his feet.

It was exhilarating to take another's possessions with no fear of reprisal. It was his right—his reward for surviving. Even as the smoke and furnace-like heat seared his eyes and throat, he felt a rush approaching giddiness. He wanted to shout and beat his chest. He was powerful. Far more powerful than any lord. And he had powerful brothers. They were a wolf pack. They answered to no one—well, to one man, but he was one of them.

"It is the battle fever." Rask had laughed at him, seeing the near-crazed expression in his eyes. "Have you never felt it before?"

Eamon had only been able to shake his head, unable to find proper words in that moment to come close to describing what he felt.

"It is within every man. Feel sorry for those who never get to release it."

And Eamon did feel sorry for them—those men like he used to be.

<hr />

Gunnar watched Eamon sitting amidst the other men across the fire, shocked by how well they accepted him. He was a foreigner. He received special attention. And yet they laughed and talked with him as if they'd known him for years. The Irishman sat quiet now, seeming almost subdued, but earlier had regaled them with stories, most of which could not possibly be true. He even spoke in Norse. He wasn't fluent, for he lacked a full vocabulary, but his accent was near perfect.

"So Irish, how does a lord's manservant come to be a slave?" one of the men asked. "What crime did you commit?"

"Did you pick him out stockings that didn't match?"

"Or let him go out in shoes that weren't properly shined?"

The men laughed as each tried to come up with the dubious act that had resulted in Eamon's fall from grace.

"Or are you a thief?" Olag asked. The men all grew quiet, waiting to see if Eamon would take offense. Gunnar watched, too. Olag's guess was as good as any.

"Nay." Eamon paused, pretending to give the question solemn consideration. "Unless a noble woman's heart and virtue are things that can be stolen." He grinned and took a swig of ale, then wiped the foam from his lips on the back of his hand before adding, "Though one can hardly steal what is freely given."

"You deflowered your lordship's daughter?"

"Nay, he had not a daughter and I did no deflowerin'," Eamon sputtered. "'Twas his wife, and she was far from virginal, I can assure you."

"You forced yourself on the lady of the house?"

"Force?" Eamon squawked. "Of course not. Are you not listenin'? Truth be told, it was nearly the opposite. While his lordship was a typical soft highborn, her ladyship was..." he paused and tipped his head back, "cut from a lustier cloth."

"You expect us to believe that the lady of the house lay with you of her own accord?" one of the men scoffed.

Eamon nodded.

"You're so full of shite, Irish."

"'Tis true," Eamon protested, laughing.

"So your lord found out and that's how you became a slave."

Before Eamon could respond, another joined in. "What kind of a man learns that you bedded his wife yet only sends you to a slaver? How does he not kill you?"

"To my knowledge, he still does not know of it," Eamon said.

"Then how...?"

"Who...?"

There was silence as the men all pondered his last words.

Eamon hesitated, knowing his answer would bring a storm of insults. "'Twas actually her ladyship who sent me away."

Raucous laughter erupted around the campfire.

"Have you ever heard of a man being so bad in the furs that the woman considered it a crime?" one guffawed.

"So what was it, Irish? Is your cock so tiny?" shouted another.

"Lucky for you, Leidolf, our women don't have such an option." The men laughed even harder as the ridicule was turned on one of their own.

"No wonder you didn't wish to tell it, Irish. That's a secret to be taken to the grave."

Eamon shook his head. "Laugh all you will, but I've no problem tellin' it, because once again the truth is in the opposite. Her ladyship was more than happy with the services I provided her. It was the level of service I provided her peers that she took disagreement with. She assumed by their increasingly frequent visits that she'd become quite popular. But it wasn't her they were comin' to see." He smiled slyly. "One afternoon she came upon me and one of her lady friends in a delicate position and took a jealous offense to it. Quite a jealous offense, in fact." His smile faded to a frown at the memory.

"Now you expect us to believe you slept with many noblewomen—that they sought you out for your favors? Is there no end to your shite?"

"My word to the gods, 'tis true."

Gunnar noted Eamon even referenced their gods now instead of his own. The man seemed to be shedding his past as easily as a snake shed its skin.

"Do you hear that, Gunnar?" One of the men shouted across the fire. "Eamon here wants us to believe he was sold into slavery for being too handy with his cock."

"Yes, I heard."

"Have you ever heard such a storyteller?"

"I don't believe that I have."

"Doubt it if you will," Eamon interjected. "But you asked me, and I've nothin' to gain by lyin.'"

"Unless you thought to gain reputation by having us repeat it! What did you hope to be called, Eamon the Virile? Eamon the Cock?" The men roared with laughter as the suggestions grew even more ribald.

"I can see that my experiences are not appreciated here, so I shall take my leave." With that, Eamon stood and stumbled around the fire to where Gunnar sat. "Those men wouldn't know the truth if it slapped them in the face," he chuckled as he flopped down next to him, ale sloshing over the side of his mug in the process. He looked at the symbols Gunnar was practicing with a stick in the dirt. "Nay, not like that." He wiped over Gunnar's last mark with his hand, picked up a stick, and redrew it. "Like this."

Chapter 28

"**W**ho is our guest?" Fiona asked as Meirna scrubbed at her face.

"Davin has arrived earlier than expected."

"Ow," Fiona winced. "Have a care, Meirna. That's not dirt. I swear you're removing my very skin!"

Meirna scowled and rubbed the damp cloth roughly over her cheek again. "Honestly, Fiona, whatever will he think? You're as brown as rye seed."

Fiona looked at her reflection in the polished tin plate. Her glowing tanned skin was tinged with a healthy dose of pink from the scrubbing. "Perhaps I should lower my bodice, then he'll not look to my face at all."

Meirna stared at her open-mouthed, and Siara inhaled sharply from where she'd been laying out Fiona's gown on the bed.

"'Twas only a jest, Meirna," Fiona murmured.

"Siara, please leave us," Meirna said quietly.

Siara scurried for the door. Meirna waited for it to close behind her before speaking. "Fiona, I swear you'll be the death of me, speaking that way. You're spendin' too much time with the common folk. 'Tis admirable to want to help those less fortunate, but you're carryin' it too far. While it's good *of* you, clearly 'tis not good *for* you."

"Yet 'tis true, is it not?"

"True? True?" Meirna stuttered, finding it inconceivable that Fiona would continue with the line of thought. "It matters naught if 'tis true! You're a lady, and ladies do not speak in such a manner."

"You know I'd never say such things in mixed company."

"You should not say such things at all! Nor think them either."

"You're right, Meirna, as always. Apologies," Fiona lowered her head, pretending to be suitably chastised.

Still ruffled, Meirna tipped her chin up none too gently and brushed her face with the white clay powder normally used to hide imperfections. It was something Meirna had always been proud that Fiona seldom needed with her pure skin, but today she added a layer to her entire face in an attempt to lighten its shade. As Fiona looked at her reflection, her green eyes blinking back at her from a pale white mask, she couldn't help but think of Gunnar's comment after their swim—about her looking like a corpse. She stifled a smile; she truly did look like a corpse now.

<hr />

Davin and her father were standing near the table with drinks in hand. Fiona paused to study their guest before she entered. He didn't appear to have grown an inch in the years since she'd last seen him, though he was slightly heavier and did carry himself differently. Gone were the timid, hunched shoulders that had oft reminded her of a turtle. Now he stood with his chest puffed like a rooster.

"Welcome, Davin," she murmured as she stepped inside and hugged him briefly. "It's been so long."

"Fiona, you're a beautiful woman," he exclaimed, holding her at arm's length while examining her with the same unmistakable squint.

"Davin has just returned from Frankia," her father informed her. "He was quite impressed."

"Aye," Davin admitted. "'Tis far grander than what we learned in your father's books."

"Come, let us sit, and he can tell us more about it over supper." Her father waved them to the full table.

All through the meal, Frankia this, Frankia that. Fiona could barely keep from yawning. His stories were so tedious after Gunnar's fascinating, detailed accounts. Davin described nothing other than what he'd been able to see from his carriage to and from the Frankish port of Cherbourg. From the sound of it, he'd never once left his host's estate, choosing instead to remain indoors sampling the man's wine. Which, judging by how often he had the maid refill his goblet tonight, was a pastime he'd grown quite fond of.

"All this talk of Frankia," her father laughed. "It seems you need to be reminded of the great things an Irish estate offers. Tomorrow I'll show you the new additions to my library and..."

Fiona stood. "Apologies, Papa. I shall retire and leave you men to private conversations." When Davin started to stand, she waved him back. "Please remain seated." *I would hate to see you fall down.*

Later, as Siara brushed out her long wavy hair in soothing strokes, Fiona asked, "Has Lord Davin given voice to how long he intends to stay?"

"Not that I've heard, my lady, but one more night is for certain."

Fiona nodded and prayed that it would only be one more.

The following morning Fiona feigned illness and had Siara bring her meals to her chambers. The day was frightfully boring, and as she made her way down to the dining hall that evening for supper, she prayed to hear Davin announce his departure.

"I'm so glad you're feeling better, my dear," her father said as soon as she was seated. "Davin has requested to see the horses tomorrow, if you would oblige him?"

"Your father says you have a new colt that your head stableman is quite keen on," Davin added.

"Aye, he's a fine colt out of our best mare," Fiona said, deflated. Even her favorite subject wasn't enough to offset the dread of being trapped in his boorish company, especially when she suspected it to be a ruse. Davin had never shown an interest in horses before. She doubted he even knew the difference between croup and withers. Reaching for her own glass of wine, she took a deep swallow.

"You never told us what business took you to Frankia?" her father asked.

Dear God, not more Frankia. Fiona took another swallow.

"I have distant relatives there. My father wished for me to renew ties."

"To what end?"

"To garner their support in future conflicts with the Northern O'Neill, of course."

Fiona's father frowned. "If you learned anything from your time with me, Davin, I would hope that it would be to learn from history so as not to repeat it. Do not spend your life caught up in old family feuds that have naught to do with you."

"I have also learned much *since* my time spent with you, Patrick. Those old family feuds you speak of are my legacy, and yours. 'Tis not a choice; 'tis a matter of family honor. To ignore the threat the Northern O'Neill pose, would mean to be overrun by them."

"And would that be so bad for you? Tell me, how would your daily life be different if your high king was Northern instead of Southern O'Neill? Both are your blood if you go back far enough. If this were decided once and for all, perhaps we could finally have real peace."

"How can you say that? Have you been in contact with the Northern O'Neill?" Davin asked, aghast.

"Nay, of course not."

"Then you should be very careful in whose company you utter such sentiments."

"I thought I was being careful, speaking my thoughts in the company of an educated man."

"I've come to learn that whilst education is of interest, real decisions are made by the sword."

"You cannot believe that," her father said, shocked.

"I do, and when the Northern O'Neill arrive to lay claim to your lands, you'll believe it, too. They're practically at your doorstep now, and their intent is clear. They've conquered every kingdom in the north and now boldly move south. After taking Airgialla, surely you can see that their eyes now rest here."

"They're not on our doorstep. Breifne still stands between us and it's Connacht land. Taking Airgialla and the other smaller northern kingdoms are one thing. Taking on the Connachts is entirely another. The Northern O'Neill will not do it."

"Only a thin strip of Breifne lies between us and them, and 'tis far removed from the majority of Connacht land and power. Throw into consideration that much of the land in question is Tir na Laoch, your ailing neighbor, Lord Nevyn's vast estate. 'Tis ripe for the taking."

"'Tis still Connacht land," her father disagreed.

"Perhaps, but the Connacht armies are fully occupied with Munster on their southern border. They'll not go to war on two fronts—certainly not over the tip of Breifne."

"Why are you really here, Davin?" her father asked.

"I had not thought to have this conversation so early in my visit." Davin took a drink.

Fiona cringed. *So early in his visit? How long did he intend to stay?*

"We believe the Northern O'Neill will attempt to take eastern Breifne and Tir na Laoch. To discourage them from any thoughts of continuing into Southern O'Neill territory, we think it best to show a strong front with a strengthened alliance here." Davin took another deep swallow of wine.

"You keep saying we," her father said. "Who is we?"

"King Flann and his advisors."

"Which include your father?"

"Aye."

"And how do they propose we do that—show our strengthened alliance?" Her father spoke very evenly, but Fiona could see his anger.

Oblivious, Davin took a large bite and was still chewing it as he lifted his fork and continued with his mouth half full. "By marriage, of course. Betroth Fiona to me. She and I are familiar with one another, and, well...," he glanced at her, "she is quite advanced in years. The fact that she is not yet married, suggests that 'tis not likely to happen at all. After our wedding, since you do not have an army of your own to speak of, my father would garrison a small force here—temporarily and for our protection, of course."

"It seems your father and King Flann have given much consideration to *our protection*."

Davin finally heard the tone. "Honestly, Patrick, even if you're right about the Northern O'Neill being unwilling to take on the Connachts over Lord Nevyn's land, it doesn't change anything. You yourself are in a similar position. You're not getting any younger, and should you die without Fiona having produced an heir or marrying back into the clan, your lands, especially when combined with Lord Nevyn's, could be the very spark that draws us into full-scale war."

Fiona could hold her tongue no longer. "You speak of me as if I were a broodmare. If something were to happen to my father, I am more than capable of managing Tir na Lionmhar."

"Apologies, Fiona, I had thought to have this conversation privately among men."

"Since when do you think it acceptable to decide my fate, *privately among men*, without my consideration? There was a time when you valued my opinion."

"I was but a lad then, too young to know better—to know a woman's true place. But I'm a man now, grown far beyond your father's teachings. While you've remained sheltered here, I've *seen* the world he taught us about."

"You've seen Frankia, and by your own accounts, not much of that beyond your host's wine cellar. And as far as grown, Davin, I could not disagree more. Your intellect, much like your form, is quite stunted."

"Fiona!" her father reprimanded.

"Nay, 'tis alright, Patrick," Davin said and turned back to her. "'Tis because your father has placed far too much value on your *consideration*, Fiona, that he finds himself in this precarious position," Davin retaliated. "How many men will die fighting over this land because you were not made to do your duty?"

"If men die fighting over this land, it will be because of greed and ambition and have naught to do with me," Fiona seethed.

"By saying that, you show how little you truly understand. 'Tis not greed, Fiona, 'tis necessity, and you should not direct your spiteful tongue at me; I'm merely the messenger. Perhaps 'tis better that you are here, so that you fully understand what's at stake. Whether you're capable of managing it or not, Tir na Lionmahr's location and rich lands hold too much strategic value to be left to you. Your father has allowed you to choose your own husband, and I urge you to exercise that gift. Because once he's gone, whoever lays claim to Tir na Lionmhar will not afford you such a luxury. You'll be forced to marry whomever they choose. I can tell you with all certainty, Fiona, there are far worse choices for a husband than I."

"I'm not at all convinced of that," Fiona snapped as she stood. "With your permission, Papa, I shall take my leave."

After he nodded, Fiona left without acknowledging Davin at all.

She could barely control her rage as she climbed the stairs. How dare he and his father conspire with King Flann to lay claim to Tir na Lionmhar! Her family had always been loyal to the Southern O'Neill. Not as zealous as some, perhaps, but supporting them in other ways—with food, supplies, and coin. And this is how they were repaid?

Did they honestly think she was a mindless bit of fluff who'd accept marrying Davin because she'd been fond of him as a child? There was nothing left of the young Davin she'd known. The curious, shy lad had been replaced by an ignorant, narrow-minded dolt. She despised him! And if they were right about the Northern O'Neill's intentions to attack, even a forced marriage to some unknown conqueror would be preferable to marrying that mewling, half-witted foot-licker.

"Lord Davin departed early this morning," Siara whispered eagerly as she pulled open Fiona's curtains. "Your father did not see him off. I think he may have even sent him away." She lowered her voice. "They exchanged heated words last night, and your father was up very late alone in his library."

"Probably for the best," Fiona groused as she tried to shield her eyes from the painful brightness. "Otherwise, he'd likely have stayed as long as the wine flowed—like a tick on a dog, content to sit and suck until he was too round to move."

"Fiona," Meirna chided as she entered and overheard her last words. She seemed poised to say more, but only shook her head. "Your father has gone out but wishes to speak with you later. He's asked that you not stray far from the house today."

Fiona nodded. As much as she wanted to hear what had transpired between him and Davin after she left, she was grateful for the delay; her head was hurting quite severely. "Siara, would you please bring me a tonic from Haisley? And perhaps draw the curtains again. I think I shall remain in bed for awhile. My head feels as though it will burst."

"Aye, my lady."

***

Fiona tapped lightly on the open door to her father's library.

"Ah, Fiona. Come in and sit down." A fire crackled merrily in the fireplace, and the room was uncomfortably warm. "As I'm sure you know, I'm beyond disappointed in the man Davin has become. It appears his time here was wasted; he learned nothing from me at all.

"That being said, it doesn't change the fact that the points he made about your marriage status—and what would become of you should I die before you're married, are valid ones. The O'Neill are looking for an excuse to fight. If it's not over Lord Nevyn's land, they will most certainly battle over ours, and your fate will lie in the hands of the victor. I cannot have that.

"I've given you nothing but free rein in this matter, hoping you would choose a husband, but it seems no man has been able to meet your lofty ideals." He shook his head. "I'm probably to blame. With all the books of heroes I've given you to read, it has elevated your standards beyond reasonable expectation. You may never be satisfied with the qualities of a mortal man. But how we came to be here is irrelevant. The fact is that you do need to find a husband and produce an heir. If you have a son while I yet live, he can inherit this land along with whatever title your future husband carries."

"You could always remarry, Papa," Fiona pointed out, shocked by her own forthrightness on the subject. Normally she would have never dared utter such words, but despite taking Haisley's tonic and sleeping most of the day, her headache had worsened. She was in no mood for this lecture now.

"You may be older, but you could find a young bride and make an heir. Age doesn't seem to matter in the fathering of children—not as it does for the bearing of them. Look at Lord Ayle. He is much older than you, and how old is his new wife? Fourteen? And already on his second child?"

"Fiona, there's more to marriage than just making an heir."

"Yet, by your own words, you would have me married off for no other purpose."

Her father stared at her, shocked. "That's not true, nor fair. I would have you married off to be happy—as your mother and I were happy. The fact that you are twenty and have not yet been forced to do so is a testament to that."

"But at some point, I will run out of time? What is the cutoff, Papa? Twenty-two? Twenty-three? At what age will my happiness cease to be of import, and you shall command me to begin making babies?"

"Fiona, I'm ashamed of you! I've been nothing but patient, lass, yet you appreciate none of it. You will remember your place. If I say you will marry, you'll do it and be glad for it. Did nothing of what Davin said sink in? If something happens to me, it will be a free-for-all among the O'Neill. They're already planning for it. Do you think whoever emerges victorious will allow you to choose a husband? Nay, lass! They'll have you married and bedded to someone they can control."

Fiona had never seen him so angry, certainly not with her. Had he called her here to tell her he intended to arrange a marriage? Her heart pounded steadily harder as she awaited his next words, Old Maive's prediction ringing in her head, *"You shall marry a powerful Irish lord...before the year is out."*

He took a deep breath to calm himself and continued. "I didn't call you here to frighten you with the darker sides of men. There is more to life than riding horses and reading books, Fiona. There's an entire world that you've not experienced and cannot even begin to imagine. When you love someone, everything is..." He groped for words. "...better. Even the most mundane things bring joy, and there's a sense of fulfillment that I cannot begin to describe. With the solitary life you lead now, I fear you'll never experience any of that."

Fiona bit her tongue to keep all the things she wanted to say from rushing out. That she knew his words to be true—that she knew love and how it had made even a deadly storm seem magical. But once admitted, she'd have to reveal Gunnar's identity. And she could never do that. Her father would have her married off for sure. Because despite his assurances that she marry for love, he'd never understand or accept that love was for a Viking.

Tears stung her eyes. She tried to suppress them. She couldn't remember the last time she'd cried and was angry that tears would come now. Before he could see them, she stood and fled to the safety of her room, bolting the door behind her. She curled into a ball on her bed with a pillow hugged tight to her chest and let the tears flow. She cried not for any one thing in particular, but for everything. For the tangled mess her life had become—her secrets, lies, and guilt. For Davin's cruel words, for having her father yell at her, for having been born an O'Neill, for living every day with the empty, gutted feeling Gunnar's absence had left inside her, for her doubts and fears that he might not return, and for the decisions, pain, and betrayal she faced if he did. Ignoring the knocks on her door, she cried for all of it, letting it out in great wracking sobs.

Fiona awoke disoriented and groggy. She looked around her bedchamber, squinting at the bright morning light streaming through her window. It seemed to pierce her very brain. Tentative knocks sounded on her door— likely what had wakened her. She closed her eyes and rolled over, feeling the laces of her gown biting into her skin. *She'd slept fully clothed?* The events of the previous night came rushing back. She groaned and pulled the pillow over her head.

The tentative knocks ceased, only to be followed moments later by sharper raps that increased in boldness with every set. This knocking was clearly not going away. The first would have been Siara. The second, Meirna.

Muttering under her breath, Fiona rose and unbolted the door, then returned to her bed as Meirna pushed inside.

"Your father has requested you at breakfast," Meirna announced, frowning at her wrinkled dress.

"I am ill," Fiona declined.

"He said if you do not join him there, then he shall join you here," Meirna said brusquely.

"So he has not *requested* me at breakfast, he has commanded me."

Meirna didn't respond, only started laying out fresh clothes.

"Would you at least have Siara bring me a dose of Haisley's tonic before my next round of interrogation? Perhaps something different than what she gave me yesterday; that seems to have had no effect at all. My head feels as if it shall split in two." Fiona expected an argument, but after peering at her more closely, Meirna nodded and left.

Fiona sat stiffly on the edge of her seat at the end of the table opposite her father, the plate of food in front of her untouched.

"I regret our words yesterday...my words," her father began. "I probably should have remarried after your mother died, but I had not the heart, and still do not. Forgive me for that—for placing the burden onto your shoulders. Had I a son or even other daughters, one of them could have produced an heir, and you would be free to be a spinster if that is your desire. But alas, that's not the case.

"Last night, as I considered your question as to what age you would cease to have a choice, I thought to give you an ultimatum—a deadline for you to either find someone to marry or I would do it for you. An arranged marriage is not unusual or unreasonable," he added defensively.

"I must admit, that decision caused me a long sleepless night, and I've concluded that I cannot do it. It saddens me that your life will not be full as your mother's and mine were, however brief our time together, but it is your life. If misery is in your future, I shall not be the cause of it. And I fear, more than just a little, that your mother might rise from her very grave if I were to do such a thing." He smiled a melancholy smile. "She was a very determined woman...much like you are."

"Gratitude, Papa."

"Do not thank me yet. I'm not finished, and you're not getting off so easily. There is still an ultimatum. I realize that you'll never meet a husband riding the countryside like a banshee—never leaving Tir na Lionmhar. So, from this day forward, every invitation that we receive, regardless of the event, be it a wedding or a wake, will be accepted, and we will attend. And I shall attempt to keep my mind open to meeting someone, though I see no woman for me other than your mother."

"But Papa. Surely you can't mean every..."

He held up his hand. "I've made up my mind, and on this, my decision is final. There will be no discussion. What you do when we attend is up to you. If you wish to sit to the side and refuse to engage in conversation or enjoy yourself in any way, that is your prerogative, but you will go. We will both go."

"But 'tis spring, Papa. We could receive two or more invitations in a week—some from as far away as..."

"Then we shall attend two or more," he cut her off. "And if, God forbid, you reach spinster age and are still unmarried, then you can...devote your life to God...or...I don't know." He ran his hand through his hair, looking suddenly old. "Let us just pray it does not come to that." He leaned back in his chair. "That is all."

Fiona stood, her tonic-fogged mind struggling to come up with a counter-argument.

"Oh, I almost forgot," he added. "We're attending Lord Sheron's feast tonight and shall depart immediately after the midday meal. We missed the hunt, but we shall make the feast. Have Meirna pack a trunk for you; it will be late and we shall likely stay the night."

"But Papa..."

"Honestly, Fiona, what is wrong with you?" he snapped. "What kind of young woman does not enjoy getting dressed up and going out? Now go, before I change my mind on an arranged marriage and save myself the trouble and worry."

Chapter 29

"**H**ow is it a man born to an Irish whore comes to speak Norse and tend to a lord?" Gunnar asked as he concentrated on trying to duplicate the latest string of symbols Eamon had scrawled in the sand.

"As you know, Dublin was held by Northmen until recently—and I also know a great many other languages—Frankish, Germanian, Latin—at least bits of them. There were always ships from afar in port, and men, no matter where they hail from, seek the company of a whore after time at sea. I grew up hearing many different tongues.

"And the whores all liked me. They'd have their customers hire me to run errands, fetch things or deliver messages. I learned early on that the ability to speak another tongue was invaluable. It was perhaps the single most important thing that helped me to survive when I killed my mother's murderer and ran. Around the docks, there's always need for a translator."

"That explains your knowledge of our language but not how you came to be a lord's manservant."

"Lords are not uncommon at the docks. I saw the easy life of their servants, and I wanted it for myself. I noted that my lord came to the docks every week accompanied only by an effeminate slip of a manservant. I hired local thugs to rob him, and, during the attack, I happened to come along and save the day. It was quite a gamble. Hiring the men cost me every coin I had to my name, not to mention put me in grave danger if they'd betrayed me.

"But they did not, and after I retrieved his lordship's purse and ran them off, I presented myself as an unemployed manservant with no references to offer because my previous lord had been killed...," He cocked his head and smiled a half-smile, "by Northmen of all things. How ironic is that? Of course, I played it off as no concern of his, and would accept no reward— said I was only doing my duty; I had a whole line of shite. In the end, he practically begged me to attend to him. I never looked back."

"How did you know what to do?"

"I'm a quick learner. I watch, and much like reading these symbols," he motioned toward the marks in the sand, "I read people. I read their reactions to my words or my actions. Subtle things—a slight nod or a relaxing of their stance when I do something correctly—a tenseness or perhaps a frown when I make a mistake. When something isn't as it should be, I figure out what it is and fix it. And I'm bold, or so I've been told." He grinned. "I think that's more than half of it. When you're confident, or at least act confident, people are far less likely to question you."

Eamon took a sip of ale. "And really, 'tis not difficult. Much of it is simply mimicking the behaviors of those around you. If you don't stand out as different, people feel at ease; when they're at ease, they accept you.

"So you spend your life pretending to be other men?"

"I suppose."

"And when you're not among people whom you're trying to *put at ease,* who is Eamon, the man?"

Eamon pondered for a moment, then shrugged. "I couldn't say. I've never been in a position like that." He didn't seem bothered by the thought. "I'm whoever I need to be in the moment."

"Some might see that as false."

"Or fortunate," Eamon countered. "I'm at home wherever and with whomever I find myself. Look at me now. A lad, born to a whore, became a nobleman's manservant and is now a Viking warrior. At the rate I'm going, I may one day be a king. Who knows?"

Gunnar smiled and shook his head. "You're an interesting man, Eamon."

"Nay, not like that. Like this." Eamon again swept over Gunnar's latest mark and redrew it with his own stick. "Try that one again."

Gunnar nodded and traced Eamon's mark before carefully trying it again on fresh sand. "Have you ever loved a woman?" Gunnar asked as he completed it, then moved on to the next.

"Have you not heard my stories?" Eamon chuckled. "The fact that I've loved too many is how I came to be in my predicament at Tibbot's."

"I noticed you didn't take a Germanian woman after the raid. Is it because there is someone else? Or do you take issue lying with an unwilling woman?"

"In truth, I didn't find their women to my liking. When it comes to lying with a woman, I have a strict code I follow that has never failed me. I must be confident that in a fight I could take her—at least two out of three times," he added with a grin. "With the size of those Germanian women, there were none where that outcome was assured, at least none that I saw."

Gunnar shook his head. Eamon couldn't just say that he preferred smaller women; everything had to be a tale, often embellished with humor. "Back to my previous question. I asked if you'd ever loved a woman. Not lay with, but loved—had a woman in your blood."

"You are serious?"

"I am."

Eamon was quiet for a moment while he considered the question. "I've enjoyed some more than others, but nay, I couldn't say that I loved any one in particular."

Gunnar nodded.

"But you have," Eamon murmured as he studied him. "And not your wife that everyone speaks of. There's someone else—in Ireland. That's why—that's why you also did not lay with a Germanian woman. That's why the men say you're different now, and explains your haste. They say we'll be hard-pressed to complete this trip in seven months. They assume you push them because you still rankle from not finding the culprits who attempted to sink the Huntress or because you were unable to retrieve the stolen slaves. But that's not it at all." His voice drifted off, and he cocked his head at Gunnar curiously. "There's a woman there, and you are eager to return to her. How strange. And you say that I'm interesting."

Gunnar stared at him. Had he not just explained his methods of reading people and his ability to infer, Gunnar would have sworn it was some type of magic. "That is not something I would have shared with the other men," he warned.

Eamon shrugged and nodded. "As you wish. But tell me, do you intend to take her as wife?"

Gunnar frowned. "Therein lies a bit of difficulty."

"She's already married?"

"No." Gunnar focused on the marks. He could feel Eamon's questioning eyes on him, but he'd already told him too much. Or had he? Eamon was Irish and a studier of people; if anyone might know of a solution... "She is highborn," Gunnar finally admitted.

Eamon raised his eyebrows but said nothing.

"Now you are mute?" Gunnar asked gruffly.

"In truth, I have a great many questions, but I'm not sure what is appropriate to ask."

"Ask what you will."

"So all this...my teaching you...is to impress her? To convince her to have you?"

"Nay, we are well past that."

"What then? Certainly, you don't think to somehow become acceptable to her family?" Eamon chuckled and took another drink. "That you could somehow pass yourself off as a noble."

The pure amusement in Eamon's tone told Gunnar how ridiculous his fledgling plan truly was. "My only thought, if I had one along those lines, would be to somehow become acceptable enough that we could remain in Ireland—some way for her to keep a semblance of what her life has been up until now. Could that be done? I have wealth. Much wealth."

"Aye, but..." Sensing his earlier mistake, Eamon chose his next words carefully. "You have no title...no lineage...no noble blood."

"They can sniff out noble blood better than any hound." The lizard-eyed lord's words taunted Gunnar in his mind. "And you were not a manservant, yet you managed to convince them otherwise."

"True, but...well...I am me, and...you are you. No offense, but I've spent my entire life attempting to fit in. You, on the other hand, have spent your life doing the exact opposite—forcing others to your will."

"Is my behavior so terrible that it is inconceivable? I would have your honest answer; there is no need to placate me."

"Nay, 'tis not that. I've actually seen many nobles, especially those from outlying lands, whose manners were quite appalling."

"But?"

"But they still had family history."

Gunnar frowned. He'd come to the same conclusion many times.

"And there's an arrogance and confidence—a certainty that goes with it. Although I suppose you aren't lacking in any of those qualities." Eamon's voice trailed off as something occurred to him. "And what is title?" he murmured.

"What?"

"Forgive me; that was not a question directed at you, I was only thinking out loud. Where does a title actually begin? The first of every noble line was not born with a decree stuck to his bare arse. In the beginning, they were just men who became lords by becoming powerful. Even now, titles and lands are granted by kings to men who have done them some favor."

"I've done nothing to gain the favor of any of your kings, I can assure you."

"Nay, I wouldn't think so. And if not granted by a high king then it must come from blood. Unless..."

"Unless what?"

Eamon hesitated. "I would hate to get your hopes up, absent cause."

"Speak, man!"

"I once accompanied my lord to a bishop's estate—an unimaginably rich place."

"I thought your Christian priests lived simple lives, void of material things."

"That's only true for the lower orders. Bishops are always of noble birth with their own lands and title. Initially, my lord was tight-lipped as to the purpose of his visit, but later he became quite talkative. A lord whose estate neighbored ours was ill, and the man had no heir. It was my lord's intent to have himself named as the heir to claim the lands when he died."

"How could he do that? Were they, in fact, related?"

"Not even distantly. But with certain false documents—records of baptisms and marriages secretly filed in the correct places, they could be. A bishop's position makes him the single most uniquely qualified person to do that. He travels to all of the parishes to collect the tithes and confer with the priests and monks. When he goes over their records, he has access to all their documents."

"Why would a bishop be willing to risk his position?"

"'Twas my understanding this particular bishop has high ambitions within the church. Such ambitions that will require much wealth to achieve. And I think the risk is not so great—who would oppose him, if there are no true heirs?"

Gunnar nodded as he absorbed it.

"It did not occur to me as an option for you at first, because, well, while my lord might not have been related to his neighbor, he did at least have noble blood, which you clearly do not. But that made his claim to the lands no less false. If you're sure you don't need to convince the lady herself, perhaps your contact with others could be kept limited."

"So did your lord get those lands?"

"He did not."

Gunnar scowled and threw down his stick. "Then why tell me all of that?"

Eamon held up his hands in defense. "He did not fail for lack of it being possible. He failed by being beat at his own game. I'm not sure who leaked word of his plan, but another adjacent lord became aware of the scheme, and he had more to offer." He paused and looked seriously at Gunnar. "How deep are your pockets?"

"Do you honestly think..."

"Think what? That a Northman could be long-lost kin to a lord? I'll admit, it would take a very creative story, but if you truly have the coin, creative stories, as you have seen and heard," Eamon grinned, "are my specialty."

"And you'd be able to locate this bishop upon our return?"

"Aye. But you can't just pay him a visit. You must request an audience well in advance. If you choose to attempt this, I will compose a letter of your desire. If the bishop is agreeable, he can be locating potential properties while we are away in the East."

Gunnar nodded. "I'll find someone to deliver it when we rejoin the fleet in Visby tomorrow. There will be trade ships going west."

"I must express again, this will be very costly."

"How much?" Gunnar asked grimly.

"For my previous lord's neighboring estate..." He took the stick from Gunnar and wrote two numbers in the dirt, "I heard this many pounds of gold and this many of silver."

Gunnar smiled and nodded. "Compose your message, Eamon."

"You're certain?"

"I am."

"Do you have an area in mind?"

"Have your bishop begin his search around Balbriggan and widen it from there, but the location matters naught."

"To prove the seriousness of your intent and raise you in his thoughts, I suggest you include a gift with the letter. 'Tis my understanding His Grace has a special fondness for rarities."

"I have a chest of valuables from previous raids that I brought to cover expenses. Come. You can look through it and choose whatever you feel appropriate."

Chapter 30

The ride to Lord Sheron's had been pure misery. While Haisley's most recent tonic had dulled her headache, it had done little to address the new pain in her joints. Fiona swore the carriage wheels hadn't missed a single jarring rut or stone. She'd been so relieved to finally arrive, but now, seated at the long table between the widower, Lord Alsandair, and the elderly Lord Mundy, she looked back at the time in the carriage with longing. At least it had been quiet.

Lord Mundy was not the problem. Hard of hearing, he made no attempts at conversation. Lord Alsandair was another matter. Recently returned from his pilgrimage to Rome, he seemed determined to share every mundane detail of his journey, spending an inordinate amount of time on how the unfamiliar foods had afflicted his bowels. Even though she was quite curt with him, if she responded at all, he either didn't notice or didn't care and continued to blather on.

Fiona felt for the extra vial of tonic in the small silk pouch purse suspended from her braided silver belt. She was tempted to take a little nip, but Haisley had been very strict in her warning about the potency of this new batch. She was not to take another dose until just before bed with the rest to be saved until morning.

With Lord Alsandair droning on beside her—something now about the color and consistency changes to his stool when he ate food seasoned with a spice called turmeric, Fiona's mind drifted. To exotic places with dark-skinned female warriors and great ships being dragged over land. To barbarians guarding the riverbanks in the wilds of Rusland and beyond. She wondered where Gunnar was at that moment. Was he thinking of her? How different this meal would be if she were seated at a table with him. She smiled, remembering his matter-of-fact, serious way of eating, and his chagrined response when she had teased him about it at the third inn.

"I see Lady Fiona understands me." Hearing her name snapped Fiona from her pleasant memory, and she stared blankly across the table at Lord Brannon, unsure if a response was in order. "Many people do not see the irony, but I saw you smile." He raised his silver goblet to her and took a long swallow.

Fiona stared at his sweating red face, then down the long table at the other lords seated there. Lord Cowyn, the buffoon. Lord Mago, the philanderer. Lord Fagan, with the lazy eye. Countless others who were all versions of the same. She longed for a reason to excuse herself. When she felt a tap on her shoulder and turned to find Lady Abiageal, Fiona blinked, wondering if she'd somehow conjured her.

"I'm so glad to find you here, Fiona. I've missed you greatly and have much to tell," Abiageal whispered furtively as she took her hand and pulled her from her seat. "I've met someone and I think I'm in love. He's younger than I am—considerably actually, but I believe he loves me, too, and I cannot wait to make introduction to you." She linked her arm through Fiona's and led her away from the table.

Fiona couldn't believe her good fortune. Not only was she able to escape Lord Alsandair's dreadful company, but once in private, she could confess her lie to Abiageal about spending the week with her—and hopefully convince her to support the story if she were to speak with her father. Of course, Abiageal would ask where she'd actually gone; she needed to have an answer for that. Fiona tried to quickly think of something acceptable to tell her, but came up with nothing. Her normally sharp mind was dull as mud.

Abiageal steered them away from the other guests towards the rough-hewn wooden staircase that led to the upper balcony rimming the great hall. At first, Fiona thought the deserted spot would be an ideal retreat, but as she started up the steep stairs after Abiageal, she began to have second thoughts. The heat and smoke from the candle chandeliers and torches grew thicker with every step. She steadied herself on the handrail, the little she'd managed to eat roiling in her stomach.

"Shall we sit?" Abiageal asked when they reached the top, motioning to two chairs that overlooked the great hall below.

Dizzy, Fiona nodded. Haisley's tonic was waning, and after the exertion of the climb, her pulse pounded painfully behind her eyes.

"This is grand. We can see the entire hall from here. Let me take a quick look to make sure I haven't missed Kiernan's arrival, then I shall tell you my news," Abiageal chatted, seemingly unaffected by the heat or the smoke.

While Abiageal searched for her beau, Fiona's gaze also wandered over the people below. She paused on the small crowd gathered around the Widow Evlin. Evlin's second husband was barely cold in his grave, yet here she was, not even pretending to mourn him. It was scandalous. Though scandal had a way of never sticking to Evlin. Not when all four of her siblings had died mysteriously during their childhoods. Not when both of her husbands died immediately after she bore them a son.

According to gossip, her first husband's heart had failed in their bedchamber. He was an elderly lord, and it had raised no suspicion. But her second husband had been young and healthy. Witnesses claimed he'd fallen from his horse during a hunt and was dead when they reached him—with no visible injury to account for his demise. The questionable circumstances of his death, however, did not preclude Evlin's infant son from inheriting his father's title and wealth.

Tonight, the bevy of admirers who vied for her attention seemed not the least bit concerned by the ill fortune that struck those closest to her. Though whether they were attracted to her multiple fortunes or her beauty was uncertain. For Evlin was beautiful. No one could argue that. Her skin was pure as milk, and her raven hair cascaded down her back in soft curls. Bearing two children had only added curves to her form, which she accentuated with a daringly cut blue silk gown.

Fiona had never cared for Evlin; the woman was a spiteful wretch. Though admittedly, the outright dislike Fiona felt for her now stemmed from envy. They were the same age—an age that was considered so young for a widow but old for an unmarried woman. A fact that Evlin relished pointing out to both Fiona and Abiageal at every possible opportunity. Having produced two heirs, Evlin faced no further demands, and her status as a widow held no restrictions. She wasn't required to appear chaste, and her actions reflected it. She basked in the attention, flirting shamelessly with the men around her, young and old alike.

"Who is that?" Abiageal whispered. "I've never seen him before."

Thankful for the interruption of Evlin's envious circumstances, Fiona's eyes followed Abiageal's finger through the smoke to the late arrival. "I don't know," she replied as she took in the tall thin stranger. His dark hair was pulled back tight, and he carried a cane but walked without a limp. With a look of bored distaste on his face, his eyes searched the crowded room while he paused for his name and title to be announced.

Fiona couldn't hear it over the noise of conversations, but she could tell by the overeager posturing of Lord Sheron and his wife, who had risen to greet him, that he was someone important. With a final nod, he dismissed them and made his way deeper into the great hall, seeming to be looking for someone.

"Oh, Fiona," Abiageal tugged on her sleeve, nodding to a younger man walking towards the staircase below them. "Here he comes. That's him. There. Oh, he sees me. He's coming. Oh..." Abiageal squirmed in her seat while he ascended the stairs. Even as poorly as she felt, Fiona couldn't help but smile at her friend's excitement. Though younger than Fiona by two years, Abiageal had already long dreaded the prospect of spinsterhood.

"Ladies," he addressed them with a bow.

"Good evening, my lord," a flushed but more composed Abiageal murmured beside her. "I didn't know you had arrived. May I present my good friend, Lady Fiona. Fiona, this is Lord Kiernan."

"A pleasure to meet you, Lady Fiona."

"My lord." Fiona nodded back at him.

"I would ask Lady Abiageal to walk with me if you would pardon her absence?"

Fiona felt Abiageal's pleading eyes on her. "Of course. I was just about to return to my father," she lied.

As Abiageal and the young Lord Kiernan descended the stairs and reappeared below, Fiona caught the look that passed between them. A single look that conveyed so much. Longing—admiration—respect—love. Despondent, she sank deep into her chair. Every joint in her body complained and her head pounded, but they were nothing compared to the renewed pain in her heart.

Disregarding Haisley's warning, Fiona reached for her purse. Withdrawing the vial of tonic, she removed the cork stopper and lifted it to her lips. She drained it, leaned her head back, and closed her eyes. Soothing numbness coursed through her veins.

"Lady Fiona O'Neill." A man's low voice from close behind gave her a start. "At last."

Fiona sat up in her chair. She turned to find the tall, dark-haired nobleman who had just arrived. He was alone, which was surprising; as someone important, his company would be much sought after. Up close, he was even thinner than he'd originally appeared, and his fine clothes hung on his skeletal frame. His skin had an unhealthy pallor, and his lanky hair appeared not to have been washed in weeks, but it was his odd protruding eyes that were most strange. Cold and unblinking, they appeared more reptilian than man.

It had to be the tonic playing tricks on her. Haisley hadn't said what would happen if she took too much, only not to. "My lord," she finally acknowledged him, trying to sweep the cobwebs from her mind. "Apologies, but I do not believe we've met."

"You are correct. We have not. But not for my lack of effort, I can assure you. I am Lord Artan MacTavish, and I've been very much looking forward to making your acquaintance."

A MacTavish? That would explain the bowing and scraping of the hosts, but why was he here?

"We have a mutual friend, you know," he said with a smile that did not go to his eyes.

"I'm sure we share a great many friends, my lord," she replied uneasily. Something about him was off.

"Aye, I'm sure we do, but none like this one. You and I share a very special friend, and I'll warrant that he's a friend unique to the two of us. Though I think 'tis safe to say, he's far more special to you, than I."

Alarms clamored inside her head. His words were innocent but his tone seemed sinister. Was that also the tonic? "Apologies, my lord, but I have no idea to whom you're referring. If I were to attempt to guess and name one, it would only insult others for not being considered special friends." Fiona smiled, trying to make light of the perhaps imagined tension as she prepared to excuse herself.

"Allow me to jog your memory," he said, his voice steely. "Our unique friend hails from north of here. Far north of here, in fact." He paused to let that sink in, staring at her with his strange bulging, unblinking eyes. "What? Still nothing?" he prodded. "Perhaps a physical description will aid you. He's a taller man with fair hair, and he carries a very unique sword, one with a golden hilt inlaid with jewels."

Fiona only vaguely heard him finish. The room had begun to spin.

"Are you alright, my dear?" Artan MacTavish smiled a sick triumphant smile.

Fiona glanced desperately at the beaming Abiageal who was still walking with Kiernan below, then to her father, who was locked in a spirited discussion with another lord. There would be no rescue from either of them. Artan pulled Abiageal's chair around in front of her. Fiona had the distinct impression that it was more to trap her there than to face her while speaking.

As he took his seat, he shifted his cane to his other hand before leaning it against the arm of the chair. The silver lion's head winked in the torch and candle-chandelier light, taunting her. Fiona stared at it in disbelief, her thoughts blurring to the many times she'd seen that cane before.

"Are you unwell?" Artan asked, his fake concern unable to cover his smirk. "Or are you remembering our special friend now?"

Fiona managed to gather her scattered wits. "Apologies my lord, I still don't know to whom you refer, but I am, in fact, not feeling well, and think I shall retire." She began to stand. His hand snaked out and pinned her arm to the chair.

"You know very well *to whom* I refer," he snarled as he leaned forward. "And you're not going anywhere. I've attended these odious country functions for many weeks, trying to meet you and have it appear to be by chance. I'll not have it cut short now. I know all about how you gallivanted around the countryside with your heathen lover—he told me all about it."

Fiona could only shake her head while her mind silently screamed, *Nay, nay, nay!*

"You don't believe me? Shall I recount what he told me? How he met you at the church ruins in Kilcock. Your travels to the old quarry, to Tara and Bru na Boinnes. Your ride along the beach at Clogherhead. Or how you spent your nights at small inns—first letting two rooms for appearances, but even abandoning that pretense in the end." He paused and leaned even closer. His breath stank of onions and smoke. "He was especially forthcoming with the details of your final days and nights in that cozy room while you waited out the storm."

He released his grip on her arm and sat up suddenly. A servant had climbed the stairs and was approaching them with a single chalice on a silver tray.

"A special vintage for my lord's most honored guest," the servant said as he offered up the tray. Artan snatched the chalice without a word and waved the man off. Fiona knew she should seize the opportunity to escape, but in her shock and tonic-addled state, she was paralyzed.

"It was actually our *friend's* suggestion that I seek you out," Artan continued when the servant was out of earshot. "He said he had no further use for you; he was leaving in his golden dragon ship, never to return, and you had served your purpose." He lowered his voice and leered at her. "Very satisfactorily, by all accounts."

He took a sip of wine, then spit it back into the chalice. "Swill," he muttered, pulling a silver flask from inside his tunic. He tipped it to his lips, swished some around in his mouth, then spit that into the chalice as well. After setting the cup on the floor, he stoppered the flask, laid it beside him on the chair, and looked back at her. "Now, where were we?"

When she didn't respond he slowly raised one eyebrow. "What did you think? That he cared for you? Are you really such a fool to have believed that? " He sniggered, then stared at her incredulous. "You did. I can see it in your face. How is that possible? You're a highborn and he was...a Northman." He spat the word like an epithet. "He must have been quite an accomplished liar—though he didn't lie about your beauty. I didn't believe his boasts at the time, but I must give credit where 'tis due; he was quite honest in his description of you. It makes me very eager to know if his other, more intimate descriptions, are equally as accurate."

Fiona couldn't speak. She felt as if she were being pulled along helplessly in the current of a giant whirlpool—each slow revolution, sucking her further down toward the dark center. His words couldn't be true. Gunnar could not have told him. *Could not. Could not. Could not.*

"What do you want from me?" she managed to whisper.

"What do I want? What...do...I...want?" he repeated, slowly tapping his fingers together in front of his mouth. "Hmmm." He pretended to ponder, then smiled a cold half-smile. "Since we've dispensed with the falsehoods and are being more direct with one another, I'll tell you what I want. I want you, Fiona." He laughed at her look of disgust and shook his head. "Oh, I want you in that way, too, but that's not your true appeal to me. I intend to marry you. After a brief whirlwind courtship, we shall become betrothed, then married, and, as your husband, I shall have access to your fortune."

"But my father yet lives."

"And he shall continue to—so long as he remains agreeable."

She stared at him in stunned disbelief, sure that she had misunderstood. "You wish to marry me for my wealth?"

"I wish to marry you for everything." His eyes dropped below her neckline. "And I will take full advantage of every right afforded to me by our marriage, but aye, 'tis your fortune that beckons me even more than your considerable charms."

"But you're a MacTavish; my family's fortune is surely meager in comparison to your own."

"I am the *sixth* son of Sleven MacTavish."

"Still..."

"Aye, even as the sixth son, one would expect me to be in very good standing, and there was a time when I was." He paused. "Since we're soon to be very close, I'll share a little secret with you. My family and I have had a falling out—a misunderstanding, you might say, and my access to the family fortune has been...well, limited. Limited to an extent that I find quite intolerable. It was something I had little hope of rectifying until you and your Northmen presented me with the perfect solution.

"Once we're married, I'll be able to resume some level of the lifestyle I'm entitled to. And who knows? A respectable marriage may even return me to my family's good graces. 'Tis surely something they never expected; you'll be a pleasant surprise to them. Of course, we won't tell them of your soiled condition. That, we'll keep just between us."

"You're mad," Fiona whispered. "I would never marry you."

Artan MacTavish saw red. He'd imagined her in many ways—as a bubble-headed fool—as a desperate woman on the verge of spinsterhood—even as the whorish type who shared her favors with many. But never once had he expected her to be like this—this haughty bitch who looked down on him. On him! How dare she? She, who had spread her legs for a filthy Northman, would think to refuse him? And look upon him with disdain? He was a MacTavish!

His palm itched to slap her from her chair to the floor where she belonged. To make her pay for the insult. To pay for everything. For his circumstances in life. For having to negotiate with her. Slap her like he did the whores and his maids when they displeased him. Under her fine dress, she was no different than any of them. He took a deep breath and struggled to check his anger. There'd be time for all that later. Time, when they were safely married, to discipline her as she deserved. It would be his right—his duty, in fact. For now, he'd keep track of her transgressions. Everything she made him endure, she would pay for later.

"Ah, but you will, Fiona. For if you refuse me, I will see to it that everyone knows of your sordid little adventure. If my word on the subject was not enough..." he chuckled, "which, of course, as a MacTavish it would be, there are plenty of witnesses who can be called to account. And I know just where to find them."

Artan looked up. Her friends were returning. "I shall take my leave of you now, my dear. I've given you much to ponder, and you seem quite pale. Perhaps you should retire. Once you've had time to think upon it, I'm sure we'll be of like mind on the matter. Lord Riddock is having a feast next week. We shall resume our conversation then." His eyes narrowed. "Be sure you are in attendance or I *will* call upon you at your home. I have an excuse now that we've met, though some might still view it as a bit inappropriate. And we wouldn't want anyone thinking anything inappropriate of you, now would we?" He stood and bowed deeply. "My lady. It has been my greatest pleasure." He smiled again, and for the first time, it was sincere.

"Who was that?" Abiageal whispered as she and Kiernan returned.

"Artan MacTavish." Fiona numbly heard her own voice reply.

"MacTavish?" Kiernan murmured and turned to look at the man's retreating back. "His father is rumored to have the ear of the high king of Leinster."

Fiona barely heard him. Her weary mind battled itself in sweeping circles. *Everything with Gunnar had been a lie. Every dark fear she'd imagined was true. He'd never cared for her. Nay, that couldn't be! But Artan knew everything. Gunnar had told him everything. Every single thing. But he couldn't have— wouldn't have described what they shared to that man. Artan had to be lying!*

A sparkle from the chair he'd vacated caught her attention. The silver flask remained on the seat, forgotten—the boldly engraved initials, *AMT*, winking distinctly clear in the candle-chandelier light. Her mind flashed to when she'd seen those initials before—when Gunnar had retrieved the flask from under the carriage seat after their race. And there was the cane. The carriage belonged to Artan MacTavish. Gunnar knew him. Artan wasn't lying.

Old Maive's prediction suddenly slammed inside her skull. *"You shall marry a powerful Irish lord. And it will be soon...before the year is out."*

Fiona couldn't think, couldn't breathe. She was deep in the whirlpool now, the revolutions coming faster.

"He seemed quite smitten with you." Abiageal's voice sounded far away. "Kept looking back. Perhaps we shall both be married soon," she said giddily. "Lord Kiernan is going to ask my father for my hand. Did you hear me, Fiona? Fiona, are you alright?"

She felt Abiageal's cool hand on her forehead, then heard her worried voice. "Fetch her father straight away, Kiernan. She's burning up with fever!"

Chapter 31

"**T**he men need to rest," Rask panted.

"They can rest when we reach the top of the next rise."

"But they're exhausted."

Gunnar felt the deep burn in his own calves and forearms, the knots in his back, and the blisters on his fingers and palms from the thick, coarse rope. Unlike the men, he embraced the pain; it was the only thing he'd found strong enough to overcome the pain of emptiness in his chest. "At the top of the next rise," he repeated and redoubled his grip. "Ready, men," he shouted.

Rask stood for a second, his jaw clenched against the words he clearly wished to voice. He shook his head and scowled before grabbing his rope and leaning into it.

"And heave!" Gunnar commanded.

Amidst the shouts of men struggling to control its final descent, the last ship slid down the slippery embankment, reaching the water with a resounding splash. Back in its element, it floated off light and buoyant—the opposite of its ponderous dangerous bulk on land. Eamon glanced at the other ships, floating peacefully on their moorings—the Treasure Huntress positioned in the middle like a queen surrounded by bobbing serfs.

When men began to collapse on the ground around him, Eamon immediately did the same. Respite had been scarce, and he'd learned to catch it whenever he could. Gunnar would roust them all with orders soon enough, of that he was certain.

Lying on his back in the sweet spring grass, he thought back over the past weeks. When the Northmen had first described to him their intentions to portage the ships over land, he'd thought it to be another jest to tease the Irishman. Even when he'd seen the path cleared through the forest on previous journeys, he couldn't believe it. The idea was madness. Impossible. Yet they'd done it.

They'd actually carried the smaller ships like litter bearers. Using long poles run through the oar holes, pairs of men grasped and lifted the ends protruding from either side. The larger ships were far too heavy for that. Using block and tackle, they hauled those from the water onto a system of logs, consisting of two continuous rows of long thick logs laid lengthwise, covered with countless shorter, narrower logs laid crosswise on top of them.

The design intended for the upper short logs to roll, and sometimes they did, but more often than not, especially where the ground was soft, the crushing weight of the ships pressed everything deep into the mud, holding them firm. Here they greased the keels with animal fat the Northmen had brought with them in barrels, and simply dragged them.

To keep the larger ships from tipping, men lined the sides with short prop poles. As a ship was pulled past, the men moved from the back to the front. Over and over and over it was repeated. Eamon had long lost track of how many lakes they'd traversed and through how many forests they'd trudged, some so dense that deep snow still remained.

Yet even the coldest places weren't cool enough to keep them from sweating profusely. For it wasn't just the slaves who labored as Eamon had incorrectly assumed. With ropes slung over their shoulders, he and the Northmen had pulled with them like beasts of burden. No one was exempt. Not even Gunnar, who drove them all like a man possessed as he slogged and strained alongside them.

After the first hill, Eamon had prayed for a descent to provide some relief from the backbreaking labor. But now he knew how foolish and naïve those prayers had been. Now he shared the dread of every other man at even the slightest downslope. Uphill was hard and excruciatingly slow, their progress measured in mere inches, but downhill was where the danger lay. Where the ships could shift forward without warning. Where the two Germanians had been crushed beneath a massive keel.

The sight of the two men pinned beneath the ship was yet another terrible image irrevocably seared into Eamon's mind. Mercifully, one man had been killed instantly. But the other... The other's agonized screams had rung in their ears as they scrambled to run new rigging and set new poles. Screams at first that had begged for them to hurry, but then changed to begging for someone to end his misery. Which they had—after the ship was pulled off of him, revealing his crushed pelvis and lower spine.

Eamon had vomited at the sight—the man's normal upper torso and legs connected by a thin layer of cloth and bloody paste. His stomach churned again now at the memory. Pushing the grisly picture from his thoughts, he turned to Olag who had flopped next to him. "What happens now?" he asked.

"It gets easier from here. Well, normally it does," Olag said, casting a sidelong glance toward Gunnar. "This is the Volga, and it'll take us the rest of the way to the Caspian Sea. Normally we rest and let the current take us, but who knows...Gunnar may have us at oars," he muttered under his breath.

As if on cue, Gunnar shouted to the resting men. "There's plenty of daylight left. I'll not have it wasted. We'll make camp further downriver.

Ships are to travel in single file as close to the center of the river as possible. I want every pair of eyes monitoring the banks. It's been four years. We don't know who controls these lands now, but we'll assume they're hostile. Any questions?"

The men all silently shook their heads.

"Good. Then to the ships," Gunnar commanded.

Her father had taken one look at her and insisted they leave at once.

Lord Sheron joined them in the entryway while they waited for their cloaks. "Are you sure you'll not stay? I can send for my healer," he offered.

"Gratitude, but I'll feel better having her safely home," her father replied.

"Of course. I'll see that extra traveling furs are provided. Hopefully, she can rest on the way. Would you still like to take the scrolls we were discussing earlier? We can retrieve them now while they're readying your carriage."

Her father nodded, then glanced at her with a worried frown. "I'll only be a moment," he said. "If the carriage comes before I return, don't wait for me. Get settled inside."

Fiona nodded from her dazed stupor and prepared to take a seat on the bench near the door. The smoke and noise coming from the hall changed her mind, and she stepped outside into the quiet night air instead. A thick fog had moved in since their arrival. So thick, she could feel the moisture brushing her face in a soft caress. Fiona threw back her hood and allowed her cloak to drape open, enjoying the feel of the cool damp.

She walked unsteadily down the short torch-lined path to the area where the carriages dropped and picked up passengers. The torches crackled and popped all around her, their flames painting the nebulous haze with orange and red hues.

She turned toward the sound of approaching hooves, expecting to see their two familiar chestnut geldings, but saw only mist. The sounds became distorted, one moment coming from her left where she expected, the next from behind her which was impossible.

Had they lost their way in the fog? Or, in her befuddled state, had she accidentally strayed too far and now stood in their path? The clanking of bits, the rattle of harness chains, the creaking of wood, the pounding of hooves were so loud—and getting louder!

The mist in front of her began to swirl. Fiona held her breath. It looked to be a safe distance away, not bearing down on her as she had feared. Two horses' heads appeared, then their necks and driving upper front legs. But not her chestnuts. Blacks—their breath streaming from their nostrils in long plumes that blurred back into the fog.

It was a terrifyingly awesome and darkly ethereal sight. The orange-tinged haze appeared as fiery smoke, and the animals, with their lower legs shrouded and invisible, seemed not to touch the ground—as if they were emerging through a portal from hell.

A second pair of blacks appeared behind the first. Then the carriage with the shadowy forms of its driver and two footmen. Fiona knew she should look away to avoid their embarrassing recognition of her when the carriage drew nearer, but she could not. Would they also seem sinister now? She blinked as they came into clear view. The three men were strangers to her.

"What is it, my dear?" A male voice murmured in her ear. "Looking for friendly faces?"

Fiona's stomach lurched.

"I couldn't have that, now could I? Couldn't have my servants recognizing my future betrothed as a Northman's whore and spreading vicious tales."

"What have you done with them?" she whispered.

"That answer might be a bit too much for you just yet. Suffice to say, you'll never see any of them ever again."

Fiona shuddered as he moved past her and climbed inside. She pulled her cloak back tight around her, suddenly chilled. Had her time with Gunnar cost three innocent men their lives? The question only added to her anguish. One painful thought tumbled through her mind after another. It was too much to bear. She didn't want to think about them, about Gunnar, about anything.

The tonic coursing through her veins beckoned her with blissful oblivion. She surrendered to it. She was only dimly aware of climbing into her own carriage that followed soon after. Dimly aware of burying herself in the pile of soft furs inside. Dimly aware of her fingertips absently caressing the silver flask before stashing it between the cushion and the wall. She didn't know why she'd picked it up. The warm memories she had of it and the time with Gunnar were all false. None of it had been real.

Fiona awoke in her bed in the darkness. Bits of the past days began to flit through her mind—the repeated visits from the healer—the bloodletting. She must have been quite ill, she thought drowsily, though she felt fine now. The first pale streaks of morning light softly illuminated her room as the sun began its rise in the East.

The East!

Gunnar!

Memories flooded back in a painful rush. Had that been a lie, too? His whole fantastic tale of returning to the East with his friends' wealth? Or was he off raiding somewhere else with no care for the suffering he'd left in his wake? Perhaps laughing and telling stories about her right now—stories that he'd told Artan MacTavish. Tormented by the thoughts, Fiona closed her eyes and tried desperately to go back to sleep. To no avail.

In the early dawn quiet, her mind free of fever and tonic, she faced her worst fears. Her every doubt and insecurity had been voiced by Artan MacTavish with ridicule. Gunnar had taken her virtue and her heart—so artfully that she was likely not the first naïve young woman he'd seduced. But she wasn't some simple-minded scullery maid; she was Lady Fiona O'Neill, descendant of a high King! She was educated. Intelligent. How could she have been so utterly duped?

And knowing the truth now, how could she feel anything other than fury? Why was the thought of it like a knife in her breast? What was wrong with her? How could any part of her still cling to the hope that he would return as promised?

Steeling herself, Fiona started from the beginning. With the clarity of hindsight, she examined every detail of their time together, searching for the evidence she'd missed that would have revealed his true intent.

One thing repeatedly stood out. Gunnar had honored his word at every turn. She couldn't think of a single instance when he had not. Even the night at the last inn when she'd practically leaned into him, he'd not touched her until she released him of his oath.

And he'd vowed to return to her.

Her mind shifted back to Artan and his cold parting words. "...*couldn't have my servants recognizing my future betrothed as a Northman's whore...*"

And they most certainly would have recognized her after all they'd been through. The thought jiggled something in her mind. She paused to examine it more closely. *After all they'd been through*. All *they'd* been through. Of course! It was so obvious. How could she have not seen it before? Three men besides Gunnar knew the details of their trip. Three men who were beholden to Artan MacTavish!

Heart pounding, she turned her scrutiny to what she could remember of her conversation with Artan. He'd offered not a single specific detail of the time she and Gunnar had spent in private—only referred to it with vague vulgar innuendos.

And who was more likely to lie to her? Gunnar, who had answered her every question, even when his answers painted him in a bad light? Or the despicable excuse for a man whose own family had rejected him? Her heart sang with the answer. It all made sense now. Clear-headed, the lie was obvious. Gunnar hadn't shared details of her with that repulsive cretin. He loved her and would return! And when he learned of this, he'd kill Artan MacTavish. Filled with a protective rage, his golden sword would flash red, and Artan MacTavish would be no more!

Even as she allowed herself the pleasure of imagining it, she knew it could never happen—at least not in time to help her. At best, Gunnar wouldn't return until fall, and possibly not until spring. She would have to deal with Artan well before then. Her mind began to sift through possibilities.

"My lady?" Siara whispered cautiously from the doorway. Fiona turned her head on the pillow to look at her. "Praise be to God," Siara whispered fervently. "I feared you were dead. Your eyes were open but you were still as a stone."

"Nay, I'm feeling much better, Siara."

"Praise be to God," she repeated. "I've lit a candle for you every night, my lady."

"Gratitude, Siara. How long have I slept?"

"Three days. Though your fever broke after the first night. The healer could find no reason why you didn't awaken then, and that's what frightened us most of all. Is there anything I can get you?"

"Perhaps you would help me to sit up and then bring me something warm to drink."

"With pleasure." Siara's face beamed as she adjusted the pillows behind her, then, with one last glance to be sure she did not carry false news, she fled the room.

Fiona sat looking out the window. It had been three days since she'd awakened. As much as she would have liked to ride, after days of inactivity, Barca would be quite high, and she didn't yet have the strength.

"Here's something to brighten your day," Meirna said as she placed a small silver tray on the table beside her. On it was a folded parchment, bearing a red wax seal. "Your father said that's the MacTavish seal," Meirna said approvingly.

"Aye, I met the youngest MacTavish, Artan, at Lord Sheron's the night I took ill."

"Well, you must have made quite the impression for him to send you a private message."

Meirna was clearly waiting for her to open it, but Fiona didn't dare—not with her there. Didn't dare risk having her see his threats—or worse, disclosures. "Meirna, would you please have Haisley warm me some of the soup from yesterday? I'm suddenly very hungry," she lied, knowing the prospect of feeding her would temporarily override Meirna's curiosity.

"Of course, my dear."

With Meirna safely gone, Fiona ripped open the seal. If the letter was damning, she'd burn it and blame carelessness. Her eyes raced through the looping scrawl.

Lady Fiona,

I feel so fortunate to have made your acquaintance at Lord Sheron's. I found conversing with you most interesting and was extremely disappointed to not be able to continue our discussion at Lord Riddock's. Your absence there has filled me with concern. I sincerely hope this letter finds you well. If you are not in attendance at Lord Haggan's betrothal feast next week, I hope it will not be considered too forward if I call upon you.

Artan

He signed the A in his name with a sweeping flourish that looped back on itself. Fiona let the letter fall back to the tray. There was nothing incriminating in case it were opened by someone else, but still a clear warning to her. Did he think she was hiding from him? That she was cowering at home, afraid of his threats? Her blood began to simmer. Artan MacTavish did not know her.

"You are bright-eyed," Meirna noted with a smile as she returned. "Has Lord Artan's letter sparked you, then?"

"Aye, Meirna, I believe it has. I'm feeling more myself with every moment. Would you please bring me parchment and quill? He was concerned by our early departure, and I would reassure him that I am well."

"Of course," Meirna nodded and retrieved her writing set from the other side of the room.

Lord Artan,

I'm happy to report that your gracious concern for my well-being is unwarranted. I have, in fact, been quite ill, but I assure you I'm recovering well. I'm flattered that you found conversing with me so interesting, and I look forward to speaking with you again at Lord Haggan's.

Fiona

She left it open, ostensibly to allow the ink to dry, but she wanted Meirna to read it. She would surely read Artan's letter at the first opportunity and be eager to know her response. But it wasn't satisfying Meirna's curiosity that motivated her. Meirna had her father's ear. So soon after being ill, he would likely oppose her attending Lord Haggan's feast. By feigning interest in Artan, she hoped to garner Meirna's important support.

Chapter 32

"**R**ask, signal the other ships to raise sails and put the men to oars. If we push, we can make the settlement by nightfall."

"Why not stop now, rest the men, and approach at dawn? We have no idea what we'll find there; better to arrive when they're asleep."

Gunnar knew it was the logical course of action and a decision he would have normally already made, but his nearness to the goal he'd waited so long to reach spurred him. Before he could respond, a horn sounded from somewhere near on the west bank. The signal was immediately picked up and repeated by other horns further downriver. He recognized the code relaying the number of their ships and another signal he didn't know. Gunnar smiled. The settlement was still there, and still under Norse control.

"Raise sails and put the men to oars," he repeated. "We no longer have the option of approaching unnoticed."

The first farms that appeared on the banks were separated by large tracts of forest and grasslands, coming closer together the farther south they traveled. Horns sounded as they passed, marking their progress. Whoever was in charge would know the exact moment of their arrival.

The river widened, splitting into a series of smaller waterways that made up the vast marshlands of the river delta. Surrounded by marsh grass taller than a man's head, Gunnar soon lost sight of both riverbanks as he navigated the fleet through the maze of dead-end finger bays and shallows. For miles, they snaked their way through the complex, convoluted network until one by one, the smaller tributaries converged and the river current slowed into swirling gentle eddies as it met the sea. Leaving the last of the marsh behind, the Huntress sailed out onto smooth open water.

"Unbelievable," Gunnar murmured in awe at the sprawling city on the west shore. He pulled his scope to take a closer look.

Protected by massive fortifications, the buildings were a bizarre assortment of construction styles representing a myriad of cultures: Viking longhouses of wood and thatch, round nomadic tribal tents of animal hides, and others made of stone and fired clay bricks. Everywhere he looked, people went about their end-of-day activities, seemingly unconcerned by the Viking force bearing down on them.

"Rask, signal the other ships to hold here, then take us in."

Fiona stood calmly next to her father as they were announced by Lord Haggan's manservant. She'd taken great care with her appearance tonight. Meirna had assumed it was to impress Lord MacTavish and, in many ways, it was for him. She wanted him to see that the sickly, weak woman he'd met that night was not who she was.

Normally after being announced, she would try to slip unnoticed past as many of the other guests as possible, but tonight Fiona lingered, smiling graciously and engaging in conversation with everyone who approached her.

She made sure not to look for Artan. She wanted to appear utterly unbothered by his threats, and it was almost an hour before the guests around her thinned enough for him to approach.

"I don't know what you're up to, but you do not wish to push me, my dear, or I can assure you, you'll regret it," he warned under his breath.

"Whatever do you mean, my lord? My friends were all worried about my illness—as were you. I had to assure them that I'm quite well."

He stared at her, measuring and suspicious. This was not the cowed, weepy response he was expecting at all. "So, have you considered my offer?"

"Aye, I've considered it at great length."

He smiled and nodded slowly. "Very good."

Fiona frowned. "I'm afraid it's not *very good*, my lord. I've considered it and concluded that I shall decline."

"Decline? Decline? You cannot decline," he sputtered.

"I can and I will. Your proposal did not suit me."

"Do you think I jested? I will ruin you," he seethed, biting off his next words as more well-wishers approached.

"Nay, I think you will not," Fiona continued after they'd moved away. "You could spread vicious lies about me. Perhaps even drag up false witnesses in the process, but then you'd forfeit what it is you really want."

"You and I both know they're not lies, nor would the witnesses be false!"

"I know nothing of the sort. And I do not see your family backing you in a scandalous personal attack on me, especially when every lord and lady here tonight beholds me vehemently reject your advances. 'Twill be quite the spectacle, and soon now, I think. Perhaps if you weren't the family embarrassment living on...how did you put it—a very limited income?"

He stared at her speechless, his face shifting from fury, to incredulity, to calculating. "Don't be too hasty with that public rebuff, my lady. You'll want to consider my next words very carefully first. You are correct about one thing. Ruining your reputation would do nothing to relieve my current untenable situation. And while I wouldn't hesitate to do it just for spite, I've become quite attached to the idea of improving my circumstances. You will still agree to marry me."

He held up a hand as Fiona started to protest. "Because if you do not, I will turn my wrath upon your father, and I'll go far beyond ruining his name." After a quick glance to make sure no one was close enough to overhear, he continued. "Since we are soon to be betrothed, I'll share another secret with you. How do you think my family has become so powerful? I can assure you it wasn't by working harder than everyone else.

"Nay, instead of that, they've chosen to eliminate their rivals and anyone else they considered a threat. Over the years they've become quite proficient at it. Abduction and forced slavery is by far their favorite method. Of course, it would be much safer to just kill their adversaries and dispose of the bodies, but they have a flair for the macabre. They delight in knowing that their enemies are still out there, suffering, even though each poses a significant risk. If one were ever to escape or manage to send word back of their plight, 'twould be disastrous; some of their victims have been very powerful men.

"So how do you imagine they ensure that does not happen? You'll never guess it, so I'll just tell you. First, their hands are crushed so they can never write again." At her horrified expression, he chuckled. "Oh, that's far from the worst of it. Next, they remove their tongues."

Fiona shook her head as she pressed the back of one hand to her mouth.

"Have you ever seen that done to a man? His tongue removed? I have— many times. My father insisted on it. 'Tis quite a gruesome process. First, the victim's arms are bound behind his back and two men hold him down on his knees. Then they grip a solid handful of his hair and tip his head back while a third man pries his teeth apart with a rod. Most resist quite vigorously at this point and clench their jaws very tightly." He shook his head with a sick smile. "But the rod always wins.

"They grasp his tongue with heavy tongs and pull it out quite far—much farther than you would think possible while someone else brings a red hot blade, fresh from the fire. All the while, the helpless wretch now makes the most unusual gurgling sounds. They're not screams because his tongue is pulled out so far it blocks his throat.

"Then there's sizzling and smoke as it's cut and seared at the same time," he said with a nonchalant wave of his hand. "It gives off the most unique smell—similar to roasted beef, but sweeter. They do scream then, but it's a hoarse wordless scream, for a man cannot form words without a tongue.

"And even though the stub is seared, there's always blood. They retch on it for hours. I know that because we were made to sit outside their cells and study them afterwards. To this day 'tis still amazing to me how much a man's body can endure."

Fiona swallowed hard, trying not to gag. His description was far too vivid to be made up. But his face and tone were so calm, he could have been talking about the weather. "Your father forced you to watch?" she whispered.

"Not just me—all of his sons. Though 'tis only forced initially. After several, you become accustomed to it." He shrugged. "And you'll do anything to avoid the beating that comes if you look away."

"What of your mother—why didn't she protect you?"

"My mother?" he barked a harsh laugh and took a drink. "I keep forgetting you do not yet know my family. My *mother*," he paused and took another deeper swig, "well, let's just say 'twould not surprise me at all if the methods of their disposal were her idea."

Fiona stared at him, stunned.

"Oh it's quite true, I assure you. She hides it well with her polished manners, but you seem fairly astute; you'll see it.

"Which brings me to the last tidbit about my family, lest you foolishly think I wouldn't have their full support. I may be the *family embarrassment*," he hissed, "but when it comes to protecting the family name—which I would convince them is under attack by your father, they would rally around me so fast it would confound you."

He raised his glass to her. "But gratitude, Lady Fiona, for the unexpected challenge. You're proving to be a versatile and entertaining adversary. I'm actually starting to enjoy this courtship. 'Twill make your ultimate submission all the sweeter. Now smile, my dear. Don't look so grim. Everyone needs to see what a lovely time we're having, so it will come as no surprise when we announce our betrothal...which, I've decided we shall publicly announce at my family's Midsummer Festival feast. With so many guests in attendance, the number of betrothal gifts will be substantial.

"I'll generously allow you to choose the wedding date, so long as it's before Lughnasa, the beginning of harvest. Aye, I know it seems rushed, but with our attentiveness to each other at every gathering between now and then, everyone will assume we are so in love that we just cannot wait."

He paused and took a drink, seeming very satisfied with himself. "You know, I'd hoped to be betrothed by Beltaine. When I couldn't find you initially, I worried that you'd been shipped away to bear an illegitimate child in secret. That would have caused me a very unfortunate delay."

"That could still be the case."

His eyes flew to her stomach, then he recovered. "Babies are often born early in a marriage," he dismissed, "even big healthy babies."

"Not this early—and not with fair hair. No one would ever believe a fair-haired child to be yours. Everyone would whisper you were a cuckold."

Artan chuckled. "Fiona. You must know that a fair-haired child born of me would never leave the birthing chamber alive. My mother would see to that, then report the sad news of our first child being tragically stillborn. She might even shed a tear for appearances. Stillborn would even account for the early birth." He frowned as something else occurred to him. "But if you do carry the Northman's seed, you'll be showing well before the time of even a rushed wedding. No one would think it mine," he muttered to himself.

"And that would not do...." His voice trailed away. He was lost in thought for several moments.

"Aye," he said, nodding to himself. "We'll still announce our betrothal at the Midsummer feast, but schedule the wedding for later in the fall. If the coming months do reveal you to be with child, the betrothal will be broken off, you'll be humiliated, and restitution demanded of your family for breach of promise. No one will ask for their gifts back, so you'll still have served a purpose. I'll live comfortably on them for awhile—at least until I can find another woman to take your place. Because I've come to realize, Fiona, while none will provide me with the indiscretions to use that you did, with the right lass, the threat of falsehoods would probably do just as well." He glanced up at Abiageal waving at them and sneered. "Someone like your mousy friend there; she'd be easy enough to coerce and subdue, don't you think?"

In that moment Fiona realized she had to shift all thought from escaping him to something far more permanent. She wished she had the sword skills to hack him down as Gunnar had the highwaymen. But she didn't, and to hire someone else who did would only be to invite discovery. From the little she'd learned of his family, she had no doubt their vengeance would be swift and severe. She had to find a way to rid the world of Artan without casting any suspicion upon herself, and that would take meticulous planning.

She would accept his proposal. That would give her until fall—assuming she was not with child. Plenty of time to get close to him and his horrid family, discover their weaknesses, and determine the best course of action. As ill as the thought made her, she knew she could do it. She had to.

Chapter 33

Though the man striding down the dock was still too far away to make out his features, Gunnar recognized him easily. Years of fighting side by side and back to back taught a man to distinguish friend from foe in an instant on the battlefield. That was undoubtedly Jarl.

While the crew secured the Huntress, Gunnar jumped to the dock and met him halfway. The two men embraced in a gruff hug.

"Gunnar, it is really you in the flesh. When the horns signaled ships approaching and that one was the Huntress, I could scarce believe it."

"That was the new signal? You made a code for her?"

Jarl laughed and nodded. "Though it's been so long with no use, I'm surprised they remembered it. It's been too long, my friend. I was worried ill fate had befallen you."

"Much has happened, and the journey itself gets longer every time."

Jarl nodded and turned to the ship. "She looks the same as the day you left, perhaps even better, if such a thing is possible," Jarl admired. "Watching the elements take their toll on the ships here, part of me wanted never to see her like that—to always remember her as she was, but this..., well, this is a gift."

Gunnar thought of the repair to the hull but said nothing. There'd be time to explain that later, over mead or wine...or maybe not at all. He changed the subject. "*She* may look the same, but I scarce recognize you. You've gone native." Gunnar chuckled as he looked him up and down, taking in Jarl's odd short trousers, sandals, and vest with no tunic underneath.

"You laugh now, but you'll soon envy my clothes—around mid-day tomorrow I predict."

"Perhaps," Gunnar agreed.

"It'll soon be dark. You can have the men beach the ships over there." Jarl pointed to the southern shoreline of the protected bay. "The approach is deep and the bottom smooth; it's easy to launch again with the tide. They can make camp anywhere on that hillside, and tomorrow unload cargo and see to making trades. For you, I, of course, offer the hospitality of my home."

"Gratitude, Jarl. Is that your house there?" Gunnar pointed to the huge longhouse on top of the rise where the camp was to be set up.

"No, that's the hall where tomorrow we shall all feast. Come—grab your gear. We'll arrange for food, drink, and firewood to be delivered to your men on the way to my home."

"Before I release them to make camp, what are the rules here?"

"Northman law...mostly," Jarl added. "There are a few foreign customs that you'll need to be aware of if you stay for any length of time. For now, the only thing I insist on is that there be no trouble with any of the merchants. They're all under my protection."

Gunnar nodded, and they returned to the ship where Rask and Olag were waiting. "You remember, Olag," Gunnar said. "And this is Rask, my second." The men shook hands with hearty forearm grips.

Gunnar relayed the camp instructions to Rask and retrieved his pack from the ship. "And Tryggr?" he asked as they walked down the dock.

"Fit to be tied, no doubt. He seldom leaves the city, but today of all days, he was checking on one of the outlying farms. I'm sure he heard the horns and is on his way as fast as his plow horse can carry him."

Gunnar smiled at the image. "This place is a far cry from when I left, and I must admit, not at all what I was expecting. I hoped to find a few productive farms, but part of me feared there'd be nothing and you'd be dead."

"Your fears were unfounded. All is well and we continue to grow every year. One day we may even rival Constantinople," Jarl said, his voice filled with pride.

"That's a bold claim but accounts for the fortifications. Have you come under attack?"

"A few times, but as it turns out, having an alliance with the Teclan is a powerful deterrent. It tends to make people rather agreeable."

"Imagine that," Gunnar said wryly. "So you still have contact with the Teclan?"

"Contact? Yes, you could say that; they're our largest trading partner. Their conquests continue, and we provide a trusted way for them to move their spoils."

"Chief Meln has agreed to trade?"

"Not Meln. Lothor."

"Nena's brother? The one who tried to kill you?"

Jarl nodded.

"Is he chief now? Is Meln dead?"

"No, Meln yet lives and is still chief, but he places great value on Lothor's council, and Lothor sees the future. One moment," Jarl excused himself as he knocked on a door. The man who opened it seemed shocked to see him and immediately brought a closed fist to his chest while nodding his head in deference. "My lord."

"Apologies for disturbing you, Akil, but I need firewood delivered to the southern rise—several wagon loads."

"Yes, my lord. I'll see to it immediately."

Jarl turned back to Gunnar. "Apologies, where were we?"

"You were telling me about trades with the Teclan; I thought they were opposed to trading."

"They don't trade with outsiders." Jarl pointed to the Teclan star on his upper arm. "But I'm not an outsider anymore, remember?"

"That's convenient."

"Quite," Jarl agreed.

"What do they trade?"

"Everything: horses, gems, gold, silver."

"For what?"

"Weapons mostly. They value our steel."

"Is that wise?"

"When they're our allies, yes."

"These ramparts are substantial for a place that's only come under attack a few times."

"As rich as we've become, it's only a matter of time. But we're ready."

"Do you still raid?"

Jarl shook his head. "No. As a place that encourages trade from all, it would put us in a difficult position."

"Do you miss it?"

"A bit. Though in truth," Jarl looked around to make sure he was not being overheard, "I prefer it this way. If I were to raid, then Nena would insist on going also. I understand it; battle is in her blood as much as mine, and she's flawless in a fight. To see her take down a foe is a thing of beauty, and afterward in the furs is unbelievable. But the risk so far outweighed any reward that I've lost my taste for it. She never received so much as a scratch, yet every time a sword was raised against her, all I could think of was...what if? I couldn't wait for it to be over. With such lack of focus, it was only a matter of time before I fell to mortal injury."

"I'm sure she felt the same about you."

"Perhaps," Jarl acknowledged with a chuckle even as he shook his head indicating the opposite, "but she is disciplined far beyond anyone I've ever known."

"Will it be a problem for you when we raid?"

"No. In fact, Nena prepared a map for you. Places the Teclan have not raided that should have more to offer. She made it years ago when we thought you to return so it will need to be updated, but I'm sure she still has it."

"Gratitude, Jarl."

"Thank her. It was her idea."

After several more stops to arrange for meat, bread, and ale to be delivered to the camp, they approached a sprawling structure, separated from any other buildings by a large, clear fenced-off area. A long wood platform spanned the entire front, with a red and gold awning that shaded the middle section in front of two solid-looking carved wood doors.

Two guards stood at the opening in the split-rail fence, a single red banner adorned with a gold dragon head rippling in the evening breeze above them. From their post, a wide path led to the steps to the low platform and the entrance. Two more guards stood at the base of the steps, another two at the doors, and a final two on both ends of the platform. All nodded deferentially to Jarl and raised a fist to their chest as he passed, then immediately returned to surveying, not tense but very aware. Gunnar didn't recognize any of them, but it was clear these were serious fighters.

The guards pulled open the two doors as they drew near.

With the number of guards and the obvious wealth of the city, Gunnar expected to find opulence inside, but the room they entered was narrow and sparsely decorated. Two curtained doorways, one midway down each side wall, led to unseen rooms. Straight ahead was another set of double wood doors with two more guards.

"You live here?" he asked, confused.

"Through those doors up ahead. We receive traders from many lands with very different customs, so we added two specialized private rooms here to make them feel more at ease. The rooms are identical in size and their entrances equally distant from the doors we just came through so that no one feels slighted. The importance of that was something I learned the hard way," he said ruefully. "This room here," he pulled back the curtain to the room on the left, revealing a long low table surrounded by thick plush furs and silk pillows, "is where we entertain our eastern guests, who prefer to sit on the floor."

He dropped the curtain and walked across to the room on the right. "And here is where we host our Byzantine and Northern traders." He pulled open the second curtain. This room was furnished with a high wood table and heavy chairs.

"I must admit, I never thought to see you as a merchant," Gunnar said as Jarl dropped the curtain and they turned toward the final double doors.

"A merchant, a farmer, a judge, a father. A true jarl. My days are filled."

"Did you say father?" Gunnar asked thunderstruck. "Why would you not lead with that information? Congratulations! Boy or girl?"

"Two girls."

Gunnar whistled.

"I know. Who'd have thought it?" Jarl said, perplexed. "With Nena's strengths, I knew we'd have sons. Now I sacrifice regularly to the gods for *a* son, if for no other reason than to help me keep the rogues away when the girls are older. Though I wouldn't worry near so much if Tryggr didn't have a boy."

"Tryggr's a father as well? With a child he acknowledges?" Gunnar stumbled to a halt at that news.

"Yes." Jarl laughed. "With another one on the way. And the seer predicts this next one is to be a boy as well. The thought of fending off two of that big ox's stubborn sons when I'm old..." Jarl didn't finish, only shook his head and grimaced as the guards pulled open the last doors for them to pass.

"I'm sure you've no cause for concern. With the way their mother handled you, I can't imagine your daughters will require protection." Gunnar grinned as he followed him inside.

"Gratitude, Gunnar," Nena greeted him with a smile, overhearing his last comment. "That is what I tell him as well. After everything we've been through, he still believes a woman needs a man to protect her."

"And here is where we call home," Jarl said with a relaxed sigh as he waved around the room. Like the city, the dwelling's decorations represented a myriad of cultures. The floor was covered with finely woven wool rugs and silk carpets, topped with the occasional thick sheepskin fleece and bearskin. Chairs were draped with plush pelts of fox, sable, and wolf, while on the walls hung intricate Byzantine tapestries and exotic hides—tiger and zebra and a strange spotted one that Gunnar didn't recognize. But it was the ornamental displays of weaponry that were most remarkable. Polished swords crossed in front of a painted Viking shield. Daggers with gold and silver handles. Finely carved long spears. Even a battle axe with dyed strips of leather braided in a colorful pattern along the length of the handle. All were striking and magnificent, but their razor-sharp edges and strategic placement around the room indicated they were all also quite functional.

"Your bed is through there." Jarl pointed to a doorway with a blue and gold silk rug tied open to one side. And we have a private bath through there that you are welcome to use." He pointed to a rust-colored rug on the far side.

Their tour was interrupted by a ruckus at the entry doors; a huge flame-haired man burst inside.

"Tryggr. I swear you're even larger than I remembered," Gunnar grunted as Tryggr enveloped him in a bear hug.

"Gunnar, you bastard, you finally made it! I'd begun to think we'd never see you again."

"Tryggr, did you bring your wife?" Nena asked.

"You know I did. Damn woman won't let me out of her sight," he grumbled and released Gunnar.

Jarl turned to Gunnar. "The truth in that statement would be in its opposite; Tryggr goes nowhere without her."

"You—with a wife?" Gunnar sputtered. "What happened to all your inflated talk of..."

"Now, don't go jumping to conclusions," Tryggr cut him off. "I didn't get all moon-eyed and soft-headed like Jarl here, risking my neck or anything. Me and this woman simply reached a mutually beneficial arrangement. That's all."

Jarl rolled his eyes.

"Yet you call her wife and not woman?" Gunnar prodded.

"Well, yes," Tryggr mumbled. "That was part of the arrangement."

"Hold his feet to the fire, Gunnar." Jarl laughed. "Shame him as he did me, and you know he would have done to you as well."

"Now there you go exaggerating again, Jarl," Tryggr protested. "Thankfully, now that Gunnar's finally returned, he can set the record straight. Jarl acts like I was opposed to him being with Nena. Wasn't it I who was at his side, tracking her all the way back to the Teclan mountain?"

"Complaining and trying to dissuade me the entire way," Jarl interjected.

"And wasn't it I who said we should risk life and limb to attack the Teclan stronghold to get her back?"

"No, that was Gunnar," Jarl clarified again.

Tryggr ignored him. "And was it not I—and this is the most telling, mind you, who allowed her to cut off a piece of my ear to give Jarl the excuse to have her in the first place? I could tell he fancied her."

"Allowed her?" Jarl exclaimed. "And I wasn't even there when she cut off your ear!"

"Only part of my ear," Tryggr reminded him. "I knew she'd be to your liking. I certainly don't recall any shaming."

Gunnar coughed.

"Did you hear that, Gunnar?" Jarl asked. "He doesn't recall any shaming. Tryggr recollects history to suit him."

"Yes, I can see that," Gunnar agreed.

They were interrupted by a tan-skinned little boy with dark red hair racing through the doors. "Papa, Mama wants to know what is taking you so long. She needs help carrying..."

Tryggr hoisted the boy in the air in mid-sentence. "Have you ever seen such a lad?" he asked, beaming with pride. "If your mother needs help, boy, why didn't you help her?"

"I tried," the boy said indignantly, "but some of the things are too heavy."

"Too heavy? A man never admits that! Nothing is ever too big or too heavy. Show me your muscle."

The little boy raised his arm and flexed it. Tryggr squeezed his bicep, pursed his lips, and cocked his head as he contemplated its size before nodding. "Definitely bigger."

The boy giggled.

"Brynjar, this is my good friend, Gunnar," Tryggr said as he returned the boy to the floor.

Brynjar stood up straight, placed a closed fist to his chest, and nodded his head. "An honor to meet you, my lord."

"The honor is mine, little man." Gunnar chuckled.

Tryggr swooped him up again and they headed for the door. "Let's go help your mother before she gets her ire up."

Jarl laughed out loud at Gunnar's dumbfounded expression. "You're not dreaming."

"But surely I am. There is no way that just happened. Never in this life or the next did I expect to witness such a scene."

"I fear your shocks are not yet over, my friend." Jarl grinned.

Before he could elaborate, Tryggr burst back through the doors, his arms laden with crates, Brynjar perched on top.

"Be careful with him, Tryggr," a woman's soft voice cautioned from the doorway. Gunnar tried to look past Tryggr to get a glimpse of the woman who had so utterly transformed his beast friend, but could only see her heavy silhouette. Gunnar smiled to himself. It would take a solid woman to hold up under Tryggr. But when she moved, it was with great trepidation, and Gunnar realized she was not a large woman, but a woman late with child.

"Aw, woman," Tryggr protested. "If he falls, he'll likely fall on his head and nothing will be hurt. His head is hard as a rock. Isn't it, boy?"

"Yes, Papa."

"Much like his father's, I'm afraid," came her weary, but affectionate response.

"Where would you like me to put these?" Tryggr asked.

"Over there in the corner," Nena directed as she stepped forward to address the woman, blocking Gunnar's view. "Come. Sit here and put up your feet. I've made you a tea of white willow bark, turmeric, and motherwort. It will help with the aches." She held out her hand and assisted the woman to a chair with an odd reclined back. "This is the only chair I could find comfort in when I was at your stage. I even slept in it some nights. If you'd like, Tryggr can move it to your house until the baby comes."

As the woman leaned back in the chair and Nena stepped away, Gunnar's mouth fell open. "Altene," he murmured involuntarily.

Jarl hadn't taken his eyes from Gunnar's face. "I told you, your shocks were not yet over," he said with a grin and slapped him on the shoulder. "But mention naught of her past as a whore—ever," Jarl warned quickly under his breath as Tryggr set down the crates and moved toward them.

"I would see the Huntress," Tryggr said. "No offense, Gunnar, but when I heard you'd arrived, I was torn between who to see first, you or her. You won out, but only barely."

"No offense taken; I'm not sure I would've made the same decision. And I should check on the men to see if they require anything."

"Then let's go."

"I forgot how she was," Tryggr murmured, his voice hushed as he stared up at the golden dragon in the torchlight.

"Those were my exact thoughts as well," Jarl agreed.

Fires dotted the hillside behind the two men. The smell of roasting meat and sounds of celebration filled the air. Gunnar had stopped to attend to some issue along the way and was just now returning to them, joined by another man.

"This is Rask, my second," Gunnar said to Tryggr.

"Second, you say?" Tryggr scoffed. "He's but a pup."

Rask stiffened.

"It's hard to fathom we were that age when we started." Gunnar attempted to smooth Rask's pride at the insult, but Tryggr wasn't finished.

"We were never like this one, I'm sure," he disagreed, stepping around Rask, sizing him up. "He looks to be barely free of his mother's tit. I bet if I examined him close enough, I'd find...wait, what's that I see? A bit of his mother's milk dribbling from the side of his mouth?"

"I dare you to look closer, old man," Rask invited, his voice a low growl.

"Dare me? And old man?" Tryggr straightened to his full height and puffed out his chest. Rask stood his ground. The two stood nearly eye to eye. Tryggr exhaled with a swoosh. "Ah, lucky for you, boy, at the moment I wish to see the Huntress far more than I care to whip you into shape."

Gunnar shook his head in a subtle warning to Rask not to respond. "Rask, instruct the men that they're to remain in camp or on the ships tonight. There's to be no trouble. None. I'll release them in the morning to begin trades. Leave three men to stand guard on the Huntress. We..."

"Guards aren't necessary," Jarl offered. "The area is secure."

Gunnar hesitated, the disclosure of the near-sinking of the Huntress on his lips, then instead said, "I'll sleep better for it." He turned back to Rask. "You're in charge tonight which means you're responsible if anything goes wrong."

Rask nodded and, with one last glare at Tryggr, turned and walked away.

"Well, his balls are plenty big enough to be a second, I'll give you that," Tryggr muttered. "But his mouth will likely get him killed."

"A fact that I've pointed out to him many times," Gunnar agreed.

"I don't recognize him. Do I know his family?"

"He's my sister's husband's youngest brother—and you wouldn't know him. He's a Dane."

"Your sister married a Dane?"

Gunnar nodded. "I was opposed to it at first, but he's from a strong family of warriors, and they're a good match. Rask is young, but he's proven himself to me many times in battle."

"How many battles could that whelp have possibly seen?" Tryggr scorned.

"Unfortunately, many. There's been war between two Dane kings for the past four years. It's what delayed my return."

"How did a Dane war involve you? Over what did they fight?"

"Same as what all kings fight over—more. More land. More power. One asserted some ancient claim to land which included my sister's home in Aalborg. Having just overwintered there, I could hardly leave without offering my sword."

Jarl and Tryggr both nodded.

"Gunnar, Jarl, Tryggr, come have a mead," Olag called out to them from the nearest fire. "Or two or three," he added with a laugh. The men around him cheered in agreement as stump seats were quickly vacated for the three.

When they stumbled back through the final set of doors into Jarl's home, Tryggr looked immediately to Nena. "Altene?" he asked.

"She and Brynjar have returned home. You're to take this chair with you when you go."

"Well, I better go now, or I'll never hear the end of it. Gunnar, Jarl." Tryggr nodded to them as he hastily hoisted the chair onto his shoulder and left without another word.

"I still cannot believe it—Altene and Tryggr. How did that come about?" Gunnar asked after watching his speedy departure.

"Looking back, I suspect they shared furs when we tracked Nena south, but my thoughts were far removed at the time, so I'm not sure."

"There's a huge difference between sharing furs and calling a woman wife."

"I agree, and Tryggr remained close-lipped about it for the longest time."

"Likely to avoid being on the receiving end of the ruthless shaming he dispensed."

"You mean the shaming that never occurred?" Jarl laughed.

"Yes, that shaming," Gunnar agreed with a grin.

"Have you eaten?" Nena asked.

"Yes, but I've yet to have dessert." Jarl grabbed her and pulled her in for a kiss.

Nena smiled and shook her head at his inebriated playfulness before gently extricating herself from his embrace. "The women have begun preparations for the feast tomorrow, and I need to rise early. If you need nothing further, I shall retire."

"And the girls?" Jarl asked.

"They're in bed, but I'm sure they await you. I told them you might be too busy tonight, but they did not believe me."

"Excuse me, Gunnar." Jarl left the room, returning a few moments later with a sheepish grin. "Apologies for the interruption. We have a nightly ritual that is not to be deviated from."

"No apology required. You seem to have a perfect life."

"I'm well satisfied, I must admit. Perhaps you'll join us. There's always need for another good man."

"No."

"That was a quick answer. Not a perhaps—just a no?"

"You know I never cared for the heat here," Gunnar evaded.

"It is stifling at times, but you become accustomed to it, and you don't miss the biting cold. But we have plenty of time to discuss that later. You must be tired. I'll show you to the bath and perhaps send for a woman?"

"A bath and a comfortable bed will be much appreciated."

Jarl raised an eyebrow at the omission of a female companion but said nothing.

Chapter 34

"How may I be of service today, my lady?"

"Greetings, Nolan. You've been our family's silversmith for years, have you not?"

"Aye, my lady. As were my father and grandfather."

"Then I'm sure I can count on your discretion?"

"Of course"

"I'm looking for a special gift for my future husband. We are to announce our betrothal at his family's Midsummer Festival feast, and I would like to give it to him then. He is Artan MacTavish."

"Congratulations, my lady. I know of the family." The man's eyes gleamed with the prospect.

"Have you created pieces for them?"

"Nay, my lady. I've not had that honor. Kells has naught to draw lords the likes of a MacTavish away from Dublin. "Would you like to browse my offerings, or do you have an idea for a gift?"

"I do, but it must remain a secret. Not even my father is to know." She looked at him and raised her eyebrows.

"I'll keep it in the strictest of confidence."

"When I last saw Artan, his fingers were blistered by hot wax from careless use of his signet ring," she lied. "I believe you made the seal my father uses with a cherry-wood handle to prevent that?"

"Aye, my lady, and I could make one much finer—perhaps with a handle of polished silver?"

"A wood handle will suffice." Noting his frown she added, "Because I would like for you to also make a box to store it in. Something like this." She pointed to a silver box with a pearl inlaid lid displayed on a nearby shelf. "But perhaps inlaid with gold instead of pearl?"

"Aye, my lady. I could even add gemstones if you wish," he offered eagerly. "Do you have a special design in mind?"

Did she ever. Fiona smiled. "I do. Artan is quite fond of dragons. Perhaps a golden dragon with gemstone eyes?"

"I could do that." He nodded. "'Twill be a fine gift that he'll cherish forever. All I'll need is a sample of the seal."

"Will this suffice?" Fiona asked and held out the letter Artan had sent her when she was ill.

He took it and examined the seal closely. "'Twill be no problem at all. The seal is broken here, but the lines are clear. I can duplicate it. May I keep this for now?"

"Of course," Fiona agreed as she turned for the door. *And read it if you will.*

After she'd stepped outside, and the silversmith closed the door behind her, Fiona had to forcibly restrain herself from skipping back to Barca. This was only the first small step in her plan, and many challenges still lay ahead, but it was such a successful start. She stroked the silver flask in her purse— the cherished memento of her time with Gunnar. She carried it with her everywhere now with no fear of its discovery. Since it bore Artan's initials, all would assume she carried it for him.

Jarl, Gunnar, and Nena stood at the end of a row watching the vendors opening their shops and stalls while they waited for Rask and Tryggr. Even as some called out a cheerful greeting to them, Gunnar noted that every man, no matter his culture, clasped the closed fist against his chest and nodded in deference to Jarl.

"The people here seem to worship you," he commented.

"They appreciate a safe place to trade, and our rates are fair," Jarl dismissed it. "They prosper, which draws more vendors, so we prosper as well. In your cargo, are there furs?"

"Yes."

"Good northern furs bring a premium. I'll introduce you to the vendor who gives the best price."

Once joined by Tryggr and Rask, they made their way up and down the crowded rows. Gunnar stared in awe at the abundance and variety of goods—foods, fabrics, furs, rugs, spices, weapons, pottery, wines. "I've never seen such a market," he confessed.

"They call them bazaars here, and wait until you see the stalls of the far, far easterners. They have silks of every imaginable color and figurines carved of the jade stone that you once showed me on your sword. It's considered very lucky in their culture," he added. "But the most impressive things are the huge carved tusks of ivory, some longer than two of Tryggr's lengths. I saw one that had an entire city carved upon it—and not just on the surface, they carve clear through to the other side in the minutest of detail. My words don't do them justice; I'll have to show you."

"Apologies, Jarl, I must take my leave," Nena said suddenly and moved away without waiting for a response. The men paused and watched, puzzled as she wove her way through the crowd.

"Exanthia," Nena greeted the young woman with a warm embrace. When the girl remained stiff and awkward in her arms, she released her. "Apologies for the emotional welcome; I was overcome with surprise. Look at you. A woman and a warrior," Nena said proudly, taking in the tall lithe girl in the warrior's dress. "You look grown far beyond your fifteen summers." Nena glanced at the open circle tattoo on Exanthia's arm.

"The gods have not yet chosen for me," Exanthia answered her unasked question. "It is my hope that they delay revealing their decision as long as they did with you. Several girls my age have already chosen and are mothers—when they were barely warriors," she added with a subtle shake of her head.

"Yet I'm sure many men have offered you their willingness?" Nena asked, hoping it was true. Had Exanthia been born Teclan it would have been a certainty, but being adopted as she was, Nena wasn't sure.

Exanthia nodded curtly.

Remembering her own irritation at the attention always given to her open circle, Nena changed the subject. "You've picked a very good time for your first warrior journey to the Great Sea. Some of Jarl's men have just returned from the North with many ships. It will be very busy, and there will be much to learn."

Exanthia's face went smooth.

"What is it?"

"Apologies, Nena. This girl is thankful for all that was done for her, and I know the gods, for whatever strange reason, chose Jarl for you, but the Northmen hold no place in my heart. The sooner I can return to the mountain, the better."

"I understand." Nena turned to the rest of the group. "Welcome, all of you. I will give you a tour and show you to your lodgings, but first, you must greet Jarl."

As Nena led the small group back to the waiting men and began making introductions, Rask could only stare at the young native woman who stood beside her. Her soft leather dress, tied behind her neck, covered and revealed so much at the same time. Bare smooth bronze shoulders, the swell of firm breasts, and the short skirt slit on the side showed a length of muscular slim thigh.

He smiled his half-smile that most women seemed to find irresistible and waited to gauge her reaction. When she finally glanced his way, there was no flush of flirtatious shyness that he expected from a girl her age. Instead, her eyebrows knitted and her nose twitched as if she'd smelled something foul. She looked away and didn't acknowledge him again while she waited for Nena to finish.

"Fancy yourself a native, do you, boy?" Tryggr chuckled, nudging him with his elbow as the two groups parted ways.

Rask scowled, still stung by her response. "I prefer my women ripe, not still green."

"So says your mouth now, but your eyes said plenty different a moment ago," Tryggr disagreed with a grin. "You couldn't take your eyes from her."

"I only looked at her close because of how she dressed, nothing more. Do many women dress like that?" he asked, hoping to change the subject.

"Only the warriors. And that one's out of your league, boy."

"Surely you jest," Rask snorted. "She was but a girl. And I've heard many men here have native women—that one even took pity on you, old man."

"There are native women, boy, and there are Teclan. That one was a Teclan. If you can't tell the difference by the look in their eyes that says they could kill you just as easily as speak to you, then look for the star on their upper arm. Even for a man the likes of Jarl, a Teclan woman was almost the death of him. One still wet behind the ears, such as you, wouldn't stand a chance." Tryggr grinned. "But there is an old toothless woman down by the docks who specializes in a boy's first time. She won't refuse you. You should take your coin and pay her a visit."

Rask's yelp of outrage was muffled by the other men's laughter. "I get more than my share of women, old man," he seethed when they finally quieted.

"Listen to the pup bark." Tryggr laughed. "He even shows his little needle teeth."

"You make it too easy for him, Rask," Gunnar chided, shaking his head as Tryggr moved away. "You must learn every word is not a challenge."

"That old fuck! Who does he think he is talking to me that way? I'm a second!"

"Then act like it." Gunnar dismissed him before turning to Jarl. "There are Teclan warriors here now?"

"Meln has always sent young warriors to his sister's tribe on the coast to learn and understand the power of the Great Sea. Now they come here afterward to study and practice our ways and the ways of the other foreigners before returning to the Teclan mountain. These have just arrived and Nena will see to them. Come. I will take you to the vendors who specialize in Northern goods so you can show your men."

The huge longhouse was filled to capacity with additional tables set up outside to hold all the revelers. While it appeared to be a traditional Viking hall from a distance, up close the modifications made to account for the climate were evident. Only the bottom one-third of the walls were solid. The upper two-thirds were left open to allow breeze coming off the sea to flow through. Multiple breaks along the lengths of the low walls served as door openings, but there were no doors.

The inside tables were arranged in three long rows, with Jarl, Tryggr, Gunnar, and Nena seated at one end of the center row. The crew of the Huntress was seated only a few feet away at the end of another. The crowd grew steadily louder as continuous lines of slaves and servants delivered trays of local delicacies. Roasted wild boar and lamb, sturgeon and pike stuffed with barberries and walnuts, mollusks seasoned with coriander, fava beans with onions, dried figs, plums and dates, saffron rice, warm flat breads and honey cakes—and endless pitchers of ale, mead, and wine.

Jarl pushed away his plate and leaned back in his chair. "I shall be sick if I eat another bite."

"I, as well," Gunnar grunted. "Nena, the food was outstanding."

"Gratitude, Gunnar. Your return has been long-awaited and much cause to celebrate. I've located the map Jarl mentioned to you and made alterations. Would you like to see it now?"

"I would."

Nena raised a hand and motioned to the nearest doorway. Two servants entered, carrying a large rack between them. On it, stretched an ox-hide map of the southeastern Caspian coastline. After it was positioned to be visible to both the center table and Treasure Huntress crew, Nena stood and walked to it. Beginning with the mark closest to the shore, she described each target's fortifications and primary form of assets before moving on to the next.

Gunnar doubted it was coincidence that she presented them in a sweeping arch that ultimately led back to the sea not far from the starting point; she knew how they operated. He glanced at Jarl, sure that he'd be bored of the recap, but found him drinking in Nena's every movement as if he were a man dying of thirst and she were cool water. Gunnar smiled to himself. He doubted Jarl was even hearing a word she said. She could've been describing how to bake a loaf of bread, and his friend's rapt attention would've likely been the same; he was still as mad for her as ever.

"Do you have any questions?" Nena asked when she'd finished.

When Gunnar shook his head, she began to walk back to them.

Rask had been seated with his back to the map initially but had turned his chair to face it during her presentation. Deep in his cups, he stood as she walked past and raised his tankard. "I have a question," he slurred. "It appears to me that you've given us a map to all your enemies. That seems very convenient, don't you think?"

A hush fell over their end of the room at the insult, spreading quickly through the entire hall as Rask's words were shared. Jarl bristled and sat up in his chair, but Nena held up her hand to him in a quick barely noticeable gesture. She turned and took a step back towards Rask. "You'd be correct. These are all enemies—not all that we have to be sure, but the richest ones. Would you prefer to attack our friends and allies? Is that your way?"

"I'd prefer to attack where the spoils are the greatest. If I'm to risk my life, I want it to be for worthy reward, not merely to clean these lands for you. I've done plenty of that these past years in my own homeland."

Ignoring the grumbles of the crowd, Nena nodded. "If it's the greatest spoils you seek and you're not afraid, then I know of a place where the wealth is so vast it surpasses all of these ten times over." She waved to the map.

"And they are not your enemies?"

"They are not."

"Then where is this treasure?" Rask demanded, boldly drunk.

"Ten days ride to the south on a mountain lined with red cliffs. It's guarded only by a single tribe. All you have to do is go in there and take it."

"That sounds more like it. Show us this place on the ma..." Rask's last word was drowned out by a roar of laughter, spreading like a wave through the entire hall. Even the woman smiled as she turned away and resumed walking to her seat. She'd made a fool of him, though he wasn't sure exactly how. *No one made a fool of him.*

Rask stepped after her, his free hand reaching for her hair. As his fingers closed, he pulled, expecting to feel her braids, but his fist held only air. She was gone. Before he could even turn to look for her, he felt her body pressed up against his back, her dagger blade to his throat. His tankard clattered to the floor.

"Make a move and it will be your last," she murmured calmly.

Chairs and benches scraped and slammed as everyone in the hall took to their feet. The room fell eerily silent. No one moved. All looked uneasily to their respective leaders for orders. Gunnar took a quick glance around the hall packed with seasoned fighters, fully aware of the carnage that would result if they were to set upon each other.

"I'd do as she says, boy," Tryggr said, slowly approaching the pair. "Or don't," he chuckled, trying to break the charged heaviness in the air. "Though it'd almost be a shame to lose you now; you were starting to grow on me. Truth be told, you remind me more than a bit of myself at that age."

Tryggr was close now, and Rask wondered if he was coming to his aid. Perhaps he was distracting the woman with words until he could get close enough to disarm her. Though he prayed the fool was careful. The tip of the woman's blade bit viciously into his throat, and he felt a trickle of blood running down his neck.

Tryggr leaned in towards Rask's ear and murmured, "Although I must say, it might be better for you if she were to just kill you now—at least it would be quick. I might almost choose that over what Jarl will surely have in store for you if she lets you live."

Though he said the words quietly, Tryggr's deep booming voice carried in the deathlike silence. Gunnar glanced at Jarl though he didn't need to. The fury he saw there made him think Tryggr might be right.

"Listen to me closely," Nena whispered in Rask's ear. "You have one chance and one chance only for Jarl not to kill you. When I release you, you will smile and apologize and maintain that it was all a jest—a misunderstanding. Do not fight back. Do not resist. And do not deviate from that story no matter what he does to you. Do you understand me? Nod if you do."

Rask gave a slight nod.

"Very well then. May your gods protect you."

The blade was gone. Her body was gone. She didn't seem to hurry, but somehow she was already in front of him, moving to intercept Jarl.

She reached up to touch Jarl's face. "No harm done, Jarl."

Jarl slowed only long enough to brush the back of her hand with his lips as he moved past her. Gunnar shook his head and held up a hand for the other men not to intervene.

"No harm intended, Jarl," Rask said, holding his empty hands out to the sides. "It was only a jest."

Jarl's fist smashed into Rask's jaw, snapping his head sideways and driving him backwards over a chair into the low wall. Before he could rise, Jarl had him by his tunic. His fist smashed him again.

He rocked back for a third blow, but Nena was there, touching his arm. "Jarl. You have looked forward to this night for many years. Do not spoil it with this. Do not spill blood. Return to your friends and your drink. There was no harm done, and I would not have you regret having wasted this precious time later. Come. Leave him," she beckoned. "For me."

For a long moment, Jarl remained with his fist cocked back, his rage warring with her request. He pulled Rask up until their faces were inches apart. "It seems the gods have chosen to spare you tonight," Jarl said, his voice deceptively quiet. "By her appeal and my long friendship to Gunnar, you shall live, but know that decision has tested me to my very limits. Steer well clear of me in the future, for you'll not be so fortunate a second time—no matter how slight the offense and no matter who pleads for you." He shoved Rask back to the floor.

"Gratitude, Jarl," Gunnar said as he stepped around him and grabbed Rask above the elbow. Pulling him roughly to his feet, he propelled him to the closest doorway opening and shoved him through. When they were clear of the hall, his own blow followed Jarl's to the side of Rask's jaw.

"Have you lost your fucking mind?! You attack Jarl's wife? And in front of him?"

"She mocked me! And I didn't attack her, I was just going to give her hair a yank."

Gunnar brought his open palm across Rask's cheek—a slap to convey the highest insult. Rask still staggered from the force of the blow. Gunnar pointed at him. "Shut your mouth. Shut it and keep it closed. You've given me many a cause to doubt my choice of you as second before, but never so much as tonight. Tomorrow, I shall decide if you'll hold the position any longer. Return to the ship and do not move from there unless I call for you. And thank the gods every minute you sit there, that you continue to draw breath. Of all men, Jarl is not one to cross, and certainly not when it comes to her. He considered his own life valueless without her; taking yours wouldn't even cause him to blink. Now go! Get out of my sight."

"Apologies, Jarl. And Nena," Gunnar murmured as he returned to his seat.

Jarl only acknowledged him with a stiff nod.

"No harm done, Gunnar," Nena said. She turned to Jarl. "Do not dwell on it further. It is over and past. Enjoy the night."

Jarl scowled and looked away.

Nena studied him, deliberating for a long moment. "What can I do to change your thoughts to happier ones?"

Jarl's head twitched at the suggestive shift in her tone, but he didn't give her his full attention, his mind still locked on what had transpired.

Nena picked up her gold chalice, topped it with wine, then moved to stand in front of him. "Shall I offer you a drink?" she asked, but did not hold out the cup, just stood in front of him with the hint of a smile playing at the corners of her lips.

"I already have a drink," Jarl declined, but his voice was softer—and she had his full attention now.

Nena stepped forward, straddling him on the chair. She took a long slow sip of wine, held it in her mouth for a moment, then swallowed it and ran the tip of her tongue over her lips. "My drink is better," she murmured. Jarl stared at her, mesmerized. She took a second mouthful of wine and leaned toward him. Pressing her lips against his, she pushed his head back and transferred the wine into his mouth. Jarl swallowed it, then kissed her hungrily, his hands reaching up to tangle in her hair.

"Nena," he groaned as she pulled away and stood up.

She turned to Gunnar and Tryggr. "Now he is happy again. I will leave you men to your talk and your drink. You have much catching up to do without any further diversion from a woman." With that, she made her way to the door, Jarl's eyes following her every step of the way.

Chapter 35

I t was done. She was betrothed to Artan MacTavish, with the wedding date appropriately set for Samhain, the day of the dead. Fiona knew Artan had chosen it to intimidate her, but it didn't; she intended to be rid of him long before then.

She stared out over the feasting crowd from her position of honor at the high table, frustrated by the delay the meal was causing her. So far, she'd accomplished none of her goals for the evening. Artan's father was notably absent, an unforeseen wrinkle, and she'd yet to speak with his mother alone. After practicing what she would say countless times, she'd certainly not expected getting to speak at all to be her biggest challenge. But that was how it had turned out. Lady Duvessa had been distant and aloof, bordering on rude with her and Artan, while fawning over her more important guests and Artan's brother, Tynan.

Fiona glanced to her right, past Artan to his mother and brother seated on his other side. Their obvious affection suited her plan perfectly. She'd already intended to use Tynan in her scheme because he was the eldest, and Artan had oft jealously referred to him as the favorite. But from what she'd seen tonight, he was more than that. His mother clearly adored him, and his father must feel the same to have chosen him to sit in his stead for the feast.

Fiona felt her father's worried eyes on her from where he was disrespectfully seated with the other guests below, but didn't look at him. He was opposed to the marriage—had confessed to her many times that he cared not for Artan. In the carriage earlier, he'd actually pleaded with her to reconsider before it was too late. She knew he felt guilty that the betrothal was the result of his pressure on her for an heir, but Fiona didn't dare tell him the truth.

"I'd almost forgotten what it was like to live like this," Artan sighed. "What an evening. I've received a string of invitations from other families who wish to honor our betrothal with their own feasts. They all assume I've been welcomed back into the fold and hope to improve their standing with my family through me. We shall tell them no differently, of course."

Artan had never shared with her what had caused the rift between him and his family, but it must have been something terrible. Despite his hopes to the contrary, his mother had made it clear their marriage wasn't going to mend it.

"Have you seen the gifts?" he asked. "There's a veritable mountain of them. Although I've yet to see a gift from you, my dear."

"I have it here, my lord," Fiona murmured as she reached under her chair and withdrew the small parcel wrapped in red silk, fastened with gold ribbon. "You should open it now."

Artan looked stunned as he took it from her. Setting it on the table in front of him, he untied the ribbon and peeled back the silk, revealing the inlaid silver box. He caught his breath, but Fiona knew it wasn't because of the fine craftsmanship. Accentuated by the red silk behind it, the golden dragon's ruby eye glittered menacingly back at him. Even Fiona had to admit it appeared quite hexed.

Using a single fingertip, Artan cautiously lifted the lid by one corner, as if he feared an adder or some other deadly creature lurked inside. Finding it empty, he snorted and dropped the lid, then pushed the box aside, carefully covering it with the silk.

"Do you not like it, my lord? I took such care with the design." She smiled.

Artan took a gulp of wine, then leaned towards her. "Do you still think of your Northman, then? Perhaps still hold out some hope that he'll return for you? You're such a fool. He's probably this very moment regaling anyone who will listen how he tasted the sweet cunny of a noblewoman." He sat back. "What? You find my words vulgar? He'll recount it in far more lewd detail than that, I can assure you—has probably done so hundreds of times already. Your filthy heathen lover," he muttered under his breath.

"He's far more of a man than you'll ever be," Fiona hissed, unable in that moment to hide her true feelings.

Artan laughed at that and raised his goblet in a mock toast to her. "My name and title say quite otherwise, my dear." He drained the goblet, then tossed it to the table, watching blearily as it rolled over the edge to the floor. "I must piss," he announced. Pushing back his chair, he stood and stumbled from the room, reappearing within moments, still tying his trousers.

Fiona closed her eyes and grit her teeth at the realization he'd urinated in the hallway. She took a deep breath, struggling to suppress her hatred and disgust. She had to maintain the guise of devoted betrothed. She'd already slipped once, and that could not happen again. Information, vital to her plan, had to be discovered this night.

From the corner of her eye, Fiona noticed his mother preparing to leave the table. This was the moment she'd been waiting for. She stood and stepped down from the front of the dais, moving to intercept Lady Duvessa before she could reach her other guests. Ignoring the woman's annoyed frown at her approach, Fiona pasted a cheerful smile on her face. "Your Grace," she bubbled, careful to use the title the self-important harridan insisted upon—a title normally reserved for kings and high clergy. "Gratitude for including us in this celebration. I've never attended such a feast."

"Nay, I doubt you would have."

Fiona pretended not to hear the insult. "Your Grace, I must seek your counsel. Marrying into such an important family, I wish to take all care against making any blunders."

"What is it?" Lady Duvessa snapped.

"Artan has mentioned accepting an invitation from another man who wishes to honor our betrothal—a man named Tibbot." Fiona searched the woman's face for any sign of recognition of the name. There was none.

"And?" Lady Duvessa demanded.

"Well, I've heard rumors that this Tibbot is a...slaver. Is it appropriate that we attend a gathering hosted by such a man?"

"'Tis not your place to deem what is appropriate, girl. As the future wife of a MacTavish, your only concern is to honor Artan's wishes, and you'd do well to remember that. If this man..."

"Tibbot," Fiona filled in for her.

"If this Tibbot truly is a slaver, it matters naught. As my sixth son, Artan's actions aren't scrutinized. And since his banishment, he undoubtedly knows a great many lesser people." Her gaze lingered pointedly on Fiona.

"Of course, Your Grace. Gratitude for the counsel." Fiona beamed at her like a half-wit. "I shall return to him now."

Fiona turned away, her pulse racing. The vain cow had shown no recognition of Tibbot—had even said, "*if the man truly is a slaver.*" Assuming Artan's comments about his mother and father being complicit in their despicable acts were true, then only Artan remained. If he had the same response, two potential obstacles to her plan would fall by the wayside.

Artan was sipping from a new goblet of wine as she returned to her seat. He nodded at her, seeming to have forgotten their interchange. Fiona casually took a bite of bread. "You mentioned other invitations to honor our betrothal with feasts, my lord. I, too, have received such an invitation for us, but from a merchant family. Wealthy merchants, to be sure, but I should probably still decline, don't you agree?" Fiona forced another piece of bread into her mouth, hoping her tone didn't convey the eagerness she felt.

"Wealthy merchants? Likely they intend to shower us with expensive gifts to try to earn favor." He considered out loud with a mixture of disdain and consideration.

"Aye, but I've heard rumors that he trades in slaves—from his estate. Can you imagine it? I shudder to think what that must be like. Men and women caged and chained like animals. I should not have bothered you with it. I shall, of course, decline."

"A slaver?" The image had piqued his sick interest as she'd known it would. "Is it Quillen? My family has had many *dealings* with Quillen in the past."

"Nay, his name is Tibbot." Fiona held her breath.

"And he keeps the slaves on his estate?"

"So I've heard," she murmured, noncommittal.

"Well, I see no reason why we should discriminate against any folk who desire to wish us well. You will accept for us."

Fiona opened her mouth as if to protest, then nodded demurely. "As you wish."

The sound of laughter drew their attention to his mother and brother, and a third lord Fiona didn't recognize. She turned to Artan who stared at the trio with barely disguised hostility.

"Your mother seems quite fond of your brother, Tynan," she prodded.

"Aye, they're unusually indiscreet tonight. She must have had quite a lot to drink."

"Indiscreet?" Fiona whispered.

"You heard me correctly. As young lads, we each went through a period when we were our mother's *special* favorite. To my knowledge that all stopped

as we grew older; I know it did with me. But it appears that since Father's..."
he darted a glance at her without finishing the sentence, then started over. "It
appears that perhaps Tynan is her special favorite once again. I've oft heard
the saying, there is nothing like a mother's love, but in our family it means
something quite different."

Fiona fought back her revulsion at this latest MacTavish perversity,
keying instead on Artan's haste to cover some slip about his father. "You
mentioned your father. Your mother said he was ill? Perhaps we should seek
him out and pay our respects."

Artan looked at her cagily as he considered his answer. "Since we are
now safely betrothed, I'll share another family secret with you—a secret that
only the closest family knows. My father was struck down by a strange palsy
months ago. He is alive and aware but remains trapped in his bed, unable to
move or speak, communicating only by blinking. My mother has assumed
control of all family matters, ostensibly until he recovers, but there's been no
improvement.

"I suspected her of having a hand in his condition; it was far too
convenient, but I've queried many healers and apothecaries and learned of
no poison that acts in such a manner." He paused. "If I were a religious man,
I might believe it was the wrath of God, and that my father is receiving divine
retribution for his many sins."

As will you, soon enough. Fiona savored the thought. She cared nothing
for the plight of a monster who'd married and spawned more evil. All she
could think of was one less MacTavish stood in her way.

"We were not expecting you back for weeks," Jarl said to Gunnar as he
poured them each a mead, and they moved to his living area.

"Nena's map was invaluable and much expedited our campaign. The holds are filled with treasure, the men's blood-lust is satisfied; there was no reason to continue." Gunnar took a seat on a chair covered with thick, soft wolf pelts.

"Excellent. Now you'll have time to relax and see the area. We shall organize a hunt in the mountains and..."

"Apologies, but as soon as we've finished trading for lighter goods, we'll be leaving. A few days at most."

"A few days? Why so soon?"

"To ensure we make it home before winter settles in Rusland."

"If you don't wish to tell me, then say so; don't make an excuse about the rivers freezing to the one man who's made the trip as many times as you. You're well ahead of schedule. And I thought you might even overwinter here."

"Leave him be, Jarl," Nena chided as she joined them. "Can you not see there is a woman?"

Jarl turned back to Gunnar, incredulous. "Is that true?"

Gunnar sank deeper into his chair. "Yes," he admitted reluctantly. "Though even now I'm half afraid to speak of her for fear the gods will yank her from my grasp. The thought of it gnaws at my gut every waking moment. How many times did I swear that if they would bless me again with a woman in my blood, I'd never leave her."

"Why did you not mention this before? So you've taken a wife? Who is she? Anyone I know?"

"Not yet my wife and no, you wouldn't know her."

Jarl stared at him expectantly.

"She is Irish."

"Ah, a slave then," Jarl said nodding, understanding his reluctance.

"Not a slave. She's highborn."

"You're not serious."

"I am."

"And how do you hope to win her?"

"I've already won her heart. And her bed," Gunnar added with a smile.

Jarl chuckled. "You told me once when it came to women, you were leaving no stone unturned. I thought it a jest at the time, but a highborn?"

"Lion and wolf," Nena murmured.

"What?" Gunnar asked.

"My father told me once that Jarl and I could never be together because we were like lion and wolf. Equal in strengths, but too different."

Gunnar nodded. "I've seen the similarity in our situation and yours more than once, and it seems no less impossible. Yet the fact that you've achieved such a happy resolution gives me hope."

"How did you meet this woman?" Nena asked. "Or is that for Jarl's ears only? If you would prefer, I will leave so you two can whisper in private. Though I must warn you, he will tell me all later; he cannot keep a secret from me."

Jarl shrugged and grinned ruefully. "It is true."

"I've no problem with you hearing my tale. In fact, I think you will appreciate it the most. She held a crossbow to my chest at night and demanded our swords and the slaves I'd just purchased."

Both Nena and Jarl's heads snapped up with immediate interest. "And did you?" Jarl asked.

"Did you not hear the part about the crossbow?" Gunnar chuckled.

"But you said your sword." Jarl looked pointedly at the golden sheath at his side.

"I was able to retrieve it later."

"And you said she was a highborn."

"Hush, Jarl," Nena said as she settled on his lap. "Let him tell us the whole story. So she is a raider." Nena nodded. "I like her already."

"Not exactly. And therein lies the problem. If she were only a raider, I would think we could easily be together. But by day, she's a respected noblewoman."

"What are you going to do?" Jarl asked.

"Eamon has a plan."

"Your Irish slave?"

"Equal member of the crew," Gunnar corrected him.

Jarl dismissed the correction with a shrug. "And what is this grand plan?"

Gunnar twisted his cup in his hands. "If the gods favor me, I plan to purchase lands and title in Ireland. Hopefully, you're looking at a future Irish lord."

Jarl laughed out loud. "Wait 'til Tryggr hears of this."

"It appears you've no need of Tryggr to have sport with me; you're doing fine on your own."

"Apologies, my friend, I just can't see it."

"Yet I suppose you saw yourself as a Teclan?"

"Even though I bear the Teclan star on my arm, I never had to pretend to be one of them. You don't really think you can fool them, do you? Assuming you're successful in acquiring title, how will you know how to act? They're born to it, and what's not bred into them, they're taught from birth; it takes a long time to get that stick up their arse." He chuckled and took a drink. "Even if you could do it, why would you want to? That life's not for you. Why not just take her? You said that you've won her heart, so take her to Norway or Daneland, or bring her here. You truly do adjust to the heat with time. Live among your own people, your own kind."

"Because I don't want her to change."

"And instead you will do so?"

"Yes."

"How much are you willing to give up?"

"Anything that is required."

"Raiding?"

Gunnar nodded.

"The Huntress?"

He nodded again. "I'm even prepared to be baptized by a Christian priest."

Jarl sat back, stunned. "You would give up the gods?"

"I said I would be baptized. If my wife has managed a secret life, I see no reason why I also cannot. I do not make this decision on a whim, Jarl. I've seen enough of the world to know what I want. She is what I want. She's strong and clever, but she's also...I don't know how to describe it. Gentle. Innocent. Good. She knows of the evil in this world, but hasn't been tarnished by it, and I would have it remain so. When I'm with her I feel...there's a certainty to my path. She is my destiny."

"Apologies, Gunnar," Nena interrupted. "But why is she a raider? Has her family fallen on hard times?"

"Nay. She raids not for coin, but to free slaves. Someone close to her was enslaved once, and it caused her great distress."

"Slaves are the way of the world," Jarl scoffed. "That's how it's always been and always will be. In every culture, in every corner of the world, the powerful enslave the weak. You know that. You've seen it. It's a necessity. And the Irish are some of the most notorious. It's not by chance that Dublin is a slave trading capital. It will never change."

"Perhaps. But Fiona still sees wonder and possibility in the world, and through her eyes I can see it, too. She has such an extraordinary unprejudiced mind. She's restored my faith in...well, in everything. I have hopes and plans for the future now, like my life is beginning anew."

Jarl chuckled into his cup, shaking his head. "Gunnar, I've heard many a descriptive word come from your mouth regarding a woman, but I can honestly say, not once do I recall a single one ever being in reference to their mind. Is she at least comely?"

"Comely? No," Gunnar murmured, his eyes suddenly far away. "She's the most beautiful woman I've ever encountered. As if Freya took human form."

"Well, that's more like it. For a moment, I thought you were going to say she was plain as well, and it would have shattered everything I thought I knew of you. Show us how you will act. Pretend Nena and I are fellow noblemen you are trying to impress."

Gunnar took a long swallow of ale, then shook his head with a suppressed smile. "I will not."

"Come now. If you cannot do it among friends, how do you hope to be able to convince strangers? I never knew you to be a fearful man before."

"You cannot goad me into it, Jarl," Gunnar laughed.

"Leave him be, Jarl," Nena chided. "You're hardly one to ridicule a man in love."

"Let me have my fun, woman," Jarl said with a grin.

"If you continue to torment him, I shall give him weapons with which to fight you back. I could start by telling him any number of things about you, like..."

"Alright, alright, I'll leave him be," Jarl conceded with a chuckle. "But only under protest." He turned back to Gunnar. "Since you are still months away from your love's bed, perhaps a woman tonight?" Jarl asked.

Gunnar shook his head.

"Have you been injured?"

"No. I gave her my word, I would not lay with another."

"And you've honored it? For the entire journey? Even after the battles?" Jarl asked incredulous, unable to see Nena's raised eyebrows from her position on his lap.

"Yes, Jarl."

"I can scarce believe you allowed her to extract such a promise from you."

"She did not extract, I gave it freely."

"Why?" he asked.

Nena cleared her throat.

"I only meant...um, not for me, of course," Jarl stammered.

Gunnar chuckled at Jarl's scrambling. "In truth, I do not wish to lay with another. I implore the gods every day to see it as proof of my love and keep her safe until I return."

"Well, if it was a sacrifice that was required to prove yourself to them, you'll have most certainly done it with that. I mean, because you're you and how you were before," Jarl added hastily as Nena sat up and turned to stare at him.

Chapter 36

"It was so generous of you and Tibbot to host a betrothal feast. And your offer to honor us with a wedding feast also...well, I feel truly blessed to have a friend like you," Fiona murmured.

"I assure you, my lady, 'tis my pleasure," Leona gushed and glanced triumphantly to Tibbot at Fiona's use of the word *friend*. "I'm having new fabric samples delivered next week; shall I bring them to you at Tir na Lionmhar?" Leona asked hopefully.

"Oh, I would not ask that of you; I shall return here—that is, unless I'm becoming a nuisance. If I am, simply say the word. I would not have you regret your kind gestures."

"Oh, my lady, you could never be a bother. You are my most welcome guest. And that's what friends are for," Leona purred.

"Indeed," Fiona agreed. "Well, 'tis getting late and I must be off. Tibbot, would you have your man send for my carriage?"

"At once." Tibbot snapped his fingers at a servant who scurried away.

As Fiona stood, she glanced at the secret doorway where she'd seen Gunnar the morning after she'd taken the slaves. Oh, how different her reaction would be this time, if only the door could open to reveal him there now. Realizing Tibbot and his wife were waiting for her, she pushed the thoughts from her mind. The pair followed her to the front door.

At the top of the steps, she turned back to them and forced a laugh. "How silly of me. With all the excitement of wedding plans, I almost forgot." She reached inside the silk pouch purse suspended from her belt and withdrew a folded parchment. "Artan asked me to give this to you." She held the letter out to Tibbot, making sure the red wax, boldly stamped with the MacTavish seal, was facing upwards. "He's probably expressing his personal gratitude for the betrothal feast. He's mentioned several times how much he enjoyed it," Fiona lied, then turned and descended the stairs to her awaiting carriage.

Safely inside, Fiona closed her eyes and imagined Tibbot reading the words she knew by heart. Words she'd written after mastering Artan's loopy graceful hand. For the first time ever, she found herself eagerly anticipating her next visit here—to see what fruit, if any, was born of this first contact.

"Are your trades complete?" Jarl asked.

Gunnar nodded. "I've converted most of my share to gemstones."

"Did you find the vendor I recommended for the other things you wanted?" Nena asked as she entered the living area with two freshly bathed little girls in matching long white nightdresses trailing at her heels.

"Yes, and you were right; the quality of his craftsmanship is unrivaled."

Nena sat, positioning the girls in front of her before beginning to comb out their long damp hair. The two stared silently at Gunnar with wide, curious eyes. They were a beautiful blend of their parents' best features—Nena's dark hair and Jarl's high cheekbones. But it was their matching hazel eyes that were truly extraordinary. Large and almond-shaped like their mother's, the light green color was further accentuated by their golden skin and thick black lashes. Gunnar stared back; the combination was incredibly striking and unique.

After Nena finished loosely braiding their hair for bed, Jarl patted his lap. "Come, my little lionesses." The girls climbed up, and he positioned them together side by side in the crook of one arm, leaving his other hand free to drink. Warm and snuggled close, the two were soon yawning, their eyelids sinking and fluttering as they fought to stay awake. When the littlest one's chin nodded to her chest, Nena stood to take them to bed.

"Let them stay. They're not hurting anything," Jarl said.

"You spoil them, Jarl," she admonished gently.

"I know, but all too soon, you'll be training them to be serious little warriors, and this time will be lost."

"That training should have begun already."

Their voices had awakened the youngest, and all three looked up at her with pleading eyes. Gunnar laughed out loud.

Nena held up her hands. "You see? If Jarl has his way, they'll never become warriors."

"I do see, and it's a perfect life. Though I'm glad not to be born a little boy now. Those two will leave a trail of broken hearts in their wake, of that I have no doubt."

"May the gods protect me," Jarl murmured and took a long swallow of ale. "I cringe to think of when they are older."

"Daughters suit you. I'd have never thought it, but they do."

"That's easy for you to say. I hope you have some, too. They twist your heart in knots in a way that's unfathomable. And I still intend for a boy or two."

As Jarl looked to Nena with a grin, Gunnar said a quick silent prayer to Frigg to one day have such a family—such a life with Fiona.

"My lady, would you be so kind as to deliver another message to Artan for me?" Tibbot asked as he held out a sealed parchment.

"Of course, Tibbot," Fiona said with a smile as she took it. "Though I swear you two are corresponding more than Leona and I."

"Simple business, my lady," he said glibly. "Nothing nearly so interesting as your wedding feast plans."

Though she was dying to read the contents of this particular letter, Fiona loosened the drawstring on her silk purse and carelessly stuffed it inside before resuming her conversation with Leona, as if she had no interest in it whatsoever.

"There's a bite to the air tonight that wasn't here when we passed this place in the spring," Eamon said as he warmed his hands over the fire, the flames casting long shadows on the ships moored at the river's edge. Tomorrow they would be hauled from the water to begin the first of the return portages.

"This is balmy," Gunnar disagreed. "We're early this year. It gets far worse than this, I can assure you. On our previous spring trip, we came across two ships that attempted return travel too late and didn't make it."

"And their crews?" Eamon asked, passing an uneasy glance at the dark timber all around them.

"Nothing left of them. Wolves and bear. Mostly wolves. Rusland is no place to spend a winter."

As if on cue, a wolf howled in the distance, a plaintive, eerie cry. When Eamon pulled his cape tight and stepped closer to the fire, Gunnar smiled and changed the subject. "Instead of symbols tonight, I should like to discuss some of the more prominent Irish families."

"A good idea. We can start with your woman's family if I've heard of them. What is her name?"

"She is Lady Fiona O'Neill."

"O'Neill?"

"Do you know of them?"

Eamon exhaled slowly. "Aye. The O'Neills are one of the most powerful clans in Ireland. When you said she was a highborn...well, I guess I just assumed it wasn't quite that high."

"Is that a problem?" Gunnar asked.

"After I tell you what I know, you can decide that for yourself. First, with Irish family names, an O' preceding a name, means they are descendants of one particular man. O'Sullivan, descendants of Sullivan, O'Reilly, descendants of Reilly, and so on. Similarly, Mac before a name, like MacKinnon or MacGregor, means they are descendants of Kinnon and Gregor. Mac actually means *son of* but everyone now accepts it to mean descendant, just as with your own surname, Frederiksen. You're not the son of Frederick, but someone in your lineage was."

Gunnar nodded.

"Neill was a very powerful high king who lived long, long ago. When he died, each of his seven sons was so determined to claim the title that the family splintered, and their feud continues to this day. Of the original seven, only two sons' bloodlines remain—the Northern and Southern O'Neill, and their hatred for each other is legendary.

"With her estate being somewhere west of Balbriggan, your lady's family will likely be allied with the Southern O'Neill, but I can't be certain of that; the dividing line is always shifting as both sides seek to expand their territory. Their goal is to unite all of Ireland under one king—an O'Neill king from the proper bloodline of course, and they are ruthless toward that end. It makes lands near the dividing line especially valuable, which unfortunately also makes your woman very valuable—as a bride for anyone seeking a legitimate claim to her family's estate.

"If we succeed in this, you must take care. The O'Neills are a cutthroat bunch. Through marriages and secret deals, their influence extends far beyond their individual realms. They've killed their own kin for centuries; they won't hesitate to kill an outsider if they thought them to stand in their way."

Chapter 37

"This is the last." Gunnar handed Eamon a pouch of gemstones and watched him stuff it deep under the linen cloth bindings wrapped around his chest and torso. "You're sure it will be enough?"

"Aye." Eamon nodded as he pulled his tunic over the wraps. "But I beg you to reconsider. Have someone else bring the rest of your wealth to you," he suggested, not at all comfortable with carrying Gunnar's share of the most recent raids on his person.

Gunnar shook his head. "Only I know where everything is buried, and it's been so long, some may be difficult even for me to find."

They'd had this discussion many times on the return trip, referring to Gunnar's multiple buried caches.

Eamon buckled his leather jerkin over his tunic, then draped the heavy Germanian fleece cape over his shoulders before following Gunnar out of the storage shed. The two men stood looking out over the bustling Aalborg harbor. The captain and crew of the closest ship, the Sea Falcon, had just finished loading the Eastern slaves to be sold in Dublin.

"I trust him," Gunnar answered Eamon's unspoken concern. "I've known him many years and have saved his life more than once. He will see you safely to Dublin. And no one knows of your true purpose."

Eamon nodded.

"As soon as I'm finished, I'll return to Balbriggan and wait for you there. Hopefully less than a month," Gunnar said.

Eamon nodded again, and the two men grasped forearms before Eamon turned and walked alone to the Sea Falcon. As Gunnar watched the Sea Falcon push away from the dock and the slaves begin to row, fingers of foreboding plucked at his gut. Eamon hadn't voiced his doubts, but Gunnar had read them clearly on his face. He couldn't help feeling the same. Now that it was here, their plan seemed beyond far-fetched and ridiculous. He'd just given a king's fortune to a freed slave, a man known for his elaborate stories, and sent him on a quest to attain a title. All for a woman he'd spent little over a week with. At what point had he completely lost his mind?

Gunnar exhaled and tried to quell his misgivings. He could not succumb to doubt now. He was committed. Eamon would not betray him. His chances of success were likely nil, but he would not betray him.

Eamon jumped from the boat before it bumped against the Dublin dock, barely resisting the urge to drop to his knees and kiss the wood planks. Other than the first days when he'd thought to die of seasickness, months on the Huntress had never affected him so. He scowled back at his recent transport. That ship was no Huntress. And it was no Falcon either. The stinking, waddling thing should have been called the Sea Pig.

He started down the docks, not bothering to help secure the ship; that was for her crew, which he was no part of, thank the gods. Eamon smiled at his reference. He wasn't sure exactly when he'd started referring to their gods rather than the one he'd known since birth, but now they felt as natural to him as the clothes he wore. He made a mental note to be mindful of it and any other pagan habits he'd picked up. When he changed his appearance back to that of an Irishman, his mannerisms and words had to change with it.

Looking surreptitiously over one shoulder, he gauged the reaction of the locals working the docks, but no one paid him any heed. The arrival of a single Norse ship, heavily laden with slaves and trade goods had raised no concern. He trailed one hand over the pouch of spending silver on his belt, reaffirming its presence, but resisted the urge to touch the many gemstone pouches bound tightly to his chest and torso. He dare not draw attention to them. If he was set upon by thieves, they would likely snatch the pouch of silver and run, not search his entire person—unless he gave them cause.

Ten paces shy of the dockmaster's station, he paused. In the face of this first test, doubts resurfaced and ran rampant through his mind. Gunnar's original messenger, though a trusted man, could have failed to deliver the letter and gift to the bishop. Or, if he had delivered it, it would not have been directly to the bishop's hand; it would have gone through a chain of his servants, any one of whom could have pocketed the gift and discarded the letter. Or the bishop could have been promoted within the church as was his intent and been replaced by someone more pious.

Eamon ran his hand over his beard and berated himself. This was all his own fault. He could be in Daneland or Norway, surrounded by fine Viking women, his pockets full of silver. But, nay, thanks to his mouth, which his mother always said ran like a duck's arse, instead, he was here, with the crushing weight of Gunnar's hopes settled squarely on his shoulders.

"Whining about it now isn't going to change anything," he muttered to himself and stepped up to the window. "There should be a dispatch here for me," he said to the clerk, his mouth suddenly dry.

"Name?"

"Eamon MacGarvan." Having never had a surname, he'd added Mac to the pet name the whores had given him—Garvan, the rough little one.

The clerk looked him over, his name and accent not matching his Viking appearance, before he grunted and pulled a box from a shelf over his head. After riffling through it, he said, "Nothing 'ere for that name."

Eamon's heart sank in his chest. "Would you please look again?"

The clerk glared at him and Eamon dropped a piece of silver on the worn wooden half door that doubled as a counter. "For your trouble," he said.

The man pocketed the silver, then pulled out every piece of parchment, shaking it exaggeratedly for Eamon to see, grumbling all the while.

"Are there any other places it could be?" Eamon asked, frantic. "What are those there?" He pointed to a crate of rolled scrolls.

"Those are ship manifests, and it'll cost you a sight more if you want me to go through them."

Eamon's eyes landed on a dusty scroll secured with a purple tassel. He set a larger piece of silver on the counter. "That one there, in the back. Start with it."

"No name on it," the clerk announced after blowing the dust off the protective leather cover and turning it over in his hands.

"Open it."

"There's no name," the clerk repeated. "How would I know 'tis for you?"

"With no name, how will you ever know 'tis for anyone? For god's sake, just open it, man!"

"But 'tis sealed."

Eamon took a deep breath to calm himself and set yet another piece of silver on the counter, though he wanted nothing more than to bound over the half-door and rip it from the man's hands. "Break the seal by placing something heavy on it so 'twill appear to have been crushed, not torn. If 'tis not the correspondence I seek, you can replace it in the crate and pretend to have no knowledge of it."

The man looked around, nodded, and swiped the silver. Using the point of his elbow directly on the seal, he pressed it flat, fragmenting the wax. Carefully he slipped the tassel tie off one end and unrolled the tooled leather cover. It seemed an eternity before he finally began to read out loud.

"From the hand of the Bishop of..."

"Kells," Eamon finished for him as he leaned through the opening and snatched the scroll from his hands. "Gratitude. That is the letter I seek." Dropping a final piece of silver on the counter, he turned away, his eyes racing down the page. They screeched to a halt at the words. *Audience for Eamon MacGarvan has been granted.* He read them again. Then a third time.

Audience for Eamon MacGarvan has been granted.

"I need your best private room and a bath," Eamon demanded as he laid two silver pieces on the counter. He watched the innkeeper's eyes go quickly from hooded disdain at his unkempt appearance, to wide-eyed appreciation at the coin. "I also require a tailor to be sent for immediately—a skilled one who will work all night for suitable reward—and a decent change of clothes to wear in the meantime. I can't be out of these Viking rags soon enough." He paused. "Do you have a stable? I'm in need of a horse for a fortnight...a good horse, but not too spirited. When the purpose of riding is to spare one's energy, I prefer not to waste it fighting an unruly beast."

"Apologies, my lord. We have a small stable, but no animals to let."

Eamon smiled at the man's reference to him as lord and added another coin. "Surely you know of a reputable hostler. That should cover the trouble of procuring one for me."

"Aye, my lord, that will cover it quite generously," the man said eagerly. "Follow me; your room is this way."

The innkeeper stood aside as Eamon stepped into the sparsely furnished room. "I suppose this will do," Eamon muttered. "While I'm waiting for the bath, I would have a meal and a pitcher of your finest ale. On second thought, I'll have poteen."

"I'll see to it immediately, my lord."

"Have them bring your largest tub; I don't wish to cram myself into some half barrel. And make sure they know I prefer my bathwater to be quite hot."

"Of course, my lord," the man bobbed his head and disappeared.

Eamon had just finished stashing the gemstones beneath a floorboard he'd pried loose with his dagger, when there was a knock on the door. "Enter," he called out. A lad balancing a tray and holding a small bundle of clothes tucked under one arm made his way to the table.

"My master sent both poteen and ale, my lord, and here is the change of clothes you requested. He sends his apologies for the commonness of the cloth; they're all he was able to procure on short notice close to your size. But they are clean."

"Lay them on the bed. I only have need of them for tonight. Has a tailor been summoned?"

"Aye, my lord. He's closing up his shop and gathering cloth samples. He should arrive within the hour, just after you've finished your bath. They're heating the water for it now."

Eamon nodded. After the lad left, he sat at the table and poured himself a mug of ale, saving the poteen for later. He devoured the fish and cockle stew without acknowledging the parade of servants who delivered the oversized tub and countless pails of steaming water. He was sopping up the last of the broth with bread when the lad emptied the final bucket.

"Will there be anything else, my lord?"

"Not now, but I'll require a shave when I'm done."

"Aye, my lord," he said, backing out through the door.

Eamon gingerly lowered himself into the hot water. He almost groaned from the pleasure. It was hot, nearly scalding, and he had to allow his body time to adjust to the temperature before continuing. Finally submerged, he leaned his head back against the metal rim and closed his eyes. Without opening them, he brought the bottle of poteen to his lips and took a sip of the cool liquid. This was pure indulgence. He'd paid far too much for all of it, but 'twas necessary to establish his image, he told himself. And Gunnar had authorized an unlimited stipend to that end.

As the hot water lifted the grime and stink of the Falcon from his skin, and the poteen and stew warmed him from the inside, Eamon mulled over how a few chance encounters had brought him to this enviable moment. Were they truly chance? Had it been chance that his previous lord's wife had fancied him? Chance that she'd caught him with another woman and sent him to a slaver? Chance that a Northman with such an unusual specific need would buy, then free him? Chance that he'd been privy to his previous lord's attempt to acquire another lord's lands? Any two might be considered coincidence, but all of them? Impossible.

So if not chance—what? The hand of God? But Gunnar was a pagan. The Norse gods? But Gunnar's woman was a Christian. The Huntress? He paused at that. The crew all believed the ship possessed mystical powers, and even he had to admit she was beyond very lucky. But was she able to control the actions of men and women who'd never laid eyes on her? Able to shape destiny?

It was too deep a thought to consider now, and Eamon pushed it from his mind. He took another long sip. What would make this moment perfect would be a woman to scrub his back and then take a toss in the bed. He thought about calling the innkeeper to send for a whore, then decided against it. That would have to wait until his obligation to Gunnar was fulfilled. He couldn't risk a whore discovering the gemstones.

As he stepped from the tub, a voice called from behind the door. "Are you ready for your shave, my lord?"

Eamon smiled. They'd been waiting to hear him moving about. He knew all too well what it was like to be on the other side of that door.

"One moment." He pulled on the borrowed trousers that came to mid-calf, then slipped into the snug tunic.

"Enter. I'm ready."

"I am here to see His Grace," Eamon said to the bishop's secretary, managing to keep his tone and expression calm. The man looked him up and down, but Eamon wasn't worried by the inspection. The tailor had outdone himself—the quality of cut and cloth were impeccable.

"Do you have an appointment?" the secretary asked with bored disinterest.

"I do not, but I've been granted audience, and he'll be expecting me. Tell him Eamon MacGarvan is here." Eamon pulled the leather-bound parchment from inside his silk tunic, flashing the bishop's seal.

"Apologies, my lord, if you don't have an appointment, His Grace is very busy today."

Eamon leaned over the desk and stared into the man's eyes. "Tell him Eamon MacGarvan is here," he repeated, his voice dangerously quiet.

The secretary remained seated, and for a moment, Eamon feared he'd used the wrong tactic; perhaps coin would have been better. The man was clearly no stranger to pompous lords seeking the bishop's favor and was quite arrogant himself. He stared back at Eamon for a long moment, then sniffed and pushed back his chair. He stood up with exaggerated slowness before ambling to the door of the bishop's inner chamber and disappearing inside.

He returned almost immediately with a different attitude. "This way, my lord." He beckoned for Eamon to follow. After motioning him toward the small chair in front of the bishop's enormous desk, he retreated, closing the door behind him.

"Your Grace," Eamon said, bowing his head and kissing the ring on the bishop's outstretched hand before taking his seat. "Gratitude for receiving me."

"I receive a great many requests and gifts, but yours intrigued me," the bishop admitted as he opened a drawer and withdrew a purple silk pouch. He untied the cord and poured the contents onto his palm before arranging the ruby and gold filigree earrings in a sparkling display on the desk. "The craftsmanship is extraordinary, and your letter claims you have more?"

"Aye, Your Grace."

"Of similar quality?"

"Far greater, I can assure you. But apologies, I forget myself." Eamon retrieved a black silk swatch from his pocket and unfolded it on the desk, revealing a single large emerald. "A simple token of my appreciation for you taking time from your busy schedule to receive me without appointment."

There was nothing simple about the huge gem, and the bishop's eyes lit up as he slid the cloth across the table toward him.

"Never have I been so plied toward aid of sale," he murmured with appreciation. "I've made inquiries in the area you requested and have good news for you. After many years of fighting Northmen and each other, several lords suffer from a lack of heirs. You mentioned in your letter that you wished for the swiftest resolution?"

"Aye."

"Normally, after the necessary documents are filed, one must simply wait for the existing lord to expire, which in my experience is impossible to predict; men who appear to be on death's doorstep can linger for many years. In my recent inquiries, however, I've discovered a unique opportunity—

one that would allow you to assume the mantle of lord almost immediately, though it will require more coin."

The bishop assumed the title was for him, as he and Gunnar had anticipated and concluded was to their benefit. The man would be filing false documents for someone to shed their previous identity and assume a new one; the original name would never be recorded, and the bishop was far more likely to aid a wealthy Irishman than a Northman. Once Gunnar was established and accepted as a lord, if the bishop were to discover the switch years from now, it shouldn't matter.

Eamon gave a quick nod, wondering what new scheme the bishop had come up with, and how much *more coin* would be required.

"There's a lord in Breifne whose circumstances lend themselves to your request. His health is such that his healers insist he seek a drier climate or surely perish. He fears not to survive another winter. If a deal can be struck and he claims you as his heir, it is his intent to leave at once for Italia."

"Why does he not simply go?"

"He has not the coin."

"But he's a highborn lord?"

"He is, but after the death of his last son many years ago, his estate has been...mismanaged and fallen into some disrepair."

"And the price?"

"The sum will be for you to negotiate. I'll not involve myself in such haggling. But the man is desperate. Though if you've not the resources to pay an additional sum to him, I have two other estates where the usual arrangements can be made. But you said you had haste...."

Eamon's mind whirled. For a lord not to have coin to travel, the land must be barren and the residence a pile a shite, but both were irrelevant. Only the title mattered. And a title that could be assumed immediately? It was too much to hope for. He did have extra coin—though not double.

But perhaps he wouldn't need double; the bishop's fee was not a set figure, and the conniver surely intended to extract compensation from the ill lord as well. Perhaps he could reduce the bishop's share or make some arrangement to deliver an additional payment after Gunnar's arrival. He'd think of something. He nodded.

"Very good. If you wish, I'll dispatch my personal messenger to Lord Nevyn today, announcing your arrival to discuss details—which will be when?" the bishop asked as he pulled out a sheet of blank parchment and a quill.

"Tomorrow, Your Grace."

"Tomorrow," he repeated quietly as he wrote it.

He finished the letter, signed it with a flourish, then tipped a candle over the bottom. After waiting for the pool of melted wax to cool slightly, he pressed his seal into it, then rolled the parchment inside a sheath of soft tooled leather. He tied it closed with a purple silk cord and tassel, which he secured in place with more wax and another seal.

Eamon didn't see him signal, but the door opened almost immediately, and the secretary hurried to the bishop's side. "Have this delivered with all haste to Lord Nevyn of Tir na Laoch in Breifne," he instructed and handed him the scroll.

Eamon sat back, musing over the significance of the estate's name. Tir na Laoch—Land of the Warrior. What were the odds of it being called that and not Tir na Capall—Land of the Horse, or Tir na Fearach—Land of Pasture or something else. Anything else. He wondered again of chance and destiny— and of the Huntress.

"Here, I'll show you on a map," the bishop said and unrolled a soft vellum. "This is Lord Nevyn's estate." He pointed to one of three outlined parcels. "If you can agree on terms, it will be up to you and him to decide upon the story behind you being his heir. Then you will return to me with the details.

"It matters naught what story you concoct, you can be the bastard son of a scullery maid for all I care. I need only names and dates to know what documents are required and where they must be filed." The bishop paused and looked at him. "Your timing could not be better. I'm long overdue for my annual accounting of the minsters and abbeys in that region. I normally make the trip in midsummer, but I've been delayed by other matters that required my attention. If you can return to me quickly with the information and...additional tokens of your good faith before I depart, I will see the matter concluded on this trip." He looked at Eamon expectantly.

"Gratitude, Your Grace. Would half of the gifts I've collected for you suffice to prove my good faith intentions? If so, then perhaps you can stop at my new estate for the remainder once 'tis done...since you will be in the area."

The bishop smiled. "You gaze upon my very thoughts."

Chapter 38

Eamon pulled his horse to a halt outside the perimeter wall of the stronghold and felt the first glimmer of hope. The lands of Tir na Laoch he'd seen so far had been unbelievably rich—dark, fertile soil and dense forests teeming with wild game. So rich, he'd almost turned back. What was the use in wasting everyone's time when he couldn't hope to make reasonable offer?

The structures he looked upon now were another matter. The walls of the fortress encircled a vast area—easily large enough to accommodate an entire village in the event of an attack. Though in their current condition, they'd protect no one. Only the bottom stone portion, the approximate height of a man, remained. All of the integral wood features built on top of it—the erect sharpened logs, the guard towers, the walkways rimming the inside of the parapets, lay in varying degrees of collapse, some reduced to little more than piles of twisted rotting ruins.

Eamon pushed his horse through the open gates that sagged out of kilter. The wood structures inside the abandoned courtyard, like the upper outer walls, had been decimated by time and neglect. The few that remained listed precariously. Only the imposing two-story stone ancestral home stood strong against the elements, though nature had begun to wage a different kind of war on the edifice, and one corner was obscured beneath a thick blanket of vines.

When no one came to take his horse, Eamon continued his inspection. The only signs of life were two skittish hens and a skinny hound that slinked away when he looked in its direction. No servants went about daily activities, and, now that he thought about it, there'd been no tenants working the land either. He filed the facts away to use in his negotiations along with the woeful condition of the stronghold. They weren't much to offset the considerable value of the land, but possibly enough if the man was as desperate as the bishop had claimed.

Eamon was examining the collapsed supports of what had once been a blacksmith's forge when an aging manservant called to him from the residence. After tying his horse to the sturdiest rotted post he could find, Eamon joined the man at the top of the stone steps.

"Greetings, my lord. Lord Nevyn awaits you in his study." The manservant held open the door. Eamon stepped over the threshold, stopping just inside. The interior was black as night. The manservant struck a light to a candle that was little more than a nub, then closed the door behind them and led off into the darkness, motioning for him to follow.

With the flickering light of the tiny candle illuminating only a small circle around them, Eamon's other senses became heightened. A drop in temperature combined with their now-echoing footfalls indicated they'd entered a much larger room. Creatures scurried and scratched unseen in the shadows. The hair on the back of his neck rose to stand on end.

"Stay close to the wall here, my lord. The path is clear," the manservant cautioned, seemingly unbothered by the disturbing animal sounds. "Apologies for the dark. We've run short on candles. Lord Nevyn's study is just on the other side of the great hall."

Eamon studied the wall the man had referred to. Beneath years of candle and torch soot, he could make out the stone and wood construction. Unlike what he'd seen outside, the thick wood timbers were protected and seemed solid.

The manservant pushed open a door, immediately extinguishing the candle to preserve the minuscule portion that remained. Eamon stepped past him and looked around the chamber. A broad-shouldered gray-haired man sat near a roaring fire on the other side of the room, eyeing him shrewdly. The bishop's letter lay open on a small table beside him.

"The bishop informs me you wish to claim title of lord," the man said bluntly as Eamon took a seat and accepted a tarnished silver cup of wine offered by the manservant.

Ignoring the bits floating on the surface, Eamon took a sip, forcing the sour liquid down without grimacing so as not to offend. "Aye," he agreed. "Though which one has yet to be determined. I'll also be viewing the estates of Lord Caith and Lord Emmons tomorrow," Eamon lied, repeating the other two names he'd seen on the bishop's map.

"Tir na Laoch is double their combined size," Lord Nevyn dismissed the claim, studying him all the while.

"Which is why the bishop recommended I see it first. However," Eamon glanced around the room, his eyes lingering on the faded tapestries and dust-covered paintings, "'tis not in the condition I was led to expect. His Grace said there was maintenance to be done, but this...this will require far more work than was anticipated. And I noted no servants or tenants—are there none?"

Lord Nevyn shrugged. "A fact easily remedied. I'm sure you also noted that the soil is fertile and the stands of timber unrivaled. There are even mineral deposits that you would not have seen."

Eamon hesitated, unsure of how to proceed. His only hope had been to leverage a dying man, who, though insulted by his low offer, might be desperate enough to take it. This man didn't seem desperate at all. He'd summarily dismissed the implied threat of competition from other estates, and countered the stronghold's shortcomings by revealing even more value in the land, effectively nullifying Eamon's only arguments.

With the way the man continued to boldly scrutinize him, Eamon had the strange impression that it was his own shortcomings were being measured. He had to be mistaken; the man was living like a mole—and dying, according to the bishop. He continued with his original and only strategy. "This estate undeniably holds great potential. 'Tis just that I was hoping for something that wouldn't require so much further investment of time, labor, and coin."

"But you would consider it—for the right price," Lord Nevyn concluded for him.

Eamon was sure now that he was being trifled with; the man had barely managed to conceal a smile. Irritated by the thought and having no alternative ploy, he went straight to his conclusion. "Aye, but I would need to know your best price; there's no point taking up more of your time if we are too far apart."

Lord Nevyn reached beside him and scribbled something on the corner of the bishop's letter. He tore off the piece of parchment, folded it once, and handed it to the manservant who carried it to Eamon.

"The first figure is pounds of silver, the second pounds of gold," he said as Eamon unfolded it.

Eamon stared at the two numbers, trying desperately to control his expression. The total was a fraction of what they were prepared to pay the bishop, but he couldn't let that show and have the man take back the offer thinking he'd started too low. Though he wanted nothing more than to jump up and shout, "*Agreed!*" he sat silently considering the note.

"You can dispense with the pretended deep thought. I know the price is a pittance. And I know you know it, too. I'm ill—not a fool."

Eamon stared at him dumbfounded.

"You wonder why I would accept such a price? 'Tis safe for you to ask. I'll not rescind it."

Eamon held up his hands, utterly nonplussed. "Very well. Why not sell the timber or lease the land? You'd easily collect a hundred times this." He held up the scrap of paper.

Lord Nevyn chuckled. "So you did notice. Good. You seem of sharp mind in addition to being of sturdy form. And you have the grounded, pragmatic air about you of a man who's been confirmed by battle. That's also good. The thought that after generations of warriors, Tir na Laoch would end up in the hands of some undersized lickspittle was my greatest concern. The answer to your question is simple. I've not the time left to pursue such means of profit now."

"And before?"

"Before...." Lord Nevyn paused. "Before, I had not the desire to watch vultures stripping the bones of the estate of all value. I may have failed my ancestors by not continuing our bloodline, but I'd not allow Tir na Laoch to be pillaged by scavenging scuts while I still drew breath.

"When the bishop approached me with his offer, he thought to sway me with extended life, but it was the thought that I could choose who gets these lands, rather than have them be some prize awarded by a Connacht king to an unknown usurper, that appealed to me. The price I gave you is what I require to live out my days in comfort in Italia. With no heir, I've no use for anything beyond that."

Eamon sat stunned. "Then you obviously know I accept the price." He paused. "But I also give you my word; Tir na Laoch will be restored to its former glory."

Lord Nevyn nodded. "Then all that remains to be determined are the details of *how* you are my heir."

Eamon stood and moved to stand in front of a painting—a portrait of a girl with light brown hair and unusual blue eyes sitting on the front steps of the manor with a hound. "Who is this?" he asked.

"My grandmother when she was a lass."

"And this brooch she is wearing, might it still be in your possession?"

"Aye."

Eamon smiled. "Then what would you think of this for a story...."

Lord Nevyn sat back and snorted when Eamon finished. "If that's the story you wish to be told, I'll agree to it. Though I can think of far simpler ones."

"Nay, 'tis the perfect story for me."

Chapter 39

Eamon stood in the empty courtyard watching Lord Nevyn's ramshackle carriage follow the bishop's lavish entourage through the sagging gates for the last time. His legs felt suddenly weak, and he moved to the front steps of the residence to sit.

He'd done it. What they'd expected to take months or years—if they were successful at all, he'd accomplished in a fortnight. Records were filed, compensation delivered, and in his hands were the Charters of Tir na Laoch, the family seal, the bronze and agate brooch, and a letter written in Lord Nevyn's hand detailing the story of his newly discovered heir. Even a few gemstones remained to begin basic repairs before Gunnar arrived.

But that could wait. Tonight he would celebrate his monumental accomplishment; tonight he would drink—and not soured wine. Eamon stood. Before he saddled his horse, he needed to hide his trophies. Not confident enough to venture through the hall without light, he walked around to the kitchen entrance.

"More poteen, my lord?" Cora held up the bottle.

"Aye," Eamon raised his empty cup. "One more to bolster my resolve before I must return to my impossible task."

"Will you be leavin' me today then, love?"

Eamon cocked his head and pondered. "Nay, not today. Tomorrow. I shall leave tomorrow. Though the thought of what I face..."

"You've no need to be frettin' any further over that, love. I think I may be able to help you."

"Are you offering more of your services, my lady?" he slurred with a grin. "I'll pay well. In silver."

"And leave all this?" Cora waved around the dimly lit tavern and smiled. "I think not. I've got things settled quite to my liking here. Besides, the way you've carried on these past days, it sounds like far too much toil and drudgery for me. But I do know of a woman who lost her husband and was turned out by his family. She's been tryin' to earn her keep here in Balbriggan ever since—and not on her back, mind you. Go to the row of shacks behind the Blue Ox and ask for Ania."

"You are Ania?" Eamon asked while using one hand to shield his eyes from the morning sun.

"I am, my lord."

"Not a lord, just Eamon. Cora from the Red Dragon told me where to find you."

"Apologies, my lord, but to what purpose?" She pulled two young children closer to her skirts.

"I'm in need of a housekeeper. Nay, more than a housekeeper. My lord inherited an estate that he's never seen and sent me ahead to make it ready before his arrival. I will not lie, it may have been a grand place once, but the conditions now are deplorable, and I'm quite desperate. My lord cannot see it in such a state. I will pay you well...in lodgings, food, and silver."

"And my children?"

"They appear old enough to work; I will pay them as well."

She studied him for a long moment, then nodded. "Aye, we'll come with you."

"Gratitude. Can you be ready to leave in the mornin'? Today I must acquire a horse and cart, and supplies." He glanced at their gaunt faces, tattered clothes, and the dirty bare feet of her children. "While I'm doing so, I would have you purchase cloth for garments and leather for shoes." He reached for his purse.

"I'll not accept charity," she declined, shaking her head.

"'Tis not charity, simply an advance on your earnings. Believe me, you will earn it. To work, you must all be well-clothed and well-shod. Here is silver to procure what you need."

"'Tis too much," she protested.

"Then keep receipt of what is spent to deduct from your wages and bring me what remains."

She nodded.

"I'll return here to collect you in the morning."

Eamon set the brake in front of Ania's shack, his new riding horse tied to the back of the wagon. Larkin, the hostler Cora had recommended, had agreed to return his rented horse to the innkeeper in Dublin as part of the handsome package price he'd paid for the sturdy carthorse, large open wagon, and fine new mount.

It would be a tight squeeze for Ania and her two children; the cart was piled high with provisions: boxes of candles, a barrel of pitch for torches, wool blankets, axe heads, saw blades, salted pork and fish, a bow and quiver of arrows for fresh meat, rounds of cheese, a basket of newly-harvested apples, sacks of wheat flour, oats and salt, a crate of chickens, two milk goats, several bolts of linen and wool cloth, two barrels of ale, and a small keg of honey. He even had three fresh loaves of bread for the trip. No one would be cold or hungry on his watch.

When children streamed from the doorway and stood lined up in front of the tiny shanty, Eamon thought to be at the wrong place. He glanced back down the row; this was the sixth shelter. Had he been so impaired the previous day that he'd miscounted? He looked back at the children, this time recognizing the two littlest ones from the day before. Three additional younglings stood beside them, the eldest being a lass of perhaps eleven years. All of them wore matching simple hand-made foot coverings. Ania, carrying only a small cloth bag, stepped from the shack, pulled the rickety door closed behind her and turned to face him.

"These are...all yours?" he asked.

"Aye. All five."

"But you're so young." The thought became words before he could stop it.

"I was married at thirteen," she said matter-of-factly. When he didn't respond, she set her jaw and raised her chin. "You said there was much work to be done."

"That I did." He nodded with a smile, recovering from his shock. "Can you drive the cart then? It appears I've not left enough room and will need to ride my horse."

The group arrived at Tir na Laoch the following morning after spending the night camped on the road nearby. The heavily laden cart was slow, and Eamon had seen no reason to push them to arrive just before dark. The place would be daunting enough in the light of day.

Armed with torches, he and Ania explored the abandoned hall while the children waited at the wagon. Most of the rooms appeared not to have been entered in many years. Eamon was appalled by the filth—and the rats. He'd never seen so many of the creatures. Some areas reeked of their urine, and their desiccated droppings crunched beneath his boots. Ania said not a word during the inspection, and Eamon prayed that she'd not ask to be returned to Balbriggan.

"It will take time," she finally announced. "We shall start with the kitchen."

After tethering the horses and milk goats in the deep grass outside the wall and releasing the chickens in the courtyard, Eamon started on the stables. He first knocked down what remained of the dangerously dilapidated structure, then chopped and stacked any good wood that could later be burned for heat. The rotted timbers and decomposing roof thatch he piled in the center of the courtyard and set on fire. Soon the children were adding to the flames with armloads of rubbage from the kitchen.

When Ania's oldest daughter, Vala, called him to midday meal, Eamon was grateful for the break. He joined the group on the front steps to eat a cold meal of bread, apples, and cheese.

"My lord, if I could trouble you," Ania began.

"I told you, Ania, 'tis Eamon, not lord. His lordship will arrive later."

"Is he a kind lord?" Nate, her youngest son, interrupted.

"Hush now, Nate," Ania chided.

"He's the most honorable and fair man I've ever known," Eamon replied truthfully.

"Eamon," Ania began again. "After the meal, would you be able to spare the time to block the doorway from the kitchen to the great hall?"

"Block it?"

"Only temporarily. We've chased the rats out for now, but they'll smell the food in the night and be bold in the dark. Our efforts to clean will be for naught if they're allowed back in, and I thought we'd sleep there for now. 'Twill be warmer and..."

"Aye, I'll see to it. I would not have the rats chewin' off Vala's bonnie nose while she slept." He winked.

"Or mine," Nate yelped.

"Or anyone's," Eamon added, seeing them all preparing to chime in. "Now who's still hungry?" He held up a piece of cheese.

The children all glanced hopefully to Ania before shaking their heads and looking away. Eamon frowned. They'd done the same the night before when they'd camped on the road—nibbled their food to make it last but declined further portions.

"Ania, may I speak to you for a moment in private in the kitchen? You can explain to me how you want the doorway blocked."

"Of course."

"Why do you not eat?" he asked quietly when they were out of earshot. "Why do you not let the children eat?"

"In the few days we've known you, you've been more kind to us than any soul ever has. We'll not reward your generosity by being gluttons."

"Gluttons? Ania, you don't eat enough to sustain a bird. I need you and the children strong. The assistance you are providing is... "

"We'll not shirk," she defended, raising her chin.

"Nay, I'm not suggestin' that. But you've seen there is plenty of food, and I know you must be hungry, so why don't you eat?"

She looked down.

"Ania, answer me. Please."

"I do not wish for us to be accustomed to it," she murmured without raising her eyes. "'Twill only make it more painful if we must do without again. Who knows what will become of us after his lordship arrives."

"I do. His lordship values honest work. You'll always have a place here if you want it. Your children will never be hungry again."

She looked up at him with a sad smile and shook her head. "You cannot know that."

"But I do know that. And if 'tis too much for you to believe me, then let us strike a bargain now for one year of your services. I'll even advance you your wages. If I'm wrong, which I'm not, and his lordship were to release you, that would be a breach of our agreement; you'd remain entitled to keep the full amount."

"I cannot do that."

"And I cannot continue to eat when you and the children do not. So— you leave me no choice. From now on, I'll only eat what you eat. Even though 'twill cause me great suffering, and I'll likely soon become weak, and my performance will falter, which means I'll surely fail my responsibility to his lordship and then..."

"Eamon stop; that's ridiculous."

"I swear I'll do it." He smiled at her. "You hold my fate in your hands, and I beg of you, woman, do not make me starve myself."

She gave him a small wave and nodded as her eyes filled with tears. "Very well," she whispered.

"Grand. Now that that's settled, I've a yearnin' for apple slices dipped in honey."

Late that night, when Eamon finally dragged himself around to the kitchen, he was surprised to find Ania still awake. She set the garment she was sewing on the table and lit a second candle, bringing it to him. The children were all asleep in a pile near the hearth.

"I've kept water warm if you'd care to wash?"

"Aye," Eamon murmured.

She dipped out a large bowl of water from a clean copper cauldron, added a small linen cloth, then carried it behind a blanket she'd hung in one corner for privacy. "Set aside any clothes you need washed, and I'll have Vala see to them in the mornin.'"

He nodded and pulled a clean tunic out of his pack, then stepped behind the blanket before stripping off his smelly one. Starting with his face and hair, he wiped off as much soot and grime as he could, frequently rinsing the cloth in the bowl, thinking all the while what he would give for the scalding bath he'd had at the Dublin inn. When he was finished and the water was dark gray, he joined Ania at the table.

"I poured you an ale." She nodded to a mug.

"Gratitude," Eamon said as he took a seat on the bench opposite her and took a deep swallow of the cool foamy liquid.

"Are you hungry?" she asked. "I can get you..."

"Nay. I'm too tired to eat." He drank in silence, watching her sew.

"We shall finish the kitchen tomorrow, and then I thought to start on the great hall, if you agree?"

He nodded.

"I discovered several large doors on the south side of the hall but could not get them open. If you can manage to do so, the sunlight and fresh air will be of great help."

"I'll see to it," Eamon mumbled.

"Your bedding is there." She nodded to a blanket-covered mound on the opposite side of the hearth from the children. Bits of dried grass poked out from under the edges.

"Gratitude, yet again," he said as he stood and moved to his bed. He knelt on the top, then flopped on his back. After wriggling a few times to adjust the stems beneath him, he closed his eyes and was asleep, never hearing Ania say goodnight.

"Stand clear!" Eamon shouted as the huge door crashed down onto the stone walkway that ran the exterior length of the great hall. The iron hinges had long since rusted solid; he'd had to pry and beat them loose from the aged wood. He peered inside and cringed. Beyond the cloud of swirling dust raised by the falling door, everything was covered in layers of cobwebs, dust, and soot. Everything except the rats, who stared boldly back at him, squeaking and squealing their outrage at the intrusion.

Ania glanced inside and nodded. "After you open the remaining doors, we'll start on one end and walk in a line with torches and sticks to drive the rats out."

Eamon could only nod and stare at her in awe.

For Eamon, the next two days passed in a fatigued blur, brightened only by a brief hunt when he killed a young stag that wandered too close. They suspended work early that day, feasting on fresh-roasted venison. It was mid-morning on the fifth day when two young men hailed him from the gate.

"Cora from the Red Dragon said you are in need of laborers and are paying in silver."

"I am."

"I am Donegan and this is my brother Declan."

Eamon looked at the two strapping young men and said a prayer for Cora.

Chapter 40

Eamon sat on the stone front steps with a mug of ale, surveying the new life slowly being breathed back into the old estate. Keva, Ania's middle daughter, sat on a stump milking one of the goats. The two wily hens had joined the crate chickens and the small flock pecked and scratched vigorously through the dirt for bugs. Even the hound appeared rejuvenated as it trotted by with a stag bone, looking for a safe place to bury its newest treasure.

Though it may not have been new, for the dog was constantly relocating previous caches. The only time it didn't have a bone in its mouth was when it was barking at new arrivals—of which there'd been a steady stream, thanks to Cora.

While Eamon continued to tear out and sort through the old, the other men cut and bundled thatch for roofing, wove panels of green willow twigs and saplings for animal pens, and felled trees in the forest before dragging the logs back and splitting them into lumber.

Working men weren't the only new arrivals. A giant grizzled one-eared cat appeared on the second day and had immediately taken to leaving rat remnants outside the kitchen door. It wasn't until he saw Ania rewarding the beast with a small plate of goat's milk while she gingerly disposed of the partial remains, that he understood why.

Unflappable Ania. She'd been nothing short of a miracle. The kitchen was cheery and unrecognizable. Years of soot and dirt scrubbed from the stone walls and floors. Freshly scoured pots and utensils hung neatly on the rack she'd had him build to her specifications. And always some delicious smell wafting from within. Not only did she work all day on the daunting task of the great hall and sew clothes for the children late into the night, she somehow managed to find time to keep them all well-fed.

This morning though, after gathering everyone for prayer, she'd announced that other than the necessary work of tending to the animals, they were to observe the Lord's day with rest—and baths. The bath stipulation had been met with howls of protest from her boys, but Ania had prevailed, and two, now very clean boys were stalking rats in the courtyard with the one-eared cat.

Ever since he'd offered a bounty on the vermin, they spent every free moment hunting them with sharp sticks, dreaming of great wealth. While there were certainly enough rats, so far the only carcass they'd presented for payment was wet and looked suspiciously to have been killed by teeth and claws. Still, he had paid them, redoubling their efforts.

Eamon leaned back and took another sip of ale. The tremendous progress gave him such a sense of satisfaction, he was loathe to leave, but he had one final important task to complete. He knew his unimaginable success with the lands and title would mean little to Gunnar without his woman. Tomorrow he would ride for her estate and learn what he could of her, then continue on to Balbriggan to wait.

Eamon kicked his horse forward to intercept the cart, piled high with fresh-scythed oats on their way to be thrashed into seed and straw before it reached the gates of Tir na Lionmhar.

"I know Tir na Lionmhar means Land of Plentiful, but your load makes it seem especially so." Eamon hailed the young driver as his horse fell into step alongside the cart.

"Aye 'tis a bountiful harvest this year," the lad agreed with a smile.

"I've come to see Lord Patrick and Lady Fiona. Do you know if they're about?"

"Apologies, my lord. His lordship and Lady Fiona left yesterday for Athlone to attend Lady Abiageal's wedding. I heard said they'll be away for a fortnight."

"Ah, my misfortune. I shall return to call upon them then. Gratitude." Eamon turned his horse and spurred it back the way he'd come before the lad could ask his name.

Something swelled in Eamon's chest at the sight of the golden ship cutting regally through the smooth harbor water. Expecting only a partial crew, he was shocked to find the Huntress packed with people, and a second ship, also full, rounding the breakwater behind her.

Gunnar leapt lightly onto Balbriggan's newly rebuilt dock, then strode toward him. His eyes skimmed over Eamon's clothes, and he grinned. "You look a sight different than the last time I saw you, my friend."

Eamon grinned back as they clasped arms just below the elbows. "As will you, soon enough."

Gunnar frowned at that, then shrugged before looking at Eamon expectantly. "So all went well?" As Gunnar's eyes searched his face, Eamon knew he had only one question.

"Aye. I've not yet seen your lady, but I spoke to one of her tenants. She and her father are attending a wedding..."

"She is well," Gunnar closed his eyes and exhaled as he absorbed the news.

Only then did Eamon realize the depth of Gunnar's fear. "Aye, she is well."

"I must see her at once."

"The only thing you *must* do is bathe. I've retained rooms at the inn here and procured proper clothing. The fewer who see you as you look now, the better. From this point on, you must apply yourself to shedding all trace of Northman speech and mannerisms. I suggest you hone your skills on the people here before you have need of them with her family and peers."

"Fiona knows me as I am; I've no need to practice before I see her."

"She is away."

"Away where?"

"To Athlone for at least another ten days."

Gunnar swore under his breath. He was so close, and yet no closer to actually holding her in his arms. The gods continued to toy with him.

"And the other things?"

"All according to plan. You are Lord Colin of Tir na Laoch of Breifne."

"Already? It's done?" he asked, incredulous.

"Aye."

"How have you managed that in such a short time?"

"With much luck." As he said the words, Eamon glanced toward the Huntress, unsure if luck was in any way involved.

"Is the previous lord dead already then? ...did you kill him?" Gunnar whispered.

"Nay, the man yet lives but is gone. His lordship suffered from a serious malady and, at the insistence of his healers, has sailed for the drier climes of Italia."

Gunnar stood stunned. "I have land and title?" he mumbled, shocked. "I cannot conceive it. Eamon, I don't know what to say. This is astonishing news."

"You may wish to withdraw part of that. The estate has long been neglected. I've started basic restorations, but 'twill take much coin and the work of many men to complete. Which brings me to ask—who are all the folk on the ships?"

"Norse and Danes who wish to settle. Rask is to take them on to the Viking settlement in Wexford. Though if I have land and am in need of men, perhaps they will stay."

"You are in need of men—many men, but with your noble status so newly fledged, Northmen might not be the best answer, at least not yet. Though with the story of how you came to be the heir, it might be possible later."

"And what is that story?"

"You're going to like it." Eamon grinned. "Though I must forewarn you. I may have outdone myself with this tale."

Gunnar rolled his eyes and shook his head, suppressing a smile. "Then perhaps I should continue to savor your good news instead; I'm not sure I'm prepared for a tale that even you consider far-fetched. It makes me fearful to imagine it."

"Had I known you were a jester, I would've made that your story, and you could've spent the rest of your life living up to it," Eamon retaliated.

"Apologies, of course I cannot wait to hear your incredible tale of my life." Gunnar grinned, nodding his head with exaggerated deference.

"That's more like it. The lord you are replacing sent his daughter to the abbey at Trim to bear an illegitimate child in secret. The place is well-known to have been a favored target of Northmen; it was raided multiple times over the years. During one of those raids, she was thought to have been killed, but she and her babe were actually taken."

"They were?"

Eamon raised his eyebrows at Gunnar's unusual gullibility. "Nay, of course not. The woman never existed. But new documents filed at the church in Kells list the date of her birth and baptism, and others at the Trim Abbey list the dates of her entry as a novice, and later the birth and baptism of her son—you. Miraculously, those records were stored in a wing of the abbey that wasn't burned by the raiders." Eamon winked.

"Your story picks up from there. How, after you were taken, your mother later wed her Norse captor, and you were raised as his son, unaware of your true identity and birthright. Only on her deathbed did she confess the truth to you, and, as proof, gave you a family heirloom—a bronze brooch with two unique green agate stones. 'Tis a brooch that you'll wear every day, and the same brooch that she is wearing as a young girl in a painting that we will display in a position of prominence in the great hall."

"How is there such a painting if she didn't exist?"

"The painting is actually of Lord Nevyn's grandmother as a young girl, but no one lives who will be the wiser."

"Will any oppose my claim?"

Eamon shook his head. "Other than Lord Nevyn, who has named you his heir, there are none left who could. The raids on the abbey and minster at Trim were real enough; the priests, monks, and nuns were all either taken or slain. Only the records remain."

"This is one of your boundary stones. From here, we're about an hour's ride from your ancestral home. I've yet to ride the estate perimeter, but Lord Nevyn assured me 'tis well marked."

"This is all mine," Gunnar murmured in disbelief. "You said the land was ripe with potential, but this...this exceeds wildest imaginings. The things we'll be able to accomplish—to build." His voice trailed away as he pictured it. "To that end, I told several men on the ships of my intent to call for them once I'm settled. I also instructed Rask to seek out skilled tradesmen in Wexford and extend them the same offer. But only men of proper temperament."

Eamon snorted. "You assigned that task to Rask? You assume he understands what proper temperament is?"

"Fortunately *having* proper temperament is not a requirement for understanding it. Far more of a concern is that he does it quietly. I've cautioned him that the current Viking lord of Wexford, whoever he is, will not appreciate skilled men being lured away."

"Ah, subtlety, another of Rask's qualities. I can see why you chose him."

"I think he'll surprise you. He's wanting to secure his position as next captain of the Huntress; he'll not wish to fail me now."

"When is he to return?"

"A week or two. He'll send word once he's back in Balbriggan and remain there with the Huntress. Once we feel it safe, he'll retrieve any suitable folk from Wexford."

Eamon nodded. "I've already begun circulating the news of the heir being found and a feast being planned. No date was set, pending your arrival, but I suggest we schedule it soon—perhaps a week from now."

"But Fiona will still be away."

"This feast is purely to establish your standing among the other noblemen. Her presence is not required." When Gunnar remained silent, Eamon amended it with a sigh. "Perhaps a fortnight then to account for any delays in her return?"

Gunnar nodded.

"As soon as we reach Tir na Laoch, I'll send out invitations; a local noblewoman has offered to provide a list of names."

"You've spoken with a noblewoman?"

"Aye, she came to the estate."

"She knew about me?"

"Nay, near as I could tell she came to see the old man."

"For what purpose?"

"She didn't say. Once she found out there was an heir, she never mentioned him again."

"I would not have you continue to act in this role of manservant. You know I do not consider you as such."

"'Tis the only position where I can remain close to you at all times and come to your aid if necessary. I'm happy to do it. Though there is one thing I would ask."

"Absolutely anything."

"I mentioned that I enlisted the aid of a woman and her children to help prepare the residence for your arrival."

"Aye."

"If you could perhaps take care not to be gruff with her."

"You think I'd be gruff?"

"Not intentionally, but...well, sometimes you can come across as a bit stern. She's had a very difficult life, and even though I've done my best to convince her otherwise, she fears not to have a position after your arrival."

"Say no more, Eamon. I shall be naught but amicable in her presence."

Chapter 41

"**A** carriage approaches, my lord," Donegan called down from his perch atop the first newly-hung gate.

Eamon and Gunnar stood up from securing ropes to the second and looked to the road. Eamon turned to Gunnar. "Your first test. 'Tis the widow who offered to aid with the list."

"You invited her back?" Gunnar glanced down at his smudged silk tunic. His fine garments were appropriate, but laboring beside the workers was not what he'd have chosen for a first meeting.

"Nay. But I have the distinct impression this lady does as she pleases, as you'll soon see. Now remember, when you greet her, noblewomen like to be complimented."

Gunnar frowned.

"Don't worry, not all noblemen are honey-lipped; many lords from outlying estates have manners barely above...," Eamon faltered.

"A Northman?" Gunnar finished for him with a smile.

"Well, aye," Eamon grinned. "'tis how the saying goes. My point was, if you can remember even a small part of what we've covered, you'll be well-served. Far more important is to avoid any serious offense."

"Like groping her backside or ogling her breasts?"

"Aye, like either of those things; God help us."

"But I'm supposed to look at her breasts if they're revealed or she'll also be insulted?"

"Aye, just not for too long. No more than to the count of two."

"What if they're spectacular, and in the moment, I were to lose count?" Gunnar grinned.

Eamon laughed. "You'd not be the first, so better only to pass a glance or not look at all. Now enough talk of breasts," Eamon whispered furtively. "She approaches."

"Lady Evlin, may I introduce, Lord Colin. My lord, I present to you, Lady Evlin."

Gunnar bowed his head. "My lady. Apologies for my appearance. I could not sit idle with the estate in such poor condition."

"The circumstances of Tir na Laoch are well-known, and your man has informed me of your intent to restore it. Though 'twill take much coin." Her voice trailed off with open question.

"If it were only coin that was required, 'twould already be done. Unfortunately, it will also take much time and labor."

His lack of concern about the cost seemed to impress her. "Your man mentioned to me of your upbringing by Northmen." She allowed her eyes to openly travel over him. "I must admit I expected..."

"A barbarian brute?"

"Aye," she smiled.

"And still you came. Were you not worried I would be dangerous?" He smiled back.

"Are you?"

"Quite."

She laughed. "I believe you just might be. Though people gossip that I'm dangerous as well—that I killed my first two husbands."

"Did you?"

She acted shocked that he would ask, then smiled and shook her head very slowly. "Nay, of course not. Would the idea frighten you?"

"If you know of my upbringing, then you'll understand it takes far more than rumors to frighten me."

"Of course," she nodded, considering· him again for another long moment. "I shall not keep you; 'twas not my intent to stay. I came only to see if you still required my suggestions for your guest list."

"And to assure yourself that I was not a filthy heathen before providing them."

"Perhaps," she smiled in agreement. "But rest assured, I've found you to be quite the opposite, quite intriguing and—quite agreeable." Her voice trailed off. "In fact, as a welcoming gift, I shall send out the invitations myself. My family is well-known and well-respected; I could even expand the list to include noble families from as far as Dublin, if you wish?"

"Your offer is much appreciated, but with the condition of the hall, I'm not yet able to offer overnight lodgings. I prefer to keep this initial introduction smaller and limited to local noble families. Come spring, I'll be better suited to have another larger gathering. And I thought to host this one soon—next week perhaps?"

Evlin nodded. "Then I shall draw up the invitations immediately and have a copy delivered to you."

"Gratitude for your effort."

"You can repay me later." She turned away with a smile.

Eamon returned to Gunnar's side as she climbed into her carriage.

"When you said widow, I pictured something quite different," Gunnar murmured.

"Aye, she's beautiful, but I cannot tell you how relieved I am that she is not your woman. I swear she licked her lips after she said 'agreeable' like a hungry hound."

"Do you think she killed her first husbands?" Gunnar mused.

"I couldn't say, but 'tis not something a normal person brings up in conversation. She seemed almost proud of it."

"If it were true, after the first, why would she do it again?"

"Does it matter? You don't need to know why a snake will bite to know to steer clear of the danger."

Gunnar laughed. "Agreed."

"Well, that meeting was an incredible success. Perhaps I worried needlessly about you interacting with your new peers."

"She doesn't count—a woman like that is familiar."

"A woman like that?" Eamon asked.

" A woman who knows her way around a man; they are the same in every culture."

"Still, she's an invaluable connection. Everyone would've been curious about you before, but invitations from her hand will be very well-received. Everything is falling into place."

"Everything except the most important thing. Has there been any word from the men on the road?"

Eamon shook his head. "There's been no sign of Lady Fiona yet, but I'm sure she'll return in time."

"Brace yourself, my lord, my lady. Another carriage approaches and the road is narrow here. I shall need to maneuver half off for them to pass."

Fiona gripped the edge of her seat and watched her father do the same as the carriage wheels on her side bumped over grass clumps and rocks on the roadside. At the sound of the drivers exchanging words, her father lifted his curtain, revealing the back of the dark carriage with its two footmen before it bounced past.

"'Tis Lord Artan, my lady, and he requests to speak with you," her driver, Rafferty, called down once their carriage had returned to the road.

"Will you require the step, my lady?" her footman asked.

"Aye, Dorrel," she replied. "I'll only be a moment, Papa," she added, hoping he wouldn't want to take the opportunity to stretch his legs so close to home. He nodded, and she stepped outside, meeting Artan midway between the carriages.

"How fortuitous to run into you," Artan said enthusiastically. "I've just come from Tir na Lionmahr. They said you were due back days ago and had no idea when you'd return. My mother has requested us tomorrow morning." He held out a letter. "Something about wedding plans. As my dutiful future wife, you will go and make an excuse for me."

"You will not attend?"

"Nay, I've a far more enjoyable and hopefully lucrative engagement planned. I'm meeting with friends for several days, and I intend to put the last of our betrothal gifts to good use."

Fiona unfolded the letter—more of a terse summons than an invitation. "At the mid-morning Terce bells?" she exclaimed when she noted the time. "I would have to leave before daybreak."

"An uncomfortable fact that I'm sure my mother took into account when she chose it."

"But I've been on the road for days; can this not wait?"

Artan barked a harsh laugh. "Oh aye, by all means, send a reply to my mother letting her know 'tis inconvenient for you."

"Where shall I tell her you are?" Fiona muttered, resigned.

"You'll think of something," he said over his shoulder as he walked jauntily back to his carriage.

Fiona waited until he'd climbed inside before she smiled. Even though she was exhausted, her step was also light as she returned to her own carriage. With the wedding less than a month away, the opportunity she'd been waiting for had finally presented itself. Best of all, it had come from Artan's own hand.

"Lady Duvessa will see you now."

Fiona felt a surge of panic, though she'd had plenty of time to prepare in the full hour she'd been kept waiting. She stroked the flask in her purse as she stood, strengthened by the connection to Gunnar. All of her schemes had led to this moment. She was ready. Pushing her doubts aside as best she could, she entered Lady Duvessa's receiving chamber.

"Where is Artan?" Duvessa demanded.

"Apologies, Your Grace. He had...business and could not attend."

"Business," she sniffed. "No matter. Men have little to offer in planning a wedding."

Fiona soon realized she was also not expected to offer anything; the meeting was simply for the woman to present the plans she'd already made.

"What is it, Fiona? You've scarce said a word. Is something not to your liking?"

"Nay, Your Grace. 'Tis not that. 'Tis...Artan."

Lady Duvessa scowled. "If 'tis to do with his gambling or whoring, neither is news to me."

"Nay, Your Grace. 'Tis none of those things. Artan assures me those days are behind him." Fiona twisted her hands in her lap, seeming unsure of how to proceed.

"Spit it out, lass. My time is valuable."

Fiona nodded and slowly withdrew a letter from her purse. She clutched it for a moment, then held it out to her, making sure the MacTavish seal faced up. "I must warn you, 'tis something dreadful."

Lady Duvessa leaned forward from her chair and snatched the letter from Fiona's grasp, quickly unfolding it. Her face grew pale, then red with shock and rage as her eyes flew down the parchment. When she reached the bottom she started over, reading it more slowly. By the time she finished it a second time, her face was a stony mask.

"How did you come by this?" she asked, her voice icy.

"I met Artan on the road yesterday as my father and I were returning from Athlone. That's when he gave me your invitation and this letter to deliver to Tibbot. The wax seals must have bonded together in the warmth under my cloak. When I later pulled them out, the seal of that," she nodded at the letter. "came loose. I know I should not have read it, but the seal was already lifted, and once I did, I didn't know what to do," Fiona continued in a well-orchestrated rush. "Your Grace, I fear...I fear it refers to Tynan. The letter mentions him not by name, only as...*the bean*." She lowered her voice. "But I believe I once heard Artan refer to Tynan as such."

That wasn't exactly true. Artan had never himself referred to Tynan as *the bean*; he'd once scornfully disclosed it to be his mother's secret pet name for her eldest son. "I know Artan is my intended, and I should side with him against all others, but I couldn't live with myself if I allowed Tynan to suffer such a fate. So heavy has this weighed on my mind, I slept not a wink last night. My only comfort was that I was meeting you today, and you would know what to do."

"This cannot be true; it must be a forgery." Duvessa held up the letter but did not offer it back to her.

"Aye, I'd have surely thought the same had I not received it from Artan's own hand. Then other things came to me—things he has said. All little insignificant things on their own, but when taken together with this..."

"As wicked as Artan is, even he would never dare such a thing."

Fiona nodded in agreement, but she could see Duvessa was not at all sure of what Artan would dare. "Of course, Your Grace. Your surety brings me great comfort and relief. I shall return the letter to Artan. I'm sure he has an explanation." Fiona held out her hand, holding her breath.

"Nay."

Fiona looked at her with wide-eyed innocence but smiled grimly inside.

"Do you know this man? This slaver?" Lady Duvessa demanded, waving the letter in the air dismissively.

Fiona frowned. "Aye, Your Grace; unfortunately I do. He's the one I asked you about at the Midsummer feast. He's a friend of Artan. Not only did he host a betrothal feast for us then, but Artan has also agreed for him to honor us with another feast after the wedding." Fiona raised a hand to cover her mouth, suddenly stricken.

"What is it now?" his mother snapped.

"There may be other letters, Your Grace. Artan insisted that I meet with Tibbot's wife to review and approve their plans for the wedding feast. Each time I carried letters between him and Tibbot. I assumed Artan was procuring a special slave for me as a wedding gift, but what if...what if they were other letters regarding this?" Fiona uttered a fake sob and covered her face with her hands.

"So you know the location of this Tibbot's establishment and can find it again?"

"Aye, Your Grace, I've been there at least half a dozen times. 'Tis in Swords," Fiona said hesitantly, pretending to be confused as to why she would ask.

"Seamus!" Lady Duvessa shouted to the servant waiting by the door. "Have the carriage with the fastest team brought around immediately." She turned back to Fiona. "We shall have our answers directly."

Chapter 42

The great hall was abuzz with activity—torches and candles being replaced, boughs of greenery trimmed with ribbon being hung. Gunnar nodded to the servants he passed, most of whom he didn't recognize—friends and family of the laborers Eamon had collected to aid with the feast. He closed the door to his study, thankful for the solitude.

Everything was going unbelievably well. Rask and the crew of the Huntress were safely returned to Balbriggan awaiting his word, while a messenger had reported Fiona and her father's return the night before. Since that news, he'd been filled to bursting with anticipation. He would actually see her tonight—if this day would ever pass!

His thoughts were interrupted by a brief knock on the door. Eamon entered. "A message from Widow Evlin has just arrived, my lord."

"Read it to me please, Eamon. I've no mind to struggle through letters right now."

Eamon broke the seal and unfolded the parchment.

Lord Colin,

Below is the final list of guests who will be in attendance this evening. I'm pleased to say that all who were invited have accepted, save one–Lord Patrick O'Neill. He and his daughter, Fiona, have been away and are yet to return. Although even if they had, I was unsure they would attend. They're likely quite busy finalizing plans for her upcoming wedding to Lord Artan MacTavish...

Eamon stuttered to a halt.

Gunnar's eyes bored holes through him. "Continue."

Eamon hesitated, then returned to the letter.

"*I had hoped that Lord Artan might attend with them and was even so bold as to include him in their invitation. The MacTavishs are one of the most powerful families in Dublin. If you were to become friendly with Artan, he'd be an extremely valuable...*"

"Enough," Gunnar snarled. It was all coming to pass—every fear, every nightmare. He'd broken his oath to the gods to never leave the woman he loved unattended, and this was his punishment. They'd let him believe right up to the very end that his transgression had gone unnoticed or been forgiven—that a life with her was possible.

Gunnar grabbed a candelabra and threw it against the wall, the bronze arms crumpling from the force of the impact. Next he hurled a chair— splinters showered the floor. "Call it off. Call the whole thing off."

"I believe that would be unwise," Eamon declined quietly.

Gunnar turned his fury on Eamon, pinning him against the wall with the back of his forearm against his throat. "Do not cross me on this, Eamon. You know not what you do."

"Kill me if you will, but 'tis the only way you'll silence me. I owe you my life, and because of that, I'll not hold my tongue."

Gunnar roared, slapping his palm to the wall next to Eamon's head. Eamon didn't flinch. Shoving himself away, Gunnar began pacing the room like a caged animal.

"You've come so far, accomplished so much. Do not give up. Let this play out. You must see her. You don't know..."

"What don't I know? Do I not know she is betrothed? To a wealthy powerful lord? Do I not know that?"

"You do."

"Then what don't I know?"

"You don't know why. Perhaps...perhaps," Eamon grappled for words. "You said she was older; perhaps her father arranged the marriage."

"You don't know Fiona. She is too willful."

"Perhaps she didn't believe you were coming back, and once she sees you..."

"You mean once she sees me as a lord?! Once she sees I am suitable?!"

"I did not say that."

"Do you think I should have her then? That I should accept her after she has faithlessly given her word to another?!"

"You won't know the truth until you speak to her."

"And what would you have me say to her, Eamon? Congratulations on your upcoming nuptials?"

"Nay, I would not have you say that."

"Should I tell her then how I raced halfway around the world and back to be with her? How many times my haste put the lives of my men in jeopardy?"

"Nay, I would not have you say those things either."

"Then tell me, Eamon, what is it you *would* have me say?"

"I would have you say nothing. I would have you only listen. Everything is already set. We know she returned last night. When she arrives, we will find a way for you to speak in private."

"You mean without her betrothed?" Gunnar's sarcasm barely covered the pain.

"I mean without anyone."

Gunnar swore and ran a hand over his head. "Continue with the preparations if you will. I'll decide later whether or not to attend. Now leave me."

"My business with you is private. You will remove your man." Lady Duvessa commanded Tibbot as she took a seat at his desk across from him. "Fiona, you will stay," she added.

Fiona took a seat to one side and prayed her luck would continue to hold; Tibbot's wife, Leona, was miraculously away, and Lady Duvessa's abrupt manner had so far precluded any frivolous conversation where Tibbot might have revealed knowing her before Artan. He dismissed his manservant now without even looking in her direction.

"'Tis my understanding that you deal in slaves and have ways to dispose of someone," Artan's mother began.

"My lady, I usually deal with men in business matters," Tibbot replied vaguely, smelling for a trap.

"You will address me as *Your Grace*. You do not deny it then?"

"Your Grace," he corrected himself without answering the question of slaves or disposing of anyone.

"I have an important proposal for you and need to know if I'm in the proper place. If you are not the man I seek..." She prepared to stand.

"Of course, I'm your man, Your Grace. How can I be of service?"

She tossed the letter onto his desk. "You can start by explaining to me the meaning of this."

Tibbot paled.

"You do not wish to read it?"

He said nothing, only stared at her.

"Take it," she demanded.

"I do not need to, Your Grace."

"So you don't deny being complicit in a plot against my eldest son?! I'll have you gutted and hanged!"

Tibbot reached for his drawer and slowly withdrew a small stack of letters, each bearing the MacTavish seal. "You will perhaps wish to read these first, Your Grace. You cannot see my replies, of course, but Artan's words are very clear. This was not my idea, and I did my best to dissuade him. Should these be made public, 'tis not I who would stand accused, nor should I." He slid the stack towards her.

Lady Duvessa ripped open the first, her eyes racing through the words. She reached for the second. As she discarded the open letters one by one on the desk, Tibbot casually reached across and slid them back to safety, lest she think to destroy them.

"You just mentioned your eldest son, but Artan has yet to reveal a name to me, only referred to the man as *the bean*. I would, of course, never have agreed had I known," Tibbot said when she finished the last.

Lady Duvessa sat silent, their presence in the room seemingly forgotten. Fiona held her breath. She knew there could be no doubt in the woman's mind now as to Artan's guilt. She'd made sure of that by including the MacTavish's secret favored methods of torture in these other letters—the crushing of hands and removal of tongue. She also knew her convincing act as a senseless dim-wit these past months, combined with innocently coming forth with the letter today, would exclude her from suspicion.

Yet this part of her plan still carried great risk. Risk that she had no control over. She was counting on their estrangement and the woman's contempt for Artan to be so fueled by rage at the threat to her beloved Tynan, that she'd react without confronting him. For if she did confront Artan, not only would he rightfully deny having written the letters, he would know exactly who had.

"Who have you told of this?" She held up the last letter to Tibbot.

"No one, my lady, uh, I mean, Your Grace."

"A ship still waits?"

"Aye, but I will, of course, cancel all arrangements."

"Nay...you will not."

Tibbot stared at her.

"You will still deliver *one* of my sons," she said, her voice dripping with venom. "I will see that he's delivered to you here within the week."

"Will he require the same...treatment?"

"Aye. If that's what Artan thought was appropriate, I'll defer to his judgment on the matter. He clearly has had time to think it through."

"You intend to replace Tynan with Artan," Fiona murmured as they took their seats in the carriage.

"I do. And do not think to warn him."

"I would never, Your Grace. I feel incredibly fortunate to have discovered this before we were married. What might he have done to me later if I displeased him?" She held a hand to her forehead. "Though what will become of me?" She allowed her voice to quaver. "If Artan's missing, I won't be able to break the betrothal for quite some time. I'll most assuredly end up a spinster now," Fiona sniffled, still playing the role of a self-centered featherbrain.

"My dear, I believe you've unwittingly just solved both of our problems. You will break the betrothal straightaway, and I shall make it public. Then when Artan's body is found, I will say he was so overcome with grief, that he took his own life."

"His body? But I thought..."

"Oh, Artan will still rot as a slave. I'll identify another body as his before having the casket sealed and buried in the family plot. No one will question it. Your family will be required to pay restitution for breach of promise. I know 'tis unusual for such a demand to be brought against a bride's family, but considering the grief it causes when Artan ends up dead as a result, 'twill not seem unreasonable."

Fiona bit her tongue to keep from pointing out any number of ways Artan could die other than of a broken heart. She focused instead on how close she was to realizing her goal. For the price of a breach of promise claim, which her father would be happy to pay, she'd be free, and Artan MacTavish would never threaten anyone again.

"I'll need a few days to make arrangements," Lady Duvessa continued. "When I'm ready, I'll send word to you. Do not break the betrothal until then. I trust you know not to breathe a word of this to anyone—not even your father? I would hate for anyone else to have to suffer Artan's fate."

"Aye, Your Grace," Fiona murmured, trying to look suitably terrified.

───────◆───────

As the MacTavish gates swung closed behind them, Fiona leaned her head back against the familiar cushions of her own carriage, too exhausted and drained to fully appreciate her success. After months of fear and doubt, the final step of her scheme was in motion and had gone mostly according to plan. Duvessa's decision to replace Tynan with Artan had been a surprise; she'd expected the woman to simply have him killed. She pushed the gruesome image of what lay in store for Artan from her mind. She'd not allow herself to be troubled for a single moment more over anything to do with him.

All she could do now was wait; wait for word from Lady Duvessa to break the betrothal, then wait to receive the false news that Artan was dead by his own hand. Until then, she'd have to keep up her guard. She would not underestimate Duvessa. Who knew what devious change of plans she might come up with in the coming days.

But she was safe for tonight. All she wanted now was to get home, climb into her soft bed, and sleep. Fiona gathered the travel furs and blankets into a pile on the seat beside her. After patting a small depression in the top, she leaned over and snuggled into them, closing her eyes.

"Thank the heavens you've returned and not a moment later," Meirna said as Fiona stumbled from the carriage. "You must hurry. There's still time."

"Time for what?"

"There's a feast tonight," Meirna announced.

"I cannot possibly..."

"'Tis a feast to present Lord Nevyn's heir," Meirna interrupted her.

"Lord Nevyn?"

"Aye, an heir has been found, and they're having a great feast tonight to introduce him. Your father only discovered the invitation this morning after you'd left."

"But..." Fiona rubbed her stiff neck.

"There will be no buts, Fiona. Your father is beside himself with excitement and cannot wait to meet the man. I have your gown already laid out." Meirna turned to the two men. "Rafferty, you and Dorrel are to take brief refreshment in the kitchen. Cahan has the stable boys ready to care for the horses and harness a fresh team."

Chapter 43

Eamon slipped into the study and closed the door behind him. Thankfully Gunnar had ceased pacing and now sat with his boots propped up on the desk next to an open bottle of poteen. Originally they'd planned for him to wait here until all the guests had arrived so he could make one announcement and be spared from having to repeat his story over and over. With the latest setback, it was imperative.

"She is here," he announced quietly.

"And her betrothed?" Gunnar asked bitterly.

Eamon shook his head.

"I suppose I should be thankful for that at least."

"Are you ready?"

After a long pause, Gunnar nodded curtly.

"Remember, after your speech, try to keep your conversations short. I'll be watching. If I find you stuck in one place overly long, I will interrupt with something for you to attend to. Initial conversations should center around how well you are restoring the fortress, and only if allowed to go on will they ask of your past."

Gunnar scowled at him. "I've agreed only to continue this charade long enough to speak with her. Make sure that happens quickly...or see it all undone."

Eamon nodded—and prayed.

After being announced, Fiona and her father joined the other lords and ladies milling about the great hall of Tir na Laoch.

"May I offer you an ale or wine, my lord? Lady?" A servant balancing a tray of full goblets offered. "The ale is fresh-brewed and the wine from Frankia."

"Gratitude," her father said as they each took a glass. "And where might I find Lord Nevyn?"

"He is gone, lord."

"Gone?"

"Lord Colin will make an announcement shortly to explain everything."

"How strange," her father murmured as the ringing of a small bell silenced the room. Everyone turned their attention to a manservant standing on a makeshift dais.

"Your attention, my lords and ladies. May I have your attention, please. 'Tis my great honor to present to you the heir of Tir na Laoch, Lord Colin." He waved to his left.

Fiona tiredly followed the direction of the manservant's hand, only mildly interested in seeing the heir. Before her eyes could discover the unknown man, they locked on another. Her heart seized in her chest. Her mind snapped to full awareness. Mouth dry, she stared at him, emotions sweeping through her body in a maelstrom of disbelief, shock, excitement, and fear. *Gunnar was here?!*

The initial thrill of seeing him was followed closely by terror so thick it threatened to choke her. It was too bold! He could never fool these people.

He'd be discovered! She had to do something and quickly! Now, while everyone was distracted trying to catch their first glimpse of the new heir, she had to help him escape!

Heart pounding, she took two steps in his direction. The goblet fell from her hand, spattering her skirt with red as it bounced off the stone floor. No one noticed; the sound was lost in the noise of the crowd as Gunnar climbed the steps of the dais, and the manservant bowed to him.

***

Gunnar waited for the crowd to quiet. "As some of you know, after planning this feast, Lord Nevyn received word that his ship to Rome could delay its departure no longer for fear of winter seas. He regrets not being here to make this announcement in person, but has written a letter for me to read on his behalf."

The manservant stepped toward him and offered him a scroll. Fiona held a hand to her mouth as he unrolled it. Her stomach churned. What was he thinking? Gunnar couldn't read!

"*Lords and Ladies,*

Apologies for my absence tonight, but you all know of my failing health and the healer's insistence that I seek a drier clime. To that end, you all also know of my extensive search to find an heir. I'm overjoyed to finally announce the success of that quest—and not with a distant relative, but with my own grandson."

Gunnar paused, waiting for the new swell of murmurs to subside.

"*Some of you might remember my daughter, Nola, who was presumed dead in one of the Viking raids on the abbey at Trim. What you would not know was how Nola came to be at the abbey in the first place. She did not seek a life devoted to God; Nola desired to marry a young lord from Airgialla. I refused his request for her hand, and, when he died of fever a month later, I thought that to be the end of it. But I was wrong. Nola was with child. And in my anger, I sent her to the Trim Abbey to bear her bastard in secret.*

I haven't spoken of Nola since that day. The guilt that I'd caused her death by putting her in the path of catastrophe weighed heavily upon me all these years. Until very recently—when I learned that Nola hadn't been killed in the raid. She and her newborn babe were taken, and my grandson—this man you see before you here tonight, was raised a Northman, unaware of his true identity and birthright. Only upon her deathbed did Nola reveal to him the truth.

Gunnar was forced to pause again as his last words were lost in the din of excited voices.

"When my grandson first came to me with his story, I did not believe it. It was too fantastic a tale, and I was unaware Nola had even given birth before the raid. He presented a bronze brooch with two dark green agate stones as evidence, and I felt the first hope. The brooch was a unique piece, but it wasn't the brooch itself that made me consider his words. He knew the history behind it—knew it had been my grandmother's—knew I'd given it to Nola on her twelfth birthday. The only way someone could possibly know those things was to have heard them from Nola's own mouth.

I requested the Bishop of Kells check the abbey's records, still with the thought of disproving him. 'Twas the bishop who discovered and verified the records of birth and baptism of Nola's son, Colin.

That it's a miracle is the only explanation. With Colin's return, God has blessed me with two lives—for not only did he deliver my grandson, an honorable man worthy of Tir na Laoch, he gave me Nola. Though she no longer walks among us, it gives me great comfort to know that she lived a full and happy life. As I prepare now to depart for Rome, it is with peace in my heart.

And so, under the eyes of God, I, Lord Nevyn, do hereby transfer title and all chartered lands of Tir na Laoch to my grandson and sole heir, Lord Colin.

"'Tis signed by my grandfather, witnessed by the bishop of Kells and their seals affixed." Gunnar held up the scroll before handing it back to his manservant, then once again faced the stunned silent crowd.

"I always knew my mother was Irish; 'twas no secret; she taught me her tongue. But she'd been married to Karl Frederiksen, the man who raised me as his son—the man I'd known to be my father. I didn't want to believe her. For with her words and her passing, I would lose two parents. She gave me a brooch and told me it was the proof. 'Tis the brooch I wear tonight and the same brooch she is wearing in this portrait as a young lass with her hound." Gunnar paused and turned to look at the painting in the gilded frame behind him. "She made me swear to return here—to see the painting with my own eyes—and to meet my uncles and cousins, for she had no way of knowing none remained.

"I came here only to honor her dying wish with the full intent of returning immediately to Norway. But upon my arrival, even though the estate had fallen into ruin, something stirred within me that I cannot explain. 'Twas my grandfather's firm belief that God took my mother when he did so that I would be returned to him in his hour of need. I cannot speak to that. But however I came to be here, I know Tir na Laoch is my home, and I shall make it my life's goal to see it restored."

The manservant handed him a chalice, and he held it up. "Join me in a toast to my grandfather, Lord Nevyn. Though he is absent tonight, we shall honor his wishes to feast and celebrate. May he recover his health and live a long comfortable life in Rome."

"Hear, hear!" the crowd cheered as Gunnar took a sip from his chalice. He stepped from the dais amidst applause—some clapping their hands together, others clapping a single hand against their chest.

Fiona stared at him, mouth agape. It was too impossible—too unbelievable. Only in dreams did such fanciful things occur. Yet it felt so real. She thought to pinch herself, but if it were a dream, she didn't want to awaken. Her eyes drank in the familiar details of his form while her ears still clung to the last echoes of his deep voice.

As the initial shock waned, questions began to tumble through her mind. *How had he managed all this? How long had he been back? Why had he not come to her? Or sent word?* She watched Evlin move in and touch his arm. He looked down at her, listened to something she said, then nodded. *And how did he know Evlin?*

"Fascinating," her father murmured in awe. "After all these years..."

Fiona could only nod and continue to stare. Gunnar lifted his gaze from Evlin and began to scan the room. Fiona held her breath, waiting for his eyes to find her—waiting to feel the warmth as he caressed her from afar.

His gaze paused on her fleetingly, just long enough for her to see the icy coldness in his eyes before moving on.

Her mind reeled. The breath rushed from her body as if she'd been struck in the stomach. He'd looked at her with no recognition at all. Nay, worse than that, he *had* recognized her and looked at her with hostility!

"Lord Patrick?" She dimly heard a male voice addressing her father while she struggled to come to grips with this most recent shock.

"Aye," her father replied.

"Lord Colin understands you are a scholar and historian and would like your opinion on an ancient sculpture. 'Twas just discovered in an underground chamber during the renovations and 'tis quite remarkable. He believes it might be Roman."

"Roman, you say?"

"Aye, my lord. 'Tis displayed under the portrait of his mother."

As her father moved away, Fiona moved dumbly to follow him. The man who'd spoken to him stepped in front of her, blocking her path. She looked up. Gunnar's manservant.

"I see you've dropped your wine, my lady. Can I get you another?" he asked. Before she could decline, he lowered his voice to a whisper. "In the middle of the great hall are doors open to the outside. Once through them, follow the walkway left to the very end. Past the last torch, you'll find another open doorway. Gunnar awaits you there." He waited until he was sure she'd understood, then moved to another guest when she finally nodded.

Her heart tripped over itself. She must have been mistaken. Gunnar was waiting for her! She moved through the crowd, pausing at the large doors that were cracked open to allow fresh cool air into the hall. She glanced over her shoulder. No one watched her. She slipped outside. Turning left, she hurried along the torch-lit walkway, her feet barely skimming the stones.

She slowed as she passed the last torch, feeling her way along the rough stone exterior, not wanting to wait for her eyes to adjust to the darkness. Her fingers felt the curtains that concealed the open doorway before she saw them. Taking a deep breath, she pushed through the heavy material and stepped inside.

Gunnar heard her soft footsteps pause at the curtains. He braced himself for the impact of seeing her up close, but it wasn't enough. His gut twisted. By the gods, she was so beautiful! Her wide eyes were dilated and dark, just as they'd been the first night he'd seen her in the storm. His heart wrenched in his chest. *How could she have betrayed him? And how could he still feel this way knowing that she had?*

Fiona's stomach fluttered. His form had appeared impressive from across the great hall, but in this smaller space, it was even more so. She smiled and took a few steps towards him. He remained behind a desk, staring at her. "Gunnar?"

"Lady Fiona O'Neill. Is it still O'Neill with your betrothal?"

Her mind spun. *So he knew of her betrothal to Artan; it had no bearing on them.* "Gunnar, what's wrong?"

"What's wrong? You dare to ask me what's wrong when I stand here returned to you as I swore I would. In the impossible position to marry you as I swore I would, and you... Did you even wait a month before choosing another?"

Fury blossomed in Fiona's chest. After all she'd endured because of *his* connection to Artan, he would think to criticize her? He had to know what kind of man Artan was; he was the one who'd borrowed his carriage in the first place! And he dared to believe she'd willingly chosen him? That she would ever do such a thing!

She tried to calm herself. There had to be some reasonable explanation for his bizarre behavior. Her mind scrambled to find one. He hadn't mentioned Artan's name—had instead referred to him as *another*. Perhaps he'd only heard that she was betrothed and not to whom. That had to be it. Her fury slightly abated, but still incensed that he would think that of her under any circumstances, she spoke through gritted teeth. "I didn't just choose *another*. He is Artan MacTavish."

Gunnar's fingernails bit grooves into the desk wood. She didn't ask for his forgiveness. Didn't plead with him to understand, or beg him to allow her to explain. She offered no excuse—that she thought he would never return, or that her father had forced her. Nothing for him to cling to and accept—and forgive. Instead, she boldly threw the man's name in his face as if it, alone, were reason enough to justify her betrayal!

"He is Artan MacTavish!" she repeated, her voice nearing a shout—like he was an idiot, and the name was so important that even a Northman should recognize it.

"Do not speak his fucking name to me again, woman. I am not deaf," Gunnar snarled.

Fiona stared at him, incredulous. The only other time she'd ever heard him swear was the night in the storm when the carriage had first become bogged in the mud. She stroked the silver flask in her purse out of habit, instinctively seeking some of the comfort it had provided these past months. The blissful memories attached to it always made it seem warm to the touch, but now the coldness of the metal stung her palm. She had to be rid of it. Withdrawing it from her purse, she flung it at his head with all her might. For a moment, she thought it would find its mark.

Gunnar batted the flask from the air. It bounced hard on the desktop in front of him, skittered a few inches, then spun in place, slowing with every revolution. The initials etched in the silver winked at him in the candlelight, trying to tell him something. The flask came to a full stop. He stared at it. It was familiar, and by her reaction he knew it to be important, but why?

Images flitted and flashed through his mind. The exhilaration of their race on the beach at Clogherhead. Fiona, spattered with sand, beaming and glorious in her triumph. *Why think of those things now when he was already tortured enough?!* Gunnar angrily tried to push the painful memories aside, to focus on the present, but could not. He was back in the carriage after the race, feeling the impending storm. His decision to change course and turn inland and his frustration at the slowness of their pace. Reaching under the seat, finding—the flask.

Fiona lifting it to her perfect lips. The initials engraved upon it blazed back at him in his mind. Initials he'd paid no attention to at the time; his eyes had been only for her. The same initials that taunted him now from the flask on the desk. *AMT.* Artan MacTavish. *But that meant...The carriage was...*

Fiona watched him stare at the flask, silent and unmoving. The object she'd clung to with such fondness these past months meant nothing to him. *She* meant nothing to him. The thick lump forming in her throat made it impossible to swallow. She'd suffered his absence, endured Artan's cruelty, anguished over every detail of her plan, and feared discovery so many times, yet managed to stay strong through all of it. But this...this was too much to bear.

She turned and stumbled back the way she'd come, missing the slit in the curtain in her haste. She lashed at the seemingly solid wall of fabric. She would not let him see how deeply he'd wounded her. She would not let him see her cry. *Where was the damn opening?! It had to be right here!*

Gunnar's mind raced. Lord Lizard Eyes was her betrothed? He had found her? And done what?! His stomach clenched with fear, frustration, and fury all at once. He rounded the desk and covered the distance between them in three long strides. "Fiona," he murmured as he reached for her.

She uttered a strangled cry that pierced his heart and pushed him away. "Don't touch me," she hissed.

He reached for her again, but she slapped his hands away and continued backing along the curtain, feeling behind her for the opening and escape.

"Fiona, I didn't know. Please talk to me. Please tell me what has happened."

She was close to the opening now. She didn't realize it, but Gunnar did. He couldn't let her leave. He lunged. Gripping both of her arms above the elbows, he pulled her tight against his chest.

"Let go of me!" she screamed and struggled to free herself.

He squeezed tighter and murmured into her hair. "Fiona, I didn't know. I came back for you and when I heard you were betrothed, it drove me mad. Please forgive me."

"Let me go!"

"I will not. Not ever again."

At his last words, her body went limp in his arms. Then, as if a dam had broken inside her, her shoulders began to quake and her body to shudder as anguish poured from her in a flood of wordless sobs.

"Shhh, shhh. Everything will be alright. I am here now. We are together. I will fix this. Shhh. Please don't cry." Gunnar mumbled reassurances, apologies—anything he could think of to comfort her. Tormented to see her in such pain and heart-stricken that he was to blame, he kept her locked in his embrace until she finally stilled. "Can I release you?" he asked, his voice a raw whisper. "You will not run away?"

Fiona nodded.

He tentatively loosened his grip.

"I need something to wipe my face," she mumbled.

Gunnar retrieved a square of lace-edged linen from underneath a candlestick and waited while she wiped her eyes and nose.

"What happened?" he asked.

"Artan found me," she said, her voice dull. "He found me, and he knew. Knew everything about us. Where we'd been, where we stayed. That we'd been together. He's a vile, despicable man, Gunnar. How is it that you procure a man's carriage and do not know his name?"

"I won it in a wager. A private, discreet wager. Names were not exchanged. And I truly never felt it was important."

"He first threatened that if I refused to marry him, he would ruin my reputation by revealing my indiscretions with you. When that failed, he threatened my father. His family is very powerful. My father is a good man and innocent in all this. I could not have..." Her voice broke. She paused to compose herself before continuing.

"Artan said you'd told him everything, that you'd deceived me. At first, it was hard not to believe him—he knew so much, but later I realized he must have learned those things from Bryen or Garrett or..." she hiccuped. "Oh, Gunnar, I fear they're all dead. He said he could not have them recognizing his future wife as a Northman's whore, and I believe he killed them for our secret. When he threatened my father, I agreed to the betrothal to allow myself time to find a way to be rid of him—and I have."

"Shhh. Shhh. I'm here now. I will fix this," Gunnar repeated, clenching his fists, glad for an entirely different reason that her betrothed had not arrived with her. With her last words of Artan's insult fresh in his mind, nothing would stop him from ripping the man apart with his bare hands. "I need you to tell me everything."

"I will, but there's no time now. We must get back. We've been gone too long already, and people will talk if they realize we're both absent."

"We're safe. We were last seen on opposite sides of the great hall, and we took different paths."

She smiled at his naiveté of her world. "They will still know, my love. Opposite directions have been used on many an occasion for a lord and lady to steal indiscreet moments alone."

"I won't let you leave like this. I'll claim sudden illness and send them all home. I care naught for any of it; this was all for you."

"If you do that, then I cannot stay. My father is here. And you know none of this was for me. It was for him and the other nobles, and a better introduction I could not have imagined. Tomorrow morning, follow your southern boundary to its easternmost cornerstone. I'll meet you there just after daybreak. There's a shepherd's cottage nearby. And Gunnar."

"Yes?"

"When we return to the others, you must act as if you don't know me."

"I know."

"I must look a fright." She reached up and dabbed gently under one eye. "My face always gets so ugly and red when I cry."

Gunnar kissed her—a long lingering kiss. "You are beautiful," he murmured, trying to express the intensity of all that he was feeling in those three simple words.

Fiona smiled at him before pulling away and slipping back through the curtain. The night air felt good on her face. She paused, looking out over the courtyard. The coolness would soon reduce the swelling around her eyes and add a flush to her cheeks. The additional time would also give him opportunity to return first. With all eyes upon him, no one should notice her.

Chapter 44

T hough the long table was filled with choice foods and servants laden with steaming trenchers continued to add to it, Fiona was unable to eat a single bite. *Gunnar was really here! He'd returned for her as he said he would, and in such a manner, she faced none of the impossible decisions she'd thought to have to make! He was a lord! They could marry and remain here! He loved her!* Her mind frenetically jumped from one joyous thought to the next. She fidgeted in her chair, finding it impossible to remain still when she wanted nothing more than to shout and clap, leap and dance.

As the other guests finally began to drift away from the table and return to mingling, she and her father joined them. Though she forbade herself from looking for Gunnar, she couldn't resist. Part of her had to keep verifying he was real. When she turned to find him headed in their direction, she quickly looked away, heat rising up her neck. *What was he doing? He had agreed!*

Heart pounding, she heard her father introduce himself, "I'm Lord Patrick O'Neill of Tir na Lionmahr."

"I believe we're neighbors," Gunnar responded, his tone friendly and polite.

"Aye, though our lands only touch on a corner. And this is my daughter, Fiona."

She allowed herself to look at him then. He stood so close, she could feel the raw masculine strength emanating from him in waves. She flushed deeper, sure that everyone could see it. How could they not?

"A pleasure, my lady." He bowed slightly to her, his blue eyes dancing with mischief.

"My lord." Fiona nodded, silently chastising herself. He was handling this far better than she. No one knew of their history. He would be expected to greet and converse with all of his guests. She had to change her way of thinking. They were simply a lord and lady meeting for the first time.

Gunnar turned back to her father. "Have you had time to inspect the sculpture?"

"I have and I believe you may be correct. Your manservant claimed you discovered it in a secret chamber?"

"Aye."

"Were any other objects found?"

"None yet discovered, but the chamber is dangerously collapsed; I've not yet had time to fully explore it, or anything else for that matter. The basic repairs have demanded all of my time. I've been told there are copper and iron deposits on the land and would like to see them but know not where to look; would you know if they're nearby?"

"That's a question better put to Fiona. I believe she's ridden every inch of land in the realm."

"Is that true?" Gunnar smiled at her, feigning surprise.

"My father exaggerates, but I have ridden much of your estate."

"Then there's a painting I should like for you to see. It's supposedly of another place on my lands that I would like to find. Perhaps you might recognize the spot and be able to describe to me its location? The painting is just there." He pointed to the nearest wall, then looked to her father. "If you would excuse her for one moment?"

"Of course." Her father smiled and nodded.

Fiona followed him to a painting of a lakeshore in spring. They stood side by side, pretending to look at it. "How have you managed all this?" she whispered.

"Coin, and plenty of it."

"Not the estate. You. Your manners."

"My manners? Are you saying I was uncouth before? As I recall, you were rather taken with me."

"Then your recollection is off; I found you to be quite distasteful." She pursed her lips as she lifted a hand and pointed at nothing in the painting.

"Distasteful? Then I can only imagine how you'd have responded, had you found me more to your liking," he teased, following her lead and pointing at something else.

Fiona suppressed a smile. This was them. Bantering. Innuendo. Perfection. "Who would have thought when you made up that first story about being an Irish lord who'd traveled so long that you'd forgotten your own tongue, that it would come to pass?"

"But this story is much better. My poor mother and I being captured by the dreaded Northmen when I was just a wee babe, covers all of my slips. And you said it was ridiculous—that it would never fool even common folk. What do you have to say now? Perhaps that I was right and you were wrong?"

"I would say that you clearly have yet to overcome your boorish need to gloat. And anyone with eyes could still take one look at you and see that you're little more than a beast."

"You do not seem to mind a beast."

"Likely because I spent so much time in the stables as a child. When you're raised around beasts, even large ones, you come to understand they're basically simple creatures—easy to train and bend to your will."

"Simple and train? My lady, you go too far. When the situation permits, I fear I shall have to take you to task for it."

"How I wish that could be now," she murmured.

"I cannot abide this—being so close and not touching you. I would see you alone again before you leave," he whispered fervently. "Meet me back in the study."

"We cannot. People will notice."

"Agree to meet me or see this simple beast strip away the shell of decorum that I struggle to maintain."

She smiled. "Very well. In one hour. But we must not speak again before then."

"One hour," he agreed.

"And Gunnar?"

"Yes?"

"Since we supposedly spent so much time discussing it, the painting is of Lough Ramor. 'Tis a large lake on your lands whose waters feed the River Blackwater. That river joins the River Boyne in Trim where you were so horribly abducted as a babe. From there, the combined waters flow all the way to the sea in Drogheda."

"Gratitude, my lady. I know of this River Boyne; I've heard there's an ancient palace somewhere along its banks. I believe 'tis called Bru na Boinnes?"

Fiona wanted to smile, but she'd caught his sudden return to formality and knew someone approached. "That is correct, my lord," she matched. "'Tis near Drogheda. You should be sure to see it when time avails."

"'Tis little more than a pile of turf and stones," Evlin disagreed as she stepped between them to stand at his side. "The term palace is quite misleading."

"Evlin," Fiona acknowledged.

"Fiona." Evlin nodded. "How are your wedding preparations proceeding?"

Evlin's reference to her wedding wasn't subtle, and Fiona was shocked by what it revealed. Evlin coveted him. Already. "Everything is proceeding exactly according to plan." Fiona smiled before excusing herself.

As she returned to her father, she looked to the three-hour candle clock mounted on the wall. She noted the candle's height against the lines hammered into the tin backing plate behind it—longer, deeper lines marking the hours with shorter shallow lines in-between, indicating the quarter and half hours. In an hour, she'd be back in his arms.

She glanced back at Gunnar and Evlin, though she had warned herself against it. The nearly deaf Lord Mundy had joined them, and Evlin was shouting something into the elderly man's ear. As if feeling her gaze, Gunnar turned towards her. Their eyes met, and he smiled—not a smile that showed teeth, just the slight quirk in the corner of his mouth that she knew so well. Every detail of him was still so familiar. It was as if they'd been apart for no time at all.

Fiona looked away, unable to keep the responding smile from her own face. She tried to focus on the person conversing with her father, but it was no use. Her mind far away, she nodded at what she hoped were appropriate times.

After seemingly interminable conversations with countless, faceless guests, she cast another glance at the candle clock, sure the appointed time was drawing near. The candle had burned to a hair's width below the half-hour mark. She frowned, wondering if the wick was somehow flawed, but the flame burned steady and bright. As if to mock her haste, a single droplet of melted wax flowed down the side into the tin bowl base.

She must have checked it a thousand times more before the blasted taper finally neared the one-hour mark. Never in her life had time passed so slowly. She looked for Gunnar and found him on the other side of the great hall, speaking to Lord Alsandair, Evlin still at his side. As tedious as her conversations had been, at least she hadn't had to endure graphic descriptions of turmeric and bowels. She smiled. Their eyes met. He nodded, the slightest of nods.

Fiona excused herself and made her way through the crowd to the side doors, then stepped outside. After quickly verifying the walkway was empty, she picked up her skirts and ran, wanting to shriek and laugh. Passing through the curtains, she stood waiting in the middle of the room, trying to control her racing heart.

Gunnar entered in a rush, kicking the door closed behind him. He swept her up into his arms, spinning her in a circle as his lips captured hers in a passionate kiss. He set her feet back to the floor and buried his face in her hair, inhaling deeply. "You've no idea how many hours I spent imagining your scent alone. And the other..." he groaned. "When we meet tomorrow, how much time will we have?"

"I've oft been known to ride for an entire day."

"An entire day. That's balm to my ears. I would imagine after a day of such vigorous activity as riding, you might arrive home quite spent and disheveled."

She giggled. "Aye, 'twill raise no suspicion if were I to return so again. Unlike now," she warned, breathless.

"Understood. But know that my desire to remove your dress is beyond fierce."

"As is my desire to have you do so," she murmured, nibbling the underside edge of his jaw.

He took a deep, shuddering breath and set her at arm's length. "In truth, 'tis nearly beyond my control. As much as it pains me to say this, you should return to the hall. I will already be much delayed, waiting for my thoughts of you to recede from visible sight."

Fiona glanced at the unmistakable bulge in the front of his trousers. "So I see." She stepped back into him, casually allowing one hand to run across his hardness.

"Do not tempt me, Fiona. Or I *will* have you right here, consequences be damned."

"Apologies, my love, I could not resist. 'Twill not be for much longer now. Until tomorrow." She kissed him lightly on the lips before slipping back through the curtain.

Shortly after she returned to the hall, her father announced he was ready to leave. Fiona didn't mind. Not being able to speak freely with Gunnar, or to touch him, was pure torture. The sooner she left, the sooner dawn would come, and she would be in his arms. Her entire body tingled at the thought.

"Can you believe that months ago I complained of Lord Nevyn having no son for you to marry?" Her father interrupted her imaginings with an inebriated smile as they climbed into the carriage. "I never considered the possibility of a grandson. Now there would be a good match. And though I'm no judge, I overheard several women practically swooning over how handsome he was. Did you find him so?"

Oh, how she did. "How can you ask me that, Papa, knowing I am betrothed," she teased, for the first time being able to jest of Artan MacTavish.

"A betrothal is not a marriage, Fiona." He frowned. "'Tis merely the intent to marry. Vows have not been exchanged before God, and betrothals can be broken. I'm sure the MacTavishs would demand restitution for breach of promise, but 'twould be a small price to pay."

Chapter 45

"**A**re you certain?" Gunnar asked the same question he'd asked Eamon at every other stone pillar in the dark.

"Aye. These markings indicate 'tis a corner."

"Thank the gods. I thought we'd be late for sure." Gunnar exhaled, his mood buoyed now that they'd finally reached their destination. He quickly scanned the nearby surroundings for a cottage but saw none. He widened his search over the shadowy dawn landscape, just as the outer rim of the sun breached the horizon, revealing details in the land contours with the first direct rays.

Movement to his right caught his eye. A horse and rider approached at a gallop in the distance. The animal's coat glinted bright molten copper as it passed through a beam of sunlight—a flash of color in the diffuse low light. Fiona. He watched with admiration as she guided the horse away from the faint road track they were following and up a low rise. After clearing a downed tree at the crest in a single fluid bound, the pair disappeared into a glade.

Gunnar pushed his horse down the hill in a path to intercept her. When they came together in the clearing, Fiona circled him, her face flushed, her lips parted, her breath showing white in the cool morning air. Both horses pranced and tossed their heads at the tangible excitement of their riders.

"You're early, Northman, as you were at our first meeting at Ward's Crossing. Do you fear another trap?"

"I assure you, my lady, my early arrival represents only immeasurable anticipation. Besides, your first trap still has me fully ensnared."

"And what is the enormous bundle behind your saddle? Are you traveling?" She grinned.

"I've come prepared."

"Prepared? For what?" she asked, feigning wide-eyed innocence.

"Lead the way to this damned cottage, and I'll show you."

Fiona laughed and turned the dancing Barca past him, freeing the reins and kicking the horse into a gallop. She called over her shoulder, "Follow me, Northman, and do try to keep up."

Fiona halted Barca by a tree near the front of the cottage and slid from his back. Though she tied his reins with haste, when she turned, Gunnar was already upon her, having carelessly tossed his horse's reins over a branch. Before she could chide him about the consequences of his horse escaping, his lips closed on hers.

Waves of energy flowed between them—emotion, passion, longing—binding them like a powerful living force. "Wait here for one moment." Gunnar's voice was rough when he finally broke away. He returned to his horse and the bundle behind his saddle. Fiona watched his strong hands jerking the leather ties and imagined those same hands soon to be on her skin with gentle precision. Her breath caught in her throat.

As he hoisted the pack onto his shoulder, motion behind him in the trees drew her attention. *A rider.* Her heart thumped in her chest for an entirely different reason. "Gunnar," she alerted, her voice low. "We've been followed."

Gunnar pivoted, his body instinctively poised to respond to danger. His shoulders settled almost instantly with relief. "'Tis only Eamon; he's my man. I brought him to stand guard." He smiled. " I would not be caught unaware in a compromising position."

"A compromising position?" Fiona smiled back. "My lord, you presume too much."

"My lady, you are about to realize exactly what I presume." Gunnar pushed open the door, looked around to verify it was safe, then stood aside and waited for her to enter.

Fiona had ridden by the structure many times but had never been inside. The two small window openings were shuttered closed, but light from the open doorway illuminated the single room. It was sparsely furnished with only a small, solid, waist-high table, two sturdy wood chairs, and a low bed platform that had been stripped for the season. Only the wood slats remained. Dried peat bricks were stacked neatly in the fire pit in the center with a clean empty iron pot suspended over them. A single shelf held wood plates, cups, and spoons.

Gunnar dropped his bundle on the bare bed platform before striking a light to a candle and closing the door. "This is far better than what I expected. Far cleaner," he said.

"The shepherd and his wife have just moved the flock to the nearer winter pastures. They are the only ones who ever stay here."

"Are you cold? I can build a fire."

"Nay, I would not have the room filled with smoke. And smoke rising might alert someone to our presence."

"Then I shall have to be sure to warm you." He stepped to her and placed his arms loosely around her waist.

"I still cannot believe you are truly here." She reached up to touch his face. "After seeing you last night, I slept not a wink. I feared it all to be a dream, and I could not bear the heartbreak of waking to find I had lost you again."

Gunnar reached up behind her to undo her hair. Running his fingers through it, he shook it loose until it fell wildly down her back. He cupped the sides of her face in his palms, looking deep into her eyes. His expression seemed almost pained. "I have imagined this moment so many times, yet now that it is here, I know not how to proceed. Every part of me demands to be the first to experience and reclaim all they have missed. My eyes demand the time to take in every curl in your hair, your beautiful eyes, the curve of your lips. My nose demands to breathe your scent." He pressed his face to the side of her neck beneath her ear and inhaled deeply. "Every inch of my skin longs, nay aches, to feel your silken softness pressed against it."

The pure reverence and longing in his voice sent her senses reeling. She'd forgotten how eloquent and powerfully moving his raw honesty was—how intoxicating his admitted weakness for her could be. She felt much the same with one significant difference. Her body didn't war with itself to be satisfied little by little; it wanted to experience him all at once.

The space between their bodies trapped his scent—warm and earthy, with traces of spicy soap. It was Gunnar's scent, his essence, and it made her light-headed. Fiona ran her fingers over his chest, feeling the obscured outlines of the muscles beneath his shirt and tunic, frustrated by the silk barriers. She wanted nothing between them. She reached up to unclasp her cloak, dropping it to the table behind her. Her fingers raced nimbly through the side laces of her gown as she used one foot, then the other, to remove her shoes and stockings.

Gunnar's eyes feverishly followed her every move as his own cloak joined hers on the table. He pulled his tunic and shirt over his head, dropping them carelessly to the floor. At the sight of his bare chest, Fiona's fingers wavered.

She gazed in wonder at the tattoos standing out in sharp relief against the smooth contours of his skin—the sculpted magnificence of his arms. Her gown and kirtle felt truly suffocating now. She needed to be free of them.

After unclasping her gown, she unlaced the front upper laces of her kirtle. Gunnar groaned as she shrugged one shoulder free, then the other, and shimmied the gown and kirtle together down her body. In a bold move, she reached beneath her shift and untied her underdrawers, letting them fall around her ankles. She stepped out of them, standing before him in only her thin shift.

Gunnar stared momentarily dumb-struck at the small pool of her silk underdrawers on the floor before sucking in a deep, steadying breath. His eyes never left hers as he kicked off his boots and untied his trousers, ripping them down his legs. When his manhood sprang free, Fiona knew she gaped, but couldn't help herself; it was far larger than she remembered. Before she'd recovered, he dropped to his knees in front of her and lifted her shift, bunching it at her hips.

Fiona reached to pull him up, but he pushed her hands away. "I have imagined the taste of your sweet thighs and cunny for far too long to put off the experience another moment."

"But..." Her protest was cut short as his fingers spread her slightly, his tongue masterfully discovering its goal. Fiona's legs wobbled. She gripped the edge of the table behind her. She was so sensitive there, far more sensitive than she remembered. Waves of ecstasy were already building.

"Gunnar, please," she gasped. "I want us to share this first release together—with you inside me."

He stood in one sinuous, fluid move, pulling her shift up over her head and dropping it to the table. His rough hands gripped below her buttocks, lifting her effortlessly. Fiona wrapped her arms around his neck, and when he flexed his wrists, indicating he wanted her legs around his waist, she complied, very aware that the new position opened her fully.

He kissed her—a deep kiss. As his tongue explored her mouth, his arms relaxed—slowly sliding her body down his. He paused when the blunt tip of his thick shaft pressed against her soft open cleft. Then with a ragged breath, he lowered her onto his full length.

Fiona moaned into his mouth as he filled her. He gave her only a brief moment to adjust to him before he began moving inside. Suspended as she was, every single sensation she experienced was him. No clothing, no blankets, no feel of a bed beneath her. Only Gunnar, inside and out. The hard planes of his chest rubbing against her breasts. The muscles of his flanks and back contracting beneath her thighs and calves with every thrust. His calloused hands supporting but also spreading her buttocks to allow him to penetrate even deeper.

The climax he'd so quickly initiated was reached in an instant. Her fingers dug into the back of his neck as she pulled herself even tighter against him, her insides contracting in pulsing shattering waves. He groaned and uttered her name as he buried himself with one deep final thrust.

Fiona slumped, pressing her forehead to his heaving chest, her arms now loosely looped behind his neck. He remained with feet spread and back arched for balance while they recovered from the brief, intense coupling. When his erection began to soften, he lifted her slightly to allow it to fall away, then stepped forward and lowered her onto his cloak on the table.

"Remain here and do not move," he whispered into her hair before stumbling to the bed rack and shaking out the furs. He returned to her, picked her up without a word, and carried her to them, placing her gently in the middle. After he lay down next to her, he slipped an arm under her head and pulled her close. Neither spoke.

"Apologies, for my haste," he finally murmured. "That is not at all how I imagined it would go, and I must admit I have imagined it many, many times. At times, the ache made it difficult to even walk."

"You did not lay with another?"

"I swore to you I would not, and if you had any doubts, my lack of control just now should be proof enough."

Fiona smiled. With her head on his shoulder, her fingers toyed lazy patterns on the dark gold and bronze hairs of his rippled stomach. "Should I call you Colin now?" she asked and felt him stiffen.

"Nay, you should not."

"You don't like it?"

"It's a woman's name."

"Nay, Colin is a strong Irishman's name."

"It sounds like your word for a young maiden."

Fiona giggled. "That's a colleen."

"Colleen—Colin. They sound nearly the same to me. As if someone had a child whose cock was so tiny they thought the babe to be a girl. Only later, when they realized it to be a boy, did they alter the name slightly."

Fiona stifled her laughter and pressed her rare advantage. "Perhaps I will call you my Colleen as a term of endearment. I think I might like it."

"And perhaps I will turn you over my knee and paddle your bare backside. I *know* I would like that."

"You could try...if you weren't a colleen," Fiona snorted before breaking into peals of laughter.

"Is that so?" He rolled on top of her and quickly held her pinned. She made no attempt to resist; she was laughing so hard now that tears slipped from the corners of her eyes. Frustrated by her clear lack of respect for his threat, he rolled them both over, pivoting his body to sit upright with her draped across his lap, her bare bottom pointing towards the roof.

Even with his intent obvious, she still made no move to escape, her mirth escalating to hiccups and hoarse heaves. He caressed one firm creamy cheek with his full palm, marveling at her smooth skin. He gave it a light swat before flipping her over, and pulling her up to sit cradled in his lap. "Your backside is safe. You know I could never take a hand to you, though I do not at all see what you find so amusing."

"'Tis just the thought," Fiona gasped as her laughter finally subsided. "...that you, of all men, would worry about being mistaken for a woman. Oh, Gunnar, I've not laughed like that since you left. I feel so...I cannot describe it. It's hard to believe that I'm the same person in the same life as yesterday. I feel utterly different—like every care has been lifted from my shoulders."

"And I the same. Like all is right in the world now that we are together."

"I cannot wait until we are married. Then we can...."

"Married? Now it is you who presume too much, my lady," Gunnar said with mock seriousness, watching her eyes fly open as she processed the insinuation behind his words. He tightened his arm around her, catching one of her hands in time, but was too slow for the other. She slapped his belly just beneath his ribcage. He grunted, trying not to laugh, and continued. "Surely you must understand that I'm a lord now, and as such, I have many options for a wife that will need to be explored."

"Is that so? Options like the Widow Evlin, I suppose?" Her eyes narrowed as she squirmed to free her other hand from his grasp. "How is it that you come to know her before even getting word to me that you had returned?"

"Ah, the Widow Evlin," he murmured. "With her family's lands and her late husbands' estates, she begs careful consideration."

"I would not be at all surprised if she hasn't, in fact, actually begged for your *careful consideration*—though you would hardly be her first."

"As I was your first," he murmured.

"Be mindful, Northman, I could still very well be your last."

Gunnar laughed out loud and kissed her hair. " Fiona, you will most definitely be my last."

He drew her back down onto the furs and brought one of her hands to his lips, kissing each of her fingertips. He paused to study her short, jagged fingernails.

"The last months have been trying," she answered his unasked question. "'Tis strange though; one of the most bothersome things were the words of a seer."

"You have a seer?"

"Aye, there's an ancient peasant woman who has the gift. She told me I would marry a powerful Irish lord. And before the year was out. I could see no happy way her words could be true."

Gunnar chuckled. "Then she must be a seer of great power. Not only am I an Irish lord, I can guarantee I'll not wait until the new year to call you wife."

"She also said our children will shape the future of these lands."

"Our children?" Fiona could tell by his tone the words had pleased him.

"You know, my father was quite impressed by you last night, kept talking about how fascinating your story was."

"I think he would find me far less fascinating if he could see me now," he said, nuzzling her neck.

Fiona giggled. "Aye, surely so, but he'll be happy to hear I encountered you on my ride today and invited you to sup with us tonight. He always wished for Lord Nevyn to have an heir for me to marry."

"And what of your betrothal?"

"'Twill not be a problem. He was never happy with the match, and in the carriage last night, he actually mentioned betrothals can be broken. We'll get no resistance from him." She paused. "You know, we must speak of Artan."

"There is naught to speak of. You need not concern yourself with it any longer."

Fiona bristled. "And if I were a Northwoman?"

He tipped his head to consider it. "Honestly, it could go either way. Normally it would fall upon the man, but in the case of a shieldmaiden, they might agree for it to be her. You are many things, Fiona, but you are no shieldmaiden. While I accept your strengths, you must also accept mine. Disposing of men is something I excel at."

"The killing, aye, but you're a lord now. There must be no stain on your title. I could..."

"No."

"No?" She pulled away from him and sat up. "First, you do not even hear what I have to say, and second, you think it your place to tell me no—as if I require your permission?"

"Apologies. I have no desire to quarrel with you, and it was not my intent to offend; it's just that I'm accustomed to making decisions without consultation." He held up his hand before she could protest that, too. "I know—and accept, that changes now. Though that goes for both of us," he warned, raising his eyebrows. "Since I'm responsible for bringing Artan into our lives, I should be the one to remedy it. And truthfully, I assumed you'd be relieved to be free of the responsibility."

"You would kill him?"

"Of course. Do you not wish him dead?"

"Aye, I do." She nodded. "He's a cruel, evil person, and no man deserves it more, but you cannot. It would raise too much suspicion that you arrive, he is killed, and then we are married."

"Then it must happen quickly. Now, while I've supposedly never met him and before you and I are seen together."

"'Tis too late. I met with his mother yesterday and set the final part of my plan in motion."

Gunnar took a deep breath. "Let us start over. Tell me everything of your plan, secret no detail. Then we shall decide Artan's fate together, and neither of us will act without the other's consent. Agreed?"

"Agreed."

"Good. Now lie back down while you tell it. I would have your skin against mine every possible moment."

Fiona allowed him to pull her down to the furs. With her back against his chest and his strong arms around her waist, she told him everything. Of acquiring the MacTavish seal and the engraved box. Of the correspondences with Tibbot where she'd pretended to be Artan. Of the arrangements within those letters to have his eldest brother kidnapped, maimed, and sent far away as a slave—his identity never specified, only referred to by their mother's pet name for him.

She confided her constant fear that, despite specifying in one of *Artan's* earliest letters that she was the only one he trusted to carry the messages between them, something would come up, and Tibbot would send correspondence directly to Artan, thereby exposing her.

"I realized early on that the only way to avoid his family's vengeance was if they were involved. After months of laying the groundwork, I began the final step yesterday. I didn't know if or when you'd return, and I was out of time."

"Know that I would give anything to be able to remove all thoughts of this from your memory," Gunnar whispered. "Now tell me of the last part."

Fiona explained how his mother had insisted on meeting Tibbot after she'd revealed the single damning letter. How Tibbot had corroborated everything by producing other letters from *Artan*. Letters with specific details of the family's secret favorite torture methods. Faced with the mountain of evidence and enraged at the threat to her beloved son, how she'd assumed Duvessa would have Artan killed, but shockingly the woman had instead decided to substitute him in the scheme.

Through it all, Gunnar said nothing. His breathing remained slow and steady in her hair, his chest rising and falling solidly against her back.

"After hearing those tortures, you must think me a cruel and terrible person," she said quietly when she was finished.

"No, I only wondered where you would've heard of such things— removing his tongue and crushing his hands? Have you seen such things done to a man before?"

"Nay, they were described to me by Artan himself. They were his threats against my father."

Gunnar grit his teeth, fighting back a fresh wave of rage.

"Your thoughts?" she asked.

"You took a great many risks with many opportunities for the plan to fail if someone's response had not been as you expected."

"I know."

"I'm not being critical. This is all my fault, and I regret more deeply than you can possibly imagine what you've endured. Thankfully by your wits and fate, it has worked out. That being said, I still see two flaws. The first is his mother's decision to spare his life. It's too dangerous. If Artan lives, he will always be a threat to us. As much as it would please me to know that he suffers, only one solution gives us certainty. He must die."

"You said there were two flaws. What is the second?" she asked.

"His mother. Assuming this went according to plan, once it was done, you'd remain a threat to her. You know too much, and she may very well intend for you to meet a similar end one day."

"Are you suggesting we kill her as well?"

He shrugged. "If she is to live, we'll need a plan that directs her suspicion elsewhere. Which means, before she sends word to you to break the betrothal, we must find a way to end Artan—some way that does not involve you at all."

"But he rarely leaves his estate and 'tis well fortified."

"You said when he met you on the road, he had an engagement that would take him away for a few days. Did he give you any clue as to where he might be going?"

"I'm assuming to gamble. He was in high spirits and mentioned putting the last of our betrothal gifts to good use."

"Did he mention Balbriggan?"

"Nay." Fiona shook her head. "All he said was his friends had agreed to leave Dublin and meet with him for a few days. Why?"

"It will be Balbriggan. It's midway between Dublin and Drogheda, and where I gambled with him before."

"How can you be certain? It could be anywhere."

"Because he's comfortable there. Men of low self-worth oft surround themselves with people of lower station to bolster their ego. To his family and peers, Artan is a disappointment and a disgrace, but at the tavern in Balbriggan, he's a god. He will return there. I can take a few men and intercept him as thieves on his way home."

"And his footmen and driver? I would not have more innocent men killed."

"We can spare his men, bind them, and leave them to be discovered."

"I fear that would only postpone their deaths. His mother will have them killed if Artan dies, and they do not give their lives to stop it." She paused as a new thought came to her. "But what if Artan were not killed there? What if, while his men are bound and blindfolded, they were to overhear that you weren't thieves, but men sent to capture him by a lord to whom Artan owes a great debt?"

Gunnar nodded as he continued with her plan. "...with the intent to demand ransom from his family to cover what he owes. If we ensure they hear Artan's voice as he is taken away, they will know him to be alive which will spare them from his mother's wrath. Then we'll kill him somewhere else and dispose of his body," he added, matter-of-factly.

"There's still one problem." Fiona frowned. "No one will believe he owed a debt to a Northman and even with your new mastery of the language, your accent is unmistakable. We would need Irishmen to do it, and that puts us back to involving outsiders."

"Not Irishmen," Gunnar corrected. "Artan's men need only hear one Irish voice—one who appears to be giving commands. I have such an Irishman, and I already have men in Balbriggan. Men who are loyal to their teeth and will relish the task." He frowned. "But if Artan is missing and not known to be dead, will you be bound to wait for him? I would have no delay in our marriage."

"Nay, once the word of gambling and bad debts becomes known, the scandal will be enough to justify breaking the betrothal. In fact, folk would be more surprised if I did not."

"And this plan will satisfy you?" Gunnar asked.

"Aye, but I have one condition."

"You always do."

"I wish to be there...when you do it."

Gunnar shook his head. "Fiona, it is one thing to calmly speak of Artan's death as if it were a puzzle to be solved, but another thing entirely to witness it."

"I've seen you kill men before."

"This will be different. He will not be attacking us."

"He is evil, Gunnar, and trust me, I have endured his attacks for many months now. Not physical perhaps, but attacks all the same. If ever there was a man who deserved to die, 'tis Artan MacTavish."

"Of course I don't disagree, but I would still not have you witness it."

"Please do not deny me this."

Gunnar took a deep breath. "You know I can deny you nothing, but it is only under strong protest that I agree." He kissed her. "It will require you slipping away in the night. Though I suppose that's not a problem for you."

"It used not to be, but Cahan has the stables guarded now."

"Then, on the chosen night, I'll meet you outside your gates with an extra horse." They lay side by side, each silently reviewing the plan in their minds. Gunnar propped himself up on one elbow with a groan and kissed her bare shoulder. "I intended to spend the entire day here with you in the furs, but I must go now—to send a scout to Balbriggan to verify Artan's presence there and ready the men. I will still attend supper at your house tonight and bring word to you then of what I discover."

"But we have time; Artan said he planned to be away for several days."

"As agonizing as it is for me to leave you, especially after my rushed performance," he added with a rueful smile, "we cannot risk missing this opportunity. If his gambling goes badly, he may very well run through your betrothal gifts sooner than expected."

Chapter 46

S eeing Gunnar standing in her entry, handing off his cloak, Fiona
could scarce control herself. He was so tall and strong and virile, and
so absolutely handsome. Her mind skipped back to how they'd spent
the morning. How he'd held her suspended while... Her face flushed beet red
at the wickedness of her thoughts. She looked down, not looking up again
until she heard her father greeting him.

"Lord Colin, welcome. How fortuitous that Fiona should run into you
this morning."

Gunnar smiled—the deepness of his dimples the only indication of how
hard he fought to keep from grinning as he bowed slightly to her. "Lady
Fiona," he said. "I could not agree more. How fortuitous indeed. If it were not
considered too bold, may I say you look very lovely."

"Gratitude, my lord." She dipped her head, her cheeks still flaming. "You
are too kind."

"My lady, I must apologize in advance. Should I say something out of
turn, please accept now that it is not my intention to offend. It is oft difficult
for me to know what is appropriate."

"Well said," her father interjected. "A man can never fully know a woman's mind."

"Knowing my upbringing, as you do, I mean that for you as well."

"We do not stand on such presumption in this household, I assure you. Please do not be troubled over it. May I offer you a drink before supper? Wine, ale, mead, poteen?"

"Gratitude, wine would be much appreciated."

"Fiona, would you care to join us?" he paused and looked to Gunnar. "Unless you'd prefer not to drink with a woman? Now it's my turn to apologize; my daughter's freedoms are not always well-received."

"How could anyone ever refuse the opportunity to be in the presence of such an enchanting beauty." Gunnar smiled at her.

Patrick braced himself for the tongue-lashing the poor man was about to receive, wishing he'd had the opportunity to warn him of Fiona's temper. When the obvious flirtation was met only with flushed silence, it took him a moment to recover. "Some men do not care for my daughter's strong will and sharp mind," he finally managed to say.

"I was raised among strong women. Northmen revere them. They say only a weak man is intimidated by a strong woman. And I do not consider myself a weak man."

Her father laughed. "Nay—with what you've survived, I think few would ever consider you as such."

"You must have a great many questions for me," Gunnar offered after they'd been seated for supper.

"In truth, I do, but I didn't wish to remind you of a perhaps difficult and unpleasant past."

"'Tis the only past I know, and to me it was neither difficult nor unpleasant. The man I knew as my father was well-respected, and I was well-treated."

"Do you have other family?"

"Aye, a sister—half-sister," he corrected. Eamon had drilled in him that the key to success was to use as many truths as possible, but twist the details to fit.

"Will she join you here?"

"Nay. She is happily married."

"To a Northman?" Her father was unable to hide his shock.

"Papa," Fiona chided him.

Gunnar answered with a smile. "To a Dane actually. She didn't understand my desire to come here and does not share it. Many Vikings feel—and apologies for this, a certain disdain for the Irish and English, which is why they raid here at will."

"Yet you do not share it—that disdain?"

"I did once," he admitted. "But something has drawn me here with such a powerful force, it's changed my way of thinking entirely." He directed his last comment to Fiona, who looked away and blushed again.

"How fascinating," her father said between bites, sometimes forgetting his meal entirely. "Irish noble blood flows in Daneland through your sister. Does she have children?"

"Aye."

"How fascinating," her father repeated.

"Papa, Lord Colin is recently returned from the East. He has seen Constantinople."

"Is it as magnificent as what is written?"

"I do not know what is said in your books, but it is a marvel of defensive architecture." Gunnar described the multiple walls, the moat, the chained bay, the Greek fire.

"I've read of these things, but your descriptions are so vivid, 'tis as if I can actually see them myself. Fascinating."

Fiona smiled into her hand linen at his repeated use of the word. She had worried about his reaction to Gunnar's lack of education, but he was truly enthralled by Gunnar's experiences.

"Your command of our language is extraordinary."

"My mother provided me a strong foundation, and my manservant has been quite helpful. He's attempting now to school me on the intricacies of Irish family politics, but I find it to be much like navigating a spider's web."

"My father has a library filled with the ancestral history of many of the clans," Fiona offered. "Perhaps it could be of help."

"Is this true?" Gunnar asked.

"Aye, 'twas a passion I shared with my late wife, and I've kept it up since her passing. She was from a rival clan, the Laigin, and it began as a folly for us to discover how our families originally came to be at odds. She always jested that it was likely something as simple as a horse deal gone awry. When your time permits, feel free to avail yourself of it."

"Gratitude," Gunnar said sincerely.

"Hopefully it won't only add to your confusion. In the quest to be named the high king of all Ireland, my countrymen have created shifting alliances and made war on each other for centuries. Blood has fought blood over who will unite the country, only to further divide it in the process."

"That story is not unique to Ireland, I can assure you; I've the seen the same in many lands. But I thought there were already high kings here."

"There are many who claim the title. Ireland has hundreds of kings, and whenever one conquers a neighboring territory, they see fit to call themselves a high king. Until recently we even had a Northman king of Dublin."

"Sihtric." Gunnar nodded.

"Aye. He carved a kingdom out of Mide and Leinster that never existed before. But whenever you hear of a man referred to as a high king, just remember, the Stone of Destiny at Tara hasn't roared in hundreds of years." He winked at Fiona.

"I've heard of this stone, and it seems a very pagan belief for Christian kings."

"You'll find that we Irish are a complex blending of old and new. Many of the pagan holidays and traditions still continue, but with new names given by the church. Take St Brigid's holiday, for example. 'Twas originally celebrated to honor the pagan goddess Brigid, but few know that now." He paused to take a bite.

"I must admit after hearing your story last night and meeting you, it has given me much to ponder. The idea that Northmen could be anything other than ruthless barbarians was previously inconceivable to me. There are too many brutal accounts for them all to be false. But seeing you, a mannered nobleman who was raised among them, made me consider that perhaps our all-consuming fear of them is unwarranted."

"Nay, you are correct to fear them," Gunnar disagreed. Fiona looked at him sharply. "I'll be devoting much of my resources to defenses—repairing the old and building new."

"But we are far from the coast here; we've never been attacked."

"'Tis only a matter of time."

"You know of their plans?"

"Nay, but I've known men like Sihtric. He was a king here. He will raise another army, another fleet, and he will return. And if not him, then his sons. It may be years, but he or his blood will come to reclaim what was his."

"They'll not find Dublin such an easy target now. Many reinforcements have been built since his ousting."

"Which is all the more reason for us to be concerned here. Most of those reinforcements will have been built to thwart an attack by sea. Sihtric will know that and will likely assemble his forces somewhere else nearby—at least a large portion of them. While the city is engaged in repelling a few ships that he'll likely send as decoys, he'll move across the land to take it from the inland side. 'Tis simple strategy." Gunnar shrugged at their shocked expressions

"Will being raised as one of them offer you any protection?"

"To some, my past will carry some influence, but in the end, I will stand against them as an Irish lord, and that is what they will see."

"You do not seem to fear the prospect."

"Fear serves no purpose, and 'tis one of their most valuable weapons. The more fear they can instill in their enemies, the less they actually have to fight. One can only prepare as best as possible. After that, 'tis in the hands of the gods—of God." He corrected himself.

"You spoke of defenses; do you truly think you can defeat them?"

"We do not need to defeat them, just appear to be too costly for them to take. Dublin will be the prize, and they'll choose the easiest path to get there—the path that provides the greatest reward in coin and supplies but costs the fewest number of men. I intend to ensure that path is not here. I know how they fight. I know the weapons and tactics they use, and with that information, will prepare accordingly."

"Then once opportunity avails, if you are willing, I wish for you to advise me on how to do the same on my lands. Earlier this year, I was reminded that threat may not only come in the form of Northmen."

"It would be my pleasure."

"Papa, if we may pause briefly from all the talk of war, Lord Colin has a merchant arriving at Tir na Laoch later this week and has requested a lady's eye to choose furnishings. With your permission, I have offered my assistance. It may require I travel there several days in a row."

"My housekeeper will be in attendance, of course," Gunnar interjected.

"Aye, of course," her father agreed, eager to return to the conversation, but Gunnar pushed back his chair.

"Apologies. With that reminder of all the work that awaits me tomorrow, I must take my leave. Gratitude for the delicious meal and agreeable conversation. 'Twas a pleasant change from dining alone and very well received."

"Perhaps you'd care to join us again tomorrow?" her father offered.

"If it's not an imposition?"

"Absolutely not."

"Gratitude."

They stood. As Gunnar stepped around her to follow her father to the entry, he leaned in and whispered. "Meet me outside your gates as soon as you can get away."

Tonight? So soon? She had many questions, but he'd already moved away to take his cloak. He'd been so calm during the meal, she'd assumed he had no news.

"Such an intriguing man," her father commented after the door closed behind him.

"Aye, Papa." Fiona covered a fake yawn with her hand. "'Tis been a very full few days, and I am to bed."

Fiona slipped through the gate and looked both ways on the road, empty in the moonlight. Just when she thought she must have misunderstood, Gunnar appeared coming down the road at a long trot, leading a second horse.

"Apologies for making you wait. I tied the second horse quite far away to ensure it did not alert your people if it made a ruckus." He slid from his horse, pulled her into a brief embrace, and kissed her. "Are you sure you must come? I already regret agreeing. You haven't slept, and I would not have you witness..."

"I am sure."

He handed her a set of reins. "Then we must hurry. Artan has been at the Red Dragon since you saw him, and little remains of your betrothal gifts. My men already await him on the road between Balbriggan and Drogheda."

———————————————

Fiona was trailing Gunnar's horse at a hand gallop when she heard a soft whistle. Gunnar immediately drew in rein as a man stepped from the bushes. "Any sign of him?" Gunnar asked.

"Nothing yet, but we felled a tree across the road ahead. He'll not pass."

"Good." Gunnar dismounted and turned to Fiona. "Come, we'll find a place to wait."

After tying the horses out of sight, Gunnar took her hand and led her to the base of a large oak tree, not far from where his men had blocked the road. He cleared the brush away from the base with his foot, then sat with his back against the trunk and patted the ground in front of him. Fiona sat between his bent legs and leaned back against his chest. He pulled his knees in snug against her sides and wrapped his arms around her shoulders.

"Try to get some rest," he whispered in her ear.

Rest? The thought of what was about to happen, what they were about to do—of all the ways it could go wrong. She took a deep breath and tried not to think about it. She focused on the warm solid cocoon his body created and the quiet voices of the other men positioned in various places around them—their murmurs and occasional soft laughter. Everyone was so calm.

When they heard the rumble of hooves and carriage wheels in the distance, then the low whistle from the lookout, Gunnar stood and pulled her to her feet, putting his finger to his lips. Fiona nodded and clenched her fists at her sides, trying to settle her racing heart. The two of them were to remain here out of sight, for now, to ensure they weren't seen—if things didn't go according to plan.

From their position, she couldn't actually see the road for the underbrush, but she didn't need to; she could imagine everything vividly by what she could hear—the driver shouting to the horses when he first saw the tree blocking the road—the surprised yells from the footmen as men converged on them from both sides—the scraping of boots and grunts of struggle as Gunnar's men dragged them from the back platform—the carriage door slamming against the side as it was ripped open. Finally, Artan's voice, drunken and drowsy at first, then outraged.

"What is the meaning of this?! Do you know who I am?! I am Lord Artan MacTavish! I will have your heads!" Then a yelp as he, too, was restrained, followed by muffled ranting when a cloth sack was pulled over his head.

"Gratitude for announcing yourself, Lord Artan. I would hate to have returned to my lordship with the wrong man." An Irishman's voice, she knew to be Gunnar's man, Eamon, rang out. "Though you are exactly where he said you'd be, skulking off from another gambling binge. He warned you there'd be consequences if you did not settle your debts with him, and his patience has reached its limit. He will demand what you owe from your family in exchange for your safe return. I hear it's quite a tidy sum."

After muffled squeals of rage and denial from Artan, Eamon spoke again, quieter but still very clear. "Bind him securely, then get him on a horse. And make haste; we're expected to have him back in Galway by week's end."

After the hoofbeats and Artan's muffled rants faded away, Gunnar and Fiona quietly returned to their own horses and remounted. They rode parallel to the road until they were out of earshot of Artan's men, then returned to it and picked up a gallop. Eamon was waiting for them alone in the road a few miles away. After a brief nod, he led them to a path into the forest.

When they came upon the other tied horses, Fiona knew they were quite close to the sea; she could smell the tangy salt in the night air. They dismounted, tied their own mounts, and followed Eamon on foot to the edge of a torch-lit glen. Artan lay on his side in the center, quiet and limp, arms tied behind his back, sack still on his head. Fiona wondered if he was dead.

A Northman stepped forward from the opposite side of the glen. One side of his face was twisted and puckered with terrible burn scars, ghoulish in the torchlight. He looked to Gunnar, who nodded, then pulled the sack from

Artan's head. Artan didn't move. The Northman nudged him with his boot, rolling him onto his back. Fiona wondered again if he was dead, and now that the fateful moment was here, part of her hoped that he was. The man moved around Artan's body, prodding him several more times with no response.

When the Northman stopped with his back to them, Fiona could tell he was doing something with his hands in front of his body but couldn't see what it was. Only when a stream of urine began to soak Artan's face and neck, did she realize he'd been undoing his trousers. She muffled a gag and turned to Gunnar to see if he would stop it, but he looked on, his face a hard mask. Fiona bit her tongue. He had warned her, had wanted to spare her eyes, had implored her multiple times not to come, but she'd insisted. She would see this through.

Artan sputtered awake. The Northman adjusted his trousers with a laugh. "Ah, his lordship is awake and none too soon, for I was nearly out."

"You're a dead man!" Artan screeched as he thrashed to get his legs under him. He rose to his knees. Another Northman stepped up from behind him and held down on his shoulder, preventing him from standing.

"For fuck's sake, Olag, did you have to soak him?" the second Northman grumbled. "There's no place to touch him now without touching your piss."

"I owe no one in Galway!" Artan shouted. "I owe no one anywhere! No one has extended me credit. No one would! 'Tis a mistake! I've been wrongfully detained. If you do not release me at once, I shall see that each of you receives a death so slow and painful..."

"That will be quite a feat to manage from the grave," Gunnar challenged.

Artan swiveled his head toward the sound of Gunnar's voice, preparing to launch another verbal attack. His mouth fell open in stricken silence as Gunnar stepped into the ring of torchlight. "You?" he finally croaked.

"Not just me." Gunnar turned as Fiona joined him from the shadows.

"Of course—you and your whore." The last of the word had barely left his lips when Gunnar sprang forward and kicked his mouth closed. Artan's neck snapped back and his teeth clacked together, at least one of them flying from his mouth—a sparkling flash of white in a fountain of red spray.

It was all Gunnar could do not to set upon the man and beat him to a bloody pulp. He longed to feel Artan's flesh lose all texture as it became spongy and soft; to feel his smaller bones breaking while he hammered him with his fists; to pound him in a senseless frenzy until the last flicker of life faded from his despotic eyes. But he didn't. Because he knew once he started, there would be no stopping, and he didn't want Fiona to see the rage he was capable of. Summoning every trace of willpower, he stepped back to her and waited for his men to prop Artan back onto his knees.

"What shall we do to him, my lord? Flay him? Break all his bones? Burn him alive?"

"That's up to Fiona. It is she he has wronged."

Silence settled over the glen as all eyes fell upon her. Artan's harsh breathing was the only sound. He glared up at her. "Do you expect me to beg you for mercy? Beg you to spare me?"

"'Twould do no good, Artan," Fiona said softly. "You are not redeemable. For me to spare your life would only be to condemn someone else's— someone innocent. Your time as a plague on this earth is over. I give you only a moment to repent your sins. You should take it."

"You filthy cunt. You..."

"Someone shut him up!" Gunnar roared, drowning out Artan's next words. A rag was quickly stuffed into Artan's mouth, silencing him.

Fiona turned to Gunnar. "Your sword please, Gunnar."

Gunnar cocked his head and pressed his lips together in a firm line at her request before slowly pulling Maid's Dream from its sheath. He moved his grip to the blade, offering her the golden hilt but did not release it. "You have neither the strength nor the technique to remove his head in one strike," he warned. "It would require much hacking, and the blood and his screams will never leave you. If you must do this, go straight through the heart. It will not be the quickest death but less blood."

"You are worried about it being quick?" She summoned a weak smile.

"Not for his sake, my love. And I ask you again, if it will satisfy you to see him dead, then let me do it." He paused, but she did not respond. "If it must be by your own hand, then straight through the center of his chest, here." He placed a hand on his own chest.

Fiona took the sword and turned to face Artan. His eyes were glazed with madness, his lips twitching as he continued to shout into the rag. Bloody foam spittle seeped around the cloth and ran down his chin, soaking the front of his tunic. Fiona placed her second hand on the hilt. The unusual curved sword felt heavy and awkward in her grasp, even with both hands. She looked to the target spot on Artan's chest.

Should she just run forward, holding it outstretched in front of her? How much force would it take? What if it only pierced partway and she could not finish it? Or what if he moved? Of course he would move! Gunnar was right; she was no shieldmaiden. And did it matter that she do it? If Artan was dead and they were safe, did it matter if it came by her hand? Gunnar wanted so desperately to be the one to kill him—why not let him? She no longer had to bear this or any other burden alone.

She felt Gunnar's warmth against her back. His strong arms slid around her sides, and his hands covered hers on the hilt. "Please. Allow me," he whispered in her ear. She nodded. He gently peeled her fingers free and took the sword into his right hand.

Without another word, he stepped around her. His left hand joined the right on the hilt as he pivoted his body in a complete revolution, building speed and rotational power while keeping the sword close. At the last second, he extended his arms, transferring the centrifugal force of the spin along with the full strength of his body to the length of the blade. The razor edge flashed with righteous vengeance in the torchlight.

There was a moist thwack, then a dull quiet thunk as Artan's head fell to the ground, much like the sound of a large apple falling from a tree. It was difficult for Fiona to believe that such a simple sound could mark the end of such evil. Far more appropriate would have been to hear trumpets heralding the deed from the very heavens. Artan's head rolled once, then stopped, facing away. The blade was so sharp it had even severed his greasy black hair just above the tie, and the clump lay on the ground next to it.

Much to Fiona's horror, Artan's headless body slumped but remained upright, blood gently pulsing from the stub of his neck. Gunnar kicked the corpse's shoulder, and it fell backwards. He turned and pulled her into an embrace with one arm. "It is done. Are you alright?"

She looked up at him and nodded. "'Twas a shock, but I do not regret coming. I needed to see it."

Gunnar nodded. "I'll take you home now." He stepped forward and wiped the blood from Maid's Dream onto Artan's cloak before returning it to its sheath, then took her by the hand and led her back to the horses. He mounted his horse, then pulled her up sideways in front of him with her shoulder against his chest. After adjusting the sides of his cloak to make sure they covered her, he wrapped his arms around her, linking his hands together with the reins over the horse's withers in front of them.

"What will they do with him?" Fiona asked as Gunnar nudged the horse forward.

"They'll bury the body deep. His head they will throw into the sea."

"And his carriage and men?"

"They are unharmed. They will likely spend a long night on the side of the road, but someone will discover and free them in the morning."

Safely enveloped in Gunnar's arms with the steady rocking motion of the horse beneath her, Fiona felt suddenly exhausted. The emotional highs and lows of the past days, combined with the lack of sleep, seemed to catch up with her all at once. She nestled her cheek against his chest. When he rested his chin on top of her head to keep it from lolling, Fiona closed her eyes.

Chapter 47

"Oh, Fiona," Evlin wailed before Fiona had even fully stepped into her father's library.

"Evlin, what's wrong?"

Evlin stepped closer. "My deepest apologies to be the one to deliver such terrible tidings." She covered her mouth briefly with one hand as if she couldn't speak, but Fiona could see the glint in her eye.

"Tidings?"

"I was on my way to my youngest son's estate when we came upon the most horrible sight on the road to Drogheda. 'Twas Artan's carriage and men—abandoned."

"And Artan?" Fiona asked.

"Taken."

"Taken? Taken where?"

"He's been abducted. His men overheard he was being taken to Galway...." She paused for dramatic effect. "To be held for ransom until his gambling debts are paid by his family. Oh, Fiona, your betrothed—a man who cannot pay his gambling debts—the shame of it—you must be devastated. Once his family pays the ransom, whatever will you do? You can't possibly still consider marrying him. Though at your age..."

"Fiona will not be marrying Artan," her father interrupted. "I'll be sending immediate word to his family. Out of respect for their difficult situation, I'll not demand restitution for breach of promise, that is our due, but I shall make it clear that Artan is to have no further contact once he is recovered."

"His family! We must tell them of his abduction," Fiona exclaimed.

"'Tis already done," Evlin soothed. "I sent word with Artan's men. They will have long reached Dublin by now; I had to stop briefly to compose the other letters."

"Other letters?" Fiona asked.

"Aye, letters to all the prominent families, informing them of the tragedy—to enlist their aid in locating Artan while the trail is still fresh, of course. But I had to come to tell you personally. Such terrible news should not be received by written word."

Evlin was so transparent. She had to personally deliver the news to fully enjoy the havoc her missive would cause. Fiona had no intention of disappointing her.

"I cannot believe this to be true," Fiona stammered, trying hard to summon tears, but finding it impossible in her giddiness. Of all the people to have discovered Artan's carriage, none could be more perfect than Evlin. She was respected and well-known—and she would spread the story of Artan's scandalous abduction like wildfire.

"I assure you it is. I heard his men with my own ears. Such a terrible thing. There were always rumors about Artan, so I suppose it shouldn't come as a complete surprise, though I'm sure 'tis small consolation for you." Evlin turned to her father. "I shall be traveling to the MacTavish's next to ensure that Artan's men and my message were, in fact, received. I'd be happy to deliver that letter for you, my lord—should you wish to send word of breaking the betrothal now?"

"If you don't mind waiting for me to compose it."

"Not at all," Evlin purred.

Fiona sank into a chair, pretending to be woozy. "Apologies, Evlin. This news is most distressing."

"'Tis understandable, Fiona. Perhaps you should retire to your bed. I shall take my leave as soon as your father finishes his letter."

Fiona stood and hugged her. "Gratitude for bringing me the news in person. You have no idea how much this means to me." She bit back a sob before fleeing the room.

"I was worried it would be too late when you received word, and you'd not be able to get away." Gunnar's voice was full of question as he met her outside the cottage.

"All is going according to plan. Nay—even better," Fiona said as she slid from Barca's back into his arms. She quickly relayed who had discovered Artan's carriage and her father's decision to immediately terminate the betrothal. "Once Evlin departed, I said I needed to go for a ride to clear my thoughts. 'Tis not unusual for me and raised no suspicion."

"How long do you have?"

"Not long." She smiled a tired smile. "A lord is returning for supper, who does not yet know of our family's scandalous tragedy."

"Come inside. At least rest for a moment."

Fiona nodded and followed him. He turned one of the sturdy chairs around, sat, and drew her down onto his lap.

"Can you believe that of all people, Evlin would discover the scene?" Fiona shook her head. "Her eagerness to spread the gossip will save weeks of waiting for word to spread on its own. Do you know she'd already sent letters to other families before coming to us? It was under the guise of aiding in Artan's rescue, but she was practically salivating at the juiciness of the gossip. She's such a spiteful wretch. Yet I know I must be grateful for it. Her testimony will not be questioned and 'twill prevent his mother from altering the story. She'll be forced to acknowledge it. In fact, I expect an immediate public plea from the MacTavishs to help find their son, though knowing Duvessa, she'll not be looking for him."

"Your understanding and propensity for devious scheming are quite disturbing. Remind me never to cross you. It's so much simpler to fight."

Fiona snorted. "Says the man who evaluates even the most basic of decisions on their strategic significance."

Gunnar chuckled. "Which is why we make such a formidable pair."

Fiona waited in her room while her father received their guest and explained what had transpired. When she joined them later for the meal, no mention was made of it until Gunnar was preparing to leave.

"The merchant has sent word that he will arrive tomorrow before midday," Gunnar said to her. "Under the circumstances, I, of course, hold you to no obligation, but if you remain of a mind to assist, your opinion would still be much appreciated."

"'Twill offer a welcome and much-needed distraction from recent events. I shall arrive mid-morning."

"Gratitude." He nodded, stepping around her to take his cloak. His calloused fingers brushed hers as he pressed a small folded piece of parchment into her hand. She closed her fist and stepped back. Though she wanted desperately to read it, she waited until she was safely alone in her bedchamber. Two words were scrawled in a blocky, almost child-like hand. Fiona reread them several times, cherishing them as if they'd been a beautiful poem, recognizing their significance as likely the first things Gunnar had ever written. *Cottage tomorrow.*

Chapter 48

Fiona could not believe her eyes when she stepped inside. The cottage was transformed. Soft furs and pillows were piled on top of a thick feather tick that now covered the bare bed slats. Multiple candle trays were suspended with chains from the roof timbers, and on the table was a loaf of bread, cheese, a bowl of apples, and a small cask she assumed was wine.

"I thought to make the time we spent here more comfortable. I shall return it to its previous state once we have no further need of it, so as not to raise the suspicions of the shepherd and his wife when they return next spring."

"And Eamon stands guard?"

"Aye. He doesn't mind."

"Would he tell you if he did?"

"Probably not." He grinned.

"What of the merchant?"

"He doesn't arrive until tomorrow. There is nothing to call us away. Now, enough talk. I was far too rushed last time and would remedy that now. " He reached up and unclasped her cloak.

"That's better. I'm far more satisfied with my performance today." He kissed her shoulder. "I believe you to be properly sated this time."

Fiona smiled, her body feeling as if it had the strength of jelly. "You keep referring unfavorably to the last time, but that is your own issue; I do not share it. Surely you know I had no complaints."

"By the gods, may I never give you cause to use the word complaint in the same breath as what I do in the furs. Would you like something to eat? An apple, perhaps? I know how hungry you get," he teased. "And I would keep your strength up—I'm far from done with you."

"An apple sounds good."

As Gunnar stood from the bed, she pulled a wolf pelt over her naked torso. He reached down and tugged it from her breasts, leaving it over her waist. Satisfied with his handiwork, he continued to the table. Fiona took the moment to admire the view of his bare back—his broad shoulders, the long bands of muscle running down either side of his spine. The way they flexed and lengthened with every step. She rarely got to see any of it; he was always facing her, watching her, devouring her with his eyes.

He returned to the bed with an apple and handed it to her. He didn't join her, just stood watching her eat, his lips curved in the slightest hint of a smile. "You look like a goddess lying in a sea of furs. I would fill my mind with every inch of you."

Fiona took another small bite and smiled. She raised her arms over her head and stretched, the action lifting her breasts up toward him. She knew it was a brazen and wanton display, but his reaction made it seem right.

"Remove the fur." He hadn't moved, but his posture had changed from relaxed to something far more intense.

Fiona hesitated, then reached for the edge of the fur covering her waist, feeling entirely wicked and shocked by what she was about to do. His eyes were intent on her hand, his breaths deepening as he watched, and waited. Slowly, she lifted the fur away. But instead of revealing herself to him, she simultaneously crossed one leg over the other, effectively limiting his view. He exhaled long and slow, his eyes returning to hers. He smiled and nodded at her sauciness, then walked to the foot of the bed.

"Spread yourself for me, Fiona. I said I would see every inch." His tone was commanding, but soft and so erotic. His eyes seemed to bore into hers, transfixing her. Fiona flushed. She knew she'd started this, but it was going too far. Her confidence in being naked around him had grown substantially, but not far enough for this.

He sat on the base of the bed and reached for her closest foot. After caressing and rubbing it between his strong hands, he lifted it to his lips and suckled one toe. Shivers raced up her leg. Fiona gasped.

"Open yourself to me, Fiona. I would see all," he repeated, his voice confident and unrushed.

"I cannot."

He suckled another toe. The sensation was so shockingly pleasurable. In all the times they'd been together at the inn, never once had he done this— and never would she have dreamed she'd have wanted him to. He moved his lips to the arch of her foot. His lower teeth scraped gently against the softer skin. Fiona moaned, and he paused. "Do you want me to stop?"

"Nay." She held out her hands to him. "Come to me."

"Not yet. You have not yet given me what I want."

She didn't move, and he smiled. He took her entire big toe in his mouth, sucking it and gently raking his teeth along its length. Fiona dropped the apple and clenched her fists in the furs. The sensation that raced up her leg now was no shiver; it was a pulsing bolt of lightning directly to where her legs joined, pooling there.

"Open yourself for me," he repeated, softly running his thumbnail along the bottom of her foot—a sensation that was both pleasurable and uncomfortably ticklish at the same time.

Fiona couldn't move. *Why did he not just open her legs himself? She would not oppose him nor move once it was done, but for her to do it...*

"Do you wish for me to continue?" He bit the inside of her arch while a finger traced her ankle.

"Aye. Please, Gunnar."

"Then you know what you must do."

Fiona closed her eyes tight and slowly spread her legs apart. The soft slick fur caressed the back of her calves and thighs as they slid over the silky surface. She heard his sharp intake of breath but could not look at him, the heat in her face now matching the heat in other areas.

He released her foot and stood.

Fiona kept her eyes closed, feeling the deliciousness of the furs against her back and the cool air touching her most private of places, imagining what she must look like spread wide open for him.

"By the gods, Fiona, I swear no man has ever beheld such a glorious sight. You should never be embarrassed for me to look upon you so. You're truly the most beautiful woman I've ever seen. Look at me. See the effect you have on me."

Fiona opened her eyes. Gunnar stood at the foot of the bed, one hand resting on the base of his cock, his fingers wrapped loosely around the thick rigid shaft. *A glorious sight indeed.*

He knelt on the bed and crawled up over her body on all fours, like a blond lion stalking its prey. Fiona ran her hands over his sculpted shoulders and upper arms, then down his rippled stomach. She stroked the silken length of his shaft jutting between them. His breath hissed through his teeth.

He attempted to lower himself to her, but she gripped it tighter and began to work her hand from tip to base, pushing and pulling.

Earlier he'd brought her to multiple releases with his teasing and tormenting. Now she was set to return the favor. His cock throbbed in her hand, hot and hard. He bit her neck and growled his need, a primal combination that both demanded and begged for her submission. The sound struck a chord deep within her core. She released him, tipping her pelvis to meet his thrust.

"Woman, I swear you push me to the very limits of my control. Every time with you, I feel the excitement as if it were the first time." He seemed shocked by it. "I have something to show you," he whispered and attempted to sit up, before flopping back with a chuckle. "And as soon as I'm able to stand and walk, I will do so. I believe you have drained me of every bit of strength."

"Perhaps you should have eaten the apple," she teased.

"Perhaps," he agreed with a smile. He took a deep breath and forced himself to his feet with a groan before padding across the room to his clothes, carelessly draped across the back of a chair. He rooted through them, withdrew a small pouch, and returned to her. "It is my people's custom to exchange rings on their wedding day. I had these made for us by a master goldsmith in the East, and have carried them over my heart ever since."

Fiona opened the silk drawstring and tipped the pouch over her open hand. Two gold rings, one large, one small, fell into her palm, sparkling in the candlelight. Twisted in identical braided patterns on the outside, they were flattened smooth on the inside for the wearer's comfort. "Gunnar, these are beautiful."

"The pattern is a continuous chain to signify eternity. Try yours on. I had to guess at the size. If it needs to be altered, I will have it done before the wedding."

She slipped it on her finger to admire it. "'Tis perfect. I shall sorely hate to remove it." She kissed him.

"On that note, I intend to ask your father for your hand tonight. I know it's sudden, likely too sudden, but I shall blame it on my heathen upbringing—which, fortunately for you, will also account for my utter disregard for your current tainted reputation."

Fiona smiled and snuggled close to him. "Who'd have ever thought when we met that I'd be the scandalous one and you the respected lord."

Chapter 49

"Lord Colin, you're early." Fiona's father greeted him.

"Apologies, but I've a matter of great import to discuss with you. In private," Gunnar added before he could call for Fiona.

"Of course. We shall take a drink in my library. Would you care for wine or perhaps poteen, if your matter is serious?"

"Poteen," Gunnar replied. *Definitely poteen.* He couldn't remember the last time he'd felt this way and didn't like it. Being in the position of having to ask another man for something as important as this filled him with nervous anxiety. He knew it was irrational. He and Fiona would marry, regardless of what her father said. Yet still, he found himself desperate for the man to agree. It would make things so much more pleasant if he did.

He downed the poteen, then blurted, "I've come to ask for Fiona's hand in marriage. I apologize if my request is inappropriate or insensitively early with the recent events, but, in truth, I could not believe my good fortune when I heard the news.

"Ever since I met her, I've been unable to keep my mind on anything else," he continued truthfully. "I berated fate that I'd arrived here too late, and she was already betrothed. I will not risk missing such opportunity again, and needed to make my desires known. I'll not quibble over the bride price. I know that is poor bargaining to reveal, but I will accept whatever price you set and consider myself fortunate."

"This is most unexpected," Fiona's father said, downing his own glass with a gasp before filling them both again. "Know that you and I are of like mind regarding the breaking of her previous betrothal. And while I would like for nothing more than to accept your request, I decided long ago that it must be her choice. You do not yet know her well, but her independent streak...well, 'tis more than a streak. I make no excuses for it; I know 'tis my own doing, but I will tell you this. If you can convince Fiona to marry you, you have my blessing. But you must understand she is..."

"She has already agreed."

"What?"

"I've already asked her to be my wife, and she has agreed. I asked her as she was preparing to depart this afternoon."

Her father stared at him, incredulous. "So that explains her dreamy-eyed state when she returned today," he mused out loud.

Gunnar coughed at the actual cause of her dreamy-eyed state. He was still unsuccessfully attempting to scrub the vivid image of her languorously spread on the furs from his mind, when Fiona knocked on the door frame.

"Supper is nearly ready, Papa. Lord Colin," she acknowledged him with a flushed nod. "I didn't know you'd arrived."

"Please come in, Fiona. Lord Colin has just given me surprising news. He has asked me for your hand and says you've agreed to marry him?"

"Aye, Papa." She glanced at Gunnar and smiled.

"Are you sure this is what you want? 'Tis very sudden. Perhaps you should take some time to think it over."

"Nay, Papa. I am sure."

He studied her for a long moment. "Very well." He smiled and shrugged. "I shall not be one to look a gift horse in the mouth. You have my blessing. That is, assuming Lord Colin and I can agree on a bride price. He's revealed he'll not argue terms and will accept whatever price I set. As you are my only daughter, it shall likely be quite high."

"Papa!" Fiona whispered, appalled.

"I jest, my dear," he chuckled. "I set the price at twenty pieces of silver to be paid to the bride on her wedding day."

"Agreed," Gunnar said.

"Which will be when?" Fiona asked.

Her father looked at her curiously. "Do you have haste?" he teased, and Fiona flushed again. "You know a large wedding, while Artan has yet to be returned to his family, would be inappropriate." At Fiona and Gunnar's similar crestfallen expressions, he continued. "I shall think on it and give you my answer soon. Now come, let's eat."

"The restorations are proceeding well?" her father asked.

"Very well." Gunnar nodded as he took a bite. "There is still much work to be done, but the granaries and other food storage buildings are all complete, and one of the men designed a smokehouse for preserving meat that is quite ingenious."

"Have you had success finding tenants?"

"Aye, so many that I find it a challenge to provide enough shelters. What remained of the old tenant cottages weren't worth repairing, so I'm building new temporary shelters inside the stronghold. Later I'll convert those into a garrison."

"How goes it having Irishmen and Northmen together?"

"They're mostly keeping to themselves; I'm not housing them together. For now, I'm having the Northmen construct a large longhouse on the shore of Lough Ramor."

"A Viking longhouse? Will that not be seen as an invitation to raiders?"

"Nay, not invitation. A warning to any who venture up the River Blackwater looking to raid. They'll think twice when they see an established Viking presence and should at least make contact to gauge our strength before attacking. That will allow us opportunity to do the same and provide us advance notice to prepare."

"You said, for now?"

Gunnar glanced to Fiona, who nodded imperceptibly. "I intend to divide up a portion of Tir na Laoch into small parcels and give the tenants land."

"*Give* them?"

Gunnar nodded. "In exchange for their labor and loyalty."

"Northmen as well?"

"Aye—until the Irish are better trained, the Northmen will be invaluable for defense."

"Irish noblemen using Norse or Dane warriors to protect their lands is not unheard of, but they pay them; they don't *give* land to them."

"And that is their mistake. A man who fights for coin may very well switch allegiance if more is offered. Once this land is given, they will be tied to it, and they will fight, not for coin, not for me, but for themselves, their families, and their futures. If I've learned one thing in my years of battle, 'tis that how hard a man fights is determined by what he fights for. Men with land will fight to their deaths.

"And my goal is not to collect only warriors. I will actively seek out skilled men in every trade: weavers, potters, blacksmiths, farmers, carpenters, stonemasons, healers. Eventually, I envision goods and services from Tir na Laoch to be what all others are measured against. We'll be known for the highest quality and will command the highest prices." He paused, curbing his excitement. "I don't have all the details worked out yet, but that is my intent."

"'Tis an admirable goal. And the promise of land should be enough to convince skilled men to join you and start anew."

"The land is one way," Gunnar said and turned to Fiona. "But I'll also have men frequenting the slave traders—both Irish and Viking. You'd be surprised at the caliber of men one can find there. Many are honest men who've been unjustly detained. Returning their freedom should ensure their loyalty."

Her father frowned. "Unfortunately, we know firsthand of such things."

"What a very charitable thing to do," Fiona murmured. "Though 'tis a shame that slavers should profit from your goodwill."

"Aye, my lady. I agree. But the result for the freed man is the same, and I see no viable alternative—unless one was to take up arms and steal them—which would be quite dangerous," he added with a subtle smile.

"Are we not waiting for Eamon?" Fiona asked as Gunnar mounted and turned his horse for the gate. "Even betrothed, 'twould be scandalous for us to return to Tir na Lionmhar unescorted."

"He will join us presently. I have something to show you first."

They rode through the gates of Tir na Laoch and up the small wooded hill to the west. Fiona heard the sounds of construction before she saw the unfinished structure. "A church?"

"Aye. When we extend the walls next year, it will be inside the fortress. It's a wedding gift for you."

"Wedding gift...or some other strategy?" she asked with one eyebrow arched.

"My lady, I'm insulted. How could you possibly construe a church to be a strategy?"

"I'm not sure exactly, but I find it hard to believe you diverted men and resources from defenses and repairs to build a church for any other reason."

Gunnar laughed aloud. "Fiona, you know me too well. Actually, it is both. A church will serve to reassure the Christian tenants and any noblemen who doubt my commitment to your god—especially as word spreads of the longhouse. And since your father does not keep a priest at Tir na Lionmahr, I thought perhaps we could be married here."

"My father has had an uneasy relationship with God since my mother died," she acknowledged. "But with Northmen here, it may be difficult for you to retain a priest."

"I already have one. Eamon found a monk who is still young and idealistic, and quite excited about the opportunity to convert the heathen." He turned his head away, adding under his breath, "'Tis only by chance that his ales are unrivaled."

"You acquired a monk to make ale for you?"

"Did you not hear the part about converting the heathen?" He tried to stifle his grin. "Although, when it comes to ale, *all* men agree that monks produce the finest. Since I'm seeking skilled men in every field, I'd be remiss if I did not consider that. And it was truly, quite by chance, that his wild berry wines might be exceptional, and he may be willing to try his hand at poteen."

"You are truly incorrigible." Fiona was still smiling and shaking her head when a beaming young man in brown robes stepped away from the construction and approached them. His tonsured monk haircut had not been shaved recently, and the top of his head was covered in a layer of dark fuzz.

"My lady," he said as he bowed his head. "I am Tarmon. 'Tis my greatest honor."

His brown eyes were warm and sincere. Fiona sensed an air of calm steadiness about him. "Apologies, Tarmon, but you seem very young to be a priest; are you yet a monk?"

"Nay, my lady. I'm recently ordained into the priesthood, thanks to his lordship's request and generous donation to the church. Come, if you have a moment, I would like to show you what I envision to see if it meets your approval."

Gunnar watched her from the corner of his eye. She'd seemed pleased, but had said not a single word since they rode away.

"Fiona?" he finally asked before they reached Eamon waiting for them just outside the gates.

"Aye?" She seemed almost startled, as if she'd forgotten his presence.

"What is it? Do you not like the church...or the priest? I can have either removed."

"Nay, Gunnar, they are perfect." She pulled Barca to a halt and looked at him, her green eyes, deep, sincere pools. "But I do not wish to wait. I wish to be married now."

"Now? As in this moment?"

"Aye. We have my father's blessing. We have a church and a priest who will marry us, even a witness." She nodded ahead to Eamon. "There is no reason to wait." When Gunnar didn't immediately agree, she added, "My father said only that a *large* wedding would be inappropriate while Artan was still missing. This would hardly be a large wedding."

"You twist his words to suit you. We both understood his intent," he disagreed. "I would not start on bad terms with him if unnecessary. And there's no church, only the beginnings of a church."

"The threshold and altar are complete; they are all that we need. Even if it were finished, we would be married outside under the threshold, then enter as man and wife to receive our blessing. Both can be accomplished now in its current state."

"And it will be binding? You are sure? It cannot be undone?"

"Aye—once 'tis consummated," she added with a grin. "But feel free to verify it with the priest if you don't believe me. Gunnar, as the cautious and reluctant one, this is unexpected. I thought you'd be eager to have me in your bed every night."

He shook his head, pressing his lips together at her blatant manipulation. "You know I want nothing more than to call you wife, but I would not jeopardize anything by acting in haste. And what of your father and Meirna? Will they not be greatly disappointed?"

"I'll make them understand. They know me to be willful and impatient. And I'll convince them 'tis better. Rather than having a small subdued ceremony now, they can plan for a great celebration in the spring when a more appropriate amount of time has passed."

"Are you are sure this is what you want?"

"Aye, more than anything." She waited a long moment. When he did not respond, she asked, "Is the decision so difficult for you, Northman?"

"You know I can deny you nothing. I still carry the rings, and my only condition for the wedding was for it to be held on a Friday—Frigg's day—the goddess of marriage and fertility so that she may bless us with many healthy children. He pushed his horse next to hers and kissed her. "Today is, in fact, a Friday."

Chapter 50

Fiona followed the last of her trunks upstairs into the master chambers over Tir na Laoch's great hall. It had been a fortnight since the impromptu wedding, yet every time she entered the room and saw the colossal bed that dominated the space, she flushed. Decadently piled high with silk pillows and soft furs, one's first impression was definitely not that it was for sleeping.

It was even worse for her when servants were present. The thought that everyone knew what they did in that bed every night, and that those acts were now considered proper by marriage, was still difficult for her to reconcile. Though part of that difficulty likely stemmed from the fact that, deep down, she couldn't believe that the church with its pious priests actually knew of the things she and Gunnar shared there—at least not all of them; some of them were surely pagan delights.

"My lady, another cart has arrived from Tir na Lionmhar," Ania's oldest daughter, Vala, called from the doorway, startling her.

"Gratitude, Vala. I thought this was the last. I'll see to it." Fiona pushed the thought of possibly pagan pleasures from her mind before descending the stairs and stepping back outside into the brisk air. At the sight of the sandy-haired young man climbing down from the cart, she stopped mid-stride. "Aiden? Aiden, 'tis really you!?" Fiona flew down the steps and embraced him. "I was just at Tir na Lionmhar yesterday, and no one mentioned your return."

"I'm only just arrived, but you should've known I'd never miss your wedding. So imagine my surprise when I learned that not only was that wedding off, but you'd already married someone else? Before we unload my wedding gift to you, I must ask—are you sure about this one, or should I hold onto it in case you intend to announce an annulment and choose yet another?" he teased. "'Tis quite heavy and difficult to move."

"Aye, I'm sure about this one." She grinned. "But before we speak of anything else, I must first apologize for that night when we freed the slaves. I never meant for you to be punished and sent away. Please forgive me."

"There's nothing to forgive, Fiona. The man I've been apprenticing under is a master craftsman with skills beyond anything I dreamed possible. I have learned...well, wait until you see." He moved to the back of the cart and began to untie the ropes that held the oilcloth cover. "Fortunately, my wedding gift was not husband-specific, for I have many long hours invested in it." He winked at her and pulled back the cloth to reveal an intricately carved trunk trimmed with decorative bronze straps and hinges.

"Aiden, 'tis beautiful." Her fingers trailed over the dark stained wood. "I will cherish it always."

Embarrassed by her praise, he changed the subject. "I still cannot believe you married in secret. I'm so glad not to have been present when Meirna learned of it. Pshew," he whistled and shook his head. "She must have been fit to be tied. She still gets high color in the face to speak of it."

Fiona's brow furrowed. "Aye, I know; she and Papa were both far angrier than I expected."

"'Twill pass—not to worry. Your father mentioned to me several times how happy you are, and Meirna and Haisley are already beginning to speak of the great spring feast." He paused. "It helped that Meirna will still get to see one child she raised, married." He pretended to look up at the sky while waiting for her reaction.

"You are to marry?"

"Aye," he grinned.

"To whom?"

"To the carpenter's daughter. Oh, she's a bonnie lass, Fiona, the bonniest in all of Kilkenny. I still cannot believe she agreed to have me. So you can see again why I've naught but good thoughts to our actions that night."

"When is the wedding?"

"Beltaine."

"We will be sure to attend."

"'Twill be the talk of Kilkenny that two lords and a lady attended the wedding of a carpenter's apprentice, for your father has said the same." He smiled and glanced over her shoulder. His face blanched. "Fiona, get behind me."

Fiona turned and followed his terrified gaze, then rested a hand on his arm. "'Tis alright, Aiden. This is my husband, Lord Colin."

Aiden stood, mouth open and working, but no sound coming out, like a fish. Gunnar held out his hand. "Pleased to make your acquaintance. Fiona has told me much about you."

Aiden shook his hand but only managed a nod.

"Come with me inside," Fiona said gently and took Aiden's hand, pulling him toward the stairs. "We have much to discuss."

"I shall leave you to it." Gunnar brushed her forehead with a kiss. "Though it appears a strong ale or perhaps even poteen might be in order," he whispered into her ear as he moved away.

"Was he able to find his tongue again?" Gunnar asked as they watched Aiden climb back onto the cart and give them a wave as he drove through the gates.

"Aye," Fiona murmured. "Though seeing you did give him quite a terror. It's hard to believe that I, too, once looked at you so." She took a deep contented breath. "What a most wonderful surprise. I have carried such guilt about him being sent away, but he is truly happy for it, and so skilled. Wait until you see his gift."

"If it can wait, I have another surprise for you, several, in fact."

"You do? What are they?"

"You'll see," Gunnar said mysteriously and took her by the hand. "But you must close your eyes."

"Gunnar, really?"

He raised his eyebrows, refusing to move. Fiona looked around the courtyard, trying to discover any evidence of surprises, but saw only normal activities. "Very well," she said with an exaggerated sigh and closed her eyes.

"And don't open them until I say."

"Mmmhmm."

"Your word?"

"Gunnar, you have it," she laughed, exasperated.

"Then take my arm. They are this way."

Fiona could tell from the original direction they'd taken and the rich earthy smells of hay, straw, and manure, they were close to the stables. *Had he bought her a horse? As much as she loved horses, she had Barca and wouldn't need another riding mount for many years. A colt perhaps that she could raise and train?*

"You may open your eyes now."

There was, in fact, a horse being held by a man—nay, two men. She quickly scanned the animal, her nature having always been to look at horses before people. It was a sturdy black gelding with a high neck-set and strong legs—an attractive beast, but obviously a carriage horse. Something familiar flickered in her mind. Before she could pinpoint it, the man holding the horse spoke.

"My lady," he said. There was something in his voice that was even more familiar. Her eyes flew to his face.

"Garrett?" Unable to help herself, Fiona rushed forward and hugged him around his neck. "'Tis you, and you are well!"

"Aye, my lady," he said uncomfortably as she released him and stepped back to a respectable distance. "And Bryen is here, too."

Fiona turned to the second man. "Bryen," she said and nodded, more controlled this time, but her huge smile gave away that she was on the verge of hugging him, too.

"My lady," Bryen nodded, grinning and embarrassed.

"Apologies for my reaction; I feared you were dead," she confessed. "And Orin?"

Garrett looked to Gunnar, who nodded.

"Your fear was well-founded, my lady. Orin no longer walks this life. Artan killed him after plying him with poteen to learn the details of our time with you and his lordship. We'd all agreed not to mention you—to simply say his lordship had traveled alone, but Artan never believed it. When a maid shook Bryen and me awake in the night and told us Orin was dead, we fled."

"My deepest apologies, Garrett," Fiona began.

"'Tis not your fault, my lady. This is all on Artan. Hopefully, the devil has him now," Bryen spat.

"Are you both to take new positions here? You'd be most welcome," Fiona said, then looked to Gunnar. Everything had happened so fast, they'd not yet discussed such things as acquiring or managing staff. He smiled and nodded.

"Aye. I'm to be the new head stableman as soon as I return from fetching my wife." Garrett grinned.

"And I'll be trained with sword and shield," Bryen announced proudly.

"But however did Lord Colin find you? I asked high and low."

"He didn't find us, my lady. We found him," Garrett professed. "When word reached us that Artan had been abducted and was presumed dead—and that a fair-haired lord who'd been captured and raised by the Northmen had returned and married Lady Fiona... Well, we may not be the sharpest, but we didn't fall off the cabbage cart just yesterday. We were a bit apprehensive, mind you, but we decided his lordship had always been fair with us. So here we are."

"Oh, Garrett, I'm so pleased."

Garrett jerked the horse's lead rope up between them when it looked like she might hug him again. "A wedding gift for you."

Fiona looked at the horse again, recognizing the animal now. The horse she'd raced to victory on the beach. The young horse she had fretted over when it could not accept its previous life.

"Garrett, I cannot accept such an expensive gift, and your presence here is truly the best gift of all. You've no idea how I have worried after you."

"My lady, 'twill be a great relief for me to see him well-cared for. And in truth, the beast is not worth much. A carriage horse that believes himself to be a racehorse is of little value. Artan caught sight of his antics on a particularly bad day and insisted I dispose of him immediately, no matter the price. I took him to a local horse market with the full intention of doing so, but the only offers I received were low and from harsh men with heavy hands. They'd have starved him into submission and worked him to death; I couldn't do that to the jughead." He straightened the horse's forelock affectionately. "I'm not sure he'll ever work in harness again, but with time and good hands, I believe he'll make a fair mount. When Lord Colin mentioned you felt a special kinship with the beast, I knew you were meant to have him."

Chapter 51

"**E**amon, there are women in the longhouse, are there not?" Fiona asked.

"Aye."

"What are some of their names?"

"Is there something you require of them, my lady?" Eamon asked after listing several.

"Nay, I was just curious."

Fiona halted Barca outside the main entrance to the longhouse but didn't dismount. The men and women working outside looked at her with curiosity laced with suspicion. They were always respectful on the surface, but she knew what they thought of her—what they thought of Gunnar marrying an Irishwoman and a Christian.

"I would speak with the one called Olya." She gave the name Eamon had provided that was the easiest to pronounce.

A man disappeared inside the longhouse. A woman appeared a few moments later, but remained in the doorway. Her dark hair was braided with red ribbon close to her head in multiple braids that joined somewhere in the back. A long thick single braid draped forward over one shoulder. She stood with the confident air of a man, dagger and short sword tucked into the front of her belt, the hilt of her longsword rising from its scabbard behind her back. In that moment, Fiona understood why his people looked at her the way they did, why they didn't feel her worthy of their leader. This was the kind of woman who would fight at his side and command their respect.

"My lady. You summoned me?" Olya asked.

Fiona had intended to dismount to not appear intimidating, but the woman who stood before her was so tall and striking, that it caught her off guard. Fiona wasn't a small woman by Irish standards, but compared to this Olya, she was downright diminutive. "I would ask a favor of you," she said, remaining astride.

"And that would be?"

"Is there somewhere we can talk in private?"

The woman hesitated, then nodded. Fiona slid to the ground and followed her away from the longhouse, between the animal pens, leading Barca.

"I wish for a set of Northwoman clothes," she said when they stopped.

"You want my clothes?" Olya sized her up. "They'll not fit you."

"Nay. I want clothes of my own. Clothes like yours."

"I'm not a seamstress."

"I only require the materials, and for you to allow me to pattern after yours. I can sew them myself."

The woman frowned as she considered it. "I'm not handy with thread and needle, but there are other women here who are. I will tell them your shape and size and acquire what it is you seek. I would not have Gunnar hear that I refused you or made you sew your own."

"I'll pay you for your trouble. I do not expect it for nothing."

"Your coin is unnecessary."

Fiona shook her head. "I would make fair trade or none at all. Is there something besides coin that you want or need?"

Olya studied her for a long moment, then nodded. "There is one thing. Teach me to ride—as you do. Unless it is something that cannot be taught and is truly magic, as the men whisper. They say you are like a witch with an animal." She glanced at the giant Barca trailing meekly behind her as proof. "Though some also say the same about you and G..." She caught herself, obviously thinking better of it.

"'Tis no magic and, aye, I can teach you."

"The clothes are a secret from him?" Olya asked, then shrugged. "They must be, or he'd have sent the request himself."

"Aye. But only as a surprise to be revealed later, not a secret to be kept. And perhaps we could barter for something else. Perhaps you could teach me to fight as well? To fight as a woman fights."

Olya snorted. "There is no such thing as fighting *as a woman fights*, my lady. There is only fighting—killing, bleeding, and dying. It's not for you."

"I've seen men die before; I saw Gunnar kill them."

"I would imagine so if you've spent any time with him at all." Olya chuckled at Fiona's attempt to shock her. "Have him teach you, then. He's far more skilled than I, anyway. Or will he not allow it?" She studied her. "That's what I thought. He'll not have you in harm's way."

"All the more reason for me to learn to defend myself."

"You have him for that now—and better protection you'll not find. No," Olya said and shook her head. "I'll not do it."

"What if he were to agree? Would you teach me then?"

Olya looked at her sideways. "If Gunnar agrees for you to learn to carry sword and shield, then aye, I'll teach you. But I must hear it from his lips. No offense, my lady, but my neck is far too dear to me to risk it on your words."

Fiona nodded.

"As for the clothes, give me a week."

"Gratitude. And you're sure I can't provide anything...coin for the seamstress or materials?"

"No. But when will you begin to teach me to ride?"

"How about tomorrow?"

Gunnar stood with his arms resting comfortably on the top rail watching the two women and horses inside the small paddock. He'd been surprised and thrilled to hear Fiona had made a connection with one of the Northwomen, and had approached quietly so as not to interrupt. Olya noticed him almost immediately, but he held a finger to his lips, grateful for the opportunity to watch Fiona in her element.

Seeing her interact with a horse was one of his favorite things. He appreciated a good steed but had never really thought of them as anything beyond simple beasts of burden. Some were faster, some stronger, but with Fiona, they became so much more. She could make them sidestep and dance, pirouette, and leap in the air—without appearing to ask anything of them at all.

"Nay, sit up straight and hold both reins tight enough to keep him from going forward," Fiona directed Olya. "Then lift your right leg away while increasing the pressure with your left heel only. Like this." Gunnar couldn't see what she was doing, but Barca bunched up as if to take a step forward, was halted by the reins, then side-passed to the right. "Imagine you are creating a box with the reins and your legs. When you ask them to move and three sides of the box remain firm and closed, they will naturally go the only way that is open to them. Do you understand?"

"Aye, but your horse is well-trained. This beast is an ignorant brute; he knows nothing," Olya protested.

"That's true, and I chose him for that very reason. Your signals will have to be strong and consistent, and 'twill build the muscles that you're not used to using. Later, as you form a bond, you'll refine those to subtle cues that appear invisible." Fiona had seen Gunnar approach but had been careful not to acknowledge him. "'Tis similar to how a woman controls a man and gets him to do her bidding, even though he is larger and stronger. You secretly maneuver them like a horse, leaving the only option appear to be the task you wish for them to perform. 'Tis not magic, and with some men, 'tis not difficult at all." Olya stared at her, mouth agape, her eyes flicking fearfully from Fiona to Gunnar behind her.

"Olya, I believe your lesson is over," Gunnar said as he opened the gate and stepped inside. "You will leave us."

Olya hesitated, glanced at Fiona, then nodded. "Aye, my lord." She slid from the black gelding's back and led him out the gate, avoiding Gunnar's eyes on the way.

Fiona covered her smile with one hand, feigning surprise. "My lord. I didn't know you were there. How much did you overhear?"

Gunnar grabbed her around her waist, pulling her gently down from Barca to face him. "Enough," he replied, trying to disguise his own smile. "But that leaves me only one question for you, wife."

"Which is?"

"Does that mean when I pleasure you in the furs, I am under your control? That it is you who directs my lips and tongue to your..."

"Gunnar!" Fiona clamped her hand over his mouth. "You must not speak of such things," she whispered fiercely, trying to stifle a giggle.

"But when I do, my words must also be at your command since I'm so easily controlled."

Fiona laughed. "You've made your point, and I concede; you win this match. I saw you approach and thought to have sport with you. Now, promise me, you'll speak of it no more." She glanced around furtively, still chuckling under her breath.

"Very well, I accept your concession and agree not to speak of it, though you know I shall have to take you to task for your insolence tonight. As your husband, 'tis my duty."

Fiona smiled. "Of course. I would never have you shirk such an important responsibility." She pulled his head down to kiss him lightly on the lips. "Now come, before Olya misconstrues there is trouble between us. And I would have you reassure her that you approve of my bargain with her—to trade riding for learning Northwoman ways."

Gunnar drew her back into his embrace and kissed her deeply. Fiona felt his hardness between them. He moved his lips to her ear. "Thinking of how I shall draw out your punishment later will render my mind worthless for anything else the rest of the day."

"My lord," Fiona giggled, "we are in public."

"On my land, where my word is law."

"But such behavior, when combined with our quick wedding, will ensure that tongues never stop wagging."

Gunnar kissed her again, then slid one arm around her waist, keeping her close as they followed Olya to the stables.

"Fiona tells me you have struck a deal," Gunnar said to Olya, who, after a quick glance up verifying their arrival, kept her eyes to the task of grooming the black gelding. "Mind yourself, Olya, my wife seems gentle and benevolent, but she's always thinking one step ahead, and can be quite ruthless to get what she wants."

Olya nodded, glancing cautiously at Fiona, who'd begun grooming Barca.

"As I explained to you, Gunnar, Olya and I have made a simple bargain," Fiona said over her shoulder. "In exchange for teaching her to ride, Olya will teach me your ways. There is much I wish to learn, and she needed to be sure that you would approve."

"It's fine by me," Gunnar said absently, his eyes following Fiona's every move as she ran a bristle brush across Barca's shiny copper coat. "Teach her anything she wishes to know. You are very fortunate that she will teach you to handle a horse; I have never seen anyone more skilled with a beast."

Olya was shocked by his open admiration and softness, especially when Fiona had clearly just mocked him. This was not the Gunnar she knew at all. Perhaps Fiona did control him with invisible commands as she did a horse.

"My lord, you asked to be summoned when the new blacksmith arrived. He's here," Eamon announced, interrupting them. "My lady. Olya." He nodded, acknowledging both women.

"It appears I must take my leave now, wife. Do try not to get into any further trouble today," Gunnar said with a smile as he joined Eamon.

"Aye, my lord," Fiona replied with a demure smile.

"That was not exactly what we agreed," Olya accused quietly as they watched the two men walk away.

"I disagree. You said you needed to hear it from his own lips, and you have. His exact words were *teach her anything she wishes to know*."

"Aye, my lady," Olya said as she shook her head. "But something more than my aching muscles tells me I may regret coming out of the longhouse that day."

Chapter 52

It was early afternoon when Fiona followed Olya through the back entrance into the unmarried womens' sleeping area. She glanced around the space filled with multiple mounds of furs. Woven reed panels separated the room from the rest of the longhouse, and a thick stag hide covered the doorway into the main hall. They were alone.

"You should try them on here to make sure they fit," Olya directed as she retrieved a folded bundle of clothes from her bedding.

Fiona nodded, glancing at the two unsecured doorways.

"No one comes here this time of day," Olya reassured her.

Fiona stripped out of her gown and kirtle, pausing before removing her shift, while she determined which of the Northwoman clothes to put on first. She decided on the linen tunic since it would cover the most, then the supple leather trousers, and finally the deer-hide boots lined with soft gray rabbit fur. While Olya laced the wide leather corset belt in the back for her, Fiona pulled the pair of tooled leather wrist guards lined with matching rabbit fur over her hands, then waited for Olya to lace them, too.

"The tree carved in the belt and cuffs is Yggdrasil, the Tree of Life," Olya said as she finished the second wrist guard. "It is very important in our culture, and if you don't yet know of it, you should ask Gunnar to explain it to you." She clasped two fox pelts together at each of Fiona's shoulders, allowing them to drape in the front and the back.

When she'd finished, Fiona glanced down at her new garments, running her fingers over the soft fur and leather tooling. "They are beautiful, Olya, and so comfortable," Fiona admired. "I think I shall wear them home and surprise him now."

"Then we must see to your hair."

Olya patted a stool, and Fiona sat. After undoing Fiona's thick bun and reclaiming the gold ribbon, she braided two tight braids on both sides of her head, then a large loose raised braid with the ribbon along her crown. She ran her fingers through the long soft waves in the back. "In battle, this would be braided, too, but Gunnar will likely prefer it down; your hair is very beautiful." Olya stepped back and looked her over. She frowned. "Something is still missing." She looked her up and down several times. "Of course," she said. "You have no weapon. Here." She pulled her own dagger and sheath from her belt. "Stick this under your belt so it at least looks as though you can fight."

"Gratitude." Fiona admired the carved bone hilt as she tucked the sheath under her belt on one side.

"Aye, now you'll pass for a Northwoman." She paused. "Lady, may I ask you a question?"

"Of course."

"Are you not afraid?"

"Of what?"

"Of the Treasure Huntress. They say the bond between her and her captain is like that between lovers. Do you not fear her wrath by taking him from her?"

"I did not take Gunnar; he chose me and this life."

"The result is the same," Olya disagreed, unconvinced.

"Yet the Huntress did not come between Jarl and Nena."

"You know of Jarl and Nena?" Olya asked, surprised.

"Aye, and I know of the Huntress's power; I know all of it. And I'm not afraid. I've not taken Gunnar; he has chosen me," she repeated. "There's a difference."

Olya looked at her and nodded. "Perhaps. Are you ready to go to him then?"

Fiona nodded and turned for the door they'd entered.

"Nay, not that way," Olya said. "Let's go through the longhouse to see if anyone notices."

Fiona hesitated. The longhouse. Gunnar had never taken her inside. He hadn't forbidden it, but he'd made it clear he didn't want her there. But it was early in the day; most of the men would be working, and she was with Olya.

Olya held open the stag hide curtain with a smile. "You go first. I'll follow and gauge reaction."

Fiona stared at the two rows of tables running the length of the hall. They seemed to stretch on for miles, though thankfully, most were empty. She glanced at the walls lined with wider sleeping benches, thinking to perhaps sneak along one side but decided against it. Not only would the path be longer, several of the benches were occupied. Fixing her eyes on the large double doors at the far end, she took a deep breath and stepped forward, taking the shortest path down the center.

It felt so strange to be seen in men's trousers. They were so light and unrestrictive that she felt practically bare. She glanced surreptitiously at the men she passed to see if her concern was valid, but none paid her any heed. They remained focused on their food and drink as if she wasn't even there. Dressed as she was, she was invisible; she was one of them!

Her confidence rising with every step, she passed behind a man with a bulky, black bearskin secured over his shoulders. She was thinking how the fur likely made him appear far larger than he actually was, when his chair suddenly scraped close behind her. Before she could turn, burly arms encircled her waist, pinning one of her arms against her side in the process. He grabbed her other arm above the wrist and pulled her down onto his hulking lap. "Now, aren't you a fine piece. Where did you come from, woman?"

Fiona jerked and twisted to free either of her arms, but he squeezed her tight, crushing her against his chest. With her face pressed deep into the thick black fur, she was unable to speak—unable to breathe.

"Release her, Bjork!" Olya demanded from behind them. Someone else's hands, that Fiona assumed were Olya's, joined the struggle.

"Get away from me, Olya," Bjork growled. "This does not concern you." The man batted her would-be rescuer away with one arm, the slight release allowing Fiona to gulp in much-needed air, before the constricting squeeze resumed.

"I'm trying to save your life, you damn fool!" Olya swore, launching herself onto his back and biting down on his ear.

The Northman roared with pain and stood, knocking Olya to the hard-packed earthen floor. Gasping for air, Fiona tried frantically to free herself, but it was hopeless; his grip was like iron. He lifted her and threw her over his shoulder, knocking the last of her remaining breath from her lungs, before he turned and headed for the door.

Head down and vision fading to black, Fiona dimly heard scrambling and swearing as he carried her out into the sunlight. She saw a blur and simultaneously felt the impact as a running man hit her abductor low on his legs, attempting to tackle him. Bjork staggered but somehow remained on his feet. She felt another blow from the side reverberate through his massive body and heard excited shouting in Norse with Gunnar's name mentioned many times. The iron grip loosened from her lower legs. Hands gently lifted her down from his shoulder. Fiona stood unsteadily, trying to catch her breath, surrounded by a small group who stared at her with mixed degrees of fear and accusation.

"I didn't recognize her with the clothes," Bjork mumbled.

"Do you think Gunnar will find that an excuse?" Olya snapped.

"You needn't worry," Fiona reassured them, still gasping and dizzy. "Gunnar will not hear of this—not from my lips. Make sure it is the same with all of you. 'Twas a misunderstanding, and no harm was done...other than to you." She pointed to the blood seeping from the bite on Bjork's ear.

"'Tis nothing, my lady."

"Have the healer see to it. We don't want you to have to explain to Gunnar how you took a fever."

Olya followed her back to Barca, her face grim. Fiona tried to cheer her. "Well, the clothing handiwork was clearly exceptional. They had no idea I wasn't one of you." She summoned a weak smile.

Olya did not smile back.

"All will be well." Fiona placed a hand on her arm to reassure her before mounting and turning Barca for home. Only when she was safely out of sight over the rise did she pull Barca to a halt, no longer able to control the shaking. She reeled from the force of the encounter. The violence. The sense of utter helplessness no matter how hard she'd resisted. Had Olya not been there...

She closed her eyes and tried to think of something else—of anything else. Olya *had* been there, and others had come to her rescue. Even her attacker had been remorseful and subdued when he learned her identity. She was safe. She was on Barca, returning home. Everything was fine. She needed to put it behind her and try to regain a suitable mood to present Gunnar with her surprise.

Even though she wanted nothing more than to delay it, dressed as she was, she had no choice; she'd have to explain the garments somehow. Her gown and kirtle were still somewhere in the longhouse, and there was no way she was going back there to retrieve them now. She loosened Barca's reins and let him wander, nibbling grass, while she tried to compose herself.

Fiona tied Barca and entered through the kitchen. Eamon sat at the heavy wood prep table, chatting with Ania. He turned to look at her, his eyes widening with interest as they moved over her body, then widening even more with shock when they reached her face. He immediately looked away.

"Apologies for staring, my lady. I didn't recognize you."

"Where is he, Eamon?"

"In his study."

"Is he alone?"

"Aye." He grinned now and shook his head. "Apologies again. I can still scarce believe 'tis really you."

Fiona crept down the hallway, then paused briefly outside the door. Taking a deep breath, she pushed it open and stepped inside.

Gunnar looked up from the parchment he was reviewing and froze. Fiona stepped closer. Still, he said nothing, his eyes covering every inch of her. "What is this?" The hint of dimples suggested the smile he suppressed. "A beautiful Northwoman come to tempt me? Apologies, woman, you are too late; I am married. Now be gone before my wife sees you and does us both in. She has a fearful temper."

Fiona smiled. "That she does, and do not forget it," she warned before turning a full circle for his inspection. "Do you like them?"

"Aye, I like them, but *like* doesn't do justice to what I feel. I would *like* you in a sack."

"I could dress this way from time to time," she said suggestively.

"I would like *that* very much." Nodding slowly, he pushed his chair back.

Fiona's skin began to tingle at his obvious desire. "Perhaps we could both dress this way on occasion and spend time with your people in the longhouse."

He frowned slightly and shook his head. "You see my people all the time, but only after they know and accept the rules here. The longhouse is different. With new arrivals and occasional travelers, 'tis too rough a place for you."

Fiona understood what he meant all too well now. "But I'd be safe with you."

"Your body would be safe, but your eyes would not."

"I would still like to go there sometime with you, as your woman."

"As my woman." He smiled. "Come closer, woman. Was this the deal you made with Olya?"

"Aye."

"I shall be sure to thank her." He held out his hand.

She stepped closer and reached up to take it. Her sleeve slid back, revealing something dark on her forearm. Horrified, Fiona jerked her arm away in an attempt to conceal it, but the quick move only caused him to follow her gaze. She silently berated herself. She should have simply turned her arm over, or stepped closer and put it behind his neck. There were any number of ways it might have escaped his notice, but her reaction had drawn his attention to it like a beacon.

"Fiona?" he asked, his eyes probing her face. "What happened?"

"'Twas nothing—an accident in the stables," she said with a smile, hearing her voice come out a little too bright.

Gunnar didn't return her smile. Instead, he took her wrist and turned her arm to examine the bruise. Fiona also took the opportunity to look at it more closely. Her heart sank. The outlines of fingers—very large fingers were unmistakable.

"Someone laid a rough hand on you?" Gunnar asked in sheer stunned disbelief.

She shook her head.

"Who was it?" His voice was quiet but sharp as a blade. "You went to the longhouse, didn't you? That's why the sudden mention of it. You went there unescorted for these." He motioned to her clothes. "What happened?" he demanded.

"Gunnar, I am unharmed."

"Your arm says differently." He cut her off, then closed his eyes and twisted his head as if trying to relieve severe cramping in his neck. She could see the war going on inside him to maintain his composure. He took a deep breath and opened his eyes again, fixing her with a serious stare. "Who did this to you?" he repeated.

Fiona wasn't fooled; she could feel the dark tension in him. Setting her mouth in a stubborn line, she gave a quick, silent shake of her head.

"Very well. If you won't tell me, someone there will." He stood, releasing her wrist.

She stepped in front of him, and placed her hands on his chest. "Gunnar, it was my fault. And I am well."

He kissed the top of her head. "Fiona, you do not understand my people. This cannot go unaddressed. You will remain here until I return." With that, he set her from his path and strode from the room. His voice echoed through the great hall as he yelled for a horse.

Remain here? Who did he think she was? Remain here while he punished someone for something she'd brought about? Nay! She had to stop him. His people would never accept her if she allowed it. She would not be the mistress everyone despised!

Fiona raced back through the kitchen and out the door to where Barca was tied. Yanking his reins free from the post, she flew onto his back—even in her desperation, marveling at the ease with which she was able to do so in the unrestrictive clothes. She dug her heels into Barca's sides. As he bounded forward, Fiona felt that everything could be alright. It would take time for

Gunnar to saddle a horse. And even then, no horse was as fleet as Barca; she'd arrive at the longhouse well before him. She settled into the saddle and let Barca race full out.

A small group of Northmen and Olya were standing outside. Their faces fell when they saw it was her.

"Gunnar's coming," she said, breathless from the pace. "I didn't say anything, but he saw the marks on my arm, and with the clothes, he knew. When I would not tell him what happened, he said he's coming here for answers." No one ran or scurried away as she expected. "You don't understand. You need to leave. Just for awhile until he calms down. He's furious."

"Aye, he would be," Olya said, resigned.

"Then hide yourselves! You don't have much time. I raced the whole way here, but he won't be far behind me!"

"You should go, my lady," Bjork said.

"I will not," she said indignantly. "Are you not hearin' me? Gunnar is coming here to punish you!"

Still, no one moved.

Fiona stood stunned, her mind tumbling. She'd never considered this— that they would refuse to heed her warning. "Very well, if you will not leave, then I shall face him with you. This was my doing. You shall not pay for it." She dismounted, tied Barca, and stood waiting near the silent group.

They didn't have to wait long. Gunnar appeared over the hill, his horse at a dead gallop. He pulled it to a stop, the horse's hooves leaving deep furrows in the damp sod. Dropping the reins, he leapt to the ground before it had even come to a complete stop and glared at her.

"Fiona, you need to leave."

"I will not."

"Fiona!"

She stared at him defiantly and shook her head.

"Very well, then." He turned away from her, addressing the others. "Who laid a hand on my wife?"

"It is my fault, my lord," Olya volunteered.

"'Twas not." Fiona stepped in front of her. "This is my doing, and I'll not have her punished. I'll not have anyone punished."

Gunnar looked past her as if she'd not even spoken. "Those were not the marks of Olya's fingers I saw on her arm. Who laid a hand on her?" Gunnar repeated, his voice quiet as death.

"It was I, my lord," Bjork confessed. "I didn't recognize her. I thought she was a newly arrived Dane."

Fiona cringed. *That was the best excuse he could think of?*

Gunnar brushed past her and closed the distance to Bjork in two long strides. He laid him out on the ground with one blow, then stood over him and shouted, "Get up!"

As Bjork struggled to his knees, Gunnar hit him again.

"I said, get up!" Gunnar roared.

When Bjork's response was too slow to suit him, Gunnar lifted him by the front of the black bearskin with one hand, while his other rocked back to deliver the next blow.

"Gunnar, you must stop!" Fiona screamed.

He ignored her and hit Bjork a third time. She was close enough to hear the sickening sound of Bjork's nose crunching. Blood poured from his face. She looked frantically to the others for help, but they stood watching in stricken silence; she knew they would not intervene. She grabbed Gunnar's arm. He shook her off as if she were no more than a fly. He was so consumed by the thought of injury to her, that he might kill this man!

The thought of injury to her...the thought of injury to her. Fiona knew what she had to do.

"Gunnar!" she shouted, stepping backwards and pulling Olya's dagger from her belt. "If you do not stop at once, I will cut myself, here and now. I swear it. I am the one to blame. I am the one you should be angry with." She pressed the blade to her forearm directly over the bruise and continued to back away.

Gunnar paused with his fist still raised and stared at her, his eyes blazing. "Fiona, drop the knife."

She shook her head. "I will not."

He released his grip on Bjork and stood in one powerful, fluid motion to face her, his expression changing briefly to calculating.

Fiona took another step backwards. "I know you're judging the distance between us, and I know how fast you are. You're not fast enough. 'Twill be done before you reach me. And do not doubt for an instant that I will do it. I will—and forever bear the mark."

"Fiona." His voice twisted with pain and anger.

"I need your word that you'll take no action against anyone here for what has transpired. I am the one responsible. If you need to punish someone, it must be me."

The others watched the standoff in shocked disbelief.

"Fiona. Drop the knife," he repeated and took a step towards her.

"Not another step, my love," she said as she applied more pressure to the blade and winced. "Not without your word."

Gunnar stared at the blade pressed deep against her soft pale skin, horror warring with his anger. He raised his gaze to meet hers and stared at her, measuring her resolve. "I give you my word," he said, his voice clipped.

Fiona lifted the blade from her arm, held it out, and dropped it to the ground in front of her. He was on her in a flash with the same unbelievable speed he'd used with the highwaymen. She'd never seen him like this. His jaw was clenched tight, his nostrils flared, his body hard as stone. He reached behind her head and took a handful of her hair. She wondered if he was about to strike her but oddly didn't fear it. Strangely calm, she looked up at him and waited.

"Do not ever threaten me with harming yourself again. Ever!" he demanded. "Now you will give me your word."

"You have it."

He pulled her in against him, his body still rock-hard. "I could never bear to see harm come to you, and certainly not be the cause of it. But by the gods, you are stubborn! And a fool!"

He was still angry, but she could feel it lessening with every breath.

Chapter 53

ONE MONTH LATER

The excitement in the air was palpable. Fiona looked out over the small crowd gathered in the courtyard, split equally with Northmen to the left, Irish to the right. Gunnar raised his fist, and the crowd noise quickly subsided.

"You all know why we're here, and we'll get to it shortly. First, I have a few announcements to make. The land granted to you here today will be yours—to grow what you wish, raise what you wish—yours to pass down to your children and their children. Your land," he repeated. "But from this day forward, all who accept land, also accept their new kinsmen. You will no longer stand divided as you are today but as one clan."

He turned to the group on the right. "If an Irish army comes, they'll not be coming to drive out only your Norse and Dane neighbors; they'll be coming to strip you of your land and return you to serfdom on another lord's estate." He turned to the left. "Likewise, a Viking force will not raid only Irish parcels. No matter who threatens us, it will be their intent to cut down any who stand in their way—and they will succeed if we are divided. Think long and hard on that. Your future and the future of your children depends on all of us working together—standing together as free men. Men with land. Against any and all who would try to take it from us.

"I will demand that everyone here learn both tongues, and every man, woman, and child who is old enough, be trained to fight."

"Apologies, my lord, but women and children?" An Irishman called out.

"If an enemy comes, your women and children—and mine—may be forced to face them. I would have them able to defend themselves."

Fiona stepped forward. "Lord Colin and I are in agreement on this. I will also begin training. Should we be attacked while you men are away, I, for one, do not wish to be helpless."

"But my lady, you cannot possibly think that you or my young Deirdre could hold a sword against a Northman...or another force," he added after her disapproving glance at his choice of words.

"Nay, Farrel, I do not, but I can learn to loose arrows from the parapets, and I can learn to wield a dagger with effectiveness. These are also things that Deirdre can learn. If attackers were to take us by surprise or break through your ranks, don't you want your family to have the best chance to survive?"

"Aye, my lady."

"Training will begin immediately." Gunnar continued when the crowd was once again silent. "I know there is much work to be done—land to clear, homes to build, fields to reclaim, but you cannot wait to learn to fight any more than you can wait to plant oats until you need them to feed your families. You must think ahead and plan for the future. To help alleviate the burden losing this time will cause, I will continue to provide grain until the first crops are harvested, and we will organize hunts for meat to share."

This statement was met with surprised smiles, nods, and relieved murmurs.

"You all know of my wishes that whatever your chosen trade, your wares be of the highest quality possible. Because I know many of you lack the resources to begin such endeavors, I am prepared to assist in the purchase of initial supplies, be it seed, premium livestock, equipment, or specialized training. Any who desire such aid will come to me with a list of what you require and we will discuss terms of a loan.

"All disputes will be settled by myself and Lady Fiona together. Neither of us will show any favoritism, nor will we tolerate it. None. If anyone here finds themselves unable to abide by what I've put forth, they should leave now." He paused, looking out over the split group, wondering if what he'd proposed was possible. Could these men ever overcome their differences, their history, and stand as one?

"Then let's get to it." A wave of excited murmurs rippled through the crowd. "Behind me is a map of Tir na Laoch. On it are the available parcels of land. Each is marked with an X or an O, which I will explain in a moment. In this pouch," he nodded at Fiona, who held up a large silk bag. "are stones with numbers painted on them. Each man seeking a parcel will come forward and pull a stone."

"Or woman, lord," Olya shouted.

"Aye, apologies, Olya. Man or woman. Fiona will read your number, and Eamon will record your name next to it on his list." Eamon held up a parchment. "When everyone has taken a stone, whoever has drawn the #1, will come forward and make their choice. I will write their number on that parcel on the map, and it will no longer be available.

"The next man is free to choose any other parcel with only one restriction. If the first to choose is Irish, and they pick a parcel with an X, then every Irishman after him may only choose from parcels marked the same. If the first is a Northman, the same applies." He held up his hand, and the crowd quieted again. "There are no better lands marked by X or O; they are divided equally."

"But my lord, every X is separated by an O, and every O the same separated by an X."

"Aye. That is correct. This mixing of neighbors will further encourage the melding of our peoples and hopefully put an end to the separation I see before me here today."

This latest announcement was followed by grumbling and knitted brows in both groups as they discussed its significance. Gunnar waited for the subtle nods as they accepted it before he proceeded.

"If there are no more questions or concerns, then form a queue in front of Lady Fiona to draw your stones. There is no need to rush; the number on your stone will determine the order in which you get to choose land, not your place in line."

Fiona was surprised when she looked up to find Ania standing before her. "You wish to choose?"

"Aye, my lady, if 'twill be allowed. I greatly appreciate my position in the residence and all that's been done for me, but I cannot pass up such an opportunity for my family."

"I will not lie; you'll be sorely missed, but I do understand." Fiona smiled and held up the pouch. "Choose your stone, Ania."

"Is that everyone?" Gunnar called out.

"Aye, my lord."

Eamon handed him the list, and he glanced down at the first name before looking back to the crowd. "Then Declan, come forward to claim your land."

Gunnar said nothing as the parcels were chosen in clusters with empty gaps between them, or when lesser lands were selected to avoid having a neighbor. When it was Ania's turn, she stepped to the map and pointed to one of the prime parcels. A stream ran through it for water, and the lands required the least work to clear, yet it had remained unchosen halfway through because it was neighbored on all sides by parcels chosen by Northmen.

Gunnar wanted to lift her hand and shout to the others that this young widow had more courage than any of the men present, but he didn't need to. He heard the surprised whispers, saw the discussions, and knew they'd already recognized it. After Ania, the best lands were chosen, regardless of neighbor.

"Does anyone remain?" he asked the crowd. No one answered. "Then proceed to your new land and meet your neighbors. Tonight, we shall all feast in the great hall to celebrate this day. Eamon will draw up your individual charters and have them ready for you later."

As the crowd dispersed, Gunnar, Eamon, and Fiona sat together on the top step. Gunnar slipped his arm around Fiona's waist and took a deep breath. "Well, 'tis done, for better or worse. Hopefully for the better, for when the loans are given, we will have invested all."

"'Twill be for the better, I'm sure of it," Fiona reassured him, then turned to Eamon, "Your idea of mixing the properties was genius, Eamon."

"Gratitude, my lady. When the choosing first started, I wasn't sure it would work. Ania was quite a surprise." He frowned. "Though 'twill be difficult for a woman and children to work land alone."

"Perhaps they'll not farm it all. Perhaps they'll raise sheep or goats," she offered.

"Perhaps, but we all know tending animals is no less labor."

"An attractive young widow needing additional aid might not be a bad thing," Gunnar suggested. "We're doing everything we can to encourage unity, and she'd make some lonely Northman an excellent wife; she's clearly fertile." He grinned.

"Gunnar!" Fiona elbowed him in the stomach. "Women are not merely broodmares for men."

"I did not say they were," he grunted, chuckling. "But for a man who wants his own children, you must admit that she obviously...well..." He slouched and covered his stomach with one hand to protect himself from another blow, adding, "A woman would, of course, be justified to have the same concern in a man—that he be able to sire children. And how are my words in any way different than what you're hoping for with your other ideas?"

"Other ideas?" Eamon asked.

Fiona glared at Gunnar before turning to Eamon. "In addition to the weapons training and language lessons, which should in and of themselves encourage mixing, I am thinking to hold feasts on special Irish and Norse holidays. Men and women may find it easier to consort with one another in celebration."

"With her intent being that *consorting* lead to marriage—and childbearing," Gunnar interjected with a grin.

"Based on mutual love and affection, not the fruitfulness of their loins," Fiona retorted. She turned quickly to Eamon. "Apologies, Eamon, for speaking so basely in front of you."

"None required, my lady." Eamon smothered a smile.

She turned back to Gunnar, who was still grinning. "I must take my leave now to oversee the preparations for tonight's feast." When he opened his mouth, she placed her finger over his lips. "Not another word on the subject." She shook her head with a smile. "But do not think you've heard the last of this discussion."

After Fiona left, Eamon produced a jug and two cups, and the two men sat on the steps drinking in companionable silence.

"The success of your marriage will be a strong example for everyone," Eamon observed.

"I ask you again to choose land for yourself. You know you don't have to pick from the remaining parcels. Any land that you desire, just say the word, and it's yours."

"I can't believe I'm saying this, but I do not desire any of it."

"I thought perhaps you and Ania..."

Eamon shook his head. "I've thought of it many times, but Ania is a good woman."

"All the more reason."

"I would not do that to her. I'll not be staying. I'll be sailing with Rask. We are of like mind, he and I. We've talked of a great many places we intend to explore."

"He's lucky to have you. Your mastery of languages will be invaluable, and your skills with sun-stone and sun-compass are already impressive."

Eamon fingered the pale yellow crystal he wore on a cord around his neck—a smaller version of the one that remained in a safe crate on the Huntress at all times. "I must admit I find it fascinating—such power in a stone." He lifted it toward the sky, turning it slowly, watching with wonder as it turned from yellow to pale purple when it hit a right angle to the sun.

"Did he offer you a ranking position?"

"Nay, and I did not expect it. I still have much to learn. And to be quite honest, I prefer not to have the responsibility of rank—to look out only for myself."

"You say that, but...

"I did not say I was incapable of looking out for others; it's just that it weighs on me like a heavy burden."

"That's because you care."

"I'd say it's because I don't care at all and have to work so hard at it." He grinned.

"I don't believe that, but I do understand your feeling," Gunnar conceded. "Jarl asked me once if I wished to replace him as leader. I told him no and meant it. But then things changed." He leaned back and stretched his legs out in front of him with a sigh. "And now I have everything."

"One might argue, you had everything before."

"Then they would know nothing. I tell you with all certainty, naught compares to having a woman in your blood. I shall pray to the gods for you to one day know it, too."

Eamon coughed and held up his hands with a laugh. "Do not pray too hard for me. I'm quite happy with the way things are."

"You know you have my deepest gratitude. None of this would have been possible without you."

"Your gratitude is unnecessary. You gave me my life, and not just the physical drawing of breath; you gave me my true life. You asked me once who I was when I wasn't mimicking others. I didn't have an answer then, but I do now. I'm a raider, a trader, an explorer—I'm a Viking. When we first met in Tibbot's cavern, I jested that we could be brethren, but perhaps it was true. The life suits me so well; perhaps 'tis in my blood. I owe you everything, and I'll not forget it."

Chapter 54

TWO MONTHS LATER

Fiona paused at the top of the steps and took a deep breath of fresh spring air, her eyes panning over the courtyard. To her right, Gunnar was talking to the blacksmith who'd arrived the day of Olya's riding lesson. Gunnar spoke very highly of the man—said his ideas and techniques were far advanced from anything he'd ever seen; he was quite thrilled to have him.

She glanced to her left, catching a glimpse of Rask before he turned a corner and was lost from view behind the great hall. Even though she'd only seen his departing back, and that very briefly, she'd easily recognized him. Rask was very conspicuous. With two swords criss-crossed on his back, his long thin braid, and the sides of his head that were always fresh shaven. He was also taller than most, almost a full hand taller than even Gunnar.

Fiona rarely saw Rask. He refused to stay in the residence even though Gunnar had offered him large private quarters, preferring instead to stay in the longhouse. He said it was to remain close to the Treasure Huntress, and the ship was beached there for the winter, but Fiona didn't believe that was the truth. At least not all of it. She had the distinct impression he went out of his way to avoid her.

She wasn't sure if he disagreed with Gunnar's choice of her as wife, or if it was unresolved resentment over the near sinking of the ship. She suspected it might be the latter, but either way, he remained distant and aloof. She sighed. All of his people had embraced her after word of her defense of Bjork had spread. All but Rask.

She continued down the steps into the courtyard toward Gunnar.

"Riders approaching, my lord." Someone shouted down from the nearest guard tower just as she reached him.

"How many?" he asked.

"Twenty men. Heavily armed and riding with haste. They fly the banner of King Flann of the Southern O'Neill."

"Archers to the ramparts," Gunnar called out. "The rest of you have weapons ready but not drawn. No man makes a move without my command." He turned to Fiona. "Gather the women and children and go inside."

"But..."

"Fiona, I need you to go inside now and send messengers out the back to the fields. I need all men to assemble with arms, but quietly. I do not wish to sound the alarm and have them race in with weapons drawn, thinking we are under attack. I'd prefer not to spark just such an event if it can be avoided." Fiona nodded and fled up the steps.

"Shall we close and bar the gates, lord?" Bryen shouted.

"Nay. Let them pass."

Gunnar stood in the open at the base of the stone steps, evaluating the riders as they galloped into the courtyard, scattering chickens with their horses' hooves. Battle-hardened men to a one, riding powerful chargers and armed to the teeth, with one exception. Their leader. He was a small man, and though he wore fine-tooled expensive leather plate armor, Gunnar could find neither scratch nor stain on it.

"I bear message from King Flann for the new lord," he announced.

"I am Lord Colin."

He kicked his horse forward, bumping Gunnar with the animal's shoulder. Gunnar stepped to the side, ignoring the insult, his hand resting on the hilt of Maid's Dream. From the corner of his eye, he could see the first of his men quietly arriving from the fields.

"The king demands that you swear allegiance to the Southern O'Neill. Here is his decree and demands." He held out a leather-bound scroll and squinted down at him.

Gunnar ignored it. "This is Connacht land and will remain so. Even if it were not, I'd acknowledge no decree from a king who can only muster the support of half of his own kin. I'd certainly not bend a knee to such a man—a half-king." Gunnar nodded to Rask, who had silently joined him at his right side.

"How dare you!" The outraged rider shook the scroll at him again. "If you do not accept these demands, this land will be stripped from you by force!"

"What have I missed, lord?" Eamon panted as he trotted to his place on Gunnar's other side.

"They bring threats from their king," Gunnar replied.

"The half-king?" Eamon asked, having heard the last of the exchange, and following Gunnar's lead. "Do you think that's why he sent a half-man to deliver it?"

"Perhaps," Gunnar agreed as the courier turned red and gurgled at the insult.

"And what is their intent?" Eamon asked.

"We were just getting to that, but first..." Gunnar nodded to his men by the entrance. The reinforced heavy gates swung closed with an echoing boom.

Eamon chuckled. "Well, now we know their intent will not be to run away."

The riders' mood shifted instantly from arrogant to wary at the unexpected move.

"You will all dismount now and address me with the proper respect due a lord." Gunnar spoke to the one in charge, but loud enough for all to hear.

"I am the king's emissary!" the leader squealed.

"Aye. You are merely a messenger, not the king, and you will dismount..." Gunnar raised one hand and gave a subtle flick with his fingers. The archers on the wall drew back their bows—the squeak of straining wood and well-resined bowstrings resonating in the silent courtyard. "...either willingly or by my command."

"Lord Davin," one of the soldiers whispered. "He has readied archers behind us."

"I am not deaf." The stunted commander glanced furtively around the courtyard at the assembled men—only now aware of the force that seemed to have materialized from thin air. His eyes paused on the brawny Irish blacksmith who stood in the front of the closest group, his huge hammer hanging carelessly at his side, his expression unforgiving. "Dismount," he called to his men over his shoulder and stepped from his horse. He glared up at Gunnar, his eyes little more than slits. "This is a grievous mistake for you," he seethed.

"You would do well to hold your tongue, as I've not yet decided whether or not to kill you." Gunnar dispensed with any further feigned courtesy.

"You wouldn't dare harm the king's messenger."

Gunnar lowered his tone and spoke very clearly. "I will kill the king himself if he brings threat here, and that is the message you will take back to him. Now you will remove your weapons and place them in a pile. Then stand near the gate—without your horses. You will tell your king that his generous gifts of steel and mounts were well received."

"I will do no such thing!"

"You will, or you will all return to your king in pieces. In either form, you will successfully convey my message. My grandfather is gone, and the time when this land could be easily taken is past."

The man's eyes darted to the right, then left, openly frantic now.

Gunnar pulled Maid's Dream, the blade singing softly as it left its sheath. He pointed it at him. "Know that yours will be the first head taken, but once I give the command, all will die."

"That's the last," Rask reported.

Gunnar turned from the pile of weapons and small herd of horses to the men who stood huddled by the gate. "Should another force arrive here, there will be no negotiation and none of the mercy I've shown today. Make sure your king knows that as well. Open the gates," he called out.

He turned to Rask and Eamon. "Send riders to follow them and report back to me with their progress. Release most of our men, but have them remain on the ready. Keep enough to increase the watch and monitor the gates. No one enters the fortress who is not known or vouched for." When they nodded, he climbed the steps to address the men. "Well done today, men. Just the sight of us standing together made them tuck tail and run. Before dispersing, all of you are to report to Eamon or Rask. They will have further assignments for some of you. Once we have verified the threat is past, we shall feast to celebrate the enormous success of this first challenge."

"Do you think it was wise to humiliate them?" Fiona asked after Gunnar relayed everything to her.

"Our response needed to be unequivocal. Not only for their king, but for our people as well. They needed to see that my word to them was true—that

I will stand with them against anyone who threatens us—even a king. And they needed to see we can be victorious." He smiled. "I wish you could have seen them. Northmen and Irish standing shoulder to shoulder, unified in the face of a common foe. It was a sight to behold. Assuming the scouts report back with good news, I should like to call a feast tonight, if you can manage it with such little notice—to further cement the brotherhood shown today while it remains fresh."

"Aye, I'll see to it."

"Though we can attribute much of the ease of our success today to King Flann's choice of emissary. The man was nothing more than a squinting whelp. Why would a king send such a man?"

"Did you say squinting?"

"Aye, the worst I've ever seen. And he was small, like an elf."

"Davin," Fiona murmured.

"One of his men called him such. Do you know him?"

"Aye, he was a student of my father's."

Gunnar frowned. "Apologies, I..."

"Nay, nay, do not worry yourself over it. Davin is persona non grata to our family."

"Persona what?"

"'Tis Latin," she clarified. "It means he is no longer welcome. While you were gone to the East, he came to Tir na Lionmhar demanding my hand in marriage—using implied threats from the king even then. My father ran him off, and we heard not another word. I'd actually forgotten all about it because then there was Artan." She was quiet for a moment, then smiled.

"What do you find amusing?"

"I was just thinking of something Davin said the last time I saw him. He told my father that, while education was of interest, real decisions were made with a sword. I suppose that means he'll be making no real decisions since his sword remains here."

Gunnar chuckled and pulled her close.

"Do you think King Flann will return with an army?" she asked. "Even if it wasn't his original intent, it will be hard for him to ignore such insult as he received today."

"He may, but I think it doubtful. He was overstepping his bounds, and he'll know it. In my experience, men in this position will name a scapegoat for the failure—in this case, likely Davin, then deny all knowledge of it. He'll also know that word of the attempt, and our loyalty will reach the ear of the Connacht high king. While he may be able to pass off one incident as the actions of an overzealous underling lord, he wouldn't be able to do it a second time."

"Perhaps I should still increase our food stores. If they were to return and lay siege..."

"That's not necessary."

"But you just said he may..."

"Even if he does, 'tis unnecessary because I have a secret. I was waiting to show you until they were fully cleared and reinforced, but I'll tell you now. Do you remember the statue that your father verified was Roman?"

"Aye. You said you discovered it in a collapsed underground chamber."

"The chamber was only partially collapsed, and, in truth, I exaggerated that to prevent your father from asking to see it. Tir na Laoch was built on top of an old Roman foundation. From that chamber, tunnels lead outside the walls in multiple directions—some large enough even for horses. If an army ever attempts to lay siege,..."

"We can escape," Fiona finished for him.

Gunnar chuckled. "Nay. We can sneak out in the night and slay them. I have no intention of ever leaving this land. In fact, instead of bringing threat here, they'd do well to think of preparing their own defenses against us. By our marriage, two of the most powerful Irish clans, Connacht and O'Neill, are combined. Strategically, that places our family in a position as powerful as any to be considered for high king."

"Do your ambitions include the high throne now?" She laughed.

Gunnar smiled and shook his head. "Nay, I have everything I desire. But our sons' or grandsons' desires could be different than mine—perhaps one of them will be the man who makes the Stone of Destiny roar again. It is a pagan stone, after all. Perhaps it's been waiting for a king who can reconcile the old gods with the new—a man who can command the respect and support of both Viking and Irish."

"Ever the strategist. If I didn't know better, I might think you planned this from the beginning."

"In truth, I gave no thought to it until you told me the words of your seer."

"Old Maive," Fiona murmured.

"It was she who said our children will shape the future of these lands."

Gunnar watched Fiona moving among the feasting people below. Though spirits were high, and drink had flowed heavily all night, he was pleased to see that all were carefully respectful in her presence, and that she was greeted equally warmly by Viking and Irish alike.

"Assuming there are no signs of storm, I intend to sail at the next waning moon," Rask announced from his seat at Gunnar's right. Gunnar had insisted he sit at the high table for the feast tonight.

"So early? The seas will be unpredictable."

"I have something important I must do before journeying again to the East. It may take some time...."

"What is it?"

Rask hesitated. "I do not wish to insult you."

"Insult me?"

"It's the repair to the Huntress. Even though I know it to be sound, it galls me every time I look upon it. It's a constant reminder that I failed her. Once I've made arrangements in Aalborg to return to the East, I will sail to Norway and seek out this Sigurd, the man who built her, and convince him to return her to her original form."

Gunnar rubbed his chin.

"You think it a foolish waste of coin?"

"Nay, it's not that. From Jarl's account, Sigurd swore never to build another ship."

"This will not be building a ship."

"True, but Sigurd is rumored to be beyond disagreeable. Dangerous even. It was supposedly only his wife who kept him temperate. With her gone, you know not what form of man you'll encounter. I would not get your hopes up."

Rask frowned. "I, too, have heard stories of Sigurd, and they are all as you say, but I must try. Perhaps he will agree—if not for me, then for the Huntress."

"Perhaps," Gunnar agreed and clasped him on the shoulder. "Let us drink to your success." The two men clacked their oxhorn cups together and took deep swallows. "I do have one request before you go."

"Anything."

"I should like to sail on her one last time—with Fiona."

Rask paused, then nodded. "As you wish." He started to say something else, then clamped his mouth closed.

"What is it?" Gunnar asked.

"There is something that has long plagued me, and since we're speaking of Fiona and the damage to the Huntress...."

Gunnar stared at him, saying nothing.

"All this time, you knew she was responsible, and still..."

"Fiona and this life are my destiny. I know that as surely as I draw breath. Had the Huntress not been disabled, I never would have realized it; nothing less would have kept me here. I don't know if it was the will of the gods or the work of the three spinners..." He paused. "Or the will of the Huntress herself, but I do know a man cannot fight his destiny. Just as you'll not be able to fight yours when it is revealed to you, despite your well-laid plans." Gunnar smiled. "I've heard the men have begun calling her the *Marriage-maker*. That to captain the Huntress means to soon be blessed with a wife."

"That would be a curse, not a blessing," Rask muttered. "And rest assured, if there is such a curse, it ends with me."

Chapter 55

"Why are we meeting them at Clogherhead? Why not at Lough Ramor?"

"I'll not have my last memory of the Huntress to be sailing about a placid lake. Clogherhead is on their way, and the sandy beach a perfect place to make land. Are you ready? We need to leave soon or we'll miss the tide."

"Aye," Fiona stepped shyly from behind the privacy screen in the Viking clothes she'd not worn since the first harrowing day.

Gunnar paused to admire her, but his perusal was far more brief than normal. His almost boyish excitement to be on the ship again was unmistakable.

"Do you think I should have blood from a sacrifice?" she asked.

"For what purpose?"

"Olya said it will summon the protection of Freya."

"Do you fear a ship?" he teased.

"Olya says the bond between the Huntress and her captain is like that of a lover's, and if she were to feel jilted..."

"You don't need blood. You'll be safe."

"How can you be sure?"

Gunnar hesitated, then answered truthfully. "Because, if the Huntress disapproved of you—of us, I fear something tragic would have befallen you already. I believe her power extends far beyond line of sight."

Fiona had seen the Treasure Huntress several times, but never in clear view. After the ship had been pulled up onto the bank of Lough Ramor near the longhouse, a structure had been built around it to protect it from winter weather. The building was little more than a roof with wide-spaced slat walls, and while she'd been able to see through the gaps to the ship inside, it was always in shadow and appeared nothing like what she saw before her now.

Standing on the beach in the bright sun and stiff bracing wind, she stared at it in awe. Plunging into the shallow troughs, then breaking through the crests of the white-capped waves in a breathtaking shower of spray, the golden dragon seemed to be rising from the very sea itself. In that moment, it was easy to understand why the crew felt as they did about it; the ship was truly a wonder.

When it slid to a stop in the shallows and Rask came ashore to speak with Gunnar, Fiona stepped closer to admire the fine carvings within the scales.

"I offer you one last opportunity to change your mind and remain as her captain," Rask said to Gunnar. "You have your woman, and she is now safely your wife. Many married men return to raiding and leave their wives at home. And it's not as if you'd have to worry about her safety. With the way our people and hers have sworn loyalty to her, she may even be able to raise a greater army than you." Rask grinned.

"Are you afraid to take her? Afraid to be the next target of the Marriage-maker?" Gunnar teased.

"Nay, it's not that," Rask scoffed. "But I would have the Huntress know I did not prey upon your weakness for my own gain." He glanced back at the dragon. "That I gave you every opportunity to reconsider."

Gunnar smiled. "She knows, Rask. This is what she wants. Though I understand how you feel. I felt the same when Jarl gave her to me. I saw no reason why he and Nena would not sail her together—she was a warrior equal to any shieldmaiden."

"A fact I remain very well aware of without being reminded," Rask said ruefully and rubbed the small scar on his throat.

"Aye, I guess you would," Gunnar laughed. "If it will reassure you for me to say it in her presence, I will do so; I have absolutely no doubts. And you won't either. The only thing left is for you to swear to gift her to someone else when that time comes and make them swear the same."

"I swear it."

"Then let's be off. The tide and winds are perfect. I'll not delay you much longer." Gunnar turned to Fiona. "Are you ready?"

Fiona nodded and watched Rask wade out a short distance, grab the boat high on the side at the base of the sweeping arch of the dragon's neck, then vault effortlessly aboard. To reach the lowest point, midway back where the ship was the widest, she would have to wade waist-deep into the surf. Even from there, it would be an embarrassing scramble—if she could make it at all. She hesitated. Her new clothes would be ruined—rendered stiff by the salty seawater. "You just wade out?" she asked, unintentionally glancing back at her soft rabbit fur-lined boots.

"What is it, shieldmaiden?" Gunnar grinned at her. "Afraid to get wet?" Without waiting for her to answer, he scooped her into his arms and splashed towards the ship. "To spare your new clothes," he said into her ear, "so that they may remain supple for you to wear for me other times." He waded deeper, turning his body against the next wave, bracing himself as it washed around his thighs before continuing alongside the ship. As he lifted her over the side, surprisingly, Rask was there to steady her while Gunnar climbed in.

"Where to?" Rask asked him.

"Just let her run—I would drink the wind," Gunnar replied. He led Fiona to the bow and put his arm around her waist.

Rask strode back down the center of the ship between the men seated at their oars on either side. "Take oars," he called out. Laughing and smiling, the crew did as told. They were well-rested after an easy winter and were eager to be away.

"Brace yourself," Gunnar whispered in Fiona's ear with a smile.

"On my mark...and...Pull!" Rask shouted the command just as the wave passing beneath them lifted them incrementally from the sand. The great ship trembled, torn between the force of the water and incoming tide driving it further up the beach, and the force of the men pulling it out to sea. It inched backwards, then shuddered to a stop as the wave retreated. "Pull," Rask called again with the next wave. And the next.

Each time, Fiona held her breath, enthralled by the battle of wills between the men and the sea. Then, with a final rub of sand, they were free. Even Gunnar's warning did not prepare her for how suddenly the ship lurched, or how the wood beneath her feet went from solid to seemingly alive. Gunnar chuckled as he steadied her.

The men rowed now in steady, experienced unison—the ship coasting when their oars skimmed through the air, before surging again as they were plunged back into the sea with the combined weight of the crew pulling against them.

Once beyond the breakers, Rask gave the order to raise the sail. Oars were stowed with a clatter of wet wood, and the sail secured. There was another gentle lurch as the wind began to fill it. Then the sail snapped taut, and the ship sprang forward, steadily picking up speed.

Faster and faster, they flew until they were skimming across the surface. The bow waves that had started as gentle curls of displaced water, now shot out in long sprays to either side, splattering white across the deep blue.

Fiona had to shout to Gunnar to be heard over the wind, even though he stood touching her. She'd never experienced such euphoria. The power and speed took her breath away—similar to when she galloped Barca full out, but this was so different—so effortless.

Even in her exhilaration, Fiona wondered if he would be saddened to realize this was the last time he would experience it. She tipped her head to look at him. He stood, legs braced, body moving easily with the rolling deck of the ship, looking out beyond with a contented smile on his face. She saw no trace of sadness or regret, but still, she couldn't help but worry.

As they walked through the sand towards higher ground, Fiona couldn't help but think of how this place had provided her with two of the most moving experiences of her life. First, their race here with the carriage horses, that now seemed eons ago, and today.

Gunnar stepped up onto a large flat stone protruding from the dunes, then reached down and pulled her up in front of him. They stood in silence, her back leaned against his chest, his arms around her waist, watching the ship sail away up the coast. With each mile, it shrank before their eyes, appearing little larger than a toy, when the first of the lengthening land shadows, cast over the sea by the setting sun, reached it. The ship's body was soon shrouded in darkness, but the higher dragon's head remained in the light, the last evening rays sparking molten off the gold.

Then with one final flash, it, too, was gone.

Fiona took a deep breath and asked the only question that had marred her perfect day. "Will you miss it?"

"My life will be far too full to miss it," Gunnar said with a smile, resting his chin on top of her head and locking his long fingers protectively over the small, barely discernible bump in her stomach.

Epilogue

"**I** heard the most unbelievable story today, Leila," Sigurd said as he poured the now-ritual oxhorn cup of mead into the fjord before taking his seat on the rocks that jutted out over the water. "And, woman, I came to hold you to account for this one. I can see the appeal of an Irish noblewoman; they say she's not only a beauty, but intelligent and brave and kind. But to turn him into an Irish lord?" He huffed. "Was that necessary? Why not simply have him capture her and bring her home? There was a Scottish princess at the auction last year; an Irish noblewoman would not be unusual."

" ..... "

"I'll try to calm down, but it's getting me all riled up just thinking about it again." He took a swig of mead from his own oxhorn cup and looked back out over the water. "What is your thinking? Do you intend to abandon all of our great warriors in foreign lands to be swallowed up by their cultures?"

" ..... "

"That *is* your goal?!

" ..... "

"I know you don't like that tone, but..."

"....."

"Apologies," Sigurd muttered and tipped his head. "Aye. I'm listening now."

"....."

"You're not abandoning them—you're planting them like seeds? Seeds of the best of our culture to leave their mark and shape the futures of many lands?" He took another sip. "How does that benefit our people if we are lost?"

"....."

"It ensures we'll never be lost? How can you say that if our customs become so melded, they cannot be told apart? I agree with extending our people's reach to distant lands, but not like this. We should be conquering and bringing the world to our heel. We are more than capable of it. No one compares to our warriors."

"....."

"We're too ambitious? There is no such thing," he scoffed.

"....."

"Not for the conquering, but for the ruling?" He paused. "You think our leaders are too ambitious to accept another's rule. So your solution is, rather than conquer and then fight amongst ourselves for the spoils, we will adapt and rule from the inside. Woman, you are a wily one. This is a bold new proposal, and I shall have to think on it. I'd already set my mind to be opposed, but this gives me much to ponder. I shall return to discuss it with you again, when I've made my own conclusions."

He refilled his oxhorn cup and tipped his face up to take in the warm spring sun. "I suppose you knew what you were doing with Gunnar. He must truly love her to give up everything and live among the Christians. And I know there's no accounting for love. Your loving me was a testament to that, to be sure." He chuckled. "Though it sounds like you have your work cut out for you with this next one—this Dane, Rask. They say he's hot-headed, filled with wanderlust, and sworn never to marry."

" ..... "

"Oh, I know you're more than up to the task. I only wish I could be there to witness that battle of wills. What shall you do to him? And what sort of woman will you choose? There seems to be nothing in common between the warrior woman you chose for Jarl and the noblewoman you chose for Gunnar. Who will be up to the task of warming this Rask's heart? Perhaps a strong Norse woman this time?" he suggested with a smile. "Though if he's half as obstinate as they say, you may have to nigh kill him to bend him to your will."

The End

Eager to know what the Huntress has in store for Rask?
Then be sure to read

LIDA
Book Three of The **Viking Treasure Huntress** *Series*

By ANN BOELTER

For more information about the author
and other books by Ann Boelter go to her website:
www.annboelter.com

Made in the USA
Middletown, DE
03 May 2022

65113741R00350